LEONARDO'S HANDWRITING

AD VERBUM

Published with the support
of the Institute for Literary Translation, Russia

LEONARDO'S HANDWRITING
by Dina Rubina

Translated from the Russian by Melanie Moore

Published with the support
of the Institute for Literary Translation, Russia

Publishers Maxim Hodak & Max Mendor

© 2019, Dina Rubina

Introduction © 2019, Anna P. Ronell

© 2019, Glagoslav Publications

www.glagoslav.com

ISBN: 978-1-912894-45-1

DINA RUBINA

LEONARDO'S HANDWRITING

Translated from the Russian by Melanie Moore

CONTENTS

DINA RUBINA: READING
LEONARDO'S HANDWRITING IN CONTEXT
BY ANNA P. RONELL 7

PART ONE

    CHAPTER 1. 29

    CHAPTER 2. 37

    CHAPTER 3. 44

    CHAPTER 4. 52

    CHAPTER 5. 61

    CHAPTER 6. 69

PART TWO

    CHAPTER 7. 82

    CHAPTER 8. 96

    CHAPTER 9. 128

    CHAPTER 10. 143

    CHAPTER 11. 150

PART THREE

    CHAPTER 12. 156

    CHAPTER 13. 179

CHAPTER 14. 191

CHAPTER 15. 200

CHAPTER 16. 212

CHAPTER 17. 228

PART FOUR

CHAPTER 18. 241

CHAPTER 19. 272

CHAPTER 20. 279

CHAPTER 21. 285

CHAPTER 22. 295

PART FIVE

CHAPTER 23. 303

CHAPTER 24. 325

CHAPTER 25. 328

CHAPTER 26. 333

CHAPTER 27. 336

ACKNOWLEDGMENTS 343

DINA RUBINA: READING
LEONARDO'S HANDWRITING IN CONTEXT

Anna P. Ronell

Dina Rubina, who is one of the most well-known and prolific Russian-language writers in Israel, was born in Tashkent, Uzbekistan, in 1953. She moved to Israel in 1990 with the biggest Aliyah of Soviet Jews and by 2017 published 10 novels and numerous novellas and short stories whose plot lines span the world and range in genre and concept as well as literary technique. Leonardo's Handwriting (2008) occupies an important place in Rubina's overall artistic oeuvre and exhibits both intriguing continuities and breaks with the novels that preceded it, pointing to the ongoing process of rethinking and building out some of the themes she has been pursuing for more than a decade. Being located in Rubina's post-immigration phase positions Leonardo's Handwriting in a somewhat different space within the context of her writing, highlighting the centrality of history and memory in her work and bringing to the forefront a strong female character who weaves her own magic into the time and space of the novel.

Rubina's writing, although unique, typifies the cultural expressions of the latest and biggest Russian Aliyah. She began her career in the Soviet Union and was a well-known author before her immigration to Israel in 1990. While enjoying a near-celebrity status in the Russian Jewish communities of Israel, the United States, Germany, and the former Soviet Union, her works are virtually unknown to the English-speaking public. Only a handful of short stories and one of her novels, Vot Idet Messiya (1996) (Here Comes the Messiah), have been recently translated into English. While the novel received many positive reviews, some of the distinct stylistic and linguistic flavor characteristic of Rubina's writing has been "lost in translation." Equally hard to capture are the subtle literary experimentations, fictional techniques, and motifs in Rubina's writing.[1]

The new English translation of Rubina's novel Leonardo's Handwriting is a bold attempt to introduce her to a new audience and to raise awareness not only of her decades of creativity but also of the existence of a vibrant, rich artistic community of Russian-speaking former Soviet Jews in Israel. This new translation is also the recognition of the fact that since the break up of the Soviet Union, the culture of the Jewish Diaspora has been transformed by the re-emergence of the Russian-language Jewish community into the global arena. The migration of almost 2 million Jews from the former Soviet Union to Israel, the US, Canada, and various European countries greatly impacted every aspect of the Jewish Diaspora and ignited a new wave of scholarship on the history and culture of this community and its relationships with the larger Jewish world. Since then, theoretical work on the Diaspora evolved considerably yet the unique nature of the Russian-language Diaspora within the Diaspora remains underappreciated and the scholarly insight into the paradoxes of globally distributed Russian-language post-Soviet Jewish culture remains scarce. The conversation around Rubina's writing not only highlights her artistic achievements but also adds to our knowledge of the multi-faceted cultural production of the Russian-language community, positioning it within the historical context of its experiences in the Russian Empire, the Soviet Union, and the post-Soviet transnational, supra-territorial Diaspora spaces.

Rubina's writing today is an outstanding reflection of Russian Israeli immigrant culture-in-progress because it occupies a privileged position of liminality, of being at the juncture of several languages and cultures. Her writing is also revealing of her ability to raise herself above the sociolinguistic environment of which she is an integral part and to look at it from the outside, appraising new developments as they are taking place "live" in real time. Rubina's works must be situated in her socio-historic context; they cannot be separated from the legacy of Russian Jewish culture in Europe and from the emerging Russian-Israeli culture with its multilingual diversity as well as with its conflicting norms, values, and behaviors. Yet writing self-consciously at the point of convergence and interaction of the culture of the Russian Aliyah of the 1990s and contem-

---

1   Parts of this essay are reprinted with permission from Anna P. Ronell, "Some Thoughts on Russian-language Israeli Fiction: Introducing Dina Rubina" in *Prooftexts. A Journal of Jewish Literary History*, Vol. 26, No. 2 (Spring 2008), pp. 197-231.

porary Israeli Hebrew culture, as well as classic European and Russian literature, Rubina has acquired a unique artistic perspective. Her works reflect upon and simultaneously shape her culture-in-flux, providing an intriguing opportunity for cultural mediation and bridging elements of Jewish history, culture and identity from around the world.

Adrian Wanner points out that the subject of "Russianness" among Russian-language Diaspora writers remains contested, as it is not clear whether the language of writing or the subject matter take priority in the author's self-identification.[2] Can Rubina be considered a Russian writer if she writes in Russian but calls Jerusalem her home? Is the question even relevant, considering that she occupies a liminal space where the Russian cultural frameworks mixed with immigrant experiences in Israel become yet another permutation of a supra-territorial post-Soviet culture in the Diaspora? Many Russian-language Israeli authors have a peculiar brand of "Russianness" so profoundly diasporic in its nature that it can be seen as a throwback unrelated to present-day Russia proper but rather to the mythology of intelligentsia that anchors many nostalgic memories of Russian immigrants in Israel.

In this context, I will borrow Julia Lerner's term of "the post-Soviet space" that lies beyond the lands of the former Soviet Union and extends into the worldwide Russian-speaking diaspora, including "the large and heterogeneous Russian-speaking collective in Israel." Lerner further claims that "using various institutions and media channels, Russians in Israel keep both aspects of their old cultural and political identity alive, along with their affinity to post-Soviet cultures and political formations."[3] While it is clear to all observers that Russian Israelis are very diverse, and that some are not halachically[4] Jewish, it is also fairly certain that their experiences in Israel are colored by their common Soviet origin. Lerner emphasizes that instead of using "Jewishness" as a common denominator for the Russian collective in Israel, it may be more useful to see their affinity with the cultural and political ideals of Soviet urban intelligentsia as the one shared aspect of their experience. While Lerner claims that

---

2 Adrian Wanner, "Russian Hybrids: Identity in the Translingual Writings of Andrei Makine, Wladimir Kaminer, and Gary Shteyngart," in *Slavic Review,* Vol. 67, No. 3, p. 662.

3 Julia Lerner, "Post-Soviet Russians in Israel: Paradoxes and Consistencies," in *Collective Identities, States and Globalization,* ed. G. Yair and O. Gazit. Jerusalem: Magnes Press, 2010, pp. 175–202.

4 According to the Orthodox community in Israel, a person must have verifyable evidence of being born to a Jewish mother to be considered a Jew according to the Halachah or Jewish religious Law.

the old intelligentsia has been negated and deconstructed in post-Soviet Russia proper—and is replaced by two new types of "the intellectual" and "the professional"—its echoes still linger in the Diaspora.

As Mikhail Krutikov points out, "in her novels and short stories, [Rubina] focuses on the predicament of the Russian intelligentsia in Israel as it tries to have its cake and to eat it too; that is, as it strives to become part of the new society and retain its cultural identity at the same time."[5] Rubina's writing reflects the fragmented identity of many of her characters, mirroring their alienation from both the Soviet-Russian and from the Israeli aspects of their background. Her biting political satire reflects the uncertainties of the post-Zionist ideological stagnation in Israel, where the necessity of the ingathering of the exiles is intertwined with the multi-faceted, perhaps even confused, historical memory of Russian Jews as well as with the challenges of Israeli elites facing waves of Palestinian terror. In *Leonardo's Handwriting*, the Russian-language readers in the Diaspora and in the post-Soviet territories can feel this lingering attachment to the values and practices of Soviet intelligentsia integrated with the newer aesthetics of nomadism, more cosmopolitan Western cultural practices and literary trends.

Rubina's literary interests are dynamic and evolving, many of the earlier motifs are less pronounced in her later works yet some remain central for attempting to understand her oeuvre as a whole. The figure of a creative—a writer, an artist, a performer—is a consistent presence in Rubina's writing and a corner stone theme in *Leonardo's Handwriting*. The figure of the artist, often a person who creates both with their mind and with their body, is not only the linchpin of a complicated plot but also a conduit through whom other characters' backstories as well as the larger philosophical themes are conveyed and revealed. As I discussed elsewhere, the critically important figure of the artist is part of Rubina's overarching theme of theater mundi, masks, and the carnival. The focus on the performative aspects of everyday life as well as of the human condition sets Rubina apart, foregrounding her continued interest in the fate of the Jewish world and the fate of the Artist.

In her early works that understandably focused on the vagaries of immigrant experience, Rubina used elements of Bakhtinian Carnival to construct a complex image of Israel and of the Russian community there

---

5   Mikhail Krutikov, "Constructing Jewish Identity in Contemporary Russian Fiction," in *Jewish Life after the USSR*, ed. Zvi Gitelman. Bloomington: Indiana University Press, 2003, pp. 252–274.

under the overarching umbrella theme of the Carnival. In the short story "Pod Znakom Karnavala" (1999) (Under the Sign of the Carnival), Rubina describes Israeli life as a big theater, presenting the "open, brutal, murderous" carnivalesque quality of it as a uniquely attractive attribute that helps her "keep her head above water." How does the carnivalesque manifest itself in Israeli life? It is described as "the changing of faces, images, and masks; turned-inside-out meaning of existence; reversed situations with their straightforward theatricality and open idiotic farce. The masks are painted roughly, a maid is dressed as a mistress, a mistress is dressed as a courtesan, and everybody is playing somebody else's roles. They play those roles in a vulgar, simplified, superficial manner, because nothing can be done—this is, after all, a street performance."[6] Life in Israel, both its oppressive qualities as well as its richness and vitality, is associated in Rubina's writing with popular culture, with a multifaceted street life, and with the subversive nature of the immigrant experience that allows one to start over, often by acquiring a completely new mask.

Rubina is not alone in her attempts to adapt Bakhtinian concepts of the Carnival to the analysis of contemporary Israeli culture and society. A well-known Russian Israeli anthropologist, Narspy Zilberg, uses the categories of analysis of literary texts developed by Bakhtin in her interpretation of the problems of immigrant culture: "Dialogism of liminal existence, i.e., life on the edge, on the threshold, life full of change and renewal, of a particular ambivalence that expresses the inevitability of the reduction of status and the subversion of existing order, is surprisingly parallel to the dilemmas of immigrant worldview."[7] Like Zilberg who develops adaptation models of Russian Jewish intelligentsia in Israel, Rubina perceives the crucial moment of transformation of consciousness and of reemergence in a new hypostasis as a point of exceptional importance that gives her an opportunity to expand beyond the limitations of realist prose and to enter the realm of the grotesque where she manipulates linguistic structures to create a highly affective emotional atmosphere.

The post-immigration phase of Rubina's writing starts off with two intriguing novels: *On the Sunny Side of the Street* (2006) and *Leonardo's Handwriting* (2008). *Leonardo's Handwriting* is not set in Israel, nor

---

6   Dina Rubina, *Chem By Zaniatsia?* Saint Petersburg: Retro, 2001, p. 25. All translations are mine.

7   Narspi Zilberg, "Russko-Evreyskaya Intellegentsia v Israele: Poiski Novykh Modelei Integratsii," in *Migration Processes and Their Influence on Israeli Society*. Moscow: Institute for the Study of Israel, 2000, p. 204.

does it focus on the immigrant experience. The novel does not have a quasi-autobiographical authorial persona or any attempts at epic depiction of multiethnic and multilingual Israeli society. Yet, the Carnival emerges in a new manifestation becoming the Circus. The creative protagonist—a mysterious genius named Anna (and nicknamed Nyuta)—starts her professional career working as a gymnast and aerial acrobat for the circus and touring the Soviet Union with a rag-tag collection of characters who also perform familiar parts of the Masks: the clown, the animal trainer, the flame swallower, the trapeze flier, or the illusionist. The Circus, yet another creative space that takes upon many of the characteristics of the Carnival, emerges as its own world, an ecosystem where many Soviet cultural and social phenomena coalesce to produce a dangerous place fueled by alcohol and adrenalin. The Russian Circus is a profoundly dark mental and physical place where performers live the life of drudgery interspersed with moments of unimaginable risk. Darkness and light, ugliness and beauty, vile base aspects of the human nature compete with generosity and kindness, creating a complex network of characters that interact with each other inside and outside the circus tent and sustain the epic story of tortured creative souls in the USSR.

As the story of Anna progresses through a series of interviews in an Interpol investigation, the third person narrator whom many of Rubina's committed readers will undoubtedly perceive as yet another reincarnation of the familiar mask of "Dina the writer" remains much less pronounced than in her previous works. Dina Rubina the implied author emphasizes in her writings and interviews the differences between her authorial persona and "the real" Dina Rubina, a human being who lives with her family in Ma'ale Adumim and who may or may not share the views and opinions of Dina Rubina the implied author. Autobiographical details throughout her short stories, novels, and novellas—some factual, some fictional—give a sense of coherent, continuous narrative, creating an illusion of authenticity, which in turn give her readers an illusion of familiarity. The quasi-autobiographical first person narrator sometimes openly takes advantage of the readers' expectations, preconceived notions, and their comfort zone, to conflate the author as a character and the author as a human being as an intrinsic part of her creative process. Over time, similar to such celebrated and recognizable authorial personae as Sholem Aleichem or Mendele Mokher Sefarim, Rubina's protagonist-narrator Dina became a real literary presence that "managed to retain a cohesive and unified personality, a distinct and immediately recognizable voice, tonality, and manner of speech" through her entire literary corpus.[8] Thus the persona of Dina, which should not be identified with the writer, assumes both the literary function of tying together her entire Israel-related work and the social function of providing a witty—sometimes even caustic—commentary on the cultural, economic, and political situation of Russian-speaking Jews (and non-Jews) in Israel and elsewhere.

One of the most important aspects of Rubina's post-immigration phase is the new awareness of the transnational, transcultural, and translingual nature of the contemporary world, which is closely related conceptually to globalization, cultural production stemming from migration experiences, and the new identities born of displacement. The paradox is that some writers choose the language of their host countries for their creative writing on the subject of Russia, while Rubina and the majority of Soviet Jewish authors in Israel choose to write in Russian on the subject of life in Israel as well as in other places including Ukraine, Uzbekistan, Spain, and Canada. In *Leonardo's Handwriting*, many of the earlier motifs are seen in sharp relief: imaginary geography and a new focus on space where movement is part of the plot; multiple voices and changing points of view, heteroglossia and linguistic hybridity; non-linear conceptualization of time that sheds a new light on the discussions of prophesy and divinity. In the words of Maria Rubina, "Artistic imagination, shaped by dislocation, transplantation, and the ensuing defamiliarization of referential reality, fosters the superimposition of the realistic and the fantastic, the fusion of various national contexts, a commitment both to local and global points of view, and the creation of imaginary locations, alternate histories, and science-fictional worlds."[9] Rubina's artistic imagination blossoms in *Leonardo's Handwriting* representing a new phase in the development of her transcultural writing.

Rubina's depictions of geographical places always draw the readers' attention with their richness and vitality, with the atmospheric ambiance, and groups of diverse characters. "Rubina describes Kiev as she used to describe Tashkent: deliciously, in detail, with its colors, smells, and distinctive speech patterns," says one review.[10] Indeed, Rubina's portrayal of Tashkent and its environs as well as her rootedness in the mem-

---

8   Dan Miron, *The Image of the Shtetl and Other Studies of Modern Jewish Literary Imagination*. Syracuse, N.Y.: Syracuse University Press, 2000, p. 118.

9   Maria Rubins, "Transnational identities in Diaspora Writing: The Narratives of Vasily Yanovsky," in *Slavic Review*, Vol. 73, No. 1 (Spring 2014), pp. 62-84.

10   "Dina Rubina," in Read Russia: <http://readrussia.org/writers/writer/dina-rubina>.

ory of Eastern European Jewish life are autobiographically inspired, yet, transnational and transcultural in their essence. "With a wave of evacuation, a lot of people found themselves in Tashkent. Quite young, my 17-year-old mother came with the evacuation, and my father was demobilized from the army after the war. Then my mother entered the Central Asian State University (SAGU), where the Moscow and Leningrad professors taught and it was a wonderful education. Dad after demobilization from the front returned to Tashkent, to his parents. I'm from the descendants of the evacuees, we grew up on their stories, their life experiences. Tashkent was the place where a lot of things fused together."[11] Both Rubina's parents are from the Ukraine—father from Kharkov and mother from Poltava—and both found themselves in Tashkent as a result of the Jewish mass evacuation to Central Asia. And it is certain that the evacuation is central to the family history as well as to Rubina's life-long writing career.

Rubina's novellas and short stories illustrate her comfort with her home in Tashkent yet show a profound affinity to her family's deep roots in the Jewish Ukraine. This advantage of intimately knowing both worlds allows Rubina to show an unprecedented cultural fluidity, navigating between Soviet, Jewish, Russian, and Uzbek cultural, social, and political aspects. The dynamics of cultural mediation that emerges as a key concept in Rubina's writing, further carrying on into her later reflections of Russian immigrant experience in Israel, are also critically important for *Leonardo's Handwriting*. Women's writing in Russian in the present-day Israel—for example, novels by Elena Minkina or short stories by Victoria Reicher—occupy a liminal position at the intersection of multiple cultural, political, psychological, and social phenomena, their works can be often seen as instances of cultural mediation as they address all stages of adaptation from a variety of different perspectives. Rubina takes the mantle of cultural mediation and embarks on a quest to connect dispersed geographical locations across the Jewish Diaspora—and across time and space—to create a set of transcultural works with noticeable threads permeating many of them.

Addressing her childhood in Tashkent, Rubina's writing examines complex processes of identity formation among the Jewish evacuees who found themselves in Central Asia and who see themselves, for all intents and purposes, as part of the emerging concept of Soviet peo-

---

11   Dina Rubina, "Greetings to Tashkent and Tashkenters" (An Interview with Dina RUbina for KULTURA.UZ), 10.03.2016: <http://www.kultura.uz/view_9_r_6593.html>.

plehood, strengthened as a result of the Great Patriotic War and now including the far-flung periphery of the Central Asian republics. Rubina has been known to speak highly and very positively about her childhood in Tashkent, about the people of Tashkent and the inspiration she derives from her years of growing up there for her novels and short stories: "Tashkenters are people unique in their fortitude, their readiness to dive straight into life, to offer their hand, heart, shoulder to lean on, to help everybody with anything, and under the circumstances to be proactive, energetic, and productive. I would like to stress that this is the dominant feature of Tashkent, a very unusual Central Asian city."[12] Rubina often mentions that the images of Tashkent and its inhabitants are cumulative, they are inspired by people she met, people she grew up with, and people she only heard about. These people are often seen by her as a thread that connects her family's pre-war roots in Ukraine with the post-war life in Tashkent, with an "alternative universe" fantasy of family history in Spain, and further with Rubina's characters in present-day Israel as well as their travels to Europe and the Americas.

It is possible to suggest that in *Leonardo's Handwriting* one of Rubina's goals might be to downplay the familiar quasi-autobiographic authorial persona and instead to foreground the Soviet history 30 years after the collapse of the Soviet Union, reaching out to those readers who are looking to ponder the nature of the new, post-Soviet reality, both in the former Soviet space and in the Diaspora. Each voice and each individual story is uniquely important, yet in the context of emerging global literary imagination, the blending of multiple voices into a form of heteroglossia within the very fabric of fiction serves as a very successful medium to relate the Soviet and post-Soviet Jewish experience in a form accessible to the general public. Memory and history are central to all Rubina's works yet they acquire exceptional importance in *Leonardo's Handwriting*. Rubina's profound awareness of the multilayered and multifaceted sociohistorical situation in the Soviet Union corresponds to her fundamental view of history (mostly Jewish) as the foundation of her writing. Addressing the ways in which history is perceived in Rubina's fiction is central to our understanding of her entire oeuvre. Is it viewed teleologically as patterns of progress? Is history cyclical or can it be represented as alternative time lines? If there are no patterns or cycles, is human history therefore random and devoid of meaning? What is the role of human agency as opposed to the role of God?

---

12   Ibid., also Dina Rubina, "Biography": <http://www.dinarubina.com/biography.html>.

The Holocaust is a persistent presence throughout Rubina's works but in *Leonardo's Handwriting* is acquires a particularly significant prominence. As Anna grows up in Kiev, the tragedy of Baby Yar and the fate of the Jewish population of Ukraine is always part of the narrative. Sometimes, it feels that the void left behind by the thousands of Jews who disappeared during the Holocaust can be palpable in the streets of Kiev, at other times, the smallest mention in passing of somebody killed by the Germans brings the feelings of void to the surface. Rubina writes, for example, of Fira Avelevna, a blind elderly neighbor Nyuta knew in Kiev.

> "Firavelna" was the grandmother and head of the large and noisy Girshovich clan from the courtyard next door. Nyuta had been going there to play for about a year and a half. The family consisted of Uncle Zhora, a foreman at the Transsignal Electrical Engineering Factory, a cocky type with a brazen tenor voice, who wore threadbare tracksuit bottoms; Auntie Rosa, his wife and Firavelna's youngest daughter, who worked as an operating theatre assistant at the hospital; their niece, Sonya, daughter of Busa, the sister-who-was-executed-may-her-memory-be-a-blessing-and-all-who-killed-her-burn-in-hell; their older son, Borya, a student at the music school (he played the cello), and six-year-old Arisha-with-the-slight-squint. She was the one Nyuta really went to play with. (97-98)

In the USSR—unlike World War II and the heroism of the Soviet people—the Holocaust has never been the same part of collective consciousness and public discourse as it was in Israel and the US. Even now, the presence of the Holocaust in Russian-Jewish literature is only beginning to be felt, often mentioned obliquely, sometimes an open secret, other times, an un-mourned trauma never addressed and never healed.

None of the specifically Jewish aspects of the Holocaust were part of Soviet popular culture or public education. In fact, the most significant postwar ideological development was the Cult of the Great Patriotic War. Memorials were built, novels written, and songs composed to commemorate the sacrifice and courage of the Soviet people during the war. In this context, the discussion of the particular nature of the Jewish war experience—both the Holocaust and the participation of Jewish soldiers in the Red Army—was suppressed. A mass murder of East European Jews on the Soviet territories and pervasive collaborationism[13]

---

13   Rita Vanagaite, *Ours*. Vilnius: Alma Littera, 2015.

was either silently ignored or was presented as a small part of the larger context of the war and the German crimes against the Soviet people. According to Emil Draitser and other scholars, the total control of the Soviet government over all media allowed for the Soviet information policy, which Paul Ricoeur called "organized forgetting."[14]

As one of the primary sources of legitimacy, the Great Patriotic War (as World War II was called in the Soviet Union) became as much a symbol and a propaganda resource as an object of honest historic inquiry. The central aspect of this symbolic function of the war memory was the display of honoring the dead through elaborate ceremonies, oversized memorials, and, of course, highly ideological literary productions. This version of the war memory did not include the Red Army defeats in the beginning of the war, the enormous waste of human life, or the brutality of political security forces toward their own people. Neither did it include any of the specifically Jewish themes: the destruction of the *shtetlach*, the mass murder of the Soviet Jews in the occupied territories by the *Einsatzgruppen*, nor the collaboration with the Germans fueled by antisemitism as well as by anti-Soviet sentiments. The war cult and the manipulation of institutional and personal means of memorialization emptied meaning out of people's commemorative impulse while suppressing all mention of the Holocaust.[15]

Under the limitations imposed by the Cult of the Great Patriotic War as well as post-war repressions and the general restrictions on all forms of cultural production, Soviet Jewry never enjoyed an outlet for the trauma of the Holocaust. As there was little opportunity for memorialization and mourning, this trauma remained unresolved, and the grief over the loss of loved ones and entire communities went mostly unaddressed. Current literary representations of the Holocaust in contemporary Russian-language fiction in the diaspora are complex. In *Leonardo's Handwriting*, the theme of the Holocaust is directly connected to the figure of Simon and through him to Nyuta. Therefore, the lengthy epistolary memoirs of his Jewish childhood that Simon sends to Nyuta serve multiple functions: they connect the presently nomadic globalized post-Soviets to their roots in pre-Holocaust Pale of the Settlement, they shape the characters' perceptions of the present based on their sense of

---

14   Emil Draitser, "Introduction," in Friedrich Gorenstein, *Redemtion*. New York: Columbia University Press, 2018, p. xv.

15   For more in-depth discussion of this subject see Nina Tumarkin, *The Living and the Dead: The Rise and Fall of the Cult of World War II in Russia*. New York: Basic Books, 1994.

history, and they provide different perspectives on what life was in Soviet Ukraine. The Holocaust in *Leonardo's Handwriting* is not yet another moment of darkness; it is part of Rubina's historic consciousness that informs her explorations of post-Soviet Jewish identity.

Addressing different Jewish "histories" throughout the ages and territories of dispersal, including discussions of Jewish history in Spain, Eastern Europe, and contemporary as well as ancient Israel, Rubina's writing is exceedingly Diasporan. Rubina's diverse fictional territory(ies) and her treatments of space in literature and culture, including the interplay between text and world—her interpretations of the geographies of the 'real' and the geographies of the 'imaginary' are exceedingly important for appreciating the scope of her literary vision. Yet in *Leonardo's Handwriting*, the protagonist's nomadic lifestyle questions the familiar concepts of space, home, and belonging as well as the concept of time that comes undone by Nyuta's ability to use complex mirror structures in her mind to simultaneously perceive the past, present, and future at once. Time and space, perhaps even the history of a place, disappear as the figure of Nyuta comes to represent the mystery of life BEYOND time and space. Thoughtful readers would undoubtedly recognize elements of magical realism throughout the novel. Magical realism, known for its dreamlike and somewhat bizarre quality, is particularly well suited for creating a protagonist like Nyuta that echoes a religious concept as much as the human life. Critics usually associate the concept of Magical Realism with the concept of "heightened reality," with the elements of the fantastic that seamlessly become part of "normal life" or with the addition of another dimension of reality through a symbolic or metaphoric structure. While in the case of Borges and Gabriel Garcia Marquez magical realism was distinguished by the fact that its practitioners treated the fantastic as normal, without any sense of surprise or amazement, in the case of Dina Rubina, the scrambled foculization, switching points of view, and numerous alternating yet complementary narrative lines intertwine in such a way that even the characters seem to be aware of their own oddness, their unusual gifts and extraordinary circumstances. What precisely is Nyuta's destiny? And what about other characters' destinies? These intertwining destinies become a narrative knot where the small choices made by "little people" acquire cosmic proportions.

History has always been part of Rubina's writing, little echoes of history are interspersed throughout her works and we can see this technique in *Leonardo's Handwriting* as well. In Rudesheim, Simon encounters a music box exactly the same he saw all through his childhood in his Aunt Frieda's room in Zhmerinka. That exact music box, made of polished mahogany and labeled by the maker in Imperial Saint Petersburg, triggers Simon's memories and makes an unexpected connection between German Rudesheim and Jewish Zhmerinka. The material culture of the Jews has always been reflected in Jewish fiction and Rubina's writing is no exception. As things acquire their own historical significance, they become markers of Jewish identity, the milestones of family history and connectors between seemingly unrelated people. Jewish artifacts, family heirlooms and ritual articles encountered in the present unleash a flood of memories about the past. The artifacts are not depicted as being actually used in the present; instead, they function as the vehicles of the past, conduits of memory flashes. Why is there a Russian made music box in a museum in Rudesheim, Germany that is exactly like the one a Jewish family had in Ukraine? How Jewish artifacts migrate to Germany? And what do we feel when we see them in a museum? Reading Simon's letter to Nyuta, with its descriptions of Simon's Jewish family in Ukraine, can we avoid thinking about the Holocaust as Simon is sightseeing in Germany?

Anna's life trajectory is unpredictable and the feelings of ambiguity and suspense are reinforced by Rubina's pastiche of various genres, including elements of detective story, mystery, and the epistolary novel. Most questions raised in the novel remain unanswered and the readers are left to decide for themselves how they feel regarding the novel's open ending. Rubina at times hints at various possibilities concealed in the complex mystery of who—or what—Anna might be. One hypothesis may be Rubina's ongoing quest to portray the Fate of the Artist and to contemplate the nature of artistic gift that simultaneously can be a curse. Anna has a number of extraordinary abilities that at times echo the super-heroes of the Marvel universe, mutants, avengers, and others who have exceptional gifts, can bend space and time, and perform physical and mental feats beyond all imagination. On a separate, yet connected, plane, the character of Anna is bound to remind us of the prophets of the Hebrew Bible. Even though most of Anna's life is spent in Ukraine, Western Europe, and Canada, it is the ancient prophetic fervor of the Hebrew visionaries that can be felt pulsating through Anna's energy. It is Simon, an old Russian Jew who understands her the best and whose near-religious faith in her underlies much of the plot, and the person who becomes the conduit of Anna's uniqueness as well as the vehicle of Rubina's storytelling.

All three characters who believe in Nyuta and genuinely trust her abilities as a Seer or a Prophet are Jews: Simon, Eliezer, and Firavelna. Eliezer taught Nyuta about the physics of the mirrors yet the miracle of having the mirrors inside her mind was inaccessible to him. His mirrors were not inside his being and he did not have the abilities of a seer. Eliezer was a scientist who through of Nyuta as his angel. Jewish characters and their spiritual journeys with Nyuta are the narrative threads that tie together the plot lines of the novel. Simon, specifically, is intriguingly the person of profound faith yet also a Jew without a recognizably Jewish religious context. As Vladimir attempts to explain to the investigator, Simon's faith transcended both the Old and the New Testaments:

> You should have heard how he explained things! It'd blow your mind. For example, he swore she was an angel. You gotta laugh, right? Not an angel-from-heaven kind of angel but, according to him, her nature was similar to some sort of beings that appear as angels and archangels and other celestial beings in folk psychology... That people believe in them because from time to time such beings really do appear on earth among humans... Jesus, for example. Do you believe? I don't really. (209)

Leonardo's Handwriting also represents an intriguing step away from attempting to deal with the subject of immigration and to a larger, more open-ended subject of migration and nomadism in a global context. As more times passes since the Great Aliyah of the early 1990s, the more Rubina's writing acquires the characteristics associated with transcultural literary works "that engage with and express the confluential nature of cultures overcoming the different dichotomies between North and South, the West and the Rest, the colonizer and the colonized, the dominator and the dominated, the native and the (im)migrant, the national and the ethnic."[16] The earlier signs of this tendency towards transculturalism can be seen in Rubina's celebrated novel *On the Sunny Side of the Street* that purportedly draws on her childhood in Tashkent as well as on her family history in Eastern Europe.

One of the central foci throughout Rubina's works, reaching particular maturity in *On the Sunny Side of the Street* and *Leonardo's Hand-*

---

16   Arianna Dagnino, "Transcultural Literature and Contemporary World Literature(s)," in *CLCWeb: Comparative Literature and Culture*, Vol. 15, No. 5 (2013): <https://docs.lib.purdue.edu/clcweb/vol15/iss5/7/>.

writing, is the singular preoccupation with the place to live, the place that can be the mythical home or just a place where one's head hits the pillow. Both *Leonardo's Handwriting* and *On the Sunny Side of the Street* have impressively rich mix of characters that includes Eastern European Jews, ethnic Russians, Ukrainians, Uzbeks and other native Central Asian peoples as well as colorful criminals, seekers, wanderers, and trouble-makers, all come to encompass the human condition that is inseparable from the dichotomy of home/exile, being rooted/uprooted, settled/unsettled. This evolution of Rubina's artistic imagination, shaped by globalization, migration, and deterritorialization, draws a renewed focus on the spaciality of human cultures, her charaters' growing and evolving identities, and the overall importance of space and place in her discussion of the human condition.

As the plot of *Leonardo's Handwriting* follows the life of Nyuta, it becomes clear that the themes of nomadism and homelessness are central for the character development and for Rubina's explorations of the concept of the living space. Right from the beginning, Rubina emphasized that Nyuta was a highly gifted, unique and extraordinary individual who had no home:

She had her life all planned out for about the next three years. I never knew where she was living at a particular time, where she was racing off to on her bike. Generally, she lived her own way—here and there, one minute locally, the next nowhere at all. In any country, she would hire a motorbike, either a powerful sports bike if she was going off road, or a cruiser, a manoeuvrable one, if she was in the city. And no luggage. A small backpack with a change of underwear, the eternal notebook for working things out. She resolved the wardrobe issue easily: she went to the nearest shop, bought her usual green or navy sweater or tee-shirt, depending on the weather. Then she'd leave them all over the place—in her hotel room, her "nest" at Genevieve's, or on a bench—for people in need... I never knew anyone less bothered about herself than she was. (49)

This itinerant lifestyle is both the protagonist's philosophy of life and Rubina's way to highlight the newness of post-Soviet globalization, the fall of the Iron Curtain, and the opening of the flood gates that allowed individuals to leave the territorial and the familial and to escape into the transcultural space, transcending both the geographical borders and the boundaries of their identities.

Nyuta's ethnic identity is never revealed and we never learn for sure who her parents were exactly. As she rises above the very notion of identity, the reader who is aware of the central place Jewishness occupies in Rubina's writing can't help but wonder if the mystery of Nyuta's birth connects her to the Jews. As Nyuta travels the world, two male figures—both Jewish— emerge as her anchors, supporters, and partners. Both Simon and Eliezer have an inkling of Nyuta's extraordinary nature yet both remain on the margins of her genius. As in many of her other works, in *Leonardo's Handwriting* Rubina structures the movement of the plot through the movement of her characters through varied geography of Soviet and post-Soviet space. The question of identity and belonging (or not belonging) is central to the trope of journey, characters' nomadic existence, uprootedness, and dislocation. This question is raised in many of Rubina's previous works, especially in *Here Comes The Messiah*, where it is reflected through multiple characters, all of whom represent parts of the authorial persona. This authorial persona functions as connective tissue between things Soviet and things Israeli, bringing into sharp focus the confusion Russian Israelis experience while differentiating between "here" and "there" and "us" and "them." As different characters in the novel question their place in the world, the discussion extends into a larger existential quandary: Who are the Jews? What makes a person Jewish? Why are Jews destined to wander around the world? The well-known Russian literary critic Lev Anninsky, for example, sees Rubina's perception of Jewishness as "not a nationality, not a population, not a peoplehood, not a tribe, not a religion, but as some secret vow, a sign, a fate that is inescapable."[17] Does Nyuta have this sign? Rubina never gives us a direct answer.

I would also like to theorize that there is an evolutionary trajectory of the female characters from the autobiographically inspired writer Dina, the struggling immigrant intellectual in Israel, to the celebrated Tashkent artist Vera Scheglova and her mother Katya, a criminal mastermind in charge of all Tashkent drug trade, to the figure of Nyuta, an acrobat, a performer, a prophet, and a witch. Nyuta emerges as the strongest of all Rubina's female characters, she is never helpless, nor a victim. She is one of the rare people who has full confidence in her abilities, her unique role in this universe, and is in full control of her life. Nyuta is portrayed as a uniquely independent woman who makes her

---

17   Lev Anninsky, "Otsecheno? Otrubleno? Otrezano?," in *Druzhba Narodov*, No. 10 (1996), pp. 218–222.

own choices and pursues her freedom to the fullest. Even though Nyuta's speech is mediated by the third-person narrator, there is no doubt that she does not set any limitations on herself on spiritual, intellectual, or physical levels. Despite the fact that throughout the novel she is the object of the male gaze and the performer for the spectators' visual pleasure, Nyuta shapes her own life and her own story. As a highly successful aerial acrobat and later a stunt performer, Nyuta creates art with her body which is subjected to the judgment and the gaze of hundreds of spectators, actors, directors, producers, and others in her creative universe. Rubina mentions on multiple occasions both the beauty and the extraordinary physical strength of Nyuta's body, sometimes appearing as an exotic marvel bedecked in sequins and feathers flying on the trapeze, and sometimes as an almost non-gendered biker riding a motorcycle at a neck-breaking speed, wearing rough boots, jeans and leathers. Sometimes Nyuta is a boyish girl, fit, muscular, and wound up tightly as a spring, sometimes she is likened to a musical instrument attuned to a special melody while making love. The two men through whose eyes we see Nyuta—her ex-husband Vladimir and her lover Simon—are both men, their views of her body are openly sexualized both inside and outside the Circus. The Male Gaze follows Nyuta everywhere yet the readers awareness that the writer Dina Rubina is actually a woman adds an intriguing dimension to the perceptions of her male characters. Nyuta's own self-perception, presented by the third-person narrator, adds yet another level to the mystery of Nyuta's nature and identity:

> *All her life, the moment of recognizing herself in the mirror was like a delayed parachute drop. She was never able to merge with her reflection straight away. In that first moment there was an encounter, a shock, a heartbeat—someone else is wearing your clothes. She had to turn herself the other way around and every single time she had to teach herself how to look all over again.*
> *Although she could always recognize herself in any distorted surface, in water, in a spoon, in the fat belly of the enamel teapot. (58)*

The multi-dimensionality of Nyuta's body imagery, the portrayals of her strength and self-confidence, acceptance of her sexuality and her being, is perhaps Rubina's subversive incursion into the territory of male foculization.

Quite a few readers noticed the polyphonic quality of Rubina's writing, often attributing it to the experience of growing up in Tashkent:

"It may partially derive from the fact that Dina was born and spent her childhood years in Tashkent, a sun-soaked Central Asian city where representatives of different cultures and ethnicities lived side by side. The scorching sun, the polyphony of an Oriental city, various episodes from her early and teenage years come up again and again in Rubina's novels and short stories."[18] Although it is undoubtedly true that the multiculturalism of post-war Tashkent is the basis for Rubina's polyphonic writing style, it is possible to suggest that over time it developed into one of the most fundamental qualities of her entire artistic oeuvre. The richness of Rubina's multi-faceted depictions of the diversity of the Tashkent's human multitudes—similar to her later depictions of the carnavalesque life in Israel—stems from her affinity for exploring the multi-lingual and multi-cultural coalescence. As I previously argued, Rubina is known for her complex dialogic imagination, incorporating and inter-weaving various voices to create an image that represents an all-encompassing mode of existence in Israel as well as in Tashkent.[19] Unfettered by the conventions of one particular genre or literary style, Rubina engages as many socially and historically charged voices as possible. Her continuous effort at heteroglossia and a multilingual milieu create an intricate, polyphonic textual quality. Thus Rubina's texts are implicitly dialogic, not only because she addresses her reader as a potential interlocutor, but primarily because her tropes, as complex networks of meaning, represent a variety of voices deeply rooted in languages. The totality of these often disaccorded voices is more generative than each one taken separately; they function together to produce a heterogeneous collective—the characters of the novel that span the width and breadth of what was coined as Soviet People. Rubina's *Leonardo's Handwriting* emerges at the crossroads of cultures, where Israeli, Russian, and other cultural, intellectual, and aesthetic trends come to bear fruit unseen anywhere else.

---

18   Alena Tveritina, "Dina Rubina: Turning the Central Asian Sun into Words," in *Russia Beyond*, 14.01.2015: <https://www.rbth.com/literature/2015/01/14/dina_rubina_turning_the_central_asian_sun_into_words_42855.html>.

19   Anna P. Ronell, "Some Thoughts on Russian-language Israeli Fiction: Introducing Dina Rubina" in *Prooftexts. A Journal of Jewish Literary History*, Vol. 26, No. 2 (Spring 2008), pp. 197-231.

LEONARDO'S
HANDWRITING

To Lina Nikolskaya,
Aerial Tightrope Walker

*And Jacob was left alone and
a man wrestled with him until the breaking of the day.*

Genesis 32:24

So let nobody expect us to say anything about angels.

Benedict/Baruch Spinoza, *Of the Human Mind*

PART ONE

*Mancinism or leftsidedness is today regarded
as a character of atavism and degeneration…*

Cesare Lombroso, *The Man of Genius*

*It appears, then, that left-handed people
are more numerous among criminals,
and sensitive left-sided people among lunatics.*

Cesare Lombroso, *Left-Handedness
and Left-Sidedness*

CHAPTER 1.

The phone rang, drawn-out and insistent, like the whistle of a train: long distance.

It was in the hall beneath a large oval mirror, and when her husband's relatives rang, it seemed to Masha that the mirror shook as if rocked by a passing train and was about to fall off the wall.

A flat, official voice: "Please hold. Mariupol for you." Do they pick these people for their voices?

It was Tamara, her husband's cousin.

She usually called to say Happy New Year or to report the death of yet another aunt—Anatoly had a whole set of ageing relations in Mariupol.

Masha wanted to put him on right away but Tamara said,

"Hang on a sec, Masha. It's actually you I want to talk to..."

And spluttering self-consciously she said that Aunty Lida's niece had passed away after a failed appendix operation in Yeysk. There now.

"What Aunty Lida?"

"Oh, you have met her and you met her niece at my wedding. Aunty Lida—she's dead now—she wasn't related on our side, she was an in-law."

And she was off ... In short, Aunty Lida was an in-law, not on the Mariupol side, on the Yeysk side.

It was a long time since Masha had abandoned her attempts to remember all the family connections of her husband's abundant relations.

"And, just listen, the niece might be gone but she's left a little girl. She's only three."

"Yes, and?"

And, clearly anxious, Tamara hastily relayed the fact that none of their relatives wanted to take the little girl even though those same relatives were really pretty well-off: the dead woman's cousin was a dental technician, didn't want for anything.

Since in that family the living and the dead marched amicably arm-in-arm from one generation to the next with cheery banter and bickering, still arguing, still singing, still draining their glasses, it was really strange that not one of them wanted to take the child in.

Masha gritted her teeth. Don't get worked up, she told herself, no one meant to insult you. No one's thinking about what you're going through.

"Tomka," she eventually brought herself to say calmly, "Why are you telling me all this?"

Tamara halted. An indifferent swell of voices boomed in the receiver and Masha suddenly realized that, in order to have this conversation, Tamara had gone to the telegraph office and waited in line for a booth…

"Well, maybe have a think, Masha," Tamara said, as if apologizing. "After all, you don't have any children. Perhaps this is a chance? No matter how you look at it, you're already, what, thirty-six?"

"Thirty-four," Masha broke in. "And I'm not giving up hope. I'm having treatment."

"Well, you know best…" Tamara immediately sounded deflated, she had lost interest in further conversation. "So, you won't even take the phone number of that woman, the dentist? Just in case?"

And for some reason Masha wrote it down, so as not to upset Tomka—after all, she meant well, fool that she was.

It was all so easy for them, those milk cows in Mariupol with their full udders.

She put the receiver down and raised her head. A woman, still young, her mobile face sprinkled with an enchanting smattering of freckles, gazed out of the oval mirror in its black frame. Her husband, resting after his shift, could be seen behind her in the gap of the open bedroom door. One bare foot swung like a pendulum keeping time either with his thoughts or with a tune he was humming silently. His face was shuttered by an open book, the title and the author's name inverted in the mirror—impossible to read.

Further in, the depths of the mirror revealed a window onto a Kiev chestnut tree, its crown studded with white candles, tossing in the wind while, higher and deeper still, the blue void of the heavens ascended as reflection merged with source and vanished into nothingness….

All of a sudden, it frightened her.

What? she asked herself, attending to an ill-defined but very keen sense of dread. What's wrong with me? What does this fear of the pit,

   LEONARDO'S HANDWRITING

wide-open in welcome, have to do with an ordinary reflection in a household mirror?

Masha lay awake all night. She got up twice to dose herself with valerian drops. Tolya said nothing although she could hear him tossing and turning until dawn.

Exactly twelve months ago, after years upon years of medical ordeals, they had become parents to a big, bonny stillborn boy.

The morning after talking to Mariupol, Masha waited for the door to close behind her husband to dial the number of the strange woman who couldn't—or wouldn't—take in her orphaned niece.

Everything went well: she got through quickly, the woman was in, the line was incredibly clear and the conversation was brief, brusque and exhaustive as if fate was in a hurry to skim through a page that had nothing much to say.

When she heard Masha's opening words, the woman said, "You won't take that child. She's incredibly thin."

"What does that mean?" Masha inquired, "Is she ill?"

"I'm telling you, you won't take her. You'll be too scared."

"So… where is she now? Who's looking after her?

"There's a neighbour, she's kind. Used to be friends with Rita, who died. She's busy trying to get the child into an institution."

"Address!" said Masha, breathing hard. The woman spelt it out.

Masha replaced the receiver in silence.

That afternoon Tolya phoned from the hospital and said there were two tickets available to see Arkady Raykin in action. "Should we go?"

"I don't really feel like it…."

And she wasn't herself the whole evening. She started going through their paperwork for some reason. She sat quietly, pensively setting out school leaving certificates, diplomas, their wedding certificate, like cards in a game of patience. The letters Tolya had written to her when he was still studying at the Military Medical Academy.

He came out of the bathroom on his way to bed and looked at his wife. She hugged herself as she hunched over the coloured cardboard files, her feet in their soft slippers tucked beneath her chair. Masha looked up with an apologetic smile.

He sighed and said, "Go on, go. See what's going on… But you'd be the one bringing her up."

***

Masha had an easy journey as far as Yeysk, with just one change of train, but when she found the address she wanted on Shosseynaya Street, the little girl turned out to have gone off with a children's home to their summer quarters.

It was Shura, that same kind-hearted neighbour, who had got her onto the trip. Every year, she helped in the kitchens of the children's home's summer quarters. "Well, judge for yourself: it's got to be worth it, free food, the sea air, you don't even touch your pay packet." It took just ten minutes for Masha to learn all this from two old ladies, the garrulous denizens of the bench always found at the entrance to any block of flats.

"Shura got herself into a right old state, worried herself sick: the child won't eat, no matter what you do. P'rhaps, out there, with the children, she'll come round? Or she's going to waste away altogether."

"What about the father?" Masha asked. "Is he around at all?"

"Him? Oh, he's around…" echoed one of the old women. "He's around alright, in a lovely place. In the nick. Nice, free lodgings."

Her companion started cackling at the joke and she laughed for a long time, spluttering, wiping her hand across her mouth and saying over and over, "Aye, that's right. In the nick. He's around, that's for sure."

Masha made her way to the bus station and bought a ticket, as instructed by the neighbours, to Dolzhanskaya village.

…The summer quarters of the children's home was in a four-storey building of what used to be a holiday centre for either the iron and steel or the textile industry.

"It's four years now since the building was transferred to the Ministry of Health and they moved the children's health and holiday centre in after renovations. They bring children with cerebral palsy along and, you know, the treatment's not too bad at all. And one of the buildings is rented out to children's homes as a summer residence."

In addition to this information, Masha was obliged to listen to various facts from the life story of an imposing gentleman in striped pyjamas: *My Life and Struggle in the Tractor Factory Assembly Shop.*

He had fetched up alongside her out of nowhere as she went for a stroll to await the children's nap time—or more precisely as she paced to and fro beside the stone parapet of the embankment—and he just kept hanging around, oblivious to her acute agitation.

It began with her being completely unable to find Shura, *the kind-hearted neighbour,* the one who had arranged for the child to go on the summer trip. Masha was sent from one floor to the next and everywhere Shura had "just been seen" or had "probably gone to buy food" until, after studying Masha keenly from head to open-toed sandals, one of the dinner ladies in the empty dining room, said:

"Shura … basically…."

"What, basically?"

"Well, she's … she's taken some time off. To have her teeth out."

Moreover, the manager, the only person Masha could talk to about the little girl, had gone off to Yeysk in the morning and was only due back around four.

Masha went out onto the embankment which was bathed in the June sunlight.

Long white beaches on a heavenly spit of land were dotted with holidaymakers in coloured bathing costumes. Clear and high, the cries and swipes of the volleyball players broke the surface of the water-laden air that had not yet been baked dry by the sun. They were using a sagging net full of holes. With a dull thud, one of the players sent the ball into the water in such a powerful spin that a suntanned girl in a blue costume squealed in delight and raced after it… The ball hung in the air for a few endless seconds, spinning amid the azure swell of the lambswool clouds, the girl, feet catching in the sand, running towards it for an eternity … until it began its fateful descent and struck the wet sand a footfall from the water, rocked listlessly to and fro and came to a dead halt.

A few steps away from Masha, a small group of men and boys huddled over someone who was sitting on a wooden beer crate, his hands rapidly moving something around on a board set up on an identical crate. From a distance, they could have been taken for stamp-collectors had the entire company not given off a peculiar sense of danger and excitement.

A belligerent silence reigned above them for two or three seconds to be shattered by disappointed cursing, laughter and threats. In an instant, the company broke apart, revealing the red tufts of the seated man's hair and his nimble, tricksy hands, seemingly about to flee the scene. Then it closed balefully around him again.

Some sort of game, Masha thought, bound to be gambling, which means cheating, losing, despair, revenge…

Blinding glints of sunlight sparkled in the ultramarine depths, on which two lilos made bright-red patches. The delicate opal lens of the smoke-grey sky ran down to the horizon. Like two gigantic mirrors, sea and sky reflected one another until each became an exultation of fathomless blue.

Why, oh, why did these waves, regularly breaking on the shore, the lazy bodies on gaudy loungers, the pure water-colour line of the horizon leave her in the grip of such incurable yearning, as if there was already no way out? As if a trap was about to spring shut? After all, no one and nothing could make her…

"… so then I went straight to the People's Control Post," the old man mumbled, excited by his own story. "What on earth's going on on your shop floors then, comrades?"

"I'm sorry!" Masha said dully. "I… I have to go."

She turned round and left.

A harsh cry, a furious expletive, the clatter of the board being overturned behind her and suddenly the redhead overtook Masha, flying along the embankment, short blue satin trousers flapping in the wind.

Two youths were in hot pursuit, whistling and yelling something after him.

***

"You can of course have a look…" said the tall, broad-shouldered director (*What a size! How much material had gone into that white coat?*). "Look, by all means."

The conversation was taking place in a long room like a spacious corridor, glass doors closing it off at both ends. It was both the weighing room and the reception area. It even came complete with a massage table.

"Just don't think we are torturing her. She's not really one of ours, after all. It's not clear who she belongs to at the moment. Sit here. Pick up a book as if you were reading and don't show any particular reaction. I mean, don't express your… No tutting, basically! Control yourself!"

Masha sat in her chair for twenty minutes, trying in vain to calm her trembling heart, staring at her open book. They had thrust some medical guide to movement therapy for cerebral palsy at her.

A sprightly old soul was wielding a mop close at hand, ramming it under tables and couches as if it was an ice-hockey stick. She was like a puck herself. Round and never still, she managed to squeeze a cloth dry as she exchanged lively comments with the nurse.

The latter spoke with a typical Baltic accent, "I don't remember zer faces, I don't. I can tell all ze children by zer little arms and legs. After all, I do ze electrophoresis wif zem every year. As soon as I saw zat little leg wif a scar on ze knee, I recognized it right away: our little Igor. Hello, my little Igor, my, how you'f grown! Don't tell me vat he looks like. Tell me ze colour of his underpants."

The glass doors kept on opening and closing. Masha cringed inwardly every time. On two occasions, some young girls wearing the very latest in short white medical attire slipped in. The door opened again.

Masha looked up and almost let out a gasp: a chill flooded her heart then subsided, burning like ice.

A small skeleton in just a pair of knickers. She had seen skeletons like that once before, behind the barbed wire of Buchenwald in a documentary shown before a film at the cinema. She remembered closing her eyes and laying her head on Tolya's shoulder.

How the child, the knobbly stem of her spine visible through its mantel of skin, could stand, move, stay on her feet at all was a mystery! And beside the enormous manager, the little girl looked like a mosquito that could be blown away with a breath.

Masha's insides shrank and she buried herself in her book. She wasn't seeing the words but the skeleton's huge green eyes and a mop of reddish, chestnut curls.

"Now, then," boomed the director, "let's move our little legs, shall we, Anya-Anyuta?" Then, as she led the little girl past, "Say hello to the lady."

Without looking up, unable to smile or even move, Masha heard a faint, dry whisper.

"...'lo..."

When the door closed behind them, Masha stood—the book fell from her knees—and said with some force, "What's going on?! How could you do this to the child?! What does she weigh? Can't you see she's wasting away?"

"Who are you talking to?" said the nurse with the Baltic accent. "To us? Zat child's been wif us for five days. What's your relationship wif her?"

Masha fled the room.

✳✳✳

The next morning, she stood outside the glass door of the holiday centre's dining room, trying to make out a mop of chestnut curls. There was no shortage of them but she couldn't see anything: her vision was blurred. (It was the tourist season and she had been unable to find a room the evening before and had spent the night in the waiting room at the station.) She had imagined all sorts of horrors, such as the little girl dying of starvation during the night.

Next she went downstairs to the manager's locked office. She waited for the burly figure in its white coat to appear at the end of the corridor, stood in her way and said with desperate determination, "I'm taking that child. Please explain the formalities."

They spent the next hour and a half in the office where, as directed, Masha noted down point by point the nine circles of hell she aimed to negotiate with all the documents in record time.

She just couldn't pull herself together, timidly attempting to put money on the table, stuff it into the pocket of the manager's vast coat or place it between the pages of some cardboard-covered account book and constantly grasping the woman's heavy work-worn hand and stammering beseechingly, "If someone could only sit with her a bit and feed her, please, even just a few spoonfuls but more often, please!" until the manager pulled her up sharply and they both burst into tears, offering one another unspecified thanks.

All this time *Shura, the kind-hearted neighbour* Masha had been unable to find, stood outside the slightly open door of the manager's office, listening, thunderstruck.

Once it was clear that everything had been arranged and this woman who was already of a certain age had burnt all her bridges, Shura screwed up her eyes then forced them open, staring at the blue square of the window at the far end of the corridor. All of a sudden and with fervour, she crossed herself awkwardly. In a flash, she realized that she had done it *the wrong way round* and her blood ran cold: Not like that, like this. She spat three times over her left shoulder and with an equally furious gesture made the sign of the cross properly over her ample bosom.

She was afraid she might scrape the parquet floor or cough. She was afraid the arrangements might fall through and the little girl would not be taken away.

But more than anything—more than of her own death—she was afraid of that little girl.

CHAPTER 2.

So, light of my life, my little mirror, would you like me to tell you a sad tale of love accursed?

Don't laugh. It was true love between Mrs. Clarkson, my landlady over here, and a wild goose that plopped down on her lawn one day.

I could write a lot about this just now because I'm all worked up. The final act of the drama played itself out before my very eyes yesterday. Or rather, I was sitting in that shed of mine, which they dignify by calling it *an annexe*—ripping me off royally in the process—and pretending to rehearse the super-virtuoso passage in the finale of Beethoven's Fourth Symphony, where the bassoons sort of chirrup and finish after the clarinets. And the Second Movement has that really difficult and saucy dalliance on tippy-toes in demisemiquaver dotted rhythm, which totally contradicts what my never-to-be-forgotten tutor, Nikolai Kuzmich, used to say: "The bassoon, my lad, is a melancholy instrument."

But unlike in the stories, this Scheherazade carries on her tale while she may. So, about three years ago, a magnificent snow-white goose fell onto the lawn in the backyard where they have a garage for the tractor, lawnmower, garden tools and other stuff.

Every so often, the Clarkson family uses it for one of their garage sales. Did I tell you that last year I paid them a dollar for a Sevres teacup from two centuries ago? The handle had come off and an ugly job had been made of sticking it back on, practically with plasticine. I steamed it, took it to pieces, fixed it with an extremely delicate specialist glue, breathed on it, licked it … and now it's there on the shelf, the almost pristine gold rim sparkling on the blue background … although my passion for antiques seems like lunacy given our homeless state.

It's just occurred to me that I have my grandfather to thank for my insatiable love of the elegance of real porcelain. He had a chocolate-coloured porcelain dog, apparently suffering from post-hunt exhaustion, behind the glass of the sideboard. It was from before the war, and do you know how I know? From the mark. The Lomonosov Porcelain Factory mark on its belly was green. After the war, they used purple ones. Then there was a white dish with Young Pioneers on the rim, a boy playing the bugle and a girl in a scarf, her hand raised stiffly to her forehead. My grandfather was always telling me it was from the 1920s. I used to ask if Young Pioneers even existed in the 20s and he'd say, "Fine, so the 30s then."

Sorry for rabbiting on! I was a Young Pioneer myself. I was, really. I remember it perfectly.

And now we make the incredible journey from Zhmerinka 1952 to the State of Kansas in 1998. It's still the same century, to be fair, utterly vile, slipping away in darkness and disgrace.

But, back to the goose. It had been left behind, exhausted, and then it turned out to have an injured wing.

Mrs. Clarkson rescued it from the neighbourhood dogs, nursed it back to health, cared for it, and all summer long it stuck to her heels, like a dog. She sent photos to all her friends. An article appeared in the local paper even, with a photo and the caption: "Mrs. Clarkson and her pet."

It left safely in the autumn as its residence papers required.

Then the following spring, it came back with a partner.

The geese sauntered around the yard as if they'd come home and he was clearly proud to be showing his girlfriend his domain. Just like the first time I showed you around Rudesheim.

Do you remember our room in Rudesheim Castle? And the *Eiswein* in the stone cellar? And the drunken local football fans bellowing out folk songs? And the metal carriage of the cable car in the fog and the funny, bug-eyed albino in the red Tyrolean hat who came out of it towards us, the one who (weirdly!) frightened you so much?

Anyway, the geese: the summer after that a whole colony arrived. They took up all the yard, wouldn't let anyone go through, hissed at and chased any trespassers. They regarded it as their territory. Their droppings fouled everything. The student daughter came home for the holidays with her boyfriend, was bitten by a goose and left the next day. The son decided not to come at all. Poor exhausted Mrs. Clarkson barely made it to the autumn and most probably had a prayer of thanksgiving said at her church, praising the merciful Lord for her seasonal deliverance. (She's very devout, actually. There's a portrait of her great-grandfather in the lounge with the touching inscription at the bottom of the canvas: "My deeds are righteous and my way is meek.")

This spring she put her trust in herself rather than higher forces and prepared in advance for that romantic time when the birds fly over. She hired two wolfhounds from a breeder at a near-by farm, which shot off like torpedoes when they spotted the flock of geese descending on the yard in the form of a great white tent and, quivering with fury, chased the poor geese until the evening so that they were unable to land.

The geese hovered above the lawn like the white blasts of a snowstorm, a blizzard poised overhead, hissing and cackling. The battle was a sight to behold! The air shook with the din: the disheartened, disgruntled calls of the geese, the gulping yelps of the hunting dogs, baying and growling.

And, in floods of tears, Mrs. Clarkson watched the combat from her kitchen window.

Something was amiss in her well-tended, well-ordered world. Something had broken down.

Even I felt uneasy and not just because it's impossible to play the bassoon when a ghastly cacophony is making the surrounding air vibrate. It's just that for some reason this sad story reminded me of guess what and whom?

Imagination's a strange thing and memory even more so.

Why do people in the backwoods of America often remind me of my neighbours in Guryev? Why is that? After all, here, you get sheer bliss at the touch of a button while there, in the town I grew up in, there were sandstorms, the murky, leaden Ural River, the endless, endless steppe, thick mud, elm trees, oleasters, stunted gardens under the windows. And allotments by the river, where people planted potatoes (that's what they used to say, "Let's go down to the allotment!") and where black nightshade ran wild. The kind we call wonderberries.

Do you even know what wonderberries are? They're a weed, small, sparse bushes with sickly-sweet black berries. Only fit for the garbage, my mother used to say, not something decent folk should eat. But when my father died and I instantly became a neglected child, I used to escape to our neighbours, the Solodovs, to eat my favourite wonderberry pirozhki. (They fried them in cottonseed oil so as not to waste the sunflower oil.) The Solodovs were sorry for me, and the unsolved murder of my father, the chief engineer at the Guryev Oil Refinery, electrified all the neighbours for many years and cast a compassionate light on the orphan.

The Solodovs plied me with my fill of wonderberry pirozhki.

They made an entertaining family: crazy, complicated, clamorous, quarrelsome—each member with their own particular character, even the littlest children. I was friends with the middle child, Genka, a liar, a troublemaker and all-round bad news. Nowadays, he's a monk at the Valaam Monastery which has always been famous for its extremely strict rule and I see no contradiction in this at all.

Their dad, Uncle Vasya, originally from some Mordvinian village or other, was a big party boss. A bright guy and honest too, he was a heavy drinker. And then he used to torment the whole family. He'd yell at his wife, "Lyolka, you are such a moron, premium grade!" He'd throw his crutch at the children, like Long John Silver, and his aim was always true. With his one leg and his obsessive approach to everything, he decided he would plant a real orchard around the house and every day he turned his dream into reality with uncommon perseverance. He would drag a spade and chair into the garden, sit on the chair and use his one leg to dig a hole for the latest fruit tree. He planted forty-seven of them. It's impossible for you, a child of Ukraine's fertile soil, to understand what a feat this was but Uncle Vasya pulled it off.

He was married to Aunty Lyolya, daughter of an enemy of the people. You can't understand or appreciate this anymore either, thank goodness.

When she was young, Aunty Lyolya was such a beauty, with her golden plait and insufferably blue eyes, that party protégé Uncle Vasya forgot all about the *intelligence, honour and conscience of our times* and took her on, along with an entire brood of younger brothers and sisters. And her elderly mother too, who must be spoken of separately and with caution. Kapitolina Timofeevna, they called her—a dried-up, tough old lady, practically of noble blood. That was on the one hand.

On the other hand, her children and grandchildren believed she was illiterate. The contradiction didn't seem strange when we were children. We simply didn't think about it. Now, though, I'm convinced that Kapitolina Timofeevna was abruptly afflicted with illiteracy when her three eldest adult children—after their father's execution—disowned their mother *via a newspaper* and she was left out on the streets with the three youngest. As for whether a particular revulsion for the Soviet written word played a part or whether it was run-of-the-mill terror … who can tell these days?

She was strict and if something wasn't the way she wanted, she would grasp her victim's hair and drag them round the house. Frenetically hard-working, she kept the entire family in clothes. There was nothing she couldn't make—trousers, coats, those tapestry portraits of Pushkin (that were fairly like him but had too ambitious a range of colours: dark-green seaweed side whiskers—all in silk embroidery thread—outlining sunken, cocoa-coloured cheeks).

And so, just imagine, Uncle Vasya did not shy away from saddling himself with all this dangerous brood. What's more, he fought with his austere mother-in-law as long as she lived and, when he died, he mourned her with real tears, went on a drinking binge even, banged his head against the wall and said, 'They don't make them like that anymore.' Sometimes, when I'd played so long that I couldn't keep my eyes open, I'd spend the night there, on the couch in the main room—although I could quite easily have crossed the road and gone home. My mother never recovered after my father died. She was numbed by a strange, tenacious pensiveness about her lot in life. When she came home from work to a cold, untidy house, she would collapse on the sofa and lie there for hours, listlessly munching apples from the ones my grandfather brought every year from Zhmerinka. She would look listlessly out of the window and she hardly spoke to me. Nowadays, it would be called severe depression and it'd be cured in about three months but back then all the neighbours criticized her for being feckless and thought she was a bad mother.

So from time to time, I stayed at the Solodovs' overnight.

I can remember waking up to the anthem of the Soviet Union coming from the radio …

Half-asleep, my eyes hardly open, I could see a bare-headed Aunty Lyolya. She would be sitting on a chair, head thrown back, resembling a mute victim, soft throat awaiting the knife-blade, full-figured, languorous in the early morning, in her lilac flannelette dressing gown: a lamb waiting to be shorn of the golden fleece. Behind her stood little grandmother Kapitolina Timofeevna raking through those incredible Samson-like tresses in broad strokes. She kneaded them with her hands first, ploughed furrows, dug deep trenches. Then, she separated them with a ten-toothed comb, spread them wide and transferred them from one side to the other. Finally, she braided and twisted the strands, moulding and sculpting a plait. When she'd finished this arduous task, she heaved the glossy golden snake over her daughter's shoulder.

I used to watch this ceremony thorough half-opened eyelids, transfixed. For some reason, when I was a boy, it seemed to me to be a sacrament of an intimate nature.

Years later, waking up beside some woman or other, I realized that everything to do with a woman's hair is an utterly unsolvable mystery.

But, there, I've let my tongue run away with me again.

I find it hard to imagine when this letter will reach you and, of course, I am no longer hoping for a reply. In any case, I prefer your silence to your otherworldly mirror writing that always fills me with the reverberating horror of a snowstorm.

When on earth are we going to meet up?

I have a contract with the orchestra in Des Moines until October. It's a bit far to travel from here but I'm settled in this sleepy little town out of state, which exists only on the county map. The linden trees are un-believably lovely and I simply can't be bothered to move house. I drive to rehearsal or take the bus if I fancy a nap en route. It takes two hours, with a stop in Kansas City.

And here, my little one, in the Midwest, people are as provincial as can be. Especially those who travel by bus, the poor. Here's an ex-ample from yesterday. A homeless black man with a wild horse's eye, a fine mellow baritone voice, a phlegmy, husky, random laugh framed by strong white teeth. A hideous outfit: ripped jeans, a faded checked shirt over a greasy 1970s turtle neck, brown trainers.

And he talked nonstop for the whole two hours in that, you know, black dialect they have, that's impossible to understand. He talked into space in a lively, friendly fashion as if he was speaking to someone in-visible. The other passengers sat staring out of the window, their ears blocked by their headphones.

During the brief stop, stretching his legs after sitting for so long, he became absorbed, dancing on the pavement to music no one else could hear, a paper cup of coffee in one hand and a lit cigarette in the other. His head seemed to be on a swivel, his shoulders, arms, hips and knees turning in circles as if he was trying over and over in vain to embrace an invisible someone, to take them in his arms.

And, pray tell, when will I take you in my arms?

I'm fed up with the local orchestra and its petty squabbles and I'm not going to renew my contract beyond October. I'll apply for somewhere nearer to you. Professor Myatlitsky is trying to persuade me to go to him in Boston.

Imagine, he's in his mid-90s and making plans for tours and mas-terclasses for another ten years. "Simon," he says to me, "don't be a fool." (The Professor says my name the way they do over here and I rather like it. There's something aristocratic about that "Simon." Not like the plebeian, playful "Senya" that has bounded along beside me all my life.) "What is it about thin and wasted Europe that draws you like a bee to honey?"

"Ah, but what honey it is!" I reply. So it won't be long till I start trying to find you. Please, show yourself. Give me some sort of sign.

Where are you now, my mirror girl? Frankfurt? Montreal? Berlin? What tricks and flirtations with the world beyond are you devising? "The Ring of Fire?" Boxes in which lovers disappear? Mirror balls and flying heads?

Who is looking into you, my darling, who is reflected in you?

Consider these rhetorical questions. I trust you're not being faithful to me? To hell with sexual fidelity!

Just come back to me from time to time. Just come back, for pity's sake…

CHAPTER 3.

The old muso, Senya, now that's who really truly loved her. And she seemed to love him back. Or, if she didn't love him, she was fond of him at least. He used to write her these letters—"*poste restante*". He had this sort of old-time formality. He never knew if the letters got through or not. After all, she either never wrote back or just dropped him a few lines in that gobbledygook writing of hers so you open the letter and stand there like a complete idiot, turning the page this way and that, upside down, over the other way, and still have no clue what it says. Like some code for spies! And it puts you in such a rage, such a fury that you could wipe the scribbles off the paper, like that spider's web off the mirror over there. You must have experts in deciphering that kind of writing at Interpol.

It didn't worry Senya, though. Nothing about her embarrassed him, nothing got on his nerves.

For example, she always drove the car—not to mention the motorbike—at bloodcurdling speeds. Even when she didn't know the road. No one except Senya could stand it. He always let her drive and always sat next to her with a lame little smile—what a jerk!—like someone riding a carriage through the Bois de Boulogne, doffing his top hat in greeting to the baronesses of his acquaintance.

He wasn't a bit jealous either. Her casual affairs didn't bother him.

Nothing really bothered either of them. Really, it didn't. They were … erm … how can I put it? In a bubble of their own love. He looked at her like looking in a mirror, never taking his eyes off her. Although he nearly always lived a long way away from her and was much, much older. Such an odd relationship…

By the way, I recognized your voice straight away—after so many years. Amazing! As soon as I heard "Vladimir?" on the line, something just went click: Investigator Kerler, Interpol.

Can I ask a question, Mr. Kerler? Why are they raking this up again? From what I understand, the case is closed. It was so many years ago. And Senya and his melancholy bassoon are no longer with us…

Do you mind if I smoke? Thank God, there are still places in Montreal where you can light up, at least on the terrace. They've all gone a bit crazy here in the West… Anyway, thanks for agreeing to question me without taking me in… That was a joke, okay?! It's just that somehow conversation's livelier over a beer and a cigarette. Although, well, you can understand … I always struggle to talk about her. In any case, I told you everything a long time ago when I was first questioned.

…Of course, she wasn't beautiful. Ordinary looking, an ordinary nose, an ordinary forehead. Sure, she had bright eyes. Restless, wandering eyes like she was always on her guard, travelling light, ready to head out... But in our line of work, the eyes don't figure. They film us to show the stunt, not our faces. The stuntman's face in the shot is a ruined stunt.

You have to stand in for the actor in such a way that the viewer can't spot the change. And wow, did she do it brilliantly! Physically, she was beyond talented. And her reactions were just crazy: she could catch a falling glass and set it in its place with both hands full. Someone I know, a physiologist, told me that forced right-handers are like that. Functions are distributed differently between the two halves of their brains. There's a scientific term: ambidextrous. And, allegedly, Australian researchers recently found that people like that assess situations and take decisions more rapidly in sport and just in life generally. Why are you smiling? Because I'm talking crap, right? Well, I don't understand a bloody thing about it. I'm just saying what I've heard. And what I witnessed too.

I'm just explaining that nature created her as one of a kind. Ideally built for jumps, somersaults, stretches and other stunts. Whatever she did, you always wanted to watch her. She drew your gaze after her then made it embroider patterns. And physically, she wasn't like those glossy porn stars with their big boob jobs. On the contrary, she was small, kind of boyish and really in proportion, you know, each part of her body running absolutely flawlessly into the next. She moved like she was answering a silent call. Like she was always on the alert. Even when she was absorbed in what she was saying. Like when a visitor you love has already packed their case, put their shoes and jacket on and is waiting for the taxi. The conversation is still animated, there's joking and laughing and yet they're straining to hear—isn't that the taxi at the door, honking its horn? And how your heart sinks: Will we ever meet again?

Damn, that's the last cigarette… No, thank you, I only smoke Du Mauriers… They should have them here. *"Monsieur, s'il vous plait, un paquet de Du Maurier et une Fin du Monde."*

You know, it's nice here. I thought it was somewhere gays hang out. No? It's all the same to me, whether they do or not. They're people too… Genevieve, for example. I respect her. You questioned her, right? You've seen her. Sure, she can drink a fair amount but that's not what I'm talking about. She's someone who has turned her fate around. The one that was written for her when she was born. Think about it: a kid from a godforsaken little village on the coast of Brittany. Wind, rain… Father's a fisherman, paid a pittance, away at sea for days at a time. Mother sells alcohol to fishermen in a bar. Five brothers and sisters and Catholicism so thick you could plug the walls with it—not a hint of humanity could get in. And what happened? When Genevieve realized she was drawn to… well, that she was … she was different, she cut herself loose from her family, went to Canada, drifted, endured hardship and, in the end, she triumphed. And it's hard to imagine Cirque de la Lune without her. She's a born trainer and a born photographer and she lives her life the way she wants to—that's what I wanted to say. And that takes strength, too, you know, and then some…

But I've wandered off the subject. Excuse me.

About our craft. Of course, we were often part of the same team on a film. They like Russian stunt performers in the West, often more than their own even. We never say no. We're crazy. Whatever we're asked to do, we do it. You want me to dive head first into concrete—you got it. The famous Russian bravery. Russian madness, more like. So, of course, we were invited to do foreign films and videos as well.

What does it mean to be a "good stunt performer"? She was the best. The best, have you got that? She was the only woman in Europe who could do a rolling stoppie! Meaning the bike picks up speed on the straight, then you brake sharply and go up on the front wheel. The main thing is for the track to be dry and the bike not to skid. When you brake, the back of the bike comes up as the rider suddenly jerks forward and you have to keep the balance and a certain angle to avoid going over the handlebars and breaking your fucking neck! It's really hard for women, physically. They haven't got the mass, the strength in their arms, see? But that girl could pull it off!

God, you're fixated on her being banned… We've already talked about it… You know, there's this psychologist, an American, Marvin Zuckerman, who believes some people's bodies need constant stress, the adrenaline rush. Their lives aren't worth living if they're not shaken to their core at least once a day. It's an addiction, habituation to the electrical impulses of fear. And I can tell you that's exactly the sort of person who goes in for stunts. Think about it— would any normal person risk their life so that some pretty-boy actor could strut around instead of you in the close-ups before and after the stunt like he was the tough guy?

No way they would. These are people... you know ... It takes a really strong nervous system. Car jumps, motorcycle jumps, horseback stunts, fencing—you're all over the place, one minute you're relying on your reactions, your training, your body. Then, there's fire ... water ... elements that have to be taken seriously...

Yes, she refused to be set on fire back then, that's true. And she ruined the shoot. But do you know how fire stunts are organized? The stunt performer wears protective clothing. It used to be made from asbestos. Then they decided that was dangerous and they started making it out of something else, a synthetic material that's supposedly fire-retardant and it doesn't distort your body shape either.

Under the asbestos or any fire-retardant suit was a thin felt lining. That's what provided the protection. Then, the costume goes on over the protective gear and is smeared with napalm... Napalm? No, course it's not. It's bone meal dissolved in petrol. A kind of gel. It's rubbed mainly onto your back. The person runs, the flames stream out behind. It makes for a dramatic shot. And there you go. Then there's the full body burn. The stunt performer wears a fire-retardant mask with tiny holes for seeing and breathing.

Excusez-moi, monsieur, pourriez-vous baisser cette musique de merde?

...Anyway, when someone's on fire, they can start to panic. The wind's in the wrong direction or something... You might get burnt. So there you go running and burning quite happily... and cut! You fall flat on your belly, they throw a tarpaulin or a blanket over you but not water—that could mean a steam burn. A fire-extinguisher puts out the flames. A couple of assistants hang around on site for that very reason. When they were filming the Joan of Arc scene, there was only one assistant. One! And he didn't put her mask on properly. A full face mask, understand. Just think what that meant!

Where was I? Oh, yes. So the flames were rising. She started gasping for breath, ripped off the mask. It left her with a fine pink scar along her left cheekbone. She used to put powder on it … it didn't help.

But she wasn't banned then. That came later, about three years later. I was there when they were filming.

We were in a team. We had a couple of stunts to do as a pair. I don't remember what the film was called in Russia. The director was Italian … I can't remember the name… it was a thriller, car chases. Utter shit. I never read their dumb screenplays. You're asked along for two fights and to overturn a car. You turn up, do the fight, flip the car and job done, fee paid and *ciao ciao!* In short, she was supposed to jump off a cliff at a dangerous spot into their fucking Gulf of Naples. She had to get it right and had to pass through a narrow gap between two cliffs.

So, action, camera, everyone on their marks, every minute costs a whole heap of dollars… She ran towards the edge and stopped short. Froze. Rooted to the spot. Suddenly, an about turn and she was out of there.

… I don't know! … I'm not sure she was scared… You see, usually, when stunt people are performing, they're close to hysterical. I tell you, I don't know what made her stop. It was as if some kind of inner lever had been pulled and in a split second she'd decided to be done with stunts once and for all. I can see her face now… so… set free, you know? Probably how people look when they're acquitted in court. She just walked, her eyes green—or blue even, like the water in the gulf. The director was yelling, the producer was in a faint, the actors were seething, the shoot was ruined … while she was as free as the air, no, as the sea!

After that, she made a living putting on mirror shows. She did the lighting, thought up designs for various mirror devices. For example, she came up with this ball she called the "invisible ball" for the most famous casino in Berlin, the Europa-Center on Breitscheidplatz.

From above it's a faceted structure, metalized plastic … but you wouldn't believe the inside. It's slid open remotely to reveal an oblong central segment and inside there's absolute, ink-black, velvety darkness. And if you stick your arm in, your arm disappears. The black hole effect. She tried to explain. I didn't understand much. I'm not much good at science, never was. All I took away was the idea of a closed system of mirrors.

And you know, there was a hell of a demand for her. She did a lot of work at the famous Tigerpalast in Frankfurt and was their chief lighting advisor, among other things. No one had a better understanding of all that equipment, spot lights, light scanners, dichroic filters and other wizardry.

She made good money. Although I've no idea where the money disappeared to. I wouldn't be surprised if it literally *disappeared*. She used to just stuff it in the pockets of her jeans or jacket… Although, I do remember her sending a fair bit to various people every month. To Ninka, whom she used to perform with. In our circus act, I mean. She felt guilty about Ninka, said it was her fault she'd lost her job and was left out in the cold. "Are you crazy?" I used to say, "She's not some poor pensioner!" Ninka's as fit as a fiddle. She's been doing famously in another act for ages. But no, she kept on sending the money, all her life. And that old crazy who filled her head with his mirrors when she was still a little girl. She sent money to Indianapolis for him too, even though he was living well on good ole American beef stew… Basically, she didn't give a damn for what they call material well-being. She worked a lot, that is true.

She had her life all planned out for about the next three years. I never knew where she was living at a particular time, where she was racing off to on her bike. Generally, she lived her own way—here and there, one minute locally, the next nowhere at all. In any country, she would hire a motorbike, either a powerful sports bike if she was going off road, or a cruiser, a manoeuvrable one, if she was in the city. And no luggage. A small backpack with a change of underwear, the eternal notebook for working things out. She resolved the wardrobe issue easily: she went to the nearest shop, bought her usual green or navy sweater or tee-shirt, depending on the weather. Then she'd leave them all over the place—in her hotel room, her "nest" at Genevieve's, or on a bench—for people in need… I never knew anyone less bothered about herself than she was. All she cared about was her biker's gear and even that only when necessary. A motorbike's a serious matter, you know. We build up speeds of well over 200 which means even a May bug can cause a fall if it hits you in the face. So you must have a leather jacket, a good pair of boots, gloves, a crash helmet—no messing around.

That last time, we weren't too far away from here, at the Figaro, a couple of months before … well, before. And she was in an excellent frame of mind, saying that next year she'd been invited to do several mirror acts here, at the Casino de Montreal, during the firework competition. She said she'd come up with an ambitious stunt especially for them, all tied in with the impact of the fireworks.

"Volodka, just imagine," she said, "two enormous natural mirrors: the black mirror of the sky and the black mirror of the gulf…"

Yes, really… She tried to explain how the trick worked, something to do with putting concave mirrors on the windows and the roof to reflect the fireworks and whatever was going on in the auditorium and all of it somehow being projected into the sky where these huge, great mirages would appear: people of mind-boggling cosmic dimensions among all the chaos of the fireworks.

I have to admit I was never very keen on her mirror stuff. I don't remember anything specific from the explanations. I just used to watch while she dug a spoon into her ice-cream and put it on her orange tongue. It was funny the way she sucked the tip of the spoon like that. Like a child…

God, Kerler. What is your name, for Christ's sake? Robert? I can remember her fifth birthday perfectly, Robert! You know, she and I are both from Kiev. We were in the same school from Grade Seven and even before that my mother cleaned their house a few times. She took me with her once. My father was drinking again and the kindergarten was closed—in quarantine yet again.

She used to say, "Volodechka, you keep your mouth shut when you're with people. Stay nice and quiet, like a dumb person."

We were so poor, it's awful to remember! Dear old Dad was none too careful in his handling of the family budget. One winter my lambswool hat went to pay for drink. Whereas her father was a military doctor, a colonel. He worked in the hospital in Pechersk and it wasn't just any old work, either. He was head of the infectious diseases ward. An enormous guy, really strong, very imposing. Her mother, too, Mariya Kirillovna, was head of classical music at the music school.

They lived on what used to be Zhilyanskaya Street, in a pre-revolutionary house with those wrought-iron railings on the balconies. It was a big flat too, with a telephone and a mysterious mirror in the hallway… For me, it was like … like being in heaven! I can remember going inside. The corridor was reflected in a mirror on the wall opposite, a bit off to one side. Anyone walking along the corridor would appear in the mirror first and only then come up to you for real.

And there was this boisterous little girl, running towards us out of the mirror, a mouth full of teeth, eyes sparkling, bursting with laughter. Running up and down along the corridor and just clattering along. As if she couldn't care less about manners.

Whereas I was a quiet boy. My dad's conversations with me were brief: Sit still, you little shit, preferably behind the cupboard. That's why I was surprised by the racket. And that no one smacked her for it. My mother said, "Sweetie, where on earth are you rushing off to, child? You're sweating like a pig." And she bursts out with, "It's not me, it's the joy inside me that wants to run!"

You know, I maybe took a whole other course in life because she was there, before my very eyes. Free, wild … different! Maybe that's why I tried to rid myself of my timid childhood, to pull it up by the roots, to crush it like a worm…

Yes… It's funny but I got in such a state when you rang and suggested meeting up. I thought, what if they've found something all of a sudden … news of some kind. Although, what … It's been four years, what could turn up now? But I'm sorry, I just don't understand. I don't. Let's assume, the body's disappeared. But the motorbike… A motorbike isn't some sort of fish to swim off into the sea, now is it? It's made of metal, for fuck's sake. What happened? Did the fish eat it? The dolphins borrow it to go for a spin?

I'm sorry… Everything's fine. Monsieur… don't worry. Everything's okay. It's okay… It happens… I lost control there for a minute.

I so hoped you'd have something new to tell me… Beer's a tricky customer, Mr. Kerler… Mr. Robert Kerler. It's a stroke of luck that you speak Russian. I really don't know what I would have done otherwise… Wept bitter tears… And beer, you drink it like water and then it turns your heart inside out… Better to go straight to the hard stuff.

One thing I do know. This beer won't help me sleep today. I'll be lying there like a log, staring into the dark but, if I close my eyes, she's stomping along that corridor, running right out of the mirror towards me: forehead sweaty, mouth full of teeth, her laugh ringing like a bell, "It's not me, it's not. It's my joy that wants to run."

CHAPTER 4.

Here's a close up of two toys.

Number one—Thumbelina. Secret prisoner of a metal flower. To release her pale figure from its dark prison, you have to press a metal plunger over and over again until your thumb is numb. A spring sets a disc in motion, the petals open and, with a strained humming sound, they start spinning faster and faster, merging into a shimmering haze. The tiny girl from the Hans Andersen fairy tale that's unbearably sad despite its happy ending can be seen through the haze, sitting inside.

She waits, unseen legs frozen and tucked up beneath her red skirt. After all, the minute you stop pressing the spring, the flower encloses its prisoner again. Quick, quick, set her free! Peel back the petals that have snapped tight shut!

But a broken petal reveals only the poorly painted head of a small plastic doll. And no matter how badly you break the latest toy Dad's bought in the hope of finding the real Thumbelina inside the flower, it is always the same cheap tat.

Toy number two is an acrobat on a horizontal bar. Like Polina's sewing machine, it moves when a handle on the side is turned. A blue costume and a celluloid face with a silly but plucky smile.

This brawny young man is on display to all and sundry and happy to loop and swing from morning till night until your hand is too tired. The handle squeaks indefatigably. The acrobat raises himself on his outstretched arms, somersaults and is back under the bar, ready to break records all over again.

"Nyu-u-ta, you might put that screechy piece of tin out of sight for a bit!"

It was the new nanny, Khristina, niece of the caretaker Markovna. She had come from Pirnovo and was now a burden on Markovna. Nyuta imagined Khristina leaving the train and instantly leaping upon Markovna as if she were a horse and urging her on and on, her fat legs dangling onto the other woman's chest.

It had been Dad's idea to summon Khristina to replace "our dear Polina," while the latter's stomach was being cut open at the hospital and stones of some kind taken out.

From below, Khristina was gargantuan, with a stupid little head. As if her body had been in a hurry to sprout its wide-planted legs and grabbing hands and to ensure it had a hefty backside. And to keep an eye on the whole of this opulent estate, the dull core of a cabbage had been planted on her shoulders, with a tightly bound bun on the back of her neck and a mouth that was never shut. And now that mouth was disgorging melodious inanities in the language Masha called "Surzhik".

"Mar'Kirilna, why's she always using her left hand to do stuff? Her right, see, it ain't no use for nothing."

Interesting—Polina was an apparently intelligent woman who could read books really quickly, something Nyuta couldn't do at all yet. What then, one might ask, was the silly old fool doing, swallowing stones?

"Nyuta is left-handed. You can't do anything about it, Khristina. It's just the way she is. Please don't pay it any particular attention."

Ma led Khristina off into the kitchen, supposedly to give her some housekeeping instructions. Really, it was to whisper directions as to how she, Khristina, should behave with the "child"—a complex, unruly child, who was incapable of concentrating. Or rather, was capable of concentrating on five things at once. At that very moment, Nyuta was still turning the squeaky handle of the toy acrobat while her left foot kicked at a rag-doll Harlequin, with a jaunty porcelain head of extraordinary beauty.

It had recently been purchased in the Toy Department of the Central Department Store on the corner of Kreshchatik and Lenin Street. Dad said the costume was "Venetian." It had two halves, one a dark blue silk, the other yellow velvet.

This wound the little girl up into a dreadful state.

"It's all wrong," she told Masha. "Buy one the other way round! With the blue on the other side!"

"Do you have any that are made the other way around?" Masha inquired of a shop assistant, pink-cheeked and scrumptious as a doll. "For some reason, my daughter would like the blue to be on the left."

"But what difference does it make?" the pink-cheeked doll demanded crossly. "Take this one. Look what a fine fellow he is."

But Nyuta snatched her hand out of Masha's and stamped her feet, saying over and over again, frenzied and miserable, "It's all wrong. It's all wrong."

"Spoil your kids and you'll live to lament it," the shop-assistant remarked damningly.

They bought the Harlequin even so. Why?! An inside-out liar, cheat and trickster! We need to find out who sent him here and why. Beat a confession out of him.

"Nyutochka, I'm off to work!" Masha called from the hallway.

She already had her hat and coat on.

"Alright." Without turning round, the little girl continued gradually kicking Harlequin under the sofa.

She never called Masha Mum although she had no problem happily addressing Anatoly as Daddy on the very first day. There were occasional periods when she called Masha "Ma," which thousands of children use for their mothers. But Masha was under no delusions: it was merely the first syllable of her name.

The door slammed shut. Khristina went through the process of locking it thoroughly and systematically, turning the key twice, drawing the chain across and inspecting the imposing oak surface carefully to see whether she had missed a lock or latch or bolt of any kind. A minute later she appeared at the door of the nursery.

"So…" she remarked. "Have Petlyura's thugs been rampaging around or does a little girl live here?"

Receiving no reply, she observed the child's actions for about a minute.

"So, I mustn't be upsetting you, Anna Anatolyevna, is it?" Then, suddenly, in quite a different voice, she said, "Get over here, you little monster!"

Oh now, this was interesting! Khristina had suddenly launched into the strange and fascinating language used by the "driver from the milk factory," the one called "Come-away-from-the-window-right-now-and-don't-listen-to-that-filth."

Early in the morning, when the gatekeeper opened the heavy panels of the milk factory's dull grey metal gates and dozens of yellow milk trucks, red brand along the sides, sneaked out of the courtyard into the street and huddled into a log jam, bellowing as long and rapturously as cows, it was then that the area around Zhadanovskogo Street, now named after a revolutionary but formerly Zhilyanskaya Street, resounded with the colourful verbal fireworks of the drivers' distinctive speech, incomprehensible but forceful.

"Get over here!" Khristina said again. "We'll fix you…Mend you, put you round the right way. So, Nyuta, are you a smart girl or a dunce?"

"Smart," Nyuta responded with conviction.

Khristina made a fist, lifted it to her round chicken's eye and looked through it like a binocular tube.

"Don't see it. Smart folks do things with their right hands. You use your left. She's says I mustn't be telling you 'mustn't say this, mustn't do that'… So, come on, let's play!" she cried abruptly. "A real fun game! Stay put, you! Don't move. We're going to have half a little girl in a minute."

Broad behind quivering, she dashed off to the kitchen. She came back with several honeycomb tea-towels and drew three almighty safety pins from the hem of her voluminous skirt.

"Don't move, my pet!"

Well, it was definitely far more interesting with Khristina than with Polina who just took Nyuta for walks in Zhilyansky Park and decorously pushed the heavy slow-moving iron swing, refusing to send it soaring into the sky. They also went to Vatutin Park in Lipki District, named for its huge, sweet-smelling linden trees, their branches putting out small green propellers with sticky tips in the springtime. You could open them up and stick them on your nose.

Besides, Polina was a constant pest with her stupid signpost reading. She sounded out the Ukrainian words in a drawl as slow as the swing: "Fa-aa-brics"… "Gro-o-ceries," "Sh-ooe Re-pa-irs"—a ludicrous task since they spoke a different language, Russian, at home. And Polina herself spoke Russian so why even bother to look at the signs?

On top of all that, she tormented Nyuta with a funny gibberish called "German". And all because Polina was a former *Froebel girl*. To begin with, Nyuta thought Polina was saying "*burble girl*". It was what Polina said whenever Nyuta played up: "Stop burbling, girl." But it turned out that once upon a time, a million years ago, there was a German Professor Froebel (a little old man, skinny as a rake, with sparse clumps of beard on his sunken cheeks) who used to give young ladies lessons in teaching—so that children weren't spoiled and didn't swear like milk truck drivers. And so, the *Froebel-Girls* (a whole bevy of them, ruffles stretched over ample bosoms and hats trimmed with cherries and apples of paradise) gathered groups of children together, seven or eight per group, and took them for walks in the park, educated them and taught them "foreign tongues". Tongues! What's there to teach? You stick your tongue out as far as you can, then a little bit more, and you touch your nose! Bravo! But it's only one tongue even then, no matter what you do!

Nyuta was quick to grasp all these stupid *"eins-zwei-trei-vier, in die Schule gehen wir's"*, sending Polina into a state of unutterable rapture. "Mashenka, Mashenka!" she would call from the doorstep when they came back from a walk. "There's just one thing I don't understand. How is that a child who can instantly remember a rhyme in a foreign tongue, can't read a word in her own language?"

But what is there to understand? There's a little mirror in your head which, if you really concentrate, reflects everything you want to remember. You just have to capture the item you need in the mirror, either a word or—much more fun—a number. And when the mirror catches what it's looking for, *it's caught forever*. Isn't it like that for everyone? And it would be fine with letters too if only they were written *properly* and not all crazily, the wrong way about, like you see all over the place outside.

There were a lot of good things about Polina as well though. After the walk, she always bought Nyuta a tasty treat. The puffy yellow log of a chocolate-covered éclair filled with magical tasting cream or custard. Or a pastry basket filled with rose-petal syrup and topped with a dark-red sour cherry.

Also, Polina was safe out of doors where she wouldn't start pestering you with her stupid vitamin C powder, the nasty acidic sour-tasting stuff she forced into Nyuta at home. She would open the flat paper packet, make it into a spout and, with the words, "Open wide!" would sprinkle the powder onto the little scoop of Nyuta's despairingly extended tongue. By contrast, outside, Polina was entirely at Nyuta's mercy. She was afraid the little girl would run away. It had happened before and Nyuta was a fast runner, nearly as fast as a motorbike. In short, unless Khristina began to engage in the same sort of nonsense, Nyuta had definitely come out on top.

It would be great too if she could stay for good although Ma had said Khristina would only be looking after Nyuta for the few days that Polina was in hospital, being cut open and neatly sewn back together again. Dad had explained how it was done once and how the stitches were removed later on.

After his entertaining account, Nyuta had cut open and disembowelled three of her dolls.

Hmmm…

And Polina wouldn't come back from the hospital, at all, ever, anyway. Maybe she likes it there so much that she'll keep on swallowing stones and then putting her fat belly under the knife?

Meanwhile, Khristina had swiftly wrapped Nyuta up tight in the towels, bound her left arm to her body and left the right free.

She made skilful use of the safety pins and spun her around by the shoulder.

"There! What a poppet!"

"Am I a mummy?"

"A what?"

"Daddy and I were looking at a picture. It's a very old dead person wrapped up in bandages."

"Yuck! So you're dead are you? Really? You're a live girl. Now, off we go, into the hall. Have a peek at yourself in the mirror!"

Nyuta tried to walk and nearly fell over.

"I can't … my legs!" she reported, frightened.

"You can do anything!" yelled Khristina. "Fibber! You can do it. You've got two legs, you know! Right foot forward! Off you go, quick march!"

It took them five minutes to hobble as far as the hall, which was home to a glorious, precious secret. But shhh, don't tell anyone.

In the afternoon, when Polina was fast asleep, all you had to do was to wait patiently but eagerly for a snore to come rumbling out of the leather chair in the dining room where she had settled down to "flick through the paper." When the first wave of a tractor's roar rose beneath the faintly fluttering newspaper, you had to dash into the nursery, almost flying, treading on the only five reliable pieces of parquet. There, on the table next to Polina's day bed, was her old round mirror on its tall stand, decorated with an enamel miniature and slightly stained with age. A threadbare Ivan Tsarevich on the mirror's enamel back was carrying off a now completely headless Marya-Iskusnitsa on a mare with a damaged leg.

And if you gingerly placed that mirror on the shoe-stand in the hall, exactly opposite the other one, the "grand" mirror in the carved black frame, and then drifted slowly into the deep space between them, which moved in taut streams, two entrances would open onto endless mirror corridors.

Nyuta had learnt to keep the game a secret because Ma was not at all comfortable with mirrors. She was reluctant to look into them and even seemed to be a little scared, which was really silly. Once, when she caught Nyuta doing her slow exhilarating dance between the two mirror flows, from which streamed a bewitching, thrumming coolness, Ma had been frightened for some reason and had taken Polina's mirror away, exclaiming helplessly: "What are you doing? I don't understand what you're up to? What is all this nonsense?"

And Nyuta now stood, one half of her in bandages, in front of the tall grand mirror with its bronze candleholders.

"Who is that?" the little girl rasped, staring at the one-armed bundle of some half-child, probing the image with her gaze as she usually did and turning it from right to left. This was much harder to do now for some reason.

All her life, the moment of recognizing herself in the mirror was like a delayed parachute drop. She was never able to merge with her reflection straight away. In that first moment there was an encounter, a shock, a heartbeat—someone else is wearing your clothes. She had to turn herself the other way around and every single time she had to teach herself how to look all over again.

Although she could always recognize herself in any distorted surface, in water, in a spoon, in the fat belly of the enamel teapot.

"There," said Khristina in satisfaction. "That's how we turn left-handers around back in Pirnovo. We'll soon have you absolutely fine!"

And for two hours Nyuta and Khristina practised how to use her weak and awkward right hand to hold a spoon, to catch a ball, to throw things and to pick them up off the floor, to comb her hair. And even to throw paper down the toilet after "doing your business."

"Khristina, please … that's enough," Nyuta said eventually. Her face was drawn, her eyes were dark and beads of sweat stood out above her upper lip. Not once in all that time had she given up, kicked an inoffensive toy or cried out. "Let me out! I'm fed up!"

Khristina gave Nyuta a fat red finger right under the nose.

"Uh-ho!" she declared. "Stop right there! No going back. Your Dad'll be home from the hospital at five so I'll let you out at half past four. The Lord loves those who are patient! But He cannot abide darned left-handers! Do you want to be hobnobbing with the devil?"

Nyuta turned sunken eyes on her nanny and tormentor. She very much did not want to be hobnobbing with some unknown and, from the tone of Khristina's voice, not very pleasant devil. Then again, she didn't much care whether the Lord loved her or not. Although, of course, it would be better if he did.

However … if her useless right hand became as quick and clever as her left, how fantastic to be able to throw five balls at once like the juggler at the circus!

The little girl sat on a stool and thoughtfully scratched her nose with her right hand—for the very first time.

God, to smell that rich and magical odour again, to take in a deep drag of it: the mixture of manure, horse sweat, fresh sawdust, hot lights and warm tarpaulin! How your heart started pounding when the orchestra struck up. The festival was under way. Streams of red and blue from the spotlights swept over your eyes and a prince in a short, spangled cloak, keeping his balance with a long pole, bore a tiny girl aloft on his shoulders. She wore almost no clothes at all but glittered and sparkled with sequins like a real live Thumbelina. All of a sudden, to the fearsome beating of a drum, she flew up and landed with a bounce, both feet on the tightrope!

Her father went crazy clapping too and bought another of the lady's crème-brulee ice-creams in a brown paper bag with a drawing of a musketeer. But Nyuta couldn't eat it. She sat, her mouth dry, eyes fixed on the ring. *In the inner mirror*, the one just above her eyes, she, Nyuta herself, balancing a long poll, was coming towards her along a tightrope. Just like that Thumbelina. But not now and not soon.

"Daddy!" she said in excitement, tugging the sleeve of her father's trench coat. "I can do that too! I can… After… after lots of days… I can do it too!"

Her father was dismissive.

"What are you burbling on about, daughter. What nonsense!" he said and ate the crème brulee himself as he would later tell her "in three bites, not even thinking, I was so on edge."

Then there was the juggler after the show…

Nyuta and her father were the last to leave because she didn't want to go. The juggler was standing or rather swaying jauntily from side to side in a dark corner near the fire extinguisher. He was practising, tossing five yellow balls up into the air and catching them. Every now and then a ball would fall. The juggler would catch the rest, fold them one after the other into his long hand and bend down to pick up the one that had fallen. Then he would release them once more, a dotted yellow line arching above his head.

"Stop, Daddy, stop," she beseeched. She stood next to the juggler and watched, concentrating hard. Somehow, she knew when a ball was going to fall or rather could see that it had dropped a little lower than the others so that it was out of step with the arc they were making. She let one go and the next and then, moving with lightning speed and precision to the left, she caught the ball as it fell and offered it to the juggler.

"Bravo!" he exclaimed, taking the ball in a burning hand. "And with your left, eh? Bravo, indeed."

And on the way home Nyuta ran and jumped and flew, racing far ahead of her father then circling back, like a happy puppy playing fetch with its owner.

He smiled at that and said, "Bravo! And with your left, eh? Bravo, indeed!"

CHAPTER 5.

…I realized right away that I had met her a long time ago, that this was the laughing, capering little girl who had made such an impression, frightened me even, many years earlier in the Kiev flat of some people who were complete strangers to me.

Our orchestra was touring the cities of Ukraine and the assistant director of the philharmonic had asked me to deliver a parcel to her relatives in Kiev ("Senechka, darling, do say you will!"). I agreed seeing that it was soft and didn't weigh much. I cannot stand traipsing around with parcels for other people when I'm already carrying my bassoon.

Add to that, the relatives in question turned out to be living on Zhadanovskogo Street, which used to be Zhilyanskaya—and still is to the ordinary residents of Kiev.

My grandfather and I used to stay there on our brief summer visits.

I loved Kiev and knew it fairly well. When I was little, I spent every summer at my grandfather's in Zhmerinka and we would always go to Kiev for a week. We stayed with a friend of his, a former circus gymnast, in an overcrowded communal flat in an old two-storey building on Zhilyanskaya Street.

The friend was called Panna Ivanovna and had an Armenian surname of some kind. If memory serves me right, she occasionally liked to make a quick buck for entertainment's sake. She used to boast that her first ever commercial transaction was when she turned soldiers' belts into sandals that she sold on the market. She claimed to have been in desperate need of the money. It was during the years that she was conducting a wildly passionate affair with a handsome ringhand.

She smoked passionately too, lighting up one after the other although she couldn't bear cigarette butts. She called them "little corpses." If she saw an ashtray full of them in the kitchen, she would give strict orders for the "little corpses" to be removed.

Some fairly colourful characters inhabited the flat as if in confirmation of its former purpose. My grandfather said it had once housed one of Kiev's respectable brothels.

Surprisingly, this motley crew managed to rub along together reasonably well without major incidents. And what an entertaining bunch they were! There was a bizarre painter, for example, not without talent, perhaps, but with no social graces whatsoever. He would wander around in extravagant, suspiciously feminine, clothing. He'd either chosen it, stolen it off washing-lines or been given hand-me-downs by his grateful muses. The Master made both me and my grandfather pose for him. True, he never gave us the portraits, and I sometimes think sadly now that I would pay good money in a flash for the one of my grandfather… (On the other hand, where would I put it, on what imaginary hook could I hang it on my endless travels?)

I remember the long industrial street with its occasional commercial apartment building embellished with ornamentation and sculptures, even caryatids. Unlike Kreshchatik, which was destroyed by bombing during the war, all the streets in this area—Zhilyanskaya, Saksaganskogo, Tarasovskaya, Starovokzalnaya, Chkalova, which used to be Stolypinskaya—had survived intact and were full to overflowing with a pullulating crowd of people of every possible stripe. The area rumbled and rattled with trams, hollered with the seasoned voices of the Central Stadium, and teemed with the hectic life of the circus at the famous Jewish Bazaar.

I remember a big, unpaved courtyard with washing hanging out, a dovecote, woodsheds, an outside toilet building made of planks and an enormous puddle by the water pump. In keeping with my grandfather's schedule—orchestra was essential and not to be cancelled—we covered vast distances of the summer city on foot or on the screeching trams.

En route, he would stock up on bits and pieces for his watchmaking.

I was mad about cars back then. The smell of the big city left me flustered and thrilled: the complex combination of hot oil and petrol from passing cars, the aroma of fried pirozhki on street stalls and of hoseddown streets. I can still remember the yard keepers, hoses at the ready. I remember too the great number of vast flowerbeds, rustling in the wind, crimson with roses, carnations and tulips.

And I loved the moustachioed Kiev trams (one of my grandfather's sayings was, "We'll survive as long as the trams keep running!"). In those days, they were painted dark blue or bright red at the bottom and a

     LEONARDO'S HANDWRITING

light pastry-coloured cream at the top. And a five-pointed star stretched across their broad flat faces that seemed to express a dull surprise.

My grandfather called the Philharmonic Hall, which had the best acoustics in Kiev, the Merchants' Assembly. He called the Pioneers' Garden behind it the Merchants' Garden as well. Always excited and emotional after a concert, he would walk me across the tramlines—he was an exceptional music lover who adored the woodwind instruments—always humming or mumbling the music we'd heard.

"All the registers of the clarinet are good, Senchis," my grandfather would say, "almost all. The basses, brooding and ominous, at the beginning of Tchaikovsky's Fifth Symphony—remember, we heard it last time? Then there are passages played in octaves that are lovely, smooth and brilliant, such emotional depth! It can cut through any orchestral *tutti*, no matter how deafening! Weeping, joy, declarations of love—the clarinet can do them all, it's good at everything. Instant attack! Dashing staccato! But the clarinet's emotions are open, Senchis, even when it sounds menacing. There's no subtext, nothing below the surface. Whereas the bassoon, Senchis, that's quite another matter. My friend used to say—and he played bassoon with the Philharmonic—that the great conductor Rakhlin—Natan Grigoryevich Rakhlin—had once said during a rehearsal of the *Pathétique*, 'Orchestra, listen to the bassoon. *It's giving the lead.*'"

My grandfather would stand still before *giving the lead* into the next cut-through courtyard and I would stop next to him docile as a tame horse. "And after the bassoon solo, when the woodwinds take up the melody, Rakhlin would mark every semiquaver with fingers as fat as bratwurst, saying 'The bassoon gives the lead! It really does!' God grant that you understand this one day, Senchis. It's such a good way of putting it."

You could cross half of Kiev by cutting through its courtyards via stone steps, gateways, changing road levels and flights of moss-covered stairs that led from one street to the next. There was the smell of layers of rotting poplar fluff and above it the heady fragrance of the linden trees and the evening scent of the velvety lilac-coloured flowers with the grandly operatic name of *matthiola*, indescribably subtle like the distant sound of a cor anglais.

But above all there was the smell of round Arnautka buns and it seems to me now that, for all his love of the woodwind section, that was in fact why my grandfather went to Kiev—for the inimitable, rich and fragrant smell of Arnautka bread.

How to describe it? I don't know. It's nothing like the sour smell of black bread or the sweetish note of white buns.

My grandfather would wake up early, shave with his cut-throat razor over the old, rust-spattered sink in the friendly communal kitchen, pull on the boots of a slaughtered Italian soldier and set off to be at the nearest bakery by opening time as if heading to meet a woman for a romantic tryst. The Arnautka bread smelt very much like a woman too—of eternally unfathomable happiness.

My grandfather was even nicknamed "Arnautkin" at the flat. They would ask, "Panna Ivanovna, when is Arnautkin coming to see you again?"

I spotted a round loaf labelled an "Arnautka bun" in a Russian shop in Boston not long ago. I bought it right there and then.

It was nothing like the heavenly smell I remember from my childhood visits to Kiev, of course.

So, I was always pleased and secretly excited to arrive in Kiev, although the city was no longer the same by the end of the 1960s.

Even so, the restaurant in the Teatralnaya Hotel on the corner of Vladimirskaya and Lenin Streets, immediately opposite the opera house, continued to serve an excellent chicken and mushroom julienne in three ramekins—and at a very reasonable price too.

The day after the concert, I finally managed to do as I had been asked.

The family, to which I was to deliver the parcel, turned out to be marvellous, welcoming and even musical, through the wife. It turned out too that my hostess had been to our concert—if only she'd known! In short, they sat me down for tea, adding a little hair of the dog—I was no slouch when it came to drinking at the time. My heart was still strong and didn't object.

A warm and friendly conversation ensued and turned—as was only too easy back then—to relatives and friends who had been victims of the purges. I grew up in Guryev and Masha, the wife, in Semipalatinsk. We were drawn to one another somehow, like long-forgotten relatives. Meanwhile, her husband, a robust and quietly genial chap, who had apparently been a military doctor and a high-ranking one at that, continued to top up my glass.

Suddenly, that little girl came tumbling out of her hidey-hole.

She was preceded by a voice booming out to all and sundry, "Nyuta! Nyuta! Nyu-u-ta!"

A scarecrow, aged around five and knee-high to a grasshopper, popped up seemingly out of nowhere, wearing a hat trimmed with flowers, her mother's long silk skirt and a blouse with a plunging neckline that revealed the two eye-like buttons of her little girl nipples.

"Do you want to see the lovely lady?"

Hup! A shoe flew into the air, the heel almost knocking her father's glass over on the table.

Hup! The other hit the heavy five-branched chandelier which swayed menacingly above our heads.

A broad-beamed young woman with a microcephalic head and great paw-like hands appeared behind the child. She was trying to catch the little monster and put it back into the Pandora's box it had escaped from at such lightning speed.

She could neither capture nor control the miniature whirlwind, however, and the little girl ran out in different costumes twice more, shrieking, "Do you want to see the lovely lady?"

I don't really like or understand children. I don't know how to talk to them. I get bored and irritated and try to slope off somewhere.

But her jumping about was so astonishing, and she even managed to throw in a twist as she jumped. She was like a grasshopper herself.

When she ran out the second time, she spotted me, stood stock still for a moment, then suddenly began to laugh a ringing comical laugh, clutching her stomach. Her mouth stretched from ear to ear, the big grown-up teeth interspersed with pointy little baby teeth. Two gaps where the eye teeth should have been. An odd little person, joy pouring out of her like a fountain. With a wild energy. And incredible eyes, like the sea, green with a hint of blue, fixing you above the laughter in such an adult way as if asking: Where do you come from? Who are you?

"What?" I asked. "What are you laughing at?"

"It's funny!" she cried. "So funny!"

"What's funny?"

"He's just like Daddy!" she cried, jumping about and pointing at me. "His birthday's the same day as Daddy's!"

Something strange occurred at this point. My hosts' faces darkened, their eyes lowered hopelessly.

"Time for bed, Nyuta!" her father said sharply.

"It's like Daddy's. The same day!" She roared with laughter.

"When is Daddy's birthday?" I asked the gap-toothed creature.

She lifted a foot to her ear, grasped her ankle and drew it towards her face.

"The nineteenth of Sep-tem-ber!" she rapped out.

I was dumbfounded. Pah! She'd got it right! And all the while she was spinning around and doing goodness knows what with her legs, arms whirling like a windmill.

Nowadays, children like this are called hyperactive but no one had heard of such a diagnosis back then. They simply referred to the child as insufferable.

"It's funny!"

And she was insufferable.

What struck me most at the time, however, were her parents' faces, their apologetic smiles and downcast eyes as if a shameful family disease had been exposed. Her father stood and began to escort her out. It would have been awkward to give her a lecture or shout at her with a visitor present. He spread his arms wide and used the whole of his large body to usher her to the end of the corridor where her room must have been. Twice more, the little girl bounced back again, gleefully yelling childish nonsense and doing tricks with her arms and legs that left me dazzled. And twice more her father withdrew in embarrassment to calm her. When he finally came back to the table, I said, "Your daughter has great sporting talent. You should send her to train as an acrobat."

And they both nodded gratefully. "Yes, yes. It's already been suggested. We'll get her into a sports club in September."

Strangely, neither husband nor wife took the slightest interest in asking me when my birthday actually was. Obviously, they knew she was accurate as a sniper. Obviously, she'd had them baffled from the start.

Unfortunately, I was already two sheets to the wind by then and it matters not one jot when you're drunk if someone is able to tell you the day you were born or even the day that you'll die.

Dear God, how we used to drink back then! Honestly!

It's a well-known fact that the conductor Mravinsky once locked the famous French horn player, Udaltsov, in his office. The latter lowered a three-rouble note out of the window on a piece of string. A boy was waiting at the bottom and hightailed it off to the liquor store. Then he tied the bottle to the same string and Udaltsov pulled up his loot. He played brilliantly after that, drunk as a lord!

Baranov, the clarinettist, and Tupikov, the bassoonist, went everywhere together. If they didn't, they fell over.

At the Kirov Theatre, they locked the alcoholic bassoon player in the orchestra room. By the end of Act Three, he was completely plastered. How had he managed to get drunk? That's those resourceful Russians for you! There's a small silver cup at the bottom of a bassoon, which seals off the double tube. Well, this inventor had soldered a second cup to it and that was where he kept his restorative tipple. He'd been drawing mouthfuls through the tube during rehearsals—an extra bocal. That was his hangover cure, poor beggar. Incidentally, he was the one who came up with the musicians' saying that "To shake the system up a bit, it is essential NOT to drink for one day of every week."

So that evening, I got roaring drunk with some very nice people and forgot about the little girl. It was the following morning when I woke up in my hotel room and splashed my puffy face with cold water a couple of times that I remembered. And it scared me! Crikey, I thought. You idiot, why on earth didn't you try to sweet talk the creepy little mite, to suck up to her? Maybe the five-year-old sibyl could have given you other dates too… Later on, I would remember the strange creature from time to time but then, as time passed, I forgot all about her.

And then, it was the autumn of 1988. Moscow. Quite by chance I was at the circus on Tsvetnoy Boulevard and a little bit tipsy to boot. I'd arrived from St Petersburg the day before to see a friend, the famous bassoonist, Misha Dyatlov. He's dead now. His sister, a receptionist at the Hotel Minsk, would always get me a decent room.

We had a friendly drink together, talked ourselves silly and, the next morning, he couldn't get out of bed. Either it was flu or his heart or kidneys were giving up. He rang me at the hotel and begged me to stand in for him at the circus. There was an evening performance then a morning rehearsal. Nothing much, just three hours.

And, of course, off I went to save my friend Misha's hide. All the more so since I'd spent a good bit of time at the circus in my youth. The dashing repertoire wasn't unfamiliar. It was only Dunaevsky and I'd have the score.

So there I was after rehearsal, putting my bassoon in its case, half an ear on the familiar sounds. The circus has its own music in the morning. The sleepy silence was broken by a predatory roar, the yell of the animal tamer, the crack of the whip. Animal rehearsals usually take place in the ring in the morning. "Early bird" performers start to wander in after ten, some for rehearsals, some just to chat.

I was listening idly to the conversation behind me. Two women. I don't remember the details but one seemed to be talking about a spring tour of Armenia. The other replied, "Relax. There won't be any tour."

"Are you crazy or what? The manager's order's on the board over there."

Whereupon the other voice, sort of low and boyish, suddenly sang out, "It isn't going to happen, to happen."

It gave me such a start!

I turned round. Of the two of them, I recognized her immediately. Not in the sense of seeing that insufferable, giggling little acrobat in the somehow toned-down young woman in jeans and a dark blue top. It was just that she was looking at me commandingly. And I realized that it had been a summons from behind me: "*Do you want to see the lovely lady*?"

Small and slight, like an arrow. Her eyes shone like a fast-flowing stream on a sunny day.

Suddenly, my hands felt so heavy I nearly dropped the bassoon case. My innards churned, dropped away. I just had time to think: Well, that's that, there won't be any spring tour of Armenia then. And that I should ask whether she was living in Kiev at the end of the 60s, when suddenly she said quite clearly, "It's funny!"

And I just stood and looked at what a narrow yet round and firm chin she had, while her lips, by contrast, were childish and trusting. And soft, even just to look at.

CHAPTER 6.

Masha said nothing as she undressed in the darkness of the bedroom, folded up her clothes on the chair by feel and pulled her nightie out from under her pillow.

"I'm not asleep," said Anatoly. "You can put the lamp on."

"You sleep … I've managed now."

She climbed under the blanket, stretched and lay still.

It had been a sad, agonizing day. They had buried Polina, Masha's old family friend, practically a relative, who had set out wanting to marry Masha's father and then, on the day he was arrested in 1936, had become her mother's friend for life.

She had come to live with them in Semipalatinsk and, throughout her years of study at the Kiev Conservatoire, Masha lived in Polina's room in a huge communal flat, spreading a thin mattress on the floor at night.

Polina had still been so active at seventy-five, had helped so enthusiastically with Nyuta. More than that, she'd literally nursed the child back to health. There had been almost nothing of her when she arrived with Masha. They'd carried her off the train and Polina had simply moved in.

And what, you would think, could go wrong during the routine removal of a gall-bladder? She'd already been recovering from the operation, completely ready to be discharged, as Tolya kept saying. And then, all of a sudden, her heart just stopped.

Masha turned her head and saw the light from the street light outside reflected in her husband's eyes.

"Tolya," she whispered. "Tell me, there was no way of imagining that clot would…"

"No, not at all. Stop going on! It was out of the blue."

"So then how…"

They were both silent and each saw again what had happened in the kitchen over dinner three days ago. Khristina had been complaining about the strange behaviour of her aunt, Markovna, the caretaker, who was renting a television that she would only switch on for a short time "for herself."

"Economizing she is, daft old brush. She thinks if she doesn't use it, she won't have to pay."

At the same time, Khristina was attempting unsuccessfully to wind a long piece of pasta onto her fork. In the end, she picked it up in her fat fingers and slurped it up noisily.

When Khristina left after dinner, planting loud kisses on both cheeks and the nose of an already sleepy Nyuta as a parting gesture, Masha grinned as she recalled some of the new nanny's comical phrases and remarked that she was a nice girl and kind but when Polina came back from the hospital, Khristina would, of course…

Whereupon Nyuta looked up from her copy of Murzilka, a children's magazine. She wasn't reading it, just looking at the pictures, starting from the back as usual. She said, "No, let Khristina stay. She's really funny. She's turning me back to front!"

"Nyuta, darling, Khristina will come and visit. Surely you don't want our dear Polina…"

"Not dear! Not Polina! Not coming back!"

"What are you talking about?" her father said, raising his voice. He and his daughter were friends and Tolya took liberties Masha would never have allowed herself. He would even smack her when she deserved it.

"Polina will be discharged the day after tomorrow. You'll welcome her back from the hospital yourself with some flowers."

The little girl looked in silence from her father to Masha, astonished and somehow helpless, as if she was trying really hard but failing to explain something obvious that had no need of evidence, something that wasn't her fault and that they either couldn't or wouldn't understand.

"But, Daddy," she whined, aggrieved, "Polina isn't coming back anyway."

Tolya freed a hand from the blanket and put the bedside lamp on.

"Mashuta," he said. "Don't imagine things. It happens. It does. Sensitive children do sometimes make these … guesses. Look at her. She's like quicksilver…"

"Tolya, maybe we should take her to see a psychiatrist all the same?"

"Rubbish! She's a perfectly normal child, just highly active."

"And do you still think she shouldn't be taught to use her right hand instead of her left? After all, eventually, at school…"

"Nonsense! What difference does it make to you which hand she uses to eat or write? What kind of medieval approach, what kind of pre-jud… Shh!"

"It's alright, she's asleep."

"Look," her husband continued, lowering his voice. "Someone forced to use their right hand can start to stammer or become neurotic or who knows what! It'll be too late to undo the damage then."

Indeed, Masha thought reproachfully, but how worried you were yourself when…

To begin with, Anatoly really had been unable to accept that a child who could instantly learn any text by heart simply couldn't learn to sound out words.

"What nonsense is this?" he fumed. "You're a clever girl, my bright little button. So, come on, say after me, 'b'… 'u'.. Makes 'bu'…"

The hapless word "bublik" led to a real row. After a storm of confusion and misunderstanding, sobs and answering back, Anatoly made Nyuta stand in the corner. He allowed her out after five minutes but she stood there stubbornly. Even her feet were wet with tears.

This time however, being, as Masha said, "pig-headed as a peasant," Tolya was determined to tough things out.

"Now then, that's enough crying. You'll turn into a puddle. Come here. I don't believe we can't do this."

And, indeed, the first syllable was immediately mastered: "Bub!" And that "bub!" was where their success ended. The next syllable simply couldn't be grasped.

"It's about a kilogram," the little girl said in the end.

"A kilogram? What kilogram, birdbrain?" He flopped down on his chair.

He said nothing for a while, calmed down and picked up the piece of paper with large, round letters written on it.

"L! I! K! 'lik,' see? What's so difficult? You've read 'bub' already. Lik, lik. L-i-k!" He turned the paper round and pushed it towards her again, looked down and suddenly leaped up like a scalded cat.

"Mashuta!"

Masha rushed in in alarm.

"Look," he said, twitchily. "She's reading from right to left. She read 'kil' instead of 'lik.'"

"Nyuta, wash your hands. Come and have some soup. And dry your eyes."

"But you don't understand. She could only read 'bub' because it's the same in both directions. And she kept on saying, 'Kilogram, kilogram…' And there's me thinking, what bloody kilogram? She read 'kil' instead of 'lik'."

"Just leave her be," said Masha sadly.

Now, after Polina's funeral, Masha was thinking back to that night on the train when she returned to Kiev with her fragile little trophy. The fleeting light of the moon rippled white on the sleeping carriage curtains. Asleep, the little girl lay curled in a tight ball on the next bunk, ethereal in the darkness.

Her little backpack swayed on a hook. Inside were two pairs of knickers, some socks and a checked dress with a torn ruffle on one puffed sleeve. "Are those all her things?" asked Masha in surprise as she received the backpack from the carer. "Yes," came the reply. "Everything she had when she came to us."

The train raced along at its top night-time speed, shying like a spooked horse at the corners, and Masha was plagued by the strange and insistent thought that they were not going home to Kiev—to Anatoly and to Polina who was waiting impatiently to see the little girl—but into some endless, inhospitable void where there would be nothing but this speed and worry and the glancing light of the moon…

All the rushing around of late, the queues to see notaries, the battles with bureaucrats, had left her utterly worn out. She was afraid the little girl would not make it, would fade away or bow out… Masha hadn't even been able to find Shura, the neighbour whom she could have questioned in more detail about the little girl, about her late mother. It was as if the elusive neighbour had hidden away on purpose to avoid a meeting.

Well, so be it. What difference did it make in the end? What was urgently needed now were tests… vitamins… Affection, love, toys, good food. What a good thing Polina was on hand with her boundless devotion and unfailing readiness to grate apples and carrots.

And, of course, they would have to try to bring the child on. There was a clear developmental delay. She just didn't speak. Thank goodness she wasn't dumb, though, and had normal hearing. It meant she would start talking properly one day.

An uncomfortable sensation of being watched closely woke Masha up. She opened her eyes and almost jumped out of her skin. The little girl was sitting on her bunk, right next to her, as close as could be—a tiny, fleshless elf in the blue glow of the carriage night-light.

She gazed silently and fixedly at Masha's face. This long, searching adult stare frightened Masha more than anything since childhood (the evening ghost stories at Pioneer Camp flashed briefly into her memory: in a dark, dark room… sat a dark, dark…)

Maybe she's a sleepwalker? Masha thought in a panic.

"Anya, Anyuta," she called softly, sitting herself up, and the little girl responded immediately with a perfectly steady gaze, wakeful and sorrowful. "Why aren't you asleep, little one?"

The child carried on watching but made no reply. Masha's throat went dry.

"Come in here with me, if you like," she said, laying back down on her pillow and patting the space alongside her. "Lie down … next to Mummy."

The little girl shifted a bit and folded hands in her lap.

"You're not Mummy," she said in a slightly throaty voice, in which such a grown-up wistfulness could be heard that Masha sat right back up again.

"Nyuta," she whispered. "Where is Mummy?"

Nyuta turned a small bluish face, in which only her enormous eyes remained, sighed and said, "Mummy's gone into the mirror."

"Tolya, do you remember," Masha began, her voice tight. "Do you remember her coming into the entryway in April and saying, 'We'll have a green door soon,' and the very next day a sign went up about renovations and the door was painted green? You talked about the theory of probability and coincidences… Tolya! I'm scared."

He held her, saying nothing. She lay for three minutes or so, nose buried under his arm. She kept waiting for him to start giving his usual, half-joking explanations of discoveries in psychology where people sometimes … but her husband said nothing. Eventually, as Masha was dropping off to sleep, Anatoly suddenly and clearly remarked, "Mashuta, you should go."

"Go where?" said Masha, frightened into wakefulness. The claret-coloured bedroom curtains glowed ominously in the light from the bedside lamp.

"Back where you found her." He was quiet for a moment then said, "You could ask around a bit… ask the things you didn't ask at the time."

***

A couple of weeks later, Masha took a few days off and went to Yeysk.

She didn't really know why she was going, what confessions she was expecting from a woman she didn't know, what evidence she might find and of what. Or what these confessions might change in their lives.

Outside the train, bare patches of meadowland blazed with yellow pools of flowering winter cress. Every shade of green flashed by in dark thickets of dense forest. A large field sown to clover clambered onto the ridge of a hill, ribbed like a washboard by the wind.

The train sped along, emerged from a sheet of rain and plunged into hazy sunshine before ripples of rain sluiced down the windows again. The abundant greenery of June breathed gratefully in the shifting downpour.

They passed an enclosure where a chocolate-coloured foal rolled on its back in the green grass, kicking its legs and revealing its pillow-soft napped-leather belly. Its mother nudged the youngster, her nose equally soft.

Masha had aged ten years over the past two. Vague childhood fears had been suddenly revived, familiar since her Semipalatinsk schooldays when she would jump over the cracks in the pavement on the way home and predict that if she didn't step on a single one, everything would be fine and her dad would come home. Inevitably she did step on one. It was an attempt to curry favour with some higher force. God didn't exist, of course, but someone was responsible for this world! She felt, she knew someone was! Well, that one, who … which … that supreme force you had to entreat somehow, to placate or better yet—make yourself as small as possible so you wouldn't be spotted. *Inevitability*—that's what had terrified her most since being little.

She was tormented by fear for the little girl and for the future but what tormented her most was shameful and deeply hidden. She couldn't admit to herself, let alone Tolya, that she was afraid of her, of her little girl. Afraid—and for the first time she said it inwardly, repulsed—of Anna.

Of Anna who knew about *inevitability* in advance, could sense it and sailed calmly towards it… Which meant that *somehow she belonged* to that mysterious higher force, the very thought of which made Masha want to shrink away.

She was in the taxi before she remembered that Shura, the neighbour, might at that very moment be making meals at the children's home's summer quarters and her heart sank. She really didn't relish the prospect of another wild goose chase.

When Masha rang the bell, however, the door opened straight away and everything worked out—just as it had during that first wretched and peculiar phone call. When she opened the door and saw her, Shura went so white that Masha could tell even in the semi-darkness of the corridor. Masha couldn't know how often Shura remembered her, walking trustingly and inescapably into a trap, or the little girl she had brought back from the very brink and taken away with her.

"What do you want?" Surprise and sudden fear made Shura slightly abrupt. She was then embarrassed and inwardly ashamed. "Who is it you're after?"

Masha stood, politely studying the thick-set elderly woman and her slightly pock-marked face.

"I'm sorry but I don't know your patronymic," she said. "It's Aleksandra?"

"Volodymerna." Shura opened the door a little wider and tucked in her stomach. "Come in, don't just stand there…"

Later, as feet were stamped on the doorstep and awkward, broken phrases exchanged, Shura suddenly realized that forgiveness had arrived, the very thing she so often asked for in her thoughts before going to sleep. And she was not letting that forgiveness get away now. For this reason, she cut off her unbidden guest's awkward preliminaries and inquiries firmly and said, "You don't need my patronymic! You're Masha, you are, ain't you? Right, then, come on through, into the kitchen. Excuse me, I'm making patties. I'll just wipe this corner of the table down and we'll have a cup of tea."

Masha sat down and for a few minutes they said nothing, each preparing for the conversation to come. Shura fussily tidied the bowl of minced meat away, put the kettle on to boil and cut up what was left of some kind of shop-bought cake.

"I haven't got much to go with the tea."

"Oh, and I've come empty-handed." They spoke at the same time and the atmosphere became lighter, simpler.

Shura brought the cups and sat at the table facing Masha.

"Well?" she said. "How are things? Why're you here?"

Masha hesitated. She didn't know where to start and asking the most important thing straight out, just like that…

"You see, I, erm, want to ask you some questions, Shura … about my little girl's parents. You must have known them well."

"Parents—that's one way of putting it!" said Shura with a smirk. "Respectful too. For parents, she had her mother, Rita, and that's it. Rita was a good, kind, girl … ordinary. May she rest in peace. What d'you want to know, Masha? Exactly? Out with it."

But Masha couldn't just come out with it. She couldn't!

"You see," she said, faltering, "the child knows hundreds of phone numbers off by heart. Just like Victor Hugo. He could remember the numbers of all the carriages in Paris."

"It happens," Shura replied. "I had an uncle who could whistle all the songs the birds sing. You could say, 'Uncle Fima, let's have a thrush!' And out would come its song… You couldn't tell the difference. And when he did the robin, well!"

And Masha opted not to say that her daughter could simply look at a stranger and tell you their telephone number and date of birth.

The kettle whistled its own song as it came to the boil. Shura got up and began to pour tea from a packet, add water and wipe up what she had split. Neither of them spoke.

"What about the father?"

"There was no father."

"I understand," Masha hastened to say. "I don't mean it like that. I really do understand everything, Shura. I just… I wanted to ask whether you know anything at all about her father. Anything?"

"Oh, yes," said Shura in surprise. "He used to skulk around here in front of everyone, did that Arkashka with his red hair. Now then, tea's up. Give us your cup. It was Uzbeks taught me to brew it like this, you know. Loads of Uzbeks used to come here, selling melons on the market. I used to put them up. Nice people. Taught me how to make a proper brew. I've never liked it any old how since then. Good tea has a character of its own, you know."

And just when Masha had already begun to think that no one would deign to tell her anything and what could she expect when she was beating about the bush herself, Shura said as if making up her mind, "So, then, Arkashka Mesin… Fine. I'll tell you. May the late Rita forgive me on the other side. He was just a kid, see? That father—so-called as I say—was only a lad himself when Anyuta was born. Fifteen, sixteen at most. What a scandal, eh? Can you imagine? The Municipal Education Authority, the District Education Authority, corruption of a minor, all that crap. Well, you can understand. They crushed her, they really did. Who didn't slag her off? Who didn't wipe the floor with her?! School librarian, they said, you're supposed to introduce the kids to books and culture and you go *corruptioning* a minor ... She would be going down the street and they practically threw stones at her. I ... I don't know ... I'd have hanged myself with the shame but Rita, she was a tough cookie. She was... well, how old was she then, to be honest? About thirty-six, that's it. She was a skinny little thing, to be fair, with a big nose ... looked just a kid herself. But it's like they say. If you can't remember your age, look at your passport. Anyway, the main thing is, the boy's trash. He used to do a bit of thieving, then he and his mates started robbing the kiosks. And now he's in the nick for thimble rigging."

"For what?" Masha asked, perplexed.

"You know, it's this game. He's a thimble rigger."

"No, I don't know," Masha replied despondently, barely listening. She was thinking how, er, colourful her little girl's inheritance was turning out to be.

"It's a game, isn't it? Thimblerig! So, some crook, he sits there and gathers a crowd around him and asks which thimble the ball's in. Then he does this stuff with his arms and moves the thimbles around. Then the tourists, stupid suckers, stand round shelling out money. And serves them right, maybe. Must be easy money. Anyway, to start with, Arkashka, when he was little, could always guess where the ball was. He was always winning. He could have kept his mouth shut but he was a nasty piece of work and couldn't keep it zipped. I, he says, I'm a Mesin, son of the real Mesin. Well, first, they just worked him over—as a warning..."

"What Mesin?" Masha inquired, bewildered.

"Oh, come on, you must have heard... there's this performer, a magician. He can read people's minds, he does hypnosis. Mesin... I even read about him in the paper not so long ago. German name... Folk, maybe. That's it: Folk Mesin."

"What?" Masha looked at Shura. "Wolf Messing?!" She flung up her arms and bust out laughing. "Oh, Lord, Shura, what rubbish!"

"Why's it rubbish?" said Shura, taking umbrage. "He did shows here for two years in a row. Performing with the Moscow Philharmonic. 'Psychological Experiments,' it was called. My late Syoma even got up on stage and afterwards he said it was all real, no tricks. And that Folk really did work out that Syoma had told him to go to row three and take a packet of Yava cigarettes out of Mikhail Stepanovich's pocket."

"But ... what does that have to do with anything? I don't understand..."

"That's what I'm telling you. Zinka used to work as a receptionist at the Cultural Centre during the summer. She was a good-looking woman, young, a natural blonde. She fell for the performer. It happens. And that's what I'm telling you—her belly started growing at about the same time. And why did she go and lumber the boy with such a foreign sounding name? Because she wanted to boast to people, to show off her how special she was."

"But … his wife was always his assistant! I know, I've heard people say…"

"Wife, shmife," Shura scoffed in reply. "What did that ever stop a man? In these things, you know yourself, if a pretty woman fancies him, a wife can stand guard with a rifle for days on end and the minute she goes off for a pee, hey presto, he's got himself another … assistant."

"Wait a minute," Masha stammered. "So what this means is … that my Nyuta…"

That your Nyuta, Shura thought sympathetically, is a bastard twice over.

She was careful not to put it so bluntly. Aloud she said, "And so what? People believe that out of wedlock children are always born beautiful and clever."

Masha sat, hunched over, shaken and depressed. She hadn't touched her tea or her cake.

Suddenly, she remembered the story of her friend, Lena Zaryadnaya, a singer with the Kiev Opera, who had bragged of once being asked, when she was training with the Sverdlovsk Philharmonic, to meet a train carrying the mysterious and by then already famous Wolf Messing who was arriving on tour.

She stood on the platform, a few roses in her trembling hands, awaiting a noble and romantic sorcerer. Instead, a short, skinny fellow stepped out of the carriage.

Of course, she didn't let on. She adopted a respectful, adoring expression but he laughed and said, "Well, I'm no giant. Nothing I can do about that. But, you, my dear young lady, sooner or later you will realize that height isn't everything!"

And now what? Masha wondered. How do we cope with all this, this genetic legacy, this cursed inheritance?

Shura, by contrast, was as relaxed as if she'd been set free. Her speech was livelier and came more readily.

"So, I think, what kind of relatives are they, abandoning an orphan to the whims of fate, as they say? Lousy relatives, that's what! They didn't even come to the funeral. Well, devil take 'em, I say. We held Rita's wake in the one room they had, just here, on the same landing. And with all the honours. I covered the mirror, set the table. Made aspic, chilled it, baked cabbage pie. We came back here after the funeral. Had a bit of a drink and a cry with her friends, sang a few songs. We did her proud. And then what? I took that little mite in till things could be sorted out. Where could I put her? I tucked her up with me, over there, by the wall. Once, I wake up in the night and I can tell there's no one next to me. I listen but no, bathroom's all quiet and the kitchen! Bless me, where the hell's she got to? I dash out of the flat—my door's open a crack … there's a light on on the landing and in their flat too—I'm barefoot, on tiptoe, heart going nineteen to the dozen. I stick my head round their door and nearly go mad with terror. There she is, that little girl, standing on a stool in front of the mirror, thin as a wafer. She's chucked the black scarf on the floor and she's staring so hard like she can see inside the mirror … like she's listening to somebody in there, inside. Creepy or what! And her little face so bright and full of joy, like I'd never seen in a child. She's running her finger over the mirror like she's drawing a person, touching it, touching someone …

"And all with her left hand. I call out quietly in a friendly voice. I don't want to frighten her and give her a stammer on top of everything else, so really quietly, I say: 'A-an-na…An-yut-ka-a… Who can you see in there?' She doesn't even turn round, just says calmly: 'Mummy…' Just telling you about it, sends a cold shiver down my spine."

At this, Masha clearly recalled the first time Anatoly had carried the little girl, light as a feather, up their tall stairs to the second floor. They opened the door, went into the flat and a happy-looking Polina was already hurrying through the rooms, flicking switches as she came, shining light everywhere in the early twilight. The Czech crystal chandelier lighting the hall was repeated in the old mirror.

All of a sudden, the child's impassive little face shuddered and glowed and she whispered, spell-bound, as if she had witnessed a miracle, "A mirror…"

Shura, meanwhile, was in full spate. The burden that had weighed on her heart for the past two years had lifted and she was in a hurry to have her say, to pour out her heart. She wanted Masha to understand her and to accept the way things were.

"And right then, Mariya, I'm sorry but I knew for sure I wouldn't be taking her in." Shura spoke rapidly and fervently. "No way! Just to be on the safe side, you know. Who was she, seeing this sort of stuff in the mirrors? My grandma, she was a fortune teller in Oster. Lots of people came to see her. From as far away as Chernigov. Anyway, she used to tell me—when you see a person eat or make the sign of the cross with their left hand, get away from them and don't look back. It isn't God's work, it's the devil's trickery."

She looked at Masha who was completely at a loss, faltered and then held her tongue.

After a lengthy pause, she continued. "And after that night, the little lass stopped eating. She just kept wasting away… As if Rita was drawing her after her. I was sure she'd follow her. I got her into the summer quarters so she'd die in public at least, otherwise who knows what people would dream up about me? But, well, look how it all turned out. It's obviously not her time yet. You never can tell—the reasons why one person goes and another lingers on into old age… God must have sent you to her."

She stopped talking and thought what else she could say to comfort the poor woman who was sitting so deep in thought, staring at the pointlessly proffered cake: It was going to go dry, now.

If only she could still fry the patties amid all this confusion.

Shura wiped her hands on the apron, sighed and said sternly but sympathetically, "And now this is the cross you have to bear."

PART TWO

...I received a great many letters from him. How nice to see them in the mirror. I once happened to show them to Mr. le Marquis de Marigny in a gallery at Versailles. He scanned several lines without apparent effort and said, "This has been written with the left hand and well written at that." "And well read too," I replied.

Henri Duchesne, *On Ambidextrous Pupils*

CHAPTER 7.

I grew up between Europe and Asia.

The town of Guryev lies on the Ural River, about which you, little one, naturally enough know nothing, but which is in fact famous for the death of Chapaev. Here is a brief geographical overview from my childhood days: Guryev is a regional centre in the Kazakh Soviet Socialist Republic—the Caspian Depression, the Mangyshlak Peninsula, oil, gas and other luxuries. As a result, Guryev, once a merchant, Cossack and fishing-industry town and subsequently pretty much destroyed by the Bolsheviks, was home to a great many specialists from elsewhere, like my father.

Immediately after the war, he took my mother and me away from the delights of Zhmerinka, something my grandfather never forgave him for.

My father died a mysterious death a long time ago. Fishermen dragged him out of the Ural River with three stab wounds to the chest and side. I was five at the time and I don't remember a damned thing but our tender-hearted teacher was subsequently permitted not to make me learn Pushkin's lines by heart:

> *"In the hut the children hasten*
> *Shouting, while their father frets,*
> *'Daddy, Daddy, won't you listen!*
> *There is a dead man in our nets!'"*[1]

My mother refused to go back to Ukraine after that, saying she couldn't "abandon Sasha's grave" although months went by when she didn't go to the cemetery and "Sasha's grave" was an extremely dismal sight—as, indeed, were all the others.

---

1   "The Drowned Man" (translated by Ephim G. Fogel in *The Slavonic and East European Review*, Vol. 26, No. 66 (Nov., 1947), p. 3.).

So then, there were specialists in Guryev, as well as people who had been sent into exile and others who had fled to the back of beyond of their own volition to get away from Soviet power… And the reason we say "the back of beyond" is precisely because it was no holiday resort. The steppes that once belonged to the Nogay Horde are made up of clay, rock and reeds … the climate is inhospitable, reaching 50 degrees in the summer and minus 40 in the winter, with snow a rare distraction. Whereas sand was constantly whipped up by the wind in both summer and winter.

Nor would Guryev's architecture have impressed a visiting Venetian. Incomprehensible Soviet buildings stood on the main street, which was, of course, Lenin Street. Later the outskirts mushroomed into prefabricated Khrushchevka slums. And when the rains came, great troughs, made of welded iron sheets and full of loamy water, were on display at the entrance to every public building. Hessian rags nailed to wooden sticks poked out of them. Comrade citizens were kindly requested to clean their footwear at the entrance. And so, here we have a picture in Sots Art style: the City Party Committee building, let's say, and outside a queue of stalwart gentlemen washing the clay off their overshoes. This required arriving everywhere, even at the cinema, well in advance. In short, the rich, loamy clay of the Kazakh steppes enriched our existence for months on end.

We, however, lived in Zhilgorodok and that, little one, was London, Paris, Constantinople and God knows where else to all the other peasants. German prisoners built the district for the leaders. It had two-storey stone houses with verandas, stained glass windows, columns, balusters and other architectural embellishments of the Baroque style. All the houses were white and set amid avenues of elm trees … in a word: Baghdad.

Zhilgorodok was right beside the Ural River, as was an enormous park, laid by those same German prisoners and magnificent later on with its dances, fairground attractions and summer draughts tournaments beneath the mature trees.

But the main entertainment of my early childhood was the mosquitoes, or rather the vicious pursuit of them. They were tracked down by a special vehicle, like a milk truck, except that its tanks disgorged puffs of toxic yellow smoke instead of milk and we would run behind as it crept along at a snail's pace, competing to see who could stay in the foul-smelling cloud the longest. The honour went to Genka Solodov, now a monk at the Valaam Monastery (also called the Mount Athos of the North because of its strict rule) and to me.

But I was talking about Europe and Asia.

The thing is that originally the bridge over the Ural River was a simple pontoon with only just enough room for two lorries to get by. Then a new one was built and a wooden diamond attached to the railings, smack dab in the middle, and divided by a vertical red line. One half said "Europe" and an arrow pointed the appropriate way. The other said "Asia" and had another arrow for lazy schoolboys such as myself.

> *"Children, be not tempted,*
> *No matter what befalls,*
> *To take a walk to Asia*
> *For anything at all."*

Twice a week, I would travel by bus over the bridge from Asia to Europe and back again.

There was a music school in Europe where a permanently tipsy Nikolai Kuzmich taught me to play the bassoon.

He was struggling to breathe even then. His wretched smoking had blackened his lungs and when yet another off-note emerged from the bassoon's ivory-ringed bell he would sigh with an embarrassed smile and say, "I could scatter gravel when I pissed once. Now, I can't even melt snow."

I suspect that once upon a time he had lived a different life, more worthy of an educated man. Be that as it may, it was from his trembling hands that I received my first instruction in the history of the woodwinds aside from my grandfather's rambling lectures.

We would sit for ages after lessons. He gave me the last slot in the timetable—19:30—and held the classes in the staff room. The school never had enough free classrooms. And it was only right and proper to have a cup of tea afterwards.

"Just imagine our shaggy ancestor," Nikolai Kuzmich used to say, turning back his worn shirt sleeves with an elderly bachelor's practised domestic gesture. "He might well live in a cave, yet he was drawn to the sublime. He carved a wooden pipe, blew into it, was astonished, drilled holes… fitted a reed to a wooden cone and there you go! The ancestor of the oboe."

He would remove the electric water-heater when the water boiled, add two or three lumps of coarse-ground brown sugar to a heap of tarry black tea and push a glass bearing a Kursk Railways monogram towards me with a gesture of invitation.

"The Russian word for 'bassoon' comes from the Italian, '*il fagotto*,' which I'm afraid means a 'bundle of wooden sticks'. It wasn't the first to come along, of course, but it's still one of the very oldest woodwinds, pretty much like the oboe. It's the lowest pitched of the woodwinds, not including the generic contrabassoon, but that really is a pile of sticks. Please..."

With habitually affectionate hands, he would lift his bassoon from its always open case like a baby from its cradle, pulling off a large offcut of tattered chamois as if it were a small blanket.

He never forgot to recall that his cherry-wood bassoon was a "copy of a Jacob Denner", and I could see it come to life at the touch of his hands even before he began to play.

"Every section of the orchestra has a base. Just as in life, there has to be some kind of support. For the brass section, it's provided by the bass trombone with quarter valve or the tuba. Have you seen a military band on parade with these enormous burnished instruments bringing up the rear? They're the helicons, tubas on the march. For the percussion, the bass is the timpani. The bass drum doesn't count since it isn't pitched. The strings are supported by the cello and the double bass while the bassoon props up the whole of the woodwind section. 'Why not the clarinet?' you ask. After all, it can drown the bassoon out easily. And my answer is that it's because the bassoon is a bass instrument and has the lowest range."

Never in all my life have I seen anyone move their lips more sensuously and erotically than Nikolai Kuzmich paying homage to his bassoon reed. And the instrument would then sing out an extensive recitative. Its soulful, constrained "voice from nowhere" hinted at the charm of a directionless sorrow, an elusive self-forgetting, a recollection of the past.

"That bassoon bit with two staccato notes followed by two slurred notes is amazing. Can you hear it? The staccato distinct, the legato lyrical and noble... And now here's something provocative: only the romantics understood the soul of the bassoon. In their music, the clarinet asks questions or makes statements. But who is it that replies? The bassoon, always. And in the tenor range—have a listen— it's so expressive that it moves you to tears." And, taking the reed from his lips, he would say: "The bassoon, my lad, is a melancholy instrument."

I happened upon his place during the spring break. I was loafing around the courtyards, missing my grandfather who died in February 1953 without living to see the putrid demise of the Big Boss. You weren't even born then, sweetheart.

Nor was I thinking in all these terms at the time, incidentally. I was a neglected thirteen-year-old simply grieving for my grandfather.

I've told you what kind of man he was, haven't I? He was born in 1890 and not one of the horrors of the twentieth century passed him by. All told, he was the best watchmaker in Vinnitsa Region and he spent his entire life in Zhmerinka although that doesn't tell you anything. He was a very deep and singular thinker—a gifted intellect. He wasn't unbiased in his approach to people, had obvious likes and dislikes and his inner life was sharply delineated, not just a hodgepodge. He was bitterly ironic at the slightest pretext with a keen sense of the absurd. There was a touch of Céline about him.

At the same time, he had a kind of folkloric quality too and would come out with all kinds of Ukrainian proverbs of the "even-the-Jew-hanged-himself-so-as-not-to-be-left-out" kind. When he was fed up of arguing with me, he would toss out a quick, "Either you play or I want my money back," and eventually out came his favourite, the standard "victory or death."

My grandfather built up an excellent library in the course of his life. He loved analysing classical music as only real music lovers do (he preferred woodwind to strings) and he spoke flawless Russian. In Zhmerinka! And this despite not even finishing *cheder*. He was obliged to leave in a clash of personalities with the *melamed*, who used to beat him for asking questions.

After that, my grandfather never burdened himself with any rote-learned wisdom from one-size-fits-all tracts. After all, he had his younger sisters to feed. Basically, he was a highly cultured person who completed three classes of *cheder* and was filled with an inner freedom, the like of which I have never encountered in anyone since, apart from your good self, my little one.

Anyway, my grandfather passed away suddenly before one of his regular visits to Guryev. He and his crates and bundles were already in Kiev where he usually changed trains for Kazakhstan. He used to come to see Mum and me every spring "to feed my hungry waifs in Kazakhstan," bringing us honeycomb from a beekeeping friend and real Ukrainian apples.

It was on top of these bundles that he passed away in the communal flat where he was staying with his old friend, the former circus gymnast. He was already dressed for the journey in his sheepskin coat and the famous boots taken from a dead Italian soldier. I'll tell you the story of those boots someday. You need to tell it with your hands. And so grief had driven me out of school for three weeks, in the best traditions of my grandfather, and then it was the holidays. And the Moustachioed One kicked the bucket and the country was shaken and started hawking up the blood and pus of its fatal affliction… But it all came too late for my grandfather.

I was as cold as a stray dog and, stumbling upon a brick hut with an unlocked door, I went inside to warm up. The dark hall smelt of damp but a door marked Staff Room stood open and a boiling kettle sang in the yellow slash of electric light. There was the fug of cigarette smoke and a heavenly aroma that I could never confuse with anything, anywhere, no matter where the rest of my life might take me.

Do you like "bread sops," little one? Or rather what I mean is do you like them the way I do? But, actually, you might not even know what they are. Let me explain. So, you're invited round to Genka Solodov's. What does he regale you with? That's right—fried potatoes. Sometimes seasoned with a bit of onion, sausage or bacon fat and you contentedly polish it off in silence and straight from the pan. How else?

And there, on the bottom of the pan, are those crunchy bits of fried food, onion, the last meat scratchings … So, when you've already scraped off everything you can and all that's left is a cloudy golden pool of oil, you tear a heel of bread into pieces, crumble it up as small as you can, press it down with a fork or a finger so that it's soaked right through to the crust… And there, little one, you have "bread sops".

I knocked and went inside. There, just as I had expected, was an unshaven guy sitting at a table in the process of eating the last fried potatoes out of the pan. The hot-plate element still smouldered, an ashy spiral on the table. He looked up briefly, nodded to me and said, "Come and join me, lad."

And so began my career in music—with a side order of "bread sops." Nikolai Kuzmich tried to offer me vodka as well but I still didn't like the taste of it back then.

Next, he looked to the side—a curl of trumpet glinted, a complicated pretzel, on the next table—and asked, "Do you like music?"

He was already well and truly sozzled. As the man wrote, "Do you like music? "No, sir, I don't drink."

"Well, yes," I replied.

"Are you Jewish, lad?" he inquired.

"Well, yes," I replied. In fact, I'm only part-Jewish but I never avoided saying I was because of my grandfather.

"Learn to play the bassoon then."

"Why?" I asked.

And Nikolai Kuzmich eagerly explained that no end of Jews played the violin or the piano but not a single one had taken up the bassoon to date. Not at the Guryev Music School, at least, which was a shame since the lungs of that nation were filled with the resonant yearning required to wrest real music from the bassoon.

"Because real music, lad, is real yearning. Especially for the bassoon which sings only of what has gone and cannot come again. I'll give you a demonstration right now."

In short, it was all very opportune, particularly since the other normal, straightforward instruments like the piano were all locked away—it was the holidays, after all,—and Nikolai Kuzmich had just finished repairing the school's one, well-worn bassoon with its leaking keys.

Whether his strength came from the "bread sops" or whether the vodka had hit the right veins, when he took up the bassoon and pressed his puffy, unshaven lips to the reed, when the bassoon's plaintively languid voice, chamois-soft and dark, rose to fill the room, I was captivated once and for all, then and forever, old woodwind player that I am.

I had my first lesson right there and then around the frying pan we had mopped with our bread crusts and without even getting up from my stool. It was about the structure of the instrument.

"Commit this to memory, lad, and don't tell me later that I'm wasting my efforts. This is the 'boot' and this is the 'bell'; there are three keys on the wing and two on the boot… This cord is attached to the boot joint and goes round your neck, leaving your right hand free. But the main thing is this curved metal tube, this one here, called the 'bocal'. It's fitted with a double reed made by cutting two blades from a reed stalk, gouging them out, thinning the inside, making a slit, folding the blades in half, then binding them with wire and inserting them into a stopper.

"And this whistle is what you'll have to hold in your mouth all your life. Please note the noble design of this early instrument: the way the yellowing ivory on the bocal harmonizes with the body's cherry colouring… The bassoon is an aristocrat like the Comte de Saint-Germain. It's carved from the mountain-growing Bosnian maple, which is yellow, but is stained a cherry colour and varnished. Our constant enemies are variations in temperature and humidity. That's why it's varnished with wood stain, an ancient, traditional way of toning wood. What does our classic writer, Griboedov, say about the bassoon? He says it snorts, as if it's being strangled. The writer got a bit carried away there, lad. Of course, the bassoon doesn't cut through the orchestra like the oboe or the clarinet, say, but it merges perfectly with the other instruments in its section, like a devoted spouse. Take Tchaikovsky's 'Queen of Spades', for example. The Overture. The bassoon and clarinet play the melody in octaves. What a combination of timbres! It makes your blood run cold! Listen…"

The bassoon sang out, syrupy, smooth and sombre. A sudden dapple of March snow fell outside and then came down in thick festive flakes.

A semi-circular, steel-coated stove was burning in the staff room, encircled by the dagger-bright glint of a streetlight outside.

Mournfully and intelligibly, the bassoon was bringing me understanding of some sort in the beloved voice of the grandfather I had been seeking everywhere in vain but had found here in the brick hut of the music school.

I was soaked from the heat, emotion and love but couldn't bring myself to take my sweater off because my grandfather's trousers were pulled right up to my armpits and I was using one of his old ties as a belt.

But I'm boring you again. Forget it, my unhappy Guryev childhood. It's all so very long ago.

Meanwhile, close at hand and all around is the little winemaking town where I've ended up quite by chance and that I'd now like to take you to. It's so close that a slab of the Rhine as grey as wet asphalt can be seen from my window, a long island, overgrown with lush vegetation, stretching out like a fox's tail in the middle of the river.

I've already written that I'm performing with the Windsbach Boys Choir in Frankfurt in October, haven't I? Their conductor, Karl Beringer, is a jolly good man. He's arranged everything in the best possible way. I am always so fervently grateful for any comfort or convenience I'm offered even if I'm entitled to it—"the Guryev pleb" in me, my mother called it. This time, Karl gave me two days off on top of everything else. Two heavenly days off, during which, like a loyal hound, I nursed dreams of being with you. But—I'll say no more. I understand—a contract's a contract and Chicago's Auditorium Theatre isn't the kind of venue you can turn down. I'm used to your wretched mirrors always stealing you away from me. Basically, I was all on my own and, for some reason, I fancied just going off wherever the whim took me.

The choir manager, Margarita, recommended Rudesheim, the home of the Rhineland wine industry. It's not far from Frankfurt. I hired a car and off I went.

You know what Germany's like on a sunny day in October. Soaring vaults of blue over your head, thickly-applied stucco clouds, as if someone had generously squeezed an enormous tube of white paint onto a dark-blue palette. The smooth beauty of the Rhine itself, meek and mild amid its steep, vine-covered banks; the towers and turrets of castles on vermillion slopes that are turning to yellow; and sunshine glinting off the black slate of the high roofs and off the weathervanes on the church steeples.

Such beauty was so effective, it took me out of myself. I drove on and on past vineyards, past dazzling yellow fields of flowering rape, and beside another, canted towards the horizon, where a sprinkler, like a great machine gun spinning in the middle, fired intermittent hazy jets of water. I missed my turning, made a U-turn and with just as much pleasure drove back the way I had come, the fields, vineyards and sprinkler now on my left.

In short, I arrived, left the car in the municipal car park and wandered the little streets at random, peering into cosy pensions and small hotels. I honestly tried to chose something relatively cheap but, as usual, what I liked was more expensive. Sadly, my mother was right. The "Guryev pleb" in me spoke louder than the voice of reason.

My mother was right and that's why she lies in the Guryev cemetery. A more dreadful place would be hard to imagine. It is an immense plot of land: the clay soil grey and dessicated, criss-crossed by deep cracks, and not a single tree or bush or even a blade of grass. In a word, a claypan.

All its enclosures, crosses and little metal pyramids had been given a coat of aluminium paint that was immediately corroded by dust. I remember the plundered and peeling little chapel, one half of its double door torn off, dark rectangles on the walls where icons once hung. And as far as the eye could see, islands of graves, crooked paths, iron pyramids and stars. How many, how many of these blasted places are there on this earth, little one?

But that's enough whinging. On to something cheerful.

I roamed the cheery, hilly, half-timbered little town in search of a cheap pension but my wandering eye veered constantly towards the tower of Rudesheim's ancient and obscenely expensive castle.

Of course, that was where I eventually took a room where I would have liked to have taken you in my arms. I'll describe it in detail now.

The hotel (our hotel, that is) is a converted castle that belongs to the Breuer family who also own the surrounding vineyards, wineries and a multitude of sales outlets. They are literally swimming in wine, this family, generously decanting it everywhere to everyone as only happens with the abundant produce of a family business. I waited in the luxurious hall for the room they were to show me to be ready and a girl in national costume—homespun grey skirt, close-fitting lace bodice, puffed sleeves—brought me a glass of tart Reisling that went straight to my head.

I immediately imagined you perched somewhat jauntily on my left knee—a nod to the hard-drinking Rembrandt and his unlovely beloved, Saskia; my left hand on your hip, groaning with longing as we take turns to sip from the glass. The pleasures of an abandoned old man. If we don't meet up soon, I'll waste away altogether.

At a counter, magnificently fitted with every conceivable electronic device, sat a German woman with a suntan, large white sparkling teeth and equally large white pearls that were oh, so like her teeth. In answer to my question as to when I should pay for my room, she waved a hand and said, "Whenever you feel like it!"

The visitor's form had no room for a passport number. I pointed this out. Breezily, she asked why ever she might need my passport.

And all of it—the silent lift, the lights that came on automatically and accompanied you along the corridors, the room, snug as a glove, the big bathroom with every alluring appliance possible, its floor a black and white chessboard as in paintings by the lesser Dutch masters, the curtains at the deep arched window the same; the mirrors—from the big one opposite the door to the round magnifying glass in the bathroom revealing the shaggy jellyfish of an astonished eye—all of it could have come straight from my dream of a "small town stopover."

I quickly undressed, ran a bath and for about forty minutes bobbed about, rolling in the foamy lather, grasping the handles on the sides. I climbed out, drowsy and groaning for you, dried myself until my skin was red and collapsed onto a very wide, very white bed, designed for us, for both of us. I slept for about three hours, deaf to the music from the restaurant below, to the excess of bells and the tourists bellowing out songs...

Basically, I spent two magical solitary days filled only with thoughts of you.

I remembered your harmonica on several occasions, the one with the two tawdry beauties in their dull enamel medallions at the edges. Once, at night, I woke up from a perfectly lifelike dream. Eyes bulging, you were painstakingly playing "Lili Marlene" clumsily and off key. Maybe I dreamt it because of the hurdy-gurdy player here who wanders around with a little lapdog, vigorously using a rasping harmonica as a mincer to disgorge an impossibly disfigured but still immortal "Lili Marlene."

Incidentally, my grandfather used to sing it fairly frequently when he was working. I can remember the cardboard eyeglass, the gentle jingle of the watchmaking tools and the very precise intonation of his mumbling. My grandfather didn't know German but of course he knew Yiddish. I'm afraid he sang his own version. I'm afraid Fritz would not have liked his performance.

For half a day I traipsed after the hurdy-gurdy man, singing along in my own Russian version, which, sadly, my grandfather never encountered. (God, that shaggy little lapdog was so touching—a wilting daisy on the pavement, pitifully heart-rending!). "Underneath the lamplight by the barrack gate … My own, Lili Marlene."

But I must tell you about our haven.

There are carved wooden heads attached to the wall in the corridor outside the door to our room. Their crowns are little shelves you want to stand a bottle on.

Each head is a symbol of something, most probably a human temperament or a particular mindset. Four even come with a clue—letters incised into the edge of the shelf above the brow: the Optimist—round cheeks, lips stretched wide in mute delight and a fool's tiny scrunched-up eyes; the Pessimist—sadly raised eyebrows, wrinkles around a down-turned mouth, a pendulous wooden nose. Next comes the Stoic, an absolutely impenetrable dimwitted mug, and the Choleric, modelled on some unfortunate sufferer from piles during an acute phase: eyes on his forehead, mouth angled down to his chin. You feel sorry just looking at the guy. There is also an obviously female face, round and smiling—probably a sanguine individual—and an old person's mask, buckteeth bared. A hypochondriac? A misanthropist? Or did some medieval witch, already condemned to the stake, worm her way in here? And in the corner above my door a hussy's face offers a wanton half-smile. I give her a surreptitious wink when I'm turning the key in the lock.

The bells on the four-sided, ivy-cloaked tower of the Rudesheimer Schloss produce not a metallic sound but rather a glass one like a celeste, especially when the tune of some folk song wreathes the town centre at noon, its refrain rising then fading away.

The weathervane on the tower is a gold-painted wine barrel. A fletched arrow lies on the barrel and a jay sits on that.

The hotel restaurant plays music even during the day. At mid-day, a maid opens the tall glass doors into the vine-tangled inner court-yard, deftly sets out tables and chairs and lays the tablecloths, flapping them like wings. And a piano dissolves into carefree mazurkas and waltzes to be joined in the evening by a flute and violin.

No wonder the entire hotel is festooned in photographs of the Breuer family vineyards in every season of the year and from every camera angle. Evidently, nothing lovelier exists in the owners' eyes. Vineyards upon vineyards in their various guises—the high banks of the Rhine looking as if a huge comb has been pulled through them, turning a tender green in May, positively aflame in September. Naked vines outlined in black, the hieroglyphs of winter branches against the snow-covered slope.

I wandered into a fifteenth-century castle while out on a stroll. It turned out to be a museum of mechanical musical instruments, a private collection put together over some fifteen years or so by an enthusiastic amateur (and, to all appearances, one who wasn't short of money, either).

Basically, I popped into the courtyard just for something to do and spotted a group of Russian tourists with their interpreter. I was thrilled at the opportunity and attached myself to the group on the sly.

It was a fine castle with the original frescoes untouched on the walls, rough floor tiles and a low, vaulted ceiling in the cellar, which was where the tour began.

It had been planned in detail with German assiduity. It was led by a young tour guide with the naïve expression of a romantic, clear blue eyes, a pleasant smile and a poor attempt at gingery whiskers and a beard, grown in all likelihood for the job, in keeping with the style of the collection as a whole. He was dressed in that style as well, wearing a frock coat with patched elbows, a wash-faded shirt and trousers with dirty knees. An organ-grinder's well-worn hat was crammed onto his head.

He went from one pianola to the next, from an eighteenth-century barrel-organ to a floor-standing musical clock, from music boxes of various shapes and sizes to a painted musical chair that began to play as soon as you lowered your bottom onto it, from a mechanical piano to a giant and most cunningly devised violin. Furthermore, he peered into the workings of the exhibits with such delight and wonder that it seemed as though he was not in fact leading the tour but had only just stumbled upon these treasures himself, upon a triumph of human ingenuity, perfect pitch and mechanical genius.

I had the fondest of encounters there. I saw a music box exactly like the one that stood on the small round table, covered with a crocheted doily, in Auntie Frida's room in Zhmerinka.

The small box of well-polished mahogany had a tiny key and a lever on the lower panel. A label pasted to the underside of the open lid read: "Fortuna. Jul. Heinr. Zimmermann. Finest music boxes." And, in smaller letters underneath, "A clear and pleasant tone. An elegant finish. A robust design."

And in really tiny letters under that: "34, Morskaya Street. St Petersburg."

For his finale, the young man wound all the music boxes up and, rattling and jerking, they hailed one another in elderly voices in the antique hall until their strength, or rather their winding mechanisms, were spent. And yet what robust designs they all were. Are we, my darling?

Rudesheim also has a cable car up to a mountain peak. As a lover of every amusement ride in the world, I bought a ticket, sat in the iron car and floated upwards, leaving the scarlet rows of wide-splayed vines below me.

Ah, the fruits of the vine!

Based upon my observations, Germans when drunk are extremely simple and good-natured and like to play practical jokes—sticking out a leg for a colleague to trip over, knocking off his cap in the black and orange of his favourite team, or something equally witty.

In the evenings, Rudesheim is full of the sound of choirs singing marches, hymns and other popular music, in the sense of music that everyone has in common. It is all performed in the loud full voices of the *Volk* and interspersed with bursts of abrupt, intimidating and implausible laughter. In short, "Marching and Tasting" wine walks.

I finish my tour in about three weeks' time and will come wherever you summon me. Just drop me a line as to where to find you—in any language or, better yet, figures so that I don't go crazy. God, I haven't seen you for three months. And, sweetheart, maybe it's time to get a mobile phone?

And if … if … but there he is again, sauntering around somewhere close by and turning the handle of an old hurdy gurdy, his version of *perpetuum mobile*, and the little dog comes bowling out from between his feet to tangle with those of the tourists. "Resting in our billet, just behind the line…" extends in a sugar-sweet stream from a music box at an unbearably funereal pace.

> "Even though we're parted,
> Your lips are close to mine…
> Your sweet face seems
> To haunt my dreams,
> My Lili of the lamplight,
> My own, Lili Marlene!"

My own, Lili Marlene!

I miss your harmonica. Do you play it when I'm not there, my beloved?

CHAPTER 8.

The woman who sold sunflower seeds lived on the corner of Krasnoarmeyskaya and Zhilyanskaya Streets, one block from the Central Stadium, and on ordinary days she plied her trade straight from the semi-basement. Cones made of newspaper and slotted one into the other lay on the ground.

She didn't have a single tooth in her head but she was always chewing seeds and the husks would bubble and seethe around her sunken mouth. She looked like a man who had soaped up his chin and already lifted his razor to scrape off the foam then been distracted so that he went about his day with soapy jowls.

The long, black wedges of the perfectly cooked seeds were popularly known as "horse's teeth." They could be cracked open by hand, not like the small pot-bellied oil seeds from Russia. The price was the same across the country: ten kopeks a glass.

On crucial-football-match days, however, the old woman sat outside. A queue would form and no one could be bothered with cones any more. The men were in a rush and simply held out their pockets.

Nyuta and her father also bought a glass of "horse's teeth" because if you're going to a match, you have to be like everyone else: gnaw on seeds, yell, whistle through two fingers and shout out the names of the players. And not forget the referee who is, of course, a wanker!

Otherwise, as the poet says, life is no life and pleasure no pleasure.

The crowd at the stadium gate would grow and swell and push then sweep across the whole square to crash in waves against the ticket offices—stone booths with tiny windows.

Dad would usually pass Nyuta over the turnstile in a trice but he would carry her through on his shoulders on championship days and for semi-finals or finals. This was called a piggyback.

If there was a huge crowd and everyone was fired up and surges of particularly sweaty and hazardous excitement filled the air, Nyuta would ask for a piggyback herself.

Her father would hoist her up, sit her on his shoulders and, from his immense height, she would be able to see the green pitch and the goals and the stands under gigantic floodlights. Ladies with trays would be making their way between the rows, saying: "Anyone for pies or pirozhki?" Then, lifting a grease-stained towel just a touch, one would say, "Pick whichever takes your fancy, sweetie."

In short, being at the stadium was tremendous fun. The roar from a hundred thousand people in the stands rose and fell or hung in the air depending on the next turn of play... And Nyuta sided honestly with her team even though she always knew what the final score would be and who was about to score and who the referee would penalize. Initially, she thought everyone knew. Apparently not, although it wasn't so hard. In her forehead, a tunnel of mirrors would unfurl, advancing towards her closed eyes, like the party horns her father could make in a flash from the page of an exercise book and blow right into Nyuta's face. As in a kaleidoscope, a circle of light would appear at the end of the mirror tunnel and numbers, or words, or shapes, or sometimes simply *silent pictures* would pulsate within it.

Barely would his daughter adopt a sly expression and drawl, "In this ma-a-atch, the fi-i-inal sco-o-ore will be...will be... shall I tell you?" than her father would become distressed. His face would take on a "vinegary" look as if he had indigestion, as if he wanted her to be quiet for the rest of her life.

"No, don't!" he would snap and turn away.

O-okay... Let's not say anything then.

Fira Avelevna was a completely different matter. Now there was someone who heard all Nyuta's predictions completely calmly, impassively even. Perhaps it was because she was old and blind? And a football fan to boot.

"Firavelna" was the grandmother and head of the large and noisy Girshovich clan from the courtyard next door. Nyuta had been going there to play for about a year and a half. The family consisted of Uncle Zhora, a foreman at the Transsignal Electrical Engineering Factory, a cocky type with a brazen tenor voice, who wore threadbare tracksuit bottoms; Auntie Rosa, his wife and Firavelna's youngest daughter, who worked as an operating theatre assistant at the hospital; their niece, Sonya, daughter of Busa, the sister-who-was-executed-may-her-memory-be-a-blessing-and-all-who-killed-her-burn-in-hell; their older son, Borya, a student at the music school (he played the cello), and six-year-old Arisha-with-the-slight-squint. She was the one Nyuta really went to play with.

Incidentally, Arisha too was studying music at school and, what's more, the piano. Mashuta was her teacher. And, Mashuta said, she had perfect pitch!

Finally, above them all, like a tribal deity, was blind Firavelna, may-she-be-with-us-in-good-health-to-a-hundred-and-twenty…

They all lived in a single room, a vast one, to be fair, in a much-divided communal flat. Boris's cello was casually propped against the wall in a dark part of the shared corridor. Sometimes, it was uncovered and its rosy, lustrous flank glinted intimately and invitingly.

In just this way the lustrous flanks of the morning prostitutes, propped casually against the wall, sleepy and uncovered, glinted in the Rue Saint Denis, Paris.

Various other interesting persons lived in the flat as well as the Girshoviches. There was the family of the alcoholic Major Petya. Judging by appearances, his redoubtable wife, Lyubov Kazimirovna, was losing her hair. She always wore a beret, puffed up like a pillow from the sleeping area. (Nyuta bumped into her once in the corridor. Lyubov Kazimirovna, wearing a flannelette dressing-gown, her nightie showing beneath it, was racing to the toilet. Tucked behind one ear was her beret, perched on her head like a pillow.) Lyudmila Kazimirovna sent her eight-year-old daughter, Nadya, for milk every morning and every time a stage-tragedy roar would boom out of their room: "Again?! Have you downed half a bucketful again? You sling that milk back like it's water!"

Fayushchenko, a bizarre old man who was a painter, lived in the small square room next to the bathroom. He was swathed in a scarf even in summer and wore women's felt boots and a woman's astrakhan hat that seemed to be attached to his head. His tight curls were a precise reiteration and a seeming continuation of the hat's grey locks.

He once appeared in the kitchen in an old kaftan, the right sleeve ripped off.

Uncle Zhora asked, "What strange kind of jacket is this, Comrade Fayushchenko?"

The latter replied, "What's strange about it, Zhora? That arm gets cold but this one, my working arm, gets hot…"

With that working hand, Fayushchenko the artist produced lavish paintings, nudes, for the most part. He would sometimes leave his room to wash his brushes in the bathroom and someone's candle-white back would flicker in the half-open doorway. And he was forever scouring the town in search of his next muse.

Once, he came home with the passport officer from the housing service. The dark-haired Ukrainian girl, the very picture of health, drank tea in the kitchen and whispered shyly to the master, "Get away with you. I'll not fit the frame."

But Fayushchenko cackled and yelled, "I'll fit you in. I'll squeeze you in! Bacon fat doesn't crease."

And he did. He created a series of Rubenesque nudes and put them up for sale at Bessarabka Market. For a week, the entire housing service trotted off to see the exhibition. The devotees of real art clustered around the pictures. Although it's true, the passport officer was dismissed in short order for "amoral conduct."

And lastly, there was the mysterious Panna Ivanna who inhabited the long, narrow room next to the kitchen. She was an incomparably ugly old woman, the blue-bleached skin of her face stretched tightly in a frightful contrast to the brick-red wrinkles of her neck. Panna Ivanna was strict. She supervised cleanliness in the kitchen and would issue reprimands if anyone left a cigarette end lying around, yelling, "Remove the little corpses!"

Furthermore, she composed her strict orders in verse form. She wrote them on half a page from an exercise book and pinned them up around the flat. One of her menacing creations hung above the gas stove, spattered with grease stains from the frying pans:

> "Steal my matches if you dare,
> You will get it, you know where."

Yet the door into this merry fellowship was always open. Or rather, to all intents and purposes it was closed but the lock could be opened with an ordinary kopek coin. Or anything else, basically. Sonya, the Girshoviches' niece, the daughter of the sister-who-was-executed-may-her-memory-be-a-blessing-and-all-who-killed-her-burn-in-hell, used a nail file while Nyuta and Arisha once managed to open it with an ice-lolly stick.

Panna Ivanna used to say that once upon a time the individual rooms in the flat had been rented by the hour. Neither Arisha nor Nyuta understood but a rusty plaque with embossed numbers was certainly attached above the door to each room.

The numerous Girshoviches lived in the room over which hung a blurry whitewashed sign saying "Dance Hall" in Ukrainian. The previous inhabitants had left them a love-seat, its exquisite flaking armrest surging up in a steep wave.

Evidently, the vast forty-metre kitchen had also been used for dancing or for entertaining in the past. It still contained a huge carved sideboard, entirely covered in intertwining oak leaves. Panna Ivanna would hang her rhyming admonitions on its fragile glass doors.

> "Add your mess to what's inside—
> In an ambulance you'll ride!"

And yet it was not Panna Ivanna but the blind Firavelna that everybody feared. Feared and respected.

When the alcoholic Major Petya was dead drunk and couldn't summon up the strength to crawl to the toilet at the end of the corridor but made it to the kitchen, he took out what Firavelna called his tomtit, and, swaying as if he was rocking a baby, ecstatically flooded the floor, eyes closed. Since all the others could see, no one wanted to look at Petya in that state and only Firavelna came out at the sound of splashing and listened closely until the process was complete.

She called Petya a *shmata* (doormat) behind his back because of his lack of willpower. She considered him henpecked.

"Emptied your bladder, have you, Petya?" she asked sternly. Petya half-opened his eyes and saw the puddle… He was gradually regaining consciousness and a sense of shame.

"I have, Firavelna," he said contritely.

"Then get yourself a big rag."

And the battle-hardened major crawled around the kitchen with his rag, uttering imprecations against vodka as he went.

Firavelna was born in Emilchino, a shtetl next to the Czech colony. She was the eldest daughter in the family and helped her father in his work as a tailor. He would send her into the colony to arrange orders, make calculations and measure waists and chests. It was there that she learned to smoke, got to grips with European style and took from the Czechs both an ability to cook and a supernatural neatness, as well as picking up Czech words and ditties. When the mood took her, she might even sing the girls a song that Firavelna said translated roughly as follows:

LEONARDO'S HANDWRITING

Anna once sang the song to a Czech violinist, a friend of Senya's who worked with him in the Boston Symphony Orchestra. He understood almost the entire thing and was delighted.

A moderately religious woman, Firavelna did nothing on Saturdays but would violate the sanctity of the day if there happened to be a football match. If our team was playing for the cup or a championship, she would fast for two days as if for the Day of Atonement. And she was most certainly a smoker! All the grandmothers received lisle stockings as presents on International Women's Day, whereas Firavelna's children bought her a gift pack of Three Bogatyrs cigarettes.

She could remember the names of all the Dynamo Kiev players as well as the leading lights of CSKA Moscow, Spartak, Dynamo and Torpedo.

And when the crowd poured down Zhilyanskaya Street after a match, she would say to Arisha or Nyuta, "Look out of the window and ask the score."

So they looked and they asked and they received their answer. Nyuta had permission to say whatever she liked at Firavelna's so she did, and when the score she'd predicted was the same as the one shouted out, interspersed with invective and flavoured with spittle hawked onto the pavement, Firavelna would pronounce with satisfaction, "Hey, you're right. Well done. There's nothing wrong with the brains in this little live-wire's head."

She had lost her sight to glaucoma even before the war and covered her face with a head square or lacy scarf. Her blindness embarrassed her.

People from home often came to visit. They spoke Yiddish in an undertone. Arisha and Nyuta would be playing dolls under the table as the unfamiliar language rustled, clanged and lamented softly overhead. From time to time, Arisha would call out: "Translation!" If she had really had enough, Firavelna would feel around beneath the table and give her a sneaky kick.

Arisha, nosy and insistent, would call for a translation even so, rather than telling the prince that Nyuta was holding whether the miller's lovely daughter would marry him or not.

Once Nyuta said, "Leave them be. They're talking rubbish: kids, grandkids; her son-in-law's a jerk; Lyusya managed to get hold of some Polish boots and only *goyim* are accepted to study medicine."

Silence fell around the table above them. The voice of a middle-aged woman asked in astonishment, "So, does she understand Yiddish then, that little girl?"

And Firavelna replied serenely and even with a touch of pride, "She understands everything!"

Like King Solomon, Firavelna dispensed advice, sat in judgement over her relatives, predicted events and handed down verdicts. Men kissed her hand as they left. Many years later Anna realized why: With her face covered by a head square, only her hand was left. It was an act of chivalry and refinement.

Firavelna didn't touch the treats people brought her. She gave them to the children straight away. After she went blind, her pathological neatness turned into a particular fastidiousness. She trusted only her eldest daughter, Manya, who lived nearby and brought her mother supper every day. She didn't entirely trust Rosa, the daughter she lived with, believing that a working woman was always slapdash and didn't have time to focus on food. Borscht for Firavelna was made without cabbage. She knew there were worms in cabbage and that every leaf had to be washed thoroughly whereas the children chopped it into big chunks. And she never tried anyone else's rissoles or stuffed fish, anything that had to be kneaded or dissected by hand. She had no faith in other people's clean hands.

Her elderly female neighbours were envious and made no bones about telling her how very good certain people were at making themselves comfortable: a daughter bringing supper over every day, a son-in-law taking out the chamber-pots and a son sending money every month. Just look at how certain people wangled things!

"Well, you try going blind," Firavelna would suggest with a smile.

The family were nice to Nyuta, which is to say that they took no more notice of her than they did of their own children. She was hanging around the place? So be it.

Especially since Arisha and Nyuta spent most of the day racing round the courtyard.

Sheds storing battered junk huddled in the vast courtyard. A few residents simply kept chickens in them. One housed a dog, Floozie, tied up and driven mad by loneliness and hunger.

Before long, however, the sheds were demolished and the courtyard came to be shared by the five-storey block, the one-storey barracks at the back and the three-storey, entirely communal block which housed a vast horde of people in its cellars, storerooms and former bathrooms.

Residents on the ground floors grew flowers in the front gardens: crimson dahlias, zinnias and velvet pansies. A small-flowered tea-rose in a corner produced a delicate and comforting fragrance in the evenings. In May the whole courtyard was so full of the scent from a little lilac's pale, unprepossessing blooms that deeper breaths were called for.

And the fibrous cobweb of a wild vine clung to the house. Once, when he lost his key, Borya clambered up its branches to the kitchen window although he could easily have used his cello mute to open the lock.

An enormous chestnut tree also stood in the courtyard. In the springtime, it was engulfed in heady cream-coloured blossom, a multitude of tapering candles, merging into a solid crown. After that, the branches sprouted their spiky fruit. Housewives dried them while they were still green to place among clothes and in flour to keep woodworm and moths at bay.

Towards the end of the summer, split green cases littered the whole area, the horse's eye of a lustrous chestnut gazing out of each one. Arisha and Nyuta threaded them on a string and ran around festooned in chestnut jewellery.

And the fascination of being up in the attics flourished through the long summer days in columns of dust motes, amid garlands of cable bundles, amid crushed aluminium kettles, broken little porcelain elephants and pieces of old vinyl records, amid boxes of pre-revolutionary books in the old script, down-at-heel, mismatched footwear and bent bicycle spokes. What magical discoveries were made here! On a poster for Van Houten's cocoa a well-padded chap with thick eyebrows and a perplexed smile, like the Good Soldier Svejk, sat at a window, the shutters thrown open. He wore a frock-coat, a bow tie and a tasselled fez on his bald pate and held a cup bearing the inscription "Van Houten's Cocoa", from which rose a constant stream of coiling steam like the smoke from the boiler of a train. Beneath the picture, in the old script, it said: "I never have the jitters and I am always in a good mood because, since I started drinking only genuine VAN HOUTEN'S COCOA for breakfast rather than stimulating coffee or tea, my muscles have been stronger, my digestion has been marvellous and my NERVES AS STRONG AS HAWSERS. A pound makes 100 cups."

Disabled war veterans began dying in droves during those years, and yellowish pink limbs began to appear more and more frequently in the attics. Nyuta found an almost complete right leg once, cut off just above the knee and wearing an excellent laced boot. She went home in it. After all, one's better than none. Her father roared with laughter but Mashuta took it out to the garbage in disgust despite Nyuta weeping and explaining that the boot came from the false leg of a hero. In the end, she and Arisha buried the prosthesis and the boot in the waste ground behind the school.

Another time Arisha dug a left hand out of a pile of rags and put on a whole show for the kids right there in the attic as if the hand was playing the piano. Lastly, the wheeled board of a "samovar" was dug out of a heap of lumber someone had thrown away. Samovars was the name given to war veterans who had lost the lower half of their bodies and used a square board with swivel wheels to get around. It was a real find.

Nyuta and Arisha immediately rushed off to find a dauntingly steep slope so that they could revel in taking off as if they had wings, the way they would fly down Batyeva Gora on sledges or in copper basins. The latter, their yellow, greenish or reddish sides flaming in the sun, were considered particularly stylish.

Nyuta made her way up to the Botanical Garden along hilly Tolstoy Street, the board under her arm, while Arisha, who had lost her nerve, trailed behind her, whining over and over again: "Nyutka, you're crazy! Nyutka, I'll tell Grandma everything, Nyu-u-tka!"

But Nyuta was off! She lay on the board on her stomach, told Arisha to give her a good push off with her foot and then there was just the wind, whistling in her ears, and the wheels clattering as they gathered ever more speed. A grey ribbon of asphalt spun before her eyes, the trams and trolleybuses of the technicolour city rang and screeched all around her, and cries and shrieks pursued her. Little by little, the board began to lose speed. Its swivel wheels no longer screeched and whirred but merely clattered fiercely. The frantic whirling in her head started to slow, reeled a little and died away.

Nyuta, still spread-eagled across the board like a baby frog, looked around. Someone nearby said loudly, "It's not a boy, see. It's a girl! She's nuts!"

Two boys, grown up already, were standing over her. One twirled his finger by his temple, looking at Nyuta disconcertedly.

"Nah! That's no girl. It's a stunt performer!"

Nyuta fell into this bustling existence thanks to Khristina to whom Masha and Anatoly had given carte-blanche, within reason, when it came to Nyuta's upbringing once they had been staggered to learn … that…

But this deserves a separate mention.

***

"Ma, I can play with the piano now," Nyuta bragged one day.

"It's *play the* piano, Nyuta darling," Masha corrected her absent-mindedly. She was setting the table for lunch. Tolya was due back from the hospital at any minute and Nyuta was already in her seat. "You know the full name is fortepiano, don't you?"

"Look!" her daughter replied without listening and ran her fingers over the tablecloth, moving them in different directions and bringing them back together, the little finger on each hand sticking out and quivering.

"We're one knife short," Masha noted then suddenly, from the corner of her eye, she saw the two nimble childish hands performing intricate but absolutely synchronized steps of some kind.

"I've got two hands now," her daughter reported, tapping out notes only she could hear.

Something inside Masha sank then soared back up again. She was balancing Nyuta's fork with the brightly coloured parrot on the handle, the one she always laid so that her daughter could use her left hand. Her throat dry, she swapped the knife and fork round, unhurriedly, without looking up. And Nyuta, continuing to chatter away, automatically picked the knife up in her right hand as if she'd been doing it all her life.

"That's interesting," Masha said, "Very interesting, my dear daughter. How did this happen?"

"Khristina taught me," Nyuta mumbled with her mouth full. "She wrapped me up, bandaged me… like a mummy, and turned me the other way around. Like a coat. And now I can do everything! I can juggle balls in the circus too, a hundred at a time… Ma? Mashuta?" and she looked at Masha in astonishment, her cheek bulging. "Why are you crying?"

Later on she could point fairly precisely to this breakthrough, to this transition when she was six years old, after which the world revealed itself from a different vantage point, as if her now developed right hand had lifted a curtain that had been closed hitherto. As if someone outside had turned on a bright spotlight on the right-hand side, illuminating the broad expanse of a hidden mirror arena around, above and inside. The world was pulled apart in both directions, found its balance and was then complete, round and profound.

And in it her body could move with great skill.

And the fearful, insatiable pull towards mirrors that reflected and complemented her right-hand side lessened and abated.

From then on, she could give a precise explanation of how her brain worked.

Bubbles would fizz in her head as they do in a glass of lemonade, her brain would effervesce and something would begin to click… Multi-coloured numbers would spring up, merging together and separating again as if they were alive… Pictures would rise chaotically to the surface, billow and gain volume, then be reflected inside her forehead in a whole gallery of mirrors, lining up in minuetting couples, floating by in garlands, arabesques and other graceful and enchanting designs. One would replace another then melt away, casting up in its wake the shimmer of a glorious dawn kaleidoscope, that would fade then bloom again like a tapestry against a pulsating velvet background of cherry-red, lilac and the dark blue of the night.

That was when she would sit and lose all track of time…

*****

Anyway, it was Khristina who dragged Nyuta along to Firavelna's family. Khristina had an interest of her own at the flat, an interest in playing patience.

The mysterious Panna Ivanna, who had once been a circus acrobat, used to play patience and "read" the cards. Her long, narrow room even contained a special table for playing cards, covered in a green cloth purchased way back when from the antique shop on the corner of Saksaganskogo and Krasnoarmeyskaya Streets. In addition to the little card table, the iron bed and a buffed and burnished wardrobe, grandly referred to as the *chiffonier*, a thin mattress lay up against the wall, on which visitors, of whom there was usually a large number, used to sleep when passing through.

"You wait over there in the kitchen for half an hour or so," Khristina commanded, "while I have my fortune told."

Nyuta could have told Khristina's fortune too if she'd ever bothered to ask but, evidently, for Khristina the greasy and much handled cards from a real Tarot deck were essential to validate the judgment of fate.

So Nyuta wandered off into the enormous kitchen where she saw a thin old lady sitting at the table, her face half-covered by a lace scarf. Next to her, on a stool, a little girl sat picking at her food with a fork. She was pretty and had curly hair. It was just a pity that her left eye kept constantly veering over to her nose as if it couldn't bear examining and inspecting everything around.

"Those footsteps don't belong… those light ones…" said the old lady all of a sudden, straightening up in her chair. "Eh, Rishele? They don't, do they?"

"Yes, they do, Granny," said the curly top, laughing and squinting. "They do."

And Nyuta was immediately drawn to them both, strongly and with all her heart!

She went over and stared at the potato pancakes the curly headed girl was picking at reluctantly.

"Granny," the latter asked. "Maybe I could let the little girl try my latkes? She's very hungry."

"But is she a good girl?" the old lady inquired. "Don't give her any if she's not."

And Nyuta and the other little girl exchanged a look and snickered, both at the same time.

So, when a flushed Khristina left Panna Ivanna's room an hour later, Nyuta and Arisha were already bosom pals and had even made arrangements to go for wafers at the milk factory with Zoyka the following day.

On the way home, Khristina told Nyuta in the strictest confidence that she would soon be getting married—in the autumn.

"In the winter," Nyuta corrected her automatically. "There will be snow everywhere."

"And the groom is almost a widower," Khristina went on excitedly, "and for some reason he never sits still."

"Because he's always travelling on the train," Nyuta explained readily. Khristina roared with laughter and drew Nyuta's head to her round solid flank as they walked, patted her on the back of the neck and said, "What a chatterbox!"

***

It wasn't worth going to the milk factory for wafers without Zoyka. Nothing would come of it. The shame was too great. Zoyka was the only one who could creep over to the semi-basement window, snivel plaintively and keep a clear conscience:

"Auntie, oh, auntie! We want something to eat! Just a little something! We're so-o-o hungry!"

Zoyka was fantastic in the role of bait. Her family inhabited the very darkest recess in what was once the pantry of the one-storey barracks. It was a shoe-box of about eight square metres with peeling walls and a tamped earthen floor. And six of them lived there—four daughters and their parents. Zoyka was the youngest. No one anywhere had ever known greater poverty.

Zoyka's father, a freight train driver, was rarely at home. He'd arrive, hit the bottle for a week, knock hell out of anyone who came within reach and go back to his train. Meanwhile, her mother had been paralysed and bed-ridden for about three years.

Zoyka was skinny, unsteady on her feet and eternally hungry. Maybe she had worms? She wanted to eat every single minute and to eat a lot. The neighbours would slip her food as best they could. If they didn't, Zoyka took it herself. Her nose was her guide: "Ooh! Berta's baking pirozhki!" Berta lived on the top floor of the three-storey block at the back of the courtyard and often made pies that she put out to cool on the balcony, still in the baking pan.

Zoyka would climb up to the roof, leaving Arisha and Nyuta on look out and hook the pirozhki with a long stick. She never took more than four: three for herself and one that the girls split between them. If, as did happen, one of the children brought a sandwich, apple or, heaven forefend, a bar of chocolate into the yard, they had to look out. "Lenin said to share!"—and she tore it from their hands.

She never used the toilet. If the need took her, she would squat under any tree, any window.

Khristina loathed Zoyka: for being dirty, for telling lies, for having a permanently outstretched hand. She called her Mowgli after the hero of a show she once took Nyuta to see at the Youth Theatre.

"And if anyone steps in shit," Khristina used to say, "there's no need for samples. It's Zoyka's."

Once, her older sister arrived at Nyuta's block looking for Zoyka—they were in Grade Eight by then and the reckless Zoyka had disappeared for a couple of days. She asked around to find out where Doctor Nesterenko lived and, arriving on the second floor, she rang the bell timidly. Khristina opened the door. Asked by the worried girl whether anyone had seen Zoyka, she replied contemptuously, "Maybe she's gone for a shit in the wild."

Zhadanovskogo Street, which was really and always will be Zhilyanskaya Street, was long and very busy with an abundance of life of all kinds.

Next to the stadium itself, at Number 6, an old, four-storey block that had a coquettish round turret on the roof and was home to artists and musicians from the Musical Comedy Theatre and even at one time, according to a stone plaque, to the illustrious Aleksey Ryabov, author of the operetta "Wedding in Malinovka," the street was a narrow tube, too tight for two cars to pass. At this point, beneath the age-old chestnuts, it was a charming, shady cubbyhole of a street. As it moved away from the stadium to Victory Square, to the Jewish Bazaar in actual fact (things often had two names, a bit like Nyuta, who had her polite, outside name "Anna" and the warm, melodious "Nyu-u-uta" at home)—anyway, en route to the immense Jewish Bazaar, the Circus under its silver helmet, the Ukraina Department Store and the Swan Hotel, Zhilyanskaya lost its scant charm, grew dull and took on an industrial appearance, becoming thoroughly repellent near the railway station like any other area of the kind… Even so it remained fiendishly interesting! What didn't it have? There was a furore of factories alone: the Lenin's Forge Shipyard, the Transsignal Electrical Engineering Plant, Heat and Power Plant No. 3, its cooling tower like an Egyptian pyramid, the Maxim Gorky Clothing Plant, formerly the deaf mutes' workshop. Then came the railway workers' cooperative, with its enormous yard where a whole heap of intriguing items could easily be collected around the barracks and sawing sheds: old bolts and screws, smashed glass to repair a broken kaleidoscope, thick, evenly smoothed wooden washers … and much more besides.

But it all paled into insignificance compared to the beguiling call of the milk factory.

The windows of the milk factory's wafer section, located in the semi-basement, looked directly onto the street.

And when the right wind blew, the wafers' rich, vanilla-tinged aroma left passers-by stupefied, driving them over to the windows.

Children would lie on the ground and stare into the bluish, tiled depths of the semi-basement. They were prepared to spend hours watching the wafers being baked. There was a fairy tale element to this, as to any, transformation.

The female staff in their white coats and gauze caps poured sizzling batter into the stoves and covered it with large, flat, iron plates. The weight pressed out tubes of batter that crept out, turning an immediate gold. The women scraped away these little tubes of wafer spillage and raked them into a huge flour scoop.

It was important not to miss the moment. Zoyka would set up a wail in a nasty beggar's voice.

"Aunties, please! Give it to us. We want something to eat!"

She would kneel down in front of the window and hold out the hem of her grubby frock and some kindly servant of the wafer room would pour in a handful of crumbly golden manna.

Nyuta, regaled by her father and Mashuta with only "the tastiest morsels" since childhood couldn't recall anything more toothsome than these heavenly windfalls and for the rest of her life she would have them with her cups of tea or coffee, asking waiters in any country's most expensive restaurants in conspiratorial tones for "two or three wafers, please. What do you mean, you don't have any?"

Most entertaining of all, however, was watching the wafer cups being baked. When the batter was poured into moulds and the lids closed, two or three cups were bound to come out substandard. The workers would toss them into a box and at that point Zoyka put on a real performance. She would sob, scrounge, hiccup and whine … it was embarrassing to look at but oh, how she longed to bite into a cup!

Nyuta and Arisha would lie still, gazing reverently at Zoyka's hysterics, no doubt the way northern tribes watch shamanic rituals from a distance with resigned apprehension.

Unable to bear the heartrending scene, one of the staff would inevitably go to the window and thrust the substandard output through the bars. Zoyka would be first to snatch the offering in her small, vice-like hands. She'd earned it!

In the USA and Canada, squirrels are shameless beggars and later they would always remind Nyuta of Zoyka as a little girl. Once, when she went to see Arisha at Middlebury College, Vermont, Anna spotted a perfect animal version of their former friend in a lane. A ginger-white squirrel was sitting on the open lid of a trash container and turning something over in its nimble little paws, while casting sly glances over its shoulder.

The aunties called Zoyka a grasping little hoyden and yelled, "Oi, you, guzzle chops, give some to the girls as well."

Once, when Khristina and Nyuta were on their way home from Panna Ivanna's (this was after Khristina's "almost-wedding" with the "almost-widower"—Zoyka's dad, Vasily Fyodorovich, who really didn't sit still but rattled from Tashkent to Irkutsk by train, although that's another story) … they were passing the windows of the wafer section when one of the workers who was smoking at the window called out to Nyuta. The little girl went over to say hello and the auntie poured her a whole heap of wafer cups and trimmings so that for two days she felt as if she was the breadwinner. She regaled the family jealously: "Ma, why don't you try the wafers?"

People began to be moved out of the communal flats in the early 1970s and Zoyka, her bedridden mother and her sisters were the first to obtain a three-room flat.

They couldn't come to terms with so many rooms to begin with and for a long time they all lived together in just one.

It seems that it was then that Khristina suddenly made her sole historic visit to the family of her "almost-widower," Vasily Fyodorovich. Either her conscience troubled her, which is unlikely, or she had decided to see whether it was time to siphon off a room for him.

His bedridden wife was still bedridden. Khristina sat on the bed next to her and started telling her that Vasya was now much better in terms of his diet and his health. After all, he would have wasted away altogether, poor thing…

"As I'm watching," Khristina recounted afterwards, "she turns red as a beetroot! And says to me, 'You are a shameless prostitute!'" At this point, Khristina sighed, smoothed her skirt with both hands over her splendid stomach and said in conclusion: "So what? I bore it all in silence."

Zoyka's hungry childhood drove her to cooking school. Many years later during a visit to her father's, Anna ran into her at the Kiev Restaurant. A curvaceous lady, bedecked and bedizened with gold trinkets, she recognized Anna at a distance and sprinted across the whole of the room. She cried and dabbed at her frosted eyelids with a tiny handkerchief, saying over and over, "Dear God, Nyutka, you haven't changed a bit."

She merely shook her head when she heard that Anna was still "turning somersaults on the tightrope."

Some fifteen minutes later, an enormous tray "from our senior chef" was placed on the table.

"Who is it from?" Anna wondered aloud.

"Zoya Vasilyevna, that's who," the waitress replied huffily.

… At home, Nyuta's father and Khristina listened to her delighted tale of the Frog Princess.

Her father commented, "And really, becoming the senior chef at the Kiev Restaurant is a long way from filching Berta's pirozhki."

(By then he was already ill on occasion although he was still refusing to be checked out properly, possibly already divining the real reasons for his morning nausea and evening pains.)

Khristina, for her part, gave a scornful grin and said, "But you didn't ask her the main thing: Where does she go to shit nowadays?"

✳✳✳

Nyuta contracted measles before the start of her first year at school and so seriously that her father, himself an expert in contagious diseases, brought an elderly lady to see his daughter on two separate occasions.

This lady was a leading light in childhood illnesses, a professor, although she didn't behave like one but like a kindly grandma. She used Nyuta's daddy's pet name, Tolenka, and seemed sorrier for him and for Ma, who was half-dead with worry, than for the patient herself. Sunlight reflected cheerily off a small round mirror above Sofia Nikolaevna's forehead as if someone had pushed her thin scalp vigorously back onto her neck, like a headscarf. The little girl, puce with fever, was delighted, licked her cracked lips and muttered, "You've got outside what I've got inside."

"Where?" asked Sofia Nikolaevna in surprise. Nyuta pointed to the middle of her own forehead.

"Right here!" she said in a friendly fashion. Masha felt as if her insides had collapsed away.

"Darling," she murmured. "It's not nice to point."

In a nutshell, when Nyuta began to recover, the first term was already well under way and Ma was inclined to keep her debilitated little daughter at home for an extra year. Khristina also believed that "such a sickly little thing will be with us a while yet." Her father, however, stood firm.

"A woman mustn't waste the years," was his somewhat peculiar remark.

So Ma took Nyuta to school. They arrived early, an hour before lessons began, as agreed with the head. They reported to the staff room where they both hung back.

"Vera Petrovna," the head told the skinny, dour, awkward woman. (Mashuta would later say that she had evidently had polio as a child since she had limited use of her left hand.) "Vera Petrovna, this is Anya Nesterenko. I told you she's been ill. She needs to be brought up to speed somehow."

Vera Petrovna led Nyuta to an empty classroom. She told the anxious Mashuta who was trying to explain something about a "special approach" to the child ("she has problems reading and writing, you see … because…") but, most significantly, was intent on hanging around the classroom for the first few days, to calm down and wait in the corridor.

Sitting Nyuta at a front desk, the teacher gave her a pencil and a piece of paper and began rapidly writing round cursive letters on the blackboard, saying, "It doesn't matter if you don't get it all at once. Write down what you see on the board. We'll look at it afterwards."

Nyuta sat, looking tensely from the board to the pencil and from the board to the lined paper. Her heart thumped clearly and precisely against her ribs. A pencil is very different to a knife or fork. Those are ordinary items, no more than they seem, dully serving a short-term end. But a pencil! The force of new words flows from it and each one is like a bud, opening up to become the candle of a chestnut tree, merging into a wondrous, luxuriant crown… 'Which hand to punish, which to spare?' They were both the same but the left… She could feel her heart pulsing in her fingertips, the droplets speeding, hurrying along…

"Off you go. Copy it out!"

Vera Petrovna sat at a table facing Nyuta, took a powder compact out of her handbag and began to smarten herself up. It was a strange kind of compact with a double mirror. It reflected on both sides. It captured Nyuta's face and hands, wanted to give her a prompt, to offer guidance…

No. I don't need to look, the little girl told herself. It's all wrong up there and I've got to put it the other way around. The other way!

Resolutely, she picked up the pencil and copied the series of letters from the board onto the paper.

"What are you doing? Writing with your left hand?" said Vera Petrovna, unpleasantly surprised and closing the compact with a click. "Are you left-handed?" She looked at the paper.

Nyuta realized immediately that something terrible had happened from the crimson cloud of fury that flooded the teacher's neck and crept on upwards. Before long, her whole face was the same, as if someone had smashed it repeatedly against the desk.

"Are you doing this on purpose?" Quietly and angrily she rapped out, "If you write like that one more time, I'll send you to the idiots' school!"

It was as though the words had hit the child across the face. Her entire body fell back against the chair. As if a sinner had been led to the pit, from which came wisps of blood-drenched steam and the visceral wail of doomed souls, and, gripped firmly and painfully by the neck, was forced to peer in…

She and Masha practised writing the letters the other way round. Nyuta could picture the blackboard hanging there—secretive, the complete opposite of a mirror's calm, transparent depth and yawning freedom. The blackness of the tightly closed school blackboard radiated a deadly horror.

Nyuta wouldn't let Masha go to bed.

"Ma," she asked, "one more go!"

"Alright…" Masha could barely keep her eyes open. Two of her music school groups had tests on the romantics the following day.

They practised with a pen rather than a pencil. Masha considered it more "promising—you won't be in Grade One for ever. And use your right hand. The right one. You can do it! That's it, clever girl! And what lovely neat letters. Just don't be shy."

And she sighed, "Right then, dear daughter, that's enough. Time for bed. It's after two…"

"No, Ma," Nyuta pleaded. "Three more letters the other way round."

She wrote properly with a pen from then on and until she finished school. If she happened to pick up a pencil or a piece of chalk, however, her willpower would freeze and startled, slanting, stunningly mysterious letters would fly from right to left beneath her hand, which only made sense in a mirror.

                                    ***

"We've had a circus performer move in!" Arisha burst out.

They were in the canteen, being jostled in the winding queue for the pirozhki that arrived on enormous trays for the lunch break, laid out in golden ranks.

The friends had been put into separate classes in Grade Four, Nyuta in A, Arisha in B. Furthermore, Arisha was doing a lot of music.

In the winter, she had won a prize in the Ukrainian Republic's "Young Talents" contest and was now working hard on the "advanced" curriculum.

Meanwhile, Nyuta had been going to the sports group at the Milk Factory Club for six months.

They missed one another a great deal and as soon as the bell went they would rush into a hug no matter where they happened to be—in the canteen, the corridor or the schoolyard if the weather was nice.

Arisha sometimes asked, "I'm not squinting so much today, am I? Am I pretty?"

And Nyuta would answer with feeling, "Awfully pretty."

"It's a clown. A real one. He's actually living with Panna Ivanna, sleeping on the mattress. She's known him for ages. They wanted him to go to a hotel but, 'No,' he says, 'it's cosier here.' He has no airs and graces. And he's really, really funny!"

And a clown now too. Wasn't life interesting? You never knew which way to turn. She had recently acquired a secret of her own as well. A shaggy secret, in thick glasses, with cut and injured fingers swathed in sticking plasters and the mysterious name of a medieval alchemist—Eliezer.

A couple of months previously, Nyuta had been running along the corridor of the Milk Factory Club after her acrobatics class. It was her Dad's day to come home earlier than usual from the hospital and he had promised to take her to the zoo. Everyone was crazy about going to the zoo to see the two baby elephants, Ravi and Shashi. They'd been given to Kiev Zoo by some Ja…wa…larlar Ner-something—the King of India, basically—but Nyuta and her Dad were going to see the monkeys. They never tired of watching them. Their leader, a stoop-shouldered old baboon, was forever turning its red bum-hole to the public… You weren't really supposed to say that; you were meant to say "bottom" but Ma didn't know that word either and used "derriere" or the even nastier "tushy". But Nyuta and Khristina knew all the correct terms. When Khristina lathered Nyuta up in the bath (and, by the way, it was time to tell her to get lost, not to come into the bathroom now!), she would say, "Now then, lazybones, stop wriggling! Rub the sponge over your bum-hole and your fanny the way you're meant to, hygiene rules."

And so, the baboon would embarrass the public with its red bum-hole.

But Nyuta and her Dad had a long-standing affection for one particular monkey, quick-moving and crafty. She was a playful little sneak thief and it was her they were going to see.

Three years earlier, Nyuta's father had outlined Darwin's theory of evolution for her outside that cage. She had listened with only half an ear, concentrating on following "their" monkey as she slinked around the tough old baboon, aware that the little one would stretch a swarthy, wrinkled and entirely human hand towards the basket and swipe a carrot as soon as his back was turned.

"And that's how the monkey became a human being!" her father said in conclusion.

His daughter looked up at him and asked quietly and sincerely, "Wasn't it surprised?"

Racing along the corridor and past the noticeboard of the Milk Factory Club, Nyuta slowed down a bit. She still needed extra seconds to make the effort involved in turning writing around. She froze. There, in a neat red frame on a sheet of exercise paper, in the *natural handwriting she was forbidden to use*—she read it in an instant—were the words: "The Intriguing World of Mirrors"—and just below the same again in black ink *but reversed*.

"You are invited to join a new club where you will be able to discover all about the mysteries of mirrors and about telescopes, binoculars and other optical marvels. Register with Eliezer in Room 3 on the first floor."

She gasped, unable to believe her eyes, took a step backwards, spun around and flew up to the first floor where she almost landed head first in someone's soft belly outside the longed-for room. A large fat man stood in front of her, with a blue-black clump of hair so thick it would need secateurs to trim it. Mischievous eyes floated like black cherries behind the lenses of his glasses.

"Whoa, there, cowboy!" issued from beneath the thick hair. "Where are you off to in such a hurry? Into the looking-glass?" And he threw the door open wide in welcome.

"Me too ... I can... Look," the girl stammered, panting.

She dashed over to a table, on which lay sheets of paper already torn from an exercise book, grabbed a pencil and a pen and quickly—just like Arisha played a contrary motion scale with both hands—wrote out Shevchenko's famous line, the writing going in different directions, *her own* to the left and *its shape-shifted version* to the right.

"The mighty Dnieper roars and bellows!!!"[2]

"Goodness gracious me!" he remarked softly and approvingly behind her. "Are you a genius, child?"

"I'm Nesterenko," she replied happily. "Nyuta!"

"Ah, so it turns out you're the one I've been waiting here for like an idiot for three days."

A week later, her fingers were just as patched with bits of sticking plastic as his because they had learnt the Ancient Egyptian method of making a mirror by polishing a sheet of bronze. The round disc, meant to represent the sun, was easily obtained from the lid of Mashuta's Mongolian jewel-box. Nyuta was rapt and impassive as she removed the lid in her parents' bedroom.

No one apart from Nyuta registered for the club with its alluring advertisement about the "World of Mirrors" and the manager "disbanded" it. After that, they held their meetings wherever they could.

Eliezer had graduated from university with a distinction in physics but was registered disabled because of some strange disease that he himself referred to as "ennui". ("Ennui, the mangy cur, comes right out of the blue, Nyuta, my angel... See, I take pills to keep it at bay.") He worked in the mirror shop at the Bozhenko Furniture Factory "to ease my mind," as he said himself with a grin.

Nyuta sometimes went to sit with him in the storeroom after school, observing keenly as his chubby yet precise hands placed amalgam on the glass, cut it to shape and prepared the backing so that the mirror wouldn't break.

"An ordinary flat mirror, Nyuta, my angel," Eliezer used to say, "reflects everything the way it is: what's on the left, the right, above, below... Everything else is about interpreting what can be seen and that

---

2   Translated by John Weir in *Taras Shevchenko, Selections*. Toronto, 1961.

takes place in our brains which are pretty ingenious constructions. You see your reflection and compare it mentally with the real thing that has crossed over into the mirror."

"But is that really possible?" she asked, holding her breath. "Without permission?"

"I don't know what permission you're talking about but some perfectly serious scientists believe in the existence of mirror universes. Do you want to hear?"

"Yes!" she breathed.

"Right, listen up… And when you get bored, wink and we'll go off and scoff some ice-cream… So, you see, there was once a scientist called Everett who realized that there was a multitude of universes parallel to our own albeit with rather different physical parameters… Wait a sec… do you know what a neutrino is? Ah-ha, so that's where we need to start. So, look, a neutrino is one of the elementary particles that go to make up matter. Okay? Physicists have discovered that the properties of particles don't change during specific spatial movements, spinning, for example. Except for the neutrino! The neutrino's properties change when it's reflected in a mirror… And there you go! So how is the complete symmetry of particle theory to be restored now?"

"How?" Nyuta repeated, following the movement of his fat fingers with fascination as they palpated the air absently. But those fingers were tracing a round shape in the air, which restored the "symmetry of particle theory."

"Each neutrino is assumed to have a mirror double. I'm the neutrino, let's say, and you're my mirror neutrino."

Nyuta starting laughing as she imagined herself, Nyuta, appearing in the mirror instead of Eliezer who was so fat. How could their faces be symmetrical? What a joke!

"And from there," he continued smoothly having waited for her to be quiet, "it's only a tiny step to the proposition that the other particles have mirror doubles too. And then… well, what then? What essentially consists of particles, Nyuta, my angel?"

"Matter!" Nyuta, his angel, hastened to say, hopping up and down, unable herself to understand where the right word came from when she was talking to Eliezer. It was just that her thoughts, like a tightrope walker on an invisible wire, could feel their way between *the mirrors* set out somewhere in the space behind her forehead and *the mirrors* beneath the spiky black clump of hair on this funny fat man's head.

"That's right! Which means that mirror particles form…?"

"Mirror matter!!!"

"Exactly. And now—time to down that ice-cream."

And off they went into the small garden opposite where pensioners sat on benches at scuffed chessboards and played for material gain.

Eliezer always bought himself two ice-creams on sticks and gobbled them up greedily, biting off large pieces as if someone was at his heels. He was hilarious as he licked off the ice-cream moustache over his thick lips and would say triumphantly, and a bit weirdly, "Let's stuff our faces while he isn't looking."

Nyuta looked over her shoulder to begin with, thinking Eliezer had encountered some unpleasant acquaintance he had to hide from. Once, though, she spotted *another Eliezer* behind him, transparent and completely white as if he had *stuffed himself* with so much ice-cream that hoar frost had covered his hair, eyebrows and eyelashes... She shivered, blinked and said, "No, no, that's not right... take it easy. You're not allowed sweet things."

It took her a long time to fall asleep at night now, as she contemplated in detail what she and Eliezer had talked about during the day. Eventually, her eyelids closed and *the mirrors* rippled lazily, quivering like duckweed on the surface of a pool. At that point it seemed that at any moment the Mirror World would at long last dissolve the thin rigid film over the entrance to the *real universe*, the parallel mirror universe Eliezer had promised, and take her into its watery rather than airy self *to luxuriate, glide gracefully and slice through the transparent mass...*

And there, where life was lived properly, where people moved properly, she was bound to meet *her real mum, the proper one.*

For some reason she knew Eliezer was the most important thing *in her life. The most important teacher*, the most important person, *essentially. She believed his every word and adjusted the mirrors, avidly capturing everything he recounted, everything he taught. And she knew that he was teaching her* the most important thing. *Because still to come in her life, hundreds and thousands of mirrors of unusual properties and designs reflected heaven and earth, corridors and auditoriums in the widest variety of countries and cities...*

Then too, like Firavelna, he was so calmly accepting of the girl's ability to see. Although sadly he could do nothing of the sort himself—

She already knew that bronze and silver reflected well and did not cloud over with oxide layers. She knew that the toxic amalgam of tin and mercury had been replaced in the previous century by the less dangerous process of silvering. She knew a great deal about the history of mirrors or "image-reflection," as Eliezer would say.

Running, she would hurtle into Arisha at break times and tell her about the Chinese warriors who used to take mirror amulets into battle or the Chinese newly-weds who held small mirrors to their hearts on their wedding day. And the Buddhist temples where mirrors were still used in the consecration of water...

Before long, Nyuta and Eliezer were ready to try Venetian glass-blowing. Eliezer's neighbour, Georgy, worked at the glass works in Stalin District, next to the brewery. Georgy, a sullen man of few words, had once organized a whole trip around the glass works for them and, as he showed them miracles and wonders, had tersely muttered things like "tin baths," "batch charger," "feeder channel."

He had a funny way of sneezing. He would bend and lift one knee, spread his elbows, prick up his ears like a wary horse then, with a quick snicker, move his arms as if he was snapping a small branch over his knee.

Afterwards, Eliezer and Georgy bought beer from the brewery shop and sat on a bench in the little square. (Mashuta would, presumably, have gone crazy if she'd seen her daughter in the company of two weird types holding mugs of beer.) Weightless poplar fluff was floating from all over the place, collecting in piles, tumbling and creeping along the ground. Not far away, three small boys were setting fire to its silvery clouds.

Whoosh! And the spectral flare went out.

And up ahead, further down the line, a sea of mirrors awaited: flat, concave and convex mirrors, with spherical or cylindrical surfaces, to use in illusions or in lighthouses, in spotlights and instruments, even in astronomical or spectral instruments!

"And the most ancient glass mirrors of all," Nyuta told Arisha at break times, "were made in Sidon even earlier than in Rome. Sidon is a really, really old Phoenician city on the Mediterranean Sea with an enormous harbour. Ships used to moor there and sailors from every country would export the glass mirrors because they gave the very purest reflections."

"The purest?" Arisha said, wrinkling her forehead.

"It means the image was reflected clearly, without any blurred lines around it. You looked at yourself and could see that, yes, it was you!"

Some twenty-five years later as she sat on the brow of a headland made of shells in Hof Dor, the ancient harbour of the Phoenician city of Dor, near Haifa, Anna remembered the lengthy vigils in Eliezer's storeroom, his black leather apron that had worn thin over his belly, the fact that his Jewish accent crept in in certain words and the utterly insatiable, unquenchable longing for constant discovery imparted to her by this morbidly fat man with the stiff clump of spiky hedging on his head.

A luxuriant sharp-ribbed palm tree on the shore creaked gently in the sea breeze.

A scattering of claret-coloured dates, their innards soft as chamois, lay in the grass under the palm tree, pecked at by the birds. 'The Phoenicians might be long gone,' Anna thought, 'but the dates still fall on the grass as regularly as they did a thousand years ago, feeding birds, ants, beetles—and people while they're at it.'

Eliezer turned out to live with his brother, and no ordinary brother at that. In her mind, Nyuta immediately dubbed him the *shapeshifter*.

They were going to visit Eliezer's house for the very first time, taking the Number 9 tram from Khaturin Street to Podol. The tram, a Kiev "push-me, pull-me," each end identical but facing the opposite way, gave occasional squeals as it went up the steep slope of Vladimirskaya Street.

Eliezer, his fat fingers comically scratching the spiky hedge on his head, said, "Just don't be surprised. My brother's my twin but he's one of a kind. Like my reflection in an unreal mirror. One day, I'll invent a mirror like that and build it. A brown-haired man will look in it and a blond-haired one will look back."

When Eliezer opened the door after rapping gently with his soft knuckles (they lived in a communal flat in a crooked little two-storey block on Heroes of Tripolya Street in a room that had been left them by an old lady, Liza) and said, "And this is my brother, Abram. Hey, Buma!"

Nyuta was rendered speechless. She simply stood there, not responding when greeted. It was Eliezer in negative that had risen from the table. Everything black about Eliezer was white: hair, eyebrows, eyelashes…

Later Eliezer said reprovingly, "You could have been a little more polite."

And he was right. But the fact was that she'd been rooted to the spot… It was impossible to explain why she'd been so frightened. She had never been frightened of anything, ever—she had come across such frightening disabled war veterans on the streets and in the parks, half-men, crippled by war and sickness; destitute, foul-smelling, drunken old men and women—beggars, scum, trash… She had never been scared or squeamish. She would offer a hand, help someone onto the tram or to sit on a bench… But she had been really frightened of the neat, rather cold man in the ironed shirt and soft smoking jacket who immediately made tea and brought over a plate of biscuits.

To be fair, Buma, despite his cosy pet name, was clearly in charge. After about forty minutes, he began to clear the cups away, saying calmly and firmly, "Well, now it's time for us all to go our separate ways." Although it was quite clear that only Nyuta really had to leave. "Elik, I think you're tired. It's time you had a rest."

He stopped Eliezer, who had jumped up to accompany Nyuta, with the palm of his hand and, grinning, added the rather odd, "No chance, it won't fall off."

And good as gold, Nyuta began *to go her separate way*. In other words, with Eliezer looking dolefully on, she went out of the room, wandered about in the darkness of the many-cornered corridor and, after knocking someone's skis over in a corner, she fumbled for the lock on the door, leapt out and was free.

She waited for the Number 9 tram in the dark for a long time. It took her a long time to get home and it felt even longer.

She spent half the night tossing and turning, unable to get to sleep. Hardly would she close her eyes than the pale shapeshifter that was Eliezer in negative would make stern and threatening gestures with one finger, shielding the *real* brother from her: It's time for all of us, all of us, I said, to go our separate ways once and for all.

***

Her father was puzzled that Nyuta was so wildly keen on mirrors and regarded Eliezer as a seriously disturbed layabout. He did not approve of her incomprehensible friendship given what he called "the age gap."

Firavelna, on the other hand, declared thoughtfully and approvingly that he had a biblical name that translated as "God is my help" ("Some help!" Arisha snorted.).

As for Mashuta, she was dreadfully worried and didn't want to hear anything about mirrors at all—there was just no understanding the child's strange enthusiasms! On one occasion Masha created an absolute uproar over a D grade for composition and screeched, high-pitched and hysterical, quite unlike her usual self, "I'll give you mirrors. I'll beat that nonsense out of you!" although it was unclear how or with what precisely the meek and mild Mashuta intended to "beat" the "nonsense" out of her daughter. By that time, however, Nyuta had learnt to slip away like a fish. At the slightest tension she simply slid out of the house, closing the door behind her without a sound. If you darted after her into the hall, all you would see would be her striped Pinocchio hat disappearing in the mirror as if she had stepped into the greenish oval and fallen through the looking glass. She would be gone for hours on end, no one knew where. She remained silent when questioned, not to be stubborn or nasty, but the way deep water is silent on a cloudy day.

On those days, Masha tore around the streets and the surrounding courtyards or, at the very least, hovered by the kitchen window, practically banging her head on the glass.

In the end, Khristina was sent to the Bozhenko Furniture Factory to find out what was going on. By then, she only dropped by twice a week, making herself out to be oh-such-a-busy mother. Although what kind of family did she have? Her almost-husband, almost-widower Vasily Fyodorovich, was almost never at home, rattling along to Irkutsk or Tashkent or Erevan for weeks on end then drinking himself into a stupor when he came home so that Khristina was free even then to some extent. Sure, her aunt, the caretaker Markovna, had shuffled off her mortal coil by then and couldn't see what the drunken Vanya was up to in her room, drinking away the dinner service her late husband had brought back as war loot from Leipzig and the Yugoslav crystal vase, obtained by standing in a horrendous queue complete with yelling and epic punch-ups.

Khristina was casually composed when she returned from her intelligence gathering.

"What?" she asked, answering the mute question in Masha's eyes. "Some fat Jewish bloke, completely off his rocker. But a decent chap.

She's safe with him. And then I didn't understand why all the fuss. Science, innit? And maybe it will come in handy in life?"

And Masha drooped. She couldn't get what she meant across to anyone.

Her daughter was leaving her, drifting further and further away and increasingly and scarily belonged more and more to the inevitable.

✳✳✳

"A jam pirozhok!" called Arisha, standing on tiptoe. "And a rice one!"

Nyuta bought one of each as well and they began to go up to the first floor, munching as they went. The bell still hadn't gone.

"Come round after school today," Arisha said. "But before five in case the clown's got a show this evening. He pulls such funny faces. You'll die laughing."

The clown didn't pull funny faces. He was very sad. Or rather, he wore a permanent expression of wistful surprise. Even when he accidentally bumped into Nyuta on his way to the kitchen with the kettle and poured water all over her and they both stood stock still facing each other, his face, with its high arched brows, registered only surprise.

"Are you Armenian?" he asked.

"No, why?" Nyuta replied, embarrassed.

"I ask everybody on the off chance," he explained. The clown's surname was Engibarov. He was slim and round-shouldered like a bent twig. His arms hung foolishly like trailing vines.

Lyubov Kazimirovna, the major's morose wife, called him a "worm." "There," she would say, "the worm's out." She didn't like other people's guests. No one ever came to visit her.

Nyuta immediately realized, however, that the awkwardness and foolishness were a pretence. The clown's hands were muscled and incredibly strong. When they had relaxed into conversation and become properly acquainted, he grabbed Arisha by the waist with one hand, tipped her upside-down, tossed her fairly high up in the air—how she shrieked, silly girl!—and caught her again under the arms like a log. It was a shame the clown hadn't thrown Nyuta in the air like that. After all, she was far lighter and nimbler than Arisha! The acrobatics coach complimented her all the time, saying she was simply born for the parallel bars and the beam and the tightrope. And although her entire body longed to do bouncing jumps, somersaults, flips and splits—how she would have soared up to the ceiling in that shared play of bodies!—Nyuta was embarrassed to perform her best move, the cartwheel, right there and then in the kitchen. She was wearing her brown school uniform dress with leggings underneath—damn that Khristina! What kind of cartwheel could she do? … She'd only disgrace herself.

Then, once they had stopped laughing and really became friends, the clown suddenly began taking his leave, suspiciously piteous as he said goodbye to them all. He shook Arisha's and Nyuta's hands for a long time as if he was leaving for good that very minute—they even exchanged a look—then vanished into Panna Ivanna's room.

Two or three seconds later—ta-dah!—the door was suddenly flung wide and out at a march came … the clown, striding along on his hands which were encased in the old boots Panna Ivanna kept in her "*chiffonier*" and polished with blacking every spring as if preparing to wear them to a show at the Musical Comedy Theatre.

He was walking on his hands in those comical laced boots while his legs gesticulated fiercely like a pair of extremely flexible arms. One minute he was wringing them in despair, then applauding, then attempting to wipe away a tear with the bare sole of a foot.

Meanwhile the boots were beating out a rhythm, tap-dancing, performing ballet steps. It was, as Panna Ivanna was wont to say, "an inimitable performance." With the performance in full swing, however, Panna Ivanna came back from the shop and, paying no attention whatsoever to the delight of the girls or the skill of the clown, said sternly, "Lyonya, put the boots down! They're a memento of my late friend."

And the clown instantly put his feet on the floor, the same surprise as ever in his raised eyebrows and spread his arms wide, the boots waggling reproachfully—tut, tut, tut.

That same evening, Arisha and Nyuta were pushing their way through the crowd to the circus gates, carrying a note from "Uncle Lyonya".

Two old women were checking tickets, one on each side of the open half of the door, making it utterly impossible to slip through the prehensile barrier of their many hands.

"What's this then?" one woman bawled when Arisha held out the note. Arisha, started babbling about Uncle Lyonya who lived with them and had invited them himself and well, you can read it yourself, while the crowd behind them pushed and swore and someone eager to get in without paying hunched over and slipped in from the side like an eel. The old women were furious and started swearing. One shouted to the other, "Damn him, he's giving his little notes out to the whole town!" whereupon she shoved Arisha back and the crowd immediately engulfed the girls and swept them off the steps and into the street.

Arisha stood and cried, squinting badly. To make matters worse, she'd lost a glove, a brand new one.

Nyuta was suddenly gripped by rage. Her body felt as if it was strong and flat like the edge of a ray of light. She became bizarrely certain that she could now cut right through the crowd, easily avoid the loathsome old women and reach the circus foyer.

"Wait here!" she said without looking at Arisha. "I'll be right back."

She took about ten steps then suddenly came back, taking out the amethyst earrings her father had given her on her ninth birthday.

"Hold these. They're in the way," she said, looking past Arisha from within herself.

And she set off at a relaxed and even pace as if allowing someone invisible to pull her along on a string. She squeezed between a man in a grey mac and two teenagers, then appeared for a moment before Arisha's startled gaze. She was already behind the old women. She didn't slide or squeeze or sneak through. She went calmly and even disinterestedly as if detached. Arisha couldn't explain it to herself rationally. She stood, clutching the amethyst earrings that had somehow offended their owner, and stared fixedly at the doors that were ingesting one fresh batch of spectators after another.

In the circus foyer, meanwhile, Nyuta flopped against a column to prevent her weak legs giving way—you could have wrung the sweat out of her. She couldn't have said how it had happened either or why the old women didn't stop her when they saw her. True, she had told herself to become transparent *from the inside out*, in other words, had kept her eyes fixed unwaveringly on *her mirrors* and, sensing a pricking in her ears, had realized the earrings had to come off. Now she was shaking with the thought that she might be arrested.

The third and final bell rang and the audience poured into the seating area.

Musicians could be heard tuning their instruments, children running in the aisles, the tip-up seats creaking and banging. From a distance, the roar of the animals sounded like faint peals of thunder. A muffled din and clamour like the sound of the surf wreathed the red floor of the ring.

Nyuta knew that now the overhead lighting would begin to dim, fade and go out. For a moment, people would hold their breath and then, all of a sudden, the orchestra would start up with a da-da-da-da dum-dum!!! Spotlights would shine on the age-old alley-way between the stands and, like gladiators, out would come two rows of semi-clad performers, sparkling like Christmas decorations. They would encircle the ring and lift their bare arms to greet the public and would be met by a gale of applause. The dazzling parade would begin, albeit with stupid words—"thanks to the beloved Party" and other such nonsense… But who was listening? Then out would come Uncle Lyonya, the sad clown in a sailor shirt…

The circus was also the most important thing.

Not because she and her father often went to see the same shows over and over again and knew the programme and the names of the performers practically by heart because they were all there, close at hand. But no, that wasn't the reason. Gazing up at the trapeze artists and the tightrope walkers balancing with fans, she walked the wire herself, gripping it with the soles of her feet, carefully keeping her back straight. The circus—and she had known it for ages—was where she belonged.

Right now, she was being desperately drawn towards the auditorium, to lean quietly against the wall of the entranceway. To stand and breathe in the specific intricate blend of warm air that belonged to the show.

But outside Arisha was waiting, frozen. Without even sneaking a look into the auditorium, Nyuta plodded over to the exit. The women, leaning against the doorposts, were chatting peaceably and keeping a look-out for any laggardly spectators.

"Where are you going?" one of them yelled after the girl. "What have you come out for? There's no going back in, girlie." Nyuta turned around and, on Arisha's behalf, said in Khristina's rich sing-song tone, "You're bloody idiots, you are, lay-yaa-dies!"

CHAPTER 9

You know, the circus is a simple business. Every idea can be tested on the audience in the evening. If you think it works, you put it in. Another time, you try and it's a complete disaster. One of our clowns, Kim Devyatkin, used to talk about an old act of his. He would come into the ring holding an umbrella, wearing a hat and coat and carrying a suitcase. Gradually, he took it all off. Then he juggled with the clothes, put them back on and left. Applause? Not so much.

And then after the show in Riga one time, a really ancient clown tells him to let the ringhand pick the stuff up—the coat, the hat, the suitcase. Don't put them on. Let the lights go down and call it a day. Don't distract the audience. So our Kim has a go, keeps it simple and it goes down a bomb. Incidentally, people said Lyonya Engibarov used to go to Odessa, to the home for retired circus performers. The old guys worked with him. They'd got nothing else to do and they helped him with his patter between acts.

Why so formal, anyway? Just call me Volodya, why not? I do hope, Robert, that you and I are not here as suspect and investigator? That's good then. In that case, I'll order another beer.

Yes, you said back then as well that you were a real circus fan. I remember. And I understand that very well … Oh, really? Is that so? There you are then, that's nice. You must have been a very little boy. Where was it? Minsk? What year?

I remember that tour, really, I do. We'd only just put our programme together. There was this one difficult trick—jump to head. It went like this. We walked out to the middle of the wire, one behind the other. I was her support and went first using a pole for balance and she followed me step for step with one hand on my shoulder. Then, I dropped to one knee and she put her right foot on my thigh. On the command of "up", I kind of pressed down on the wire and threw her up off my leg. Pushing off at the same time, she sailed up in a candlestick and came down, feet together, on my head.

You must remember. It's really complicated. I was wearing a sort of tight felt cap so she didn't rip my hair out. And she had to stand to attention, grip my head with the soles of her feet, settle into position and let me move forward a bit. Once I'd got my balance, I walked or ran to the platform. Her job was to hold the position, straight as an arrow, directly above the wire, leaving the balancing to me and without leaning to the side.

Gadzhikurbanova is the only woman who's done it, the "jump to head on the wire" and she did it onto a rounded surface not a soft cap. She jumped onto a solid papier-maché helmet—practically an airfield! How did it go for Anna? If she came down slightly crookedly, leaning slightly over on one foot, she clung on with her toes like a monkey, gripping my head as hard as she could and hanging on for dear life while I hied it over to the platform… She had barely any falls doing it. It's true that in 1985, our timing was out when we pushed off from the wire. Her timing worked against mine and made me tear a ligament. It's a good thing it was on the low wire in rehearsal. It took me a long time to recover afterwards.

We had another trick in our repertoire too, looping the loop. You must remember that as well. That's when I used to attach my feet to the wire with rope while the audience watched, slide out into the middle using just my arms to balance and then pretend to fall. A gasp from the audience, round I went and found my balance again. Then I started to loop the loop, over and over, to edgy broken chords from Pink Floyd, sliding a step closer to the platform. At the platform, I had to balance top dead centre, which was really difficult after a loop. And with one last step, I was on the platform itself. We'd asked the orchestra to synchronize my victory step with the brass chord from Dunaevsky's march. It cut in as all the lights went up—every type of spotlight on full. And they dropped the quiet opening, going straight into the victory theme. It had the audience on their feet!

The number went down a storm but it was a bit of a rest for me. It was safe—I was tied on...

...No, it wasn't possible to use a harness of any kind. I was attached by rope, nothing else. We used to buy strong, multi-strand rope, 7-8 millimetres thick, at hardware stores. It wouldn't wear through straightaway. That only happened twice maybe and then just on one foot. Then I stopped the loop, balanced on top of the wire, took the worn rope off my foot and threw it into the ring. You should have seen the reaction from the crowd. There was a roar like a big match.

Loops look good. Lots of aerial gymnasts do them as a finale. They use their hands or feet to spin around the various trapeze bars…

You're not the first person to remember only her. She really was so … dazzling in that costume. "The nude," we called it—a flesh-colour bikini in a stretch fabric: tight bottoms and a bra, thick spangles of coloured rhinestones. They twinkled under the spotlights, sparkled like the real thing! You couldn't see the fabric. Well, there practically wasn't any. Just a flesh-coloured triangle on thongs. It was daring. And drop-dead gorgeous. Over the top, she wore a transparent nylon cloak down to the ground, trimmed with white feathers. And an enormous set of plumes on her head. It wasn't comfortable but it looked good. And all this in semi-darkness, under coloured spotlights, just the glass beads glittering on her body. The public groaned…

No, for goodness sake, order something for yourself, please. I don't want to eat yet… Although, we've been sitting here a while now. I might be feeling peckish… No, why? I have a good appetite although to be honest in the beginning I didn't think I could go on living let alone eat… But, as you can see, I could… And I'm doing fine… But Senya, now.

Oh, come off it. What hurricane? We each choose our own hurricane… I preferred to live and … to wait…

I'm sorry… Excuse me, I didn't get that… What?!

Ah, so that's what this is about. Now, I see. That's why you set up a meeting in this dive!

Mr. Kerler, are you trying to say that you didn't know this before? Some breakthrough! No, I didn't mention it during the investigation. I didn't think it would help. Then again, you're right. I didn't want to. What's done is done. No, who would have thought it? Someone disappears along with their motorbike and the investigators want to know who meant what to whom twenty years ago!

Sure, she wasn't just my partner of many years. She was my wife. So what? You want to know whether I had any reason to kill her or just to want her dead? Yes, I had dozens of reasons for killing her and a passionate desire to see her dead.

Does that amuse you? Does it send the investigation down another track?

And for somebody who really tried to kill her, there's Genevieve. But you know that already. Howard stopped her… That Howard—Genevieve's parrot, the African grey, with the hunched back. He was a chick dying at some breeding farm when Genevieve rescued him. They didn't want him and it was clear why: he wasn't just hunchbacked, his feathers had some sort of disease, they kept falling out. Genevieve fed him from a pipette. And he was worth it. He was clever, chatty, funny. And he loved Anna like a person would. Seriously, as soon as he saw her, he would ruffle his feathers, preen himself and say: "Anna—boy! Have a kiss!" Have you ever seen parrots kissing? No? They stretch their beaks towards your lips … and close their eyes … like people do! It's enough to drive you crazy!

Anyway, he saved Anna.

Later, after about three months, Genevieve told me herself, sobbed out all the details. It makes your hair stand on end. How desperate the poor creature must have been—Genevieve, I mean, obviously—to attack a professional bunch of muscle. She cried so hard, poor thing, inconsolably…

To be honest, Genevieve had been hopelessly in love with her for years. Anna didn't want to go into it, reacted harshly, interrupting any hints. She could be surprisingly prudish about certain things. As if she'd forgotten that when we were students at the circus institute she and I, homeless castaways, would seek out places to slake ourselves with one another. We were so desperate we'd even use the empty kiosks in Gorky Park… You pull out two or three boards, spread a jacket on the grubby, spit-stained floor… Now that's where our acrobatic skills came in handy.

Okay. Give me a moment. Let me have a cigarette… I'm fed up with myself. And I got fed up with her, the way only a prisoner in a cell can get fed up with another one.

You know, if I close my eyes, her face comes up on my retina and it always will—till I kick the bucket.

I've already told you how I first saw her, when she was five…

The second time was in the basement at the milk factory billiard club. She used to go there with her father. He was a real sports fan and the daughter got dragged along everywhere—the stadium, the shooting range, the billiard hall. Incidentally, when she asked for a moped for her fifteenth birthday, her father got one, didn't bat an eyelid. A wonderful man, really. And a good doctor. You know, he had military awards and in peace time, too. He was head of a special hospital for infectious diseases, several times he was sent off to fight cholera. To Karakalpakia for example, in 1965, I think it was, and then to Astrakhan Region in 1970. I saw the military awards myself, all those Supreme Soviet commendations. Not to mention that he went to Chernobyl off his own bat, though he wasn't so young by then. That's what killed him, essentially. He was in the zone too long. He was a solid chap, Cossack background. Could have lived to a hundred. Mind you, Anna was sure he died because he missed his wife.

…Anyway, the billiard hall was in the milk factory club in the basement. And we kids used to drop in to watch the games.

That's where I saw her. What a billiard player she was! Incredible! A seven-year-old girl! She could barely see over the edge of the table. She had a funny way of using the cue with her left hand, although she could use the right as well, and of sticking out her lip and she was so accurate it blew the guys away! And I remember those mirrors too: great green eyes above the green billiard table…

I actually got to know her later on when she moved to our school, No. 145, in Grade Seven.

We had this maths teacher, Izolda Sergeevna. She was mean, a real nag…she practically snarled. Face like a nun, I remember, bloodless lips. And the impression that somehow she felt cold in the classroom. She'd call you up to the board and then walk backwards towards the window, chop-chop, and sit herself down on the radiator. She must have been freezing.

Anyway, she called Anna up to the board in her very first lesson. Can you imagine? Well, there's nothing to imagine and we didn't know anything either. It turned out that her father had obtained a note from her old school that she shouldn't be asked to write on the board: She could give a spoken answer or use a piece of paper. But Izolda didn't know that. Either her parents weren't quick enough off the mark or that nun of ours couldn't care less about notes, which also happened. Maybe she called her up to spite her—I wouldn't put it past her—to see what sort of fancy-pants daddy's girl she was with her special treatment.

So she called her up: "Nesterenko, Anna!"

That's when I heard her name for the first time. Already when I'd seen her in class, it was like a grenade exploding in the pit of my stomach. My insides were on fire. She was in the next row to my right and a little bit behind. I didn't dare turn round but the right side of my face was burning like an oven. An-na Nest-eren-ko! An-na Nest-eren-ko! It was like the line of a song.

Izolda said her name again. Her thin eyebrows rose in surprise and she said: "What's the matter, Nesterenko? Is there something wrong with your hearing?"

And let me tell you, even before you'd failed for real, she could scald you with such contempt that you'd feel like an utter piece of shit when you went up to the board.

I turned and there was Anna, as white as chalk, struggling out from behind her desk and dragging herself to the board like she was going to the gallows.

Izolda set her some task—I don't remember what—and Anna stood with her back to the class, not moving. She lifted both her hands like a blind person preparing to feel something horrible in front of them… Finally, she picked the chalk up in her left hand and started to write.

The gasp that swept through the class and died away and the deathly silence that followed—those I do remember… The chalk kept on clattering away. After all, she had a brilliant brain for maths, did Anna. But no one could understand anything from her slanting squiggles. Everyone kept quiet, dumbfounded and intrigued… We could all sense how alien she was, see? As if the shadow of another word had sailed silently by like a ship in the night… No, no, that's not it. I was with Senya once in Las Vegas—we ran into each other by chance in around 1998 and spent a night drinking. He kept going on about the nature of angels. Not literally heavenly angels but people who have greater abilities … who, through a divine oversight, as it were, are given more than an ordinary mortal should be… Depending on how the person handles that burden … how well they bear it, he said … no, I'm talking nonsense whereas he explained it so smoothly, so convincingly… Fine. What was I saying?

Ah, yes. As soon as Izolda Sergeevna sat on that radiator, it was as she were stuck to it. She followed the left hand of this miracle pupil closely, while Anna herself sent the chalk dancing faster and faster across the board.

She finished writing and stood, not turning round, arms down, head down. She recalled later that she'd been scared to turn round.

Suddenly, Izolda said, "Ah-ha… I thought as much."

She turned to the class and asked, "Class, does anyone know what Leonardo's handwriting is?"

Silence.

Izolda smiled, wrapped her chilly self in her thick cardigan and then off she went for almost the entire lesson.

She started to explain that it was a kind of handwriting some people, left handers, had that was also called "mirror writing" because you could only read what they'd written in a mirror. And that the great artist and inventor Leonardo da Vinci had used it in his sketches and drawings. It used to be thought that the world's most famous left-hander had been putting his brilliant inventions into code but nowadays some scientists—psychologists and physiologists—disagreed. They claimed it was his natural handwriting and down to the way the brain is configured in left-handed people. The term "Leonardo's handwriting" had even appeared in psychology to mean not just mirror writing but a whole host of differences in these unique people. As our new student, Anna Nesterenko, had just shown us. "Sit down, Anya. No mistakes. Full marks."

Anna just stood in the same position and you could see the chalk trembling in her left hand.

Well, we all pestered her at break time, everyone running over with a bit of paper and asking her to write something in "Leonardo's handwriting". And she did, for everyone. She was so happy.

After that, she and Izolda were the best of friends until she left school. That was when she was thick as thieves with that nutjob genius, Eliezer, who was drumming all his university textbooks into her for some reason. Be that as it may but even Izolda's mouth dropped open sometimes and she would ask—"And where did you learn that?"

And that's what I'm saying. She had a passion for numbers. And great abilities in maths… And everything in her life could have been different if not for … if not for that special feature… Those abilities that were more than one person needs to be happy.

What else can I tell you? How I trotted around after her for two years? Hanging round the skating rink at the Central Stadium in the evenings in winter—matches were played on the lower field and they turned the upper one to ice. They blasted out music for days at a time … the tango beat of "The Girl in Our Yard," Kola Belda's "I'll carry you off into the tundra, you and you alone." And I would wait for hours for her to show up on her skates in her fluffy green hat and her boy's jacket. And I was able to go a couple of times round the ice with her.

That moment when she took her glove off, tucked it in her belt and put her hot little hand in your icy mitt…

It was for her sake that I took up wrestling and spent a whole year boxing so as to fight off or kill anyone who might attack her… It's frightening to remember how I loved her, you know. What a torment and disaster it was. Utter physical exhaustion…

I remember once at the beginning of June before the Grade Eight exams, waiting for her on a bench near the university. She used to spend hours there in the library with that blessed fool, Eliezer. He might not have been of this world but he could call in some amazing favours at all the libraries. There I am, sitting and watching the end of the avenue where she was meant to appear. It was death-to-allergy-sufferers time, flowering poplars, the curse of the city. The fluff was swirling about everywhere, sticky, cobwebby, whole blankets of it flying about, like in a dream…

I spied on her everywhere: from one tram to the next, hung around the sheds for hours—it was easy to keep an eye on the entrance to her building from there. In the end, I lay in wait for her. I'd decided I was going to tell her everything that day. Declare my feelings. Just say that I'd kill… And when I decided I'd tell her everything, I hadn't eaten for two days, can you believe it? Not even a bit of bread. I was shaking like a leaf.

And then at last she appeared at the end of the avenue. And she was walking, walking so smoothly, her sandals parting great pools of poplar fluff. And suddenly, hunger and terror made it seem as if she was walking on air… on clouds. Can you imagine? And as I was sitting there, I fell off the bench in a dead faint.

That's how much I loved her.

What? Later—what? Later I beat her up. I put everything I had into that as well… About ten years later. And she never even whimpered but after every blow she spat the blood out and asked pitifully, "Does it hurt, Volodya? Does it?" While she could still talk, while she was still conscious. She kept on saying, "Does it hurt, Volodechka?"

"Hi, George, hello! I didn't know you were back. How was London? Everything go well? I'm good, thanks. This here's my friend, Robert. And this is George. Good to see you, old man. We'll talk on the phone. Cheers!"

… My French is awful… And my Russian's no better. You don't mind me introducing you as a friend, do you? I couldn't very well say—this is an Interpol investigator, I'm helping him with his inquiries… Okay, not "inquiries" … fine. Just a chat. Incidentally, I always used to get them mixed up, which was George and which was Roger. They're twins. One's gay. The other's normal … straight, as they say here. They both work for the Cirque de la Lune. Roger's a trapeze artist and George is in casting. The administrator's lover… When you think they're into the same things we are, you can't help it, it makes you crazy.

Mind you, it's entirely possible that I would never have told her my feelings at all. We'd have finished school, gone our separate ways. I'd have got over it, like most young men in love do. Just think, my life would have been completely different, completely! Life without her. It's strange even to think about it…

It's just that in the end she chose me. Not chose, exactly, but showed me: You're mine now.

It was in Grade Nine at the end of May, just before the holidays. The end of the year, you know, when everyone's already thinking about summer. After a sports lesson, we'd all rushed off to the changing room. I was the only one left in the gym. It was such a bright day, everything flooded with light, squares of sun shining from the enormous windows onto the painted wooden floor. I was sitting on a mat in one of those windows of sun, hugging my knees. Feeling melancholy. Suddenly, there she was in the doorway. Maybe she'd forgotten something or finally noticed me all of a sudden… Or some other fancy had come over her. I never knew what motivated her.

She came up to me, closer and closer, so that her round knees were in front of my face… I sat there like a complete idiot, almost screwing my face up. I was scared to look up at her. And suddenly she grabs me by the ears with both hands and yanks me up. I jumped up as if I'd been stung. She gave me a big hug, like a boy. Can you imagine? I stood there, driven crazy by my pounding heart, and clutched at her like a child on the edge of a precipice, frightened to let go. And we must have stayed like that for five minutes in the square of sunshine on the floor, holding each other really close, like brother and sister…

So, what else did you want to ask me? Only, if you'll excuse me, I'll be back in a minute. It's the beer…

…Right, sorry, when I was taking a piss, I remembered us running in different directions in a cornfield on the outskirts of Zhmerinka…We'd done the wall of death so many times on our motorbikes in the course of the day that in the evening we made our way out into the countryside and collapsed in a heap. We just lay there, looking up at the starry sky

… a wall of corn surrounding us, the stars in the black sky above our heads like a room full of electric light bulbs. That's where the watchman waylaid us, Panas Redko, and until we moved on, he would come along every evening and tell us stories. He was a small, stumpy guy in a padded jacket and trousers—in all that heat—with a double-barrelled gun over his shoulder and a cute little dog so unlike a guard dog to look at and by nature that it was strange the field hadn't been emptied from under them.

You don't know what the wall of death is? It's a motorcycle ride. Like a gigantic wooden barrel, four metres high, with a dome made of dirty tarpaulin as pointed as the tent of the Shemakhan Tsaritsa. A viewing gallery runs round it on the inside. They used to have them at the fairs. They weren't run by the circus but by another lot—SoyuzAttraction.

The Soviet circus only ever had one motorcycle trick and that was a long time ago: the Globe of Death. It was performed by the Mayatskys, husband, wife and daughter. It was very heavy to transport, not cost-effective, so they stopped doing it, just ignored any requests…

Plus, there's no real action when the riders are racing around in a ball up under the big tent like rats on a wheel and you're down below, sitting comfortably, looking in at them from outside. Whereas the sensations are completely different inside the wall of death, when you're being shaken and bounced around, your heart in your mouth, and the entire structure is rocking and swaying and the rider's about to fly right out over the wall. Incidentally, American circuses do lots of these stunts. They work in families, setting the equipment up, dismantling it fairly quickly and moving it around on their own trailers.

And SoyuzAttraction ran it at a great profit too.

Anyway, here's how things started between us. In Grade Nine Anna had already been all over Kiev on her moped. Khristina had made her a cool little jacket out of her father's leather one. He brought some men's boots back from Mongolia for her, made of real top-quality leather and she bought goggles from the sports section of the department store. How she used to race around, honestly! Like a foreign movie. Do you remember the motorcyclist in Fellini's "Amarcord?" So what was I supposed to do? I couldn't follow her around on foot. For a few months, I unloaded vegetable lorries at the Fridman Grocery Store after school. I was a strong kid. And by the spring, I'd earned enough to get myself a moped too. To stop my dear old Dad selling it for drink, I kept it in the Girshoviches' shed. Anna was friends with their daughter, Arisha.

Hang on—although you might have heard—she played here not long ago: Irene Girshovich, the famous bell-ringer. She performs in churches and cathedrals. You haven't come across her? You know, it's really powerful. It reduces you to tears. In general, I've no ear for music. As long as it's got a good rhythm. But it's funny, the way this had me in tears. Maybe because it was Arisha, Anna's friend, and then the bells are so heartrending … the voice of heaven, scary even. As if you're being asked straight out, "Worm, do you realize what you had and what you've lost?"

They were neighbours, basically, all on Zhilyanskaya Street. Anna spent more time at their place than she did at home. Her mum had gone off her rocker by then in any case. That was over mirrors as well. She felt as if some kind of spell was being cast on her from inside the mirror. As if, and I can't lie, someone from the mirror had replaced her daughter. Superstitious bollocks, essentially. But that's another story.

Anyway, the flat Anna lived in—and it was a luxurious communal flat, the kitchen alone was about forty square metres—was also home to an old lady, Panna Ivanna. She was a colourful old girl, an ex-circus star, right back in the 1700s probably, and pretty loopy. She was a smoker herself and graciously allowed other people—even the kids, practically—to blacken their lungs in her presence. But she couldn't be doing with cigarette butts. You'd hardly finish smoking and be just about to stub the butt out in the ashtray and she'd be: "Now, then, remove that little corpse!" That's what she called cigarette butts. Hmm. And she wrote poetry on all sorts of domestic issues. Related to sanitation, mainly. You'd go to their toilet and there'd be a small handwritten poster over the cistern:

"Citizens, the cleaner's job is not an easy one,
So when you do a number two be careful where it's gone."

Anyway, Anna had me on a tight rein, walking to heel. In winter it was skating on Trukhanov Island. You'd go to Hydropark Metro Station and there would be skis rattling, shouts of "Hey, man, you nearly took my eye out with those poles!" In summer we took the mopeds and went swimming, again on Trukhanov Island. And what a view you had from there—from the domes of St Andrew's as far as the Kiev-Pechersk Lavra. And the smell—a blend of grass and river water. Indescribable!

Anna and Arisha were like sisters, glued at the hip. Such a close friendship! So I used to sit in their kitchen and smoke as well...

And now the last school holidays were almost upon us. There we were with Arisha and her blind Grandma in the kitchen. And she was another astonishing old lady—I'll tell you at some point if we have a minute. Suddenly, Panna Ivanna comes out of her room and says, "You, youngsters, what do you think about earning a few kopeks?" She has a friend who runs a motorcycle trick show out in the sticks, she says, him and his wife. But his wife just happens to be pregnant at the moment so she's keeping off the bikes. So, she says, why shouldn't Anna take her place doing the wall of death over the summer? It wouldn't be hard to get up to speed. A week practising, two at the most. They're raking it in right now, she says. It's a shame to lose the chance. Anna jumped at it. She always loved diving into any crazy schemes. What about me? I was hers, utterly and completely.

That's how come we ran away from home for the first time. At least she left her father a note on that occasion. I remember it really well.

Anna wrote it with her right hand. It was so funny with its round childish cursive letters: "Daddy! Don't worry, I am always with you."

So what can I tell you? Our first summer together...

"Roman and Irina Kupchy—the Fantastic Fliers!" They even had posters, proper eye-catching ones. Mind you, if there had been any surprise checks, we'd have been in real trouble, Roma especially. Sixteen-year-old kids, no insurance. Come on! No one was in the least bit bothered. We couldn't give a toss. I do think now sometimes, what a crazy country we lived in. Defies description!

It was a bizarre sort of business, that I can say. New spectators were admitted to the wall of death every half hour. We sold and checked the tickets ourselves then got changed behind a curtain into helmets, protective clothing... And off we went, setting the whole province roaring. A couple of tight circles on the ground, then along the mobile circular track, then higher, higher, higher, we'd steer our birds' flight. The main thing was not to lose your mark, to keep your eye on the broad white line whitewashed onto the boards.

What does it feel like? Okay, you know, the vibration isn't a problem. You're pressed towards the wall in a way that makes your body many times heavier. It only seemed as if we were flying like birds. When you're doing 60 on the wall, it whips up such a vortex that your cheeks fill out like sails and your guts twist into a real corkscrew. The audience was thrilled and howled like the bikes. Anna and I swapped places. That Roma now, he was one tough guy. There we were clattering around on Russian Izhes while he had a BMW, war-loot. They last forever. They look simple enough but the mechanics are fantastic. The engine's like a car's, a proper one but with just one cylinder… Roma was a real ace. He could ride sitting down, side-saddle, back-to-front, even standing up.

And so as not to get the slightest bit dizzy, he'd hit the bottle first thing in the morning so that by evening the ride had a strong whiff of alcohol as well as exhaust fumes.

And the weather we had that summer! Dry and hot… We bought sleeping bags at the sports shop in Vinnitsa and spent the night as far away as we could—in the forest or the countryside…The yellow corn, the green grass, the black sky with its cut-glass stars…

Well, obviously, you understand, that's when it all happened between us…

We were both sixteen. You can imagine the tornado that swept through the long-suffering field that had been entrusted to Panas Redko's care.

When he first came across us… Or rather, his little dog was first, jumping onto our sleeping bag with a bark of delight, then someone's hand moved aside the stalks of corn and a kind face with a moustache appeared, with two barrels behind one ear. He gave a shout of surprise, "Guys! What's the heck's going on?" He took Anna for a boy to start with. I'd chopped her gorgeous hair off almost at the roots before the whole motorcycle epic so that there was no way she'd get lice and it couldn't get caught up in anything on the wall. We chatted… And you know, he grew really attached to us. He'd come and see us every blessed evening. He knew so many fairy stories, anecdotes, parables and horror stories that Gogol must have been turning in his grave. And at night, all the scents of summer came together. We had dogs fussing in the distance as a musical accompaniment, cicadas whirring loudly and, all of a sudden, the hoot of an owl from the forest. What a sound! As Pushkin said, "tranquil is the Ukrainian night." And everything written about it is absolutely true.

So there was our Panas Yagorovich with his tall tales…

He said his grandfather had worked for a Polish landlord. For some reason all his stories involved the Poles. He had such a drawn out way of talking: "He-ere co-omes his lo-ordshi-ip on his ho-orse." And there were so many evil creatures in his stories. It was dreadful. He'd go off and we'd relax and there would be something moving, racing across the sky and among the stars until daybreak: a comet or a shooting star or a witch sailing along like Baba Yaga...

Youth, in other words. There was nothing we couldn't do. We even managed to go swimming in the River Bug. We had this secret place, a steep shore with a gnarled and crooked pine tree right on the edge. Some kind soul had fixed a rope swing to a stout lower branch. You grabbed it in both hands, took a run backwards then another forwards, then flew out almost to the middle of the river or however far the rope reached. I can still see Anna flying, light as a feather. She lets go and falls. I'm standing above the water, trying to see where she'll come out. The seconds go by … more and more … my heart's in my mouth. Then suddenly, up she pops, right next to the shore!

What a summer that was—freedom, flying up into the sky, and motorcycles.

...Even so, we finished school. And with pretty good grades too. We could have gone on to a decent university. Ultimately, that goofball Eliezer, the armchair genius, could have got her obsessed with optometrics of some kind… But he'd emigrated to America by then. You know, the wave of Jewish emigration at the end of the 1970s. They said his brother took him away. They lived together, he and his brother.

They were twins, too, but very strange ones. The brother was an albino.

Imagine: the same face but with completely white hair, eyebrows, eyelashes… When they stood next to one another, it blew your mind. Only unlike Eliezer, the *bruder* was normal, a really tight-lipped, humourless individual, very stern.

He was an architect at some institute or other, designing something to do with livestock. Eliezer did everything he said, obeyed him in everything as if he were his son rather than his twin. Anna and I would often be at their place, drinking tea, enjoying a lively conversation, arguing. She and Eliezer were always arguing about something I didn't understand. You'd sit between them blinking. It was like a maths or physics conference: "invisible vacuums," "the mystery of orthopositronium," "bending light beams"… Suddenly, the brother would come in from work and it was like a blast of cold air as if the Holy Inquisition had arrived.

"Elik," he'd say, "you're overwrought. It's time for a rest." And he'd always add this weird phrase, "No chance, it won't fall off." I have no idea what it meant—what was falling off, what "it" was.

And Anna and I would set off for home, good as gold. Perhaps his brother really was looking out for him. After all, not only did her mirror hero have diabetes, he suffered from depression as well. It was a bit much for Kiev back then—a Jew with diabetes and depression. Evidently, his brother thought it would be easier for him in America.

Many years later Anna looked him up, this Eliezer. He was living in Indianapolis, in the back of beyond. She even went to see him. He helped her with the calculations for some projects or other but that was even later again, much later. By then he was living alone, a sad, fat old man in Section Eight housing… He always called Anna, "Nyuta, my angel." He's still alive, I think. The diabetes meant he'd had to have his leg off.

So, where was I?

That summer, she was crazy about getting into circus school and not in Kiev, close to home, but in Moscow. She was always hankering to be somewhere else: to get the hell out, flying, running… Where didn't matter. The main thing was away from here.

And me? I was already hers. Forever…

CHAPTER 10.

She turned up at my hotel room. I opened the door after three separate knocks—the blows of fate, heavy with meaning. The music of doom.

There she stood at the door: *Do you want to see the lovely lady?*

For the first time in my life, I felt how the floor could disappear from under you, when you hadn't touched a drop. And I was furious with myself.

Her eyes were disconcerting even at the most relaxed moments. Their unsettling colour—the transparent green of the shallow sea over grey pebbles gleaming in the crisp morning sun—changed depending on the light and, of course, on those never-ending sweaters in every shade of the sea, which suited her so well. Together with her pinkly swarthy complexion, it created an impression of windswept freshness even when she was straight off her motorcycle, all hot and sticky, forehead shining with sweat.

She was standing in the doorway. I looked at her and I saw everything, absolutely everything, in those awe-inspiring Gorgon eyes. In that split second, the whole of our life flashed by: the endless separations, the unavoidable wayfaring, the planes, trains, motorcycles … roads, cities, motels, concert halls … and some kind of snowstorm, fallen trees, a car in the snow…

The entire whirlwind went spinning past me at an unimaginable pace. Or did she communicate it to me telepathically? Set it all out honestly so that I could be certain it wasn't going to be dull.

And all this was being offered to me in, what the great writers call, my declining years!

I took a step backwards, gesturing to keep her at bay, and said, "No, no. For the love of God!"

She came in and closed the door behind her.

I was playing in an award-winning Leningrad orchestra by then and almost never had to moonlight at the circus although it did happen. It was easy money, evening work with nothing much needing to be spent on rehearsals. Marches, waltzes, foxtrots—it was hardly rocket science.

I had found my way into a circus company completely by chance back in my student days. My friend, Alyoshka, a real whizz on the trombone, dragged me off to see a friend of his, a painter. "He's bedridden," Alyoshka kept saying animatedly. "Just imagine, completely bedridden!" And until we got off the bus on the Petrograd Side and arrived at a typical brick block of flats, I simply couldn't understand why he was talking about a disabled person in such a frivolous tone. All became clear when we went in.

The painter really was lying with a languid air on a sagging couch and didn't raise his head when we arrived. Alyoshka, the trombonist, said in a practised drawl that exactly a year ago Grisha had fulfilled a major commission at the circus and earned a whole heap of money. His entire fee was paid in ten rouble notes. He took them home in a plastic wallet and told his wife he wasn't working until they ran out. All the next day he worked like a slave. He stuck the notes to the walls of the room, like fish scales—he attached a row of them with sticky labels, overlapping slightly, then another row underneath… He pasted them onto all four walls, after which he took up position on the couch for the great lie in. Waking up in the morning, he would gaze lovingly at the crimson scales on the walls and hum pensively:

> "The tender light of morning falls,
> Upon the ancient Kremlin walls."[3]

If a breeze came in through the open window, the walls would shimmer in a murmur of scarlet.

Grisha the painter had lain like this for a year already. The walls looked like the crown of a tree in autumn, with lots of its leaves missing.

He was delighted to see us and yelled, "Irka, go and get some vodka!"

She went over to the wall, carefully tore off a note and left. While we warmed up after the frost, another three people turned up—two sturdy boys and a girl who was just as sinewy and supple. Initially, I thought they were from the Kirov. Later, they turned out to be from the circus. All

---

3   Lines from the song "May Moscow" (Moskva mayskaya) written in 1937.

three were terribly inarticulate. Ballet dancers aren't exactly brain boxes either but all the same… So Alyoshka, the whizz on the trombone, and I found ourselves surrounded by pumped up muscles, crude swearing and light, extremely flexible morals. And we were both happy to dive into the whole shebang. It didn't pay much but it was better than nothing when we were students. And then later, even when I was playing with decent orchestras, I would still drop in on the circus every now and then.

I was drawn to that universe with its procession of indescribable faces, its strongmen and clowns, acrobats, conjurors, trainers and their animals, beautiful muscular bodies, as well as the wigs and false noses. And its fateful inability to live any other way. They had a carefree resilient strength, a charming insouciance. It was a festival of forgotten roads, trailers and tents … of unobtrusive ordinary love.

Basically, I had a pretty good knowledge of the circus and its denizens, was friends with a few of them, drank with a great many and the number I sat and listened to were enough to fill a dozen novels.

Circus people are animals really, people of the body. Close-knit as a pack of macaques and fearful, they are afraid of the world, trust only their own. There's a reason they live and work in families, whole generations. And they don't accept outsiders willingly. The circus is their natural habitat.

It wasn't long before I was surprised to discover a major paradox: The majority of circus people are lazy and not accustomed to systematic work. The excess of free time in their lives corrupts. An hour and a half's rehearsal and that only when an act needs some work. (Except for the jugglers who rehearse for twelve hours at a time. I knew one who practised even on the toilet.)

Comparing them to athletes, circus people may be likened to sprinters. When the pressure's on, they can spend days constantly at work, swinging from bars, setting up equipment, building new props, sewing costumes. They go all out in the evenings for the audience and hit the bottle afterwards to release the tension. On the whole, the circus community drinks like crazy, mainly beer and fortified wine.

Kim Devyatkin, a famous clown in his day, would have his first tipple at the crack of dawn the minute the drinking den opened. He held the old Agdam port wine in particular esteem. He could easily put away five bottles before an evening performance so that he was working on autopilot. He carefully kept his reprises exactly the same throughout his working life. He worked with a little dog called Manyuna for forty years, like Karandash and Klyaksa. It goes without saying that Manyunya would occasionally go to a better place but would appear in her next incarnation almost immediately. He had no desire to create or rehearse new acts. He regarded any creative effort as folly. His main challenge was not to confuse the main arena entrance with the side access at the end of his piece, not to trot off along the wrong one. His wife, Ninochka, acted as a steer, keeping her beady eye on him, standing like a watchful siren at the main entrance, calling loudly from behind the curtain: "Over here, Kimmie, darling, over here," while he walked towards the sound of her much-loved voice.

I can remember one acrobat, a confirmed sot. He would do three flips on stilts off a springboard.

"Pasha, how come you pack away so much vodka?" people asked. "How will you perform tomorrow?"

"It's like this," he explained, "the ground flashes past once, the ground flashes past twice … third time round and I steady up again."

They spent the whole of their day off horizontal, of course. And there were no holds barred after the final performance, making it clear that there would be no technicians for about three days…

The language they used among themselves was ninety per cent swearing while the remaining ten per cent consisted of verbs and nouns: "Did a handstand." Circus children are usually said to be "born in sawdust" but they themselves said that they "came out of the ring dirt" and I liked that: like coming out of Gogol's "Overcoat." I remember the trapeze artist, Doveyko, yelling at someone in the ring during a rehearsal: "I was doing this when you were still rolling around in the dirt on the ring floor!"

The "circus" as an all-encompassing concept embraced all their concerns, excitement and intrigues. All their conversations centred on the circus, all their jokes and teasing. They mocked the people on the ground—the ones who were always down below, the conjurors, clowns, comedy musicians and small-animal trainers.

The trapeze artists, acrobats and tightrope walkers, the thrill acts in other words, were regarded as the circus elite.

And they were all horribly uneducated and poor.

Among performers, circus people were the poorest of the poor. They lived like gypsies, easily adapting to any circumstances. They lived in camps, that is, in families, in buildings that went by the name of hotels or hostels where they cooked on plug-in hotplates. I ate with them many times after shows. Everyone would bring something from their room for a potluck meal. It might be potatoes fried on the hot-plate.

Because they were so poor, they all fought furiously to travel abroad. Foreign tours were the only opportunity to earn decent money. As it was for musicians, essentially. I can remember the conductor, Mravinsky, shouting in rehearsals, "I know, you just want to keep the family in bread and dripping." It was a euphemism, of course. They would bring back clothes, sell them on the black market… In other words, the "family" got its bread and dripping from those foreign tours.

People brought back what they could. There were some who brought in five hundred pairs of tights a time.

The circus people used to hide their smuggled goods in containers or in the lion and bear cages. Who's going to put their head in there? A customs officer? He's quite happy with his head where it is, thank you.

I had a fling with an aerial gymnast once. To be fair, the big time was already behind her. She worked on the trapeze, stood on her head on the swing. It was weighted and slow. She was blonde with statuesque shoulders, shapely, slightly sagging legs and a special gait that brought to mind a pacing horse. All this passed for beauty. She didn't miss a single circus hand. Sitting at the shared table, hungover, she would languidly place her foot one minute on a chair, another on the table, flex, bend forward and caress an instep or a calf as if stroking the neck of a horse. She used to sigh and say, "I'd rather be in the big top. It's safer there."

Suffice it to say that when the three knocks of Fate sounded in my life, not a single person from the business known as the Circus could have ignited a single romantic spark in me.

And I would have sent the girl packing with a slap on the rear had it not been for that long-ago evening in a Kiev flat; had it not been for the noise and cavorting, the uproar and stamping of that funny little girl and, between the pranks, the date of my birth being stated correctly. And why hide it? If it hadn't been for the strange shiver and heaviness that spread through my whole body the minute the knock came.

Incidentally, I'd seen their act the day before, the famous one using a board. If I'm going to be completely honest with myself that was why I'd postponed my trip to Leningrad by a day. I simply turned up for the evening performance.

It was a really romantic and effective number. And the music was well chosen—a track by the group Space, delicate, undulating swells, ethereal, moonlike.

In pitch darkness, follow-spot beams criss-crossed to light up a male figure in a white satin body stocking. He went to the middle of the wire, holding a board rather than a balance pole. It was about six metres long. He lowered it onto the wire and balanced it a touch with his feet. From platforms at each end, two slight female figures descended, stepping lightly and balancing with fans. Then they came together.

In as much as I understand these things, it was very complicated for the women to step onto the board with the right foot and to move the left leg at the same time. It took synchronization not to tip the balance one way or the other, to calculate how far along to place one leg, when to move the other and how to rule out any potential swing... It demanded incredible artistry from all three, in short.

Both girls began to take small, sliding sidesteps out to opposite ends of the board. It was visibly sagging and vibrating. The follow spots moved in pairs over both performers. Each one's whole body was illuminated by beams of red and green. And so they moved out to the ends and at the very tip of the board—and this was particularly striking—they dangled a foot over the void and then, as the audience gasped, went back onto the board. Both turned to face the centre at the same time and froze in a lunge pose. The audience broke into tumultuous applause.

At that point, the male performer left the wire. Two solitary figures remained at the ends of the board.

A mirror ball was brought in, casting flecks of white light around the auditorium as if snow had begun to fall slowly. To the audience's surprise, one end of the board began to go down. The girls began to rock it up and down. It was quite spectacular: a long seesaw hanging in a snowstorm, ten metres off the floor, and two slight figures balanced on the ends in the beams of the spotlights, their movement increasingly risky in the crazy spin of the mirror ball.

The audience was going wild already.

But I had eyes for one performer only. The other was a fine gymnast, an excellent professional gymnast with a magnificent and very feminine figure. But the one I couldn't take my eyes off was swooping like a swift. She was born of a slow snowstorm, of a flight to the moon, and I felt that had she slipped and fallen from the wire, she would simply have continued to soar up into the rigging, descend slowly almost to the ring floor and then fly up again...

I didn't stay to the end of the applause, to watch the congratulations and other transports of delight offered by a grateful public. I wiped my sweaty palms on a handkerchief and went out into the fresh air. I made up my mind to stop being an idiot and to go to Saint Petersburg that very evening.

And so, I had already packed my travel bag. She knocked and came in, still looking like a teenager, contemptuously dislodging me from my near hysterics: "No, no. Not in a million years."

I think she said that from now on we belonged to one another—some sordid cliché of the kind.

I asked if she was out of her mind, a mere girl, a snot-nosed child. "You do realize how much older than you I am?" I asked sternly.

"Hush," she replied. "I don't care."

I said, "No, come on. Excuse me but I'm not a paedophile. I love mature women, you know, full breasts, sagging rear, solid thighs and to go with them…"

Without a word, she shoved me in the chest with all her strength and dived onto me the way people throw themselves off a bridge and into a river. We fell to the floor and a powerful current bore us ruthlessly, implacably away, twisting and turning like twigs.

From that moment on … ah, yes: "*the effort of the calf, the quivering of the torso, rotating round its axis start a flight such as the soul has yearned for.*"[4] From that moment on—isn't that what the classic novels say?—"My fate was sealed."

---

4   From "The Classical Ballet" ["For Mikhail Baryshnikov"] in *A Part of Speech* by Joseph Brodsky, tr. by Alan Myers with the author. New York: Farrar, Straus and Giroux, 1980, p. 77.

CHAPTER 11.

The onset of Masha's illness was sudden and strange. She had gone to the television centre to accompany a balalaika ensemble from the music school. There, in the foyer, she went into the lift with a nondescript woman, turned to face the wall and, out of the blue, felt that if she looked back she would see that the woman had fangs.

Masha snatched her compact out of her bag and captured the woman's insipid face in its mirror. She was running an indifferent gaze over the wall in lacklustre fashion. What was unutterably sinister, however, was that there was someone in the mirror behind her, with her back to Masha and holding a mirror and that the number of these backs and faces went on and on, funnelling down into the compact and vanishing into its brass frame. It almost made her faint.

The lift stopped. Masha emerged, her legs weak, and repelled the hideous illusion by sheer willpower. By lunchtime, she'd forgotten all about it.

Three weeks later, she and Anatoly went to a concert by the French radio orchestra, conducted by Cluytens (a highly unusual programme, including symphonies by Lalo, for instance) and as she was washing her hands in the ladies' room of the Ukraina Film and Concert Hall, which had mirrors fitted all the way around, she looked up and saw the back of a woman washing her hands in the mirror behind her own reflection. In front of that woman, further away and off to the left, *another Masha* was washing her hands. She was quite clearly grinning and even winking at another one, symmetrically opposite her on the right…They were exchanging glances and laughing at *the real Masha* who was immediately taken poorly. Two kindly concertgoers, one of whom fortunately turned out to be a nurse at some hospital or other, missed fifteen minutes of the second part of the concert to bring Masha round. Tolya, meanwhile, had begun to worry in the auditorium to start with and had then rushed around the foyer, not knowing what on earth to think.

After which it was no longer possible to keep the whole revolting nonsense from him.

Next came Yakov Mironovich Stelkin, a well-known psychiatrist with a two-month waiting list, but, thankfully, this was their world—medics. Tolya rang him at home that same evening and Stelkin—now there's manners and solidarity for you!—was an absolute sweetheart and gave them an appointment straight away, allaying their concerns and urging "rest and recuperation."

Masha perked up. She went for walks with Tolya in the city centre. They wandered along Kreshchatik—it's not often you get the chance just to go for a walk!—popped into a department store and bought Masha a charming "vintage" hat in a 1920s style with a wisp of a veil. It was astonishing how well the veil suited Masha, the spitting image of Mary Pickford. What a shame she didn't want to see herself in the round mirror on the counter.

Afterwards, they sat in the Grotto Café and each had vanilla ice-cream. They remembered that it was in this area many moons ago that Tolya had proposed to Masha in the shabby little Druzhba cinema, so nervous he made a complete hash of it, crushing her hand and muttering, "Please, allow me to declare my love!"

And now here he was eating ice-cream and exclaiming over and over again, "Madam Nesterenko, please allow me…"

Mashuta even managed a couple of smiles.

They hadn't talked about Nyuta at all in recent weeks. Masha had forbidden it. Tolya tried to put in a good word for their daughter. He recalled his own eagerness to leave Mariupol for work when he was young, going as far as the White Sea to join a biological research station. "And it was fine, Mashuta, you see. It all worked out. None of us went to the bad." She cut him off with such an agonized twist of her mouth that she seemed to be choking back a gut-wrenching howl. He fell silent immediately. And what could he say? A chap at a biological station and a girl, burning circles on a fairground wall of death on a motorbike, surrounded by drunken men, were very different matters. The main thing was not to think about where she was tearing around at all, my motorbike angel…

… When they climbed the stairs to their door and Tolya switched on the light in the hall as usual, revealing a slight, rather stooping stranger in the mirror wearing an antiquated black porkpie hat, Masha staggered back and sank to the floor with an anguished sob. "Take it away! Take it away!" The hat fell off and rolled into a corner, a comical, black, runaway bun.

Tolya grasped his wife under the arms, dragged her into the bedroom, got her undressed and attempted to soothe her. Then he spent a long time removing old nails from the wall with a pair of pliers and swearing. He took the heavy antique mirror in its carved oval frame down and turned it to face the wall in the pantry. "Damn it, it's like having a body in the house!"

As for valocordin, valerian and other attempts at shutting the stable door, the requisite medication was lacking in a house where no one had ever been ill. There weren't even any strong sleeping pills and why should there be? They managed to make it through to the morning, whereupon Tolya took Masha in a taxi to the famous Pavlov Psychiatric Hospital in Kurenyovka, where he stayed with her until the evening.

***

That night, Nyuta had one of the worst nightmares of her life: a dishevelled Mashuta, her face swollen and unfamiliar, was smashing mirrors.

The tall institutional mirrors, set into walls, splintered with a quiet crack, a mass of curved wounds coiling away. Mashuta ran barefoot from one mirror to the next, sobbing silently and striking out to right and left with the heels of the shoes she was clutching in both hands.

Worst of all, however, was that, at one and the same time, these were the inner *mirrors* that reflected the world her daughter lived in and, with each blow and each sob from the exultant, unhinged Mashuta, this fragile world splintered into bloody cracks.

Nyuta struggled to come round.

She lay spread-eagled, as if broken, too weak to move. She tried to work out why. She sought, like a blind man, to feel her way out from beneath a whole heap of slivers. The impenetrable sky lay above her like the school blackboard. Eventually, it rippled with the green weeds of dawn. With an immense effort of will, Nyuta shot out of bed.

"Where're you going?" Volodka asked sleepily.

She said nothing, stuffing her things into a rucksack. Her body ached, her head was splitting with a shooting pain but, most importantly, the *mirrors* had been extinguished, the *mirrors* had all been smashed. And it would take a long time now, an excruciatingly long time—weeks—for them to build up a thin coating layer by layer, a film, a reflected lustre, a vibrating light...

She *couldn't see* anything just then. It was simply instinct that told her something terrible had happened to Mashuta.

In a thick, stricken voice she said, "Home, Volodya. I've got to go home. Something's wrong."

"How d'you know?" he said, taken aback. He wasn't used to it yet, hadn't felt the abyss sway beneath her feet. She kept her gaze on him: the pale crew cut, his face discomfited and childish with sleep, his lips black from the previous day's bilberries. My poor dear.

On my own, she thought hopelessly. Don't get him involved. You're meant to be on your own.

Quietly she murmured, "I just do."

***

Cruelly, Masha and Anatoly's old life followed them *along every new path* that they took. Masha had taken Anatoly to Saint Kirill's Church on the hospital's premises on their very first date to show him Vrubel's contributions to the iconostasis. She had explained that the icon of the Mother of God, with its piteous unorthodox expression, had been based on a woman called Emilia, another man's wife, with whom Vrubel had been secretly in love. And Tolya had looked at it seriously, taken it *personally*, and then said that, for the man who loves, his woman is always the Mother of God. In response to which, Masha promptly fell unreservedly in love with him for the rest of her life.

He didn't send his daughter a telegram. Where was he supposed to send it? To the village, to the wall of death?

That evening, however, as he was walking home from the hospital from Vladimirskaya Street, years of habit made him look up and he suddenly saw that the light was on in the kitchen window and he gasped and took the stairs at a young man's speed.

The hall was lit up too, unseeing and unhearing now, a great blind space left by the mirror.

Nyuta came out of the kitchen and stood in the doorway, keeping her distance.

She was lovely—tanned and slim, her short, still curly hair dark gold from the sun, splashes of the river in her bright eyes. She smelled of the fresh, healthy outdoors, of swimming in the River Bug, of all the grains, fruit and freedom of the Ukrainian summer.

Sinking heavily down onto the old settee with its threadbare cherry-coloured velvet, his eyes fixed firmly on his daughter, Anatoly said dully, "It's bad, Nyuta..." And he wondered sadly why he bothered. After all, she…

"I know, Daddy," she said calmly. She went over and held his head, folding him to her breast. And Anatoly couldn't help it, he broke down and sobbed. He sobbed for the first time in his life, not in the least bit embarrassed by his daughter's presence.

Later, when they were drinking tea in the kitchen, he said quietly, "Nyuta, how can we change our life?"

Looking him in the eye, his daughter replied, "It's already changed, Daddy. There's nothing you can do about it. But don't torture yourself. Mashuta will be back. In about five weeks."

And indeed a month and a half later Grade Six pupils at the music school were listening to a new and brittly calm Masha dictate the main dates in the life of Franz Liszt, the brilliant Hungarian composer, whose daughter Cosima was famous because, when she married Richard Wagner…

Only now the mirror was in the pantry, its secret ocean depths plashing against the blank wall.

PART THREE

…but only the Gods have put a veto on the adventures of our minds. If They do not choose to intervene, we are condemned to fashion our own laws or to wander in fright through the pathless wastes of our terrifying liberty, seeking even the reassurance of a barred gate or of a forbidding wall.

Thornton Wilder, *The Ides of March*

CHAPTER 12.

A sticky pink lollipop shaped like a cockerel and wrapped in the silver foil of an Alyonka chocolate bar lay on the kitchen window sill in the student hostel.

The cockerel was collectively-owned.

Students at the circus school used it to accompany their drinks or, to be more precise, to mask the flavour of fortified wine. They would lick it once or twice then wrap it carefully in the foil until the next drinking session. It sometimes seemed as if it had been there for ten years already, as if the golden cockerel had raised several circus generations.

In fact, you could be expelled for drinking if you were caught. Every now and then, an inspection commission combed the hostel. Two or three teachers stomped, quick march, through the rooms every once in a while, peering into every nook and cranny, inspecting cooking pots—just like the Gestapo. The offenders from the floor above, the men's floor, grabbed their bottles and hopped out of the ground-floor window of the room Anna shared with two other girls.

It was a corner room, the last on the corridor, and therein lay its advantage. Better still, a good sturdy pipe ran across the front of the building next to the window so that the ventilation pane made it possible to dive into the hostel and to dive out again just as stealthily.

In the evenings, it became a public thoroughfare. The girls even stopped bothering to lock the doors so that there was no need to wake them up. In or out, that's your business, just sneak through quietly. Let people sleep. Classes start early tomorrow.

Incidentally, there were "friends" on the teaching staff as well, former circus performers.

The morality commission showed up once and the students dashed for the precious escape hatch. Five or six people spilled silently and nimbly—they do teach something in our grand old institute, after all—out of the ventilation pane one after the other. Finally, the last one slithered out like an eel and landed softly on the ground.

Anna went over to the window to open the ventilation pane and froze. Someone had stirred in the black shadow of a tall poplar in the courtyard and the elderly juggling teacher, Firs Petrovich Zemtsev, emerged, limping, into the glow of a street lamp. He walked over to the window, shook his head and said softly with a grin, "Oh, Nesterenko, Nesterenko, you silly, silly girl." Clearly, he had been silently observing the emergency evacuation. He didn't let on to a soul.

As for the drinking sessions, what did they amount to in the main? A student grant of a massive thirty roubles meant fortified wine or the local semi-sweet Lidiya. Anna's top grades earned her a higher grant, a whole thirty-five roubles. Volodka would inevitably fail one or two subjects and then have to beaver away, agonizing over his revision, and resit… The whole process of studying was like plugging holes in the roof with just one bucket: he'd resit Foreign Theatre, only to fail Musical Education; he'd bone up on one subject and forget everything he knew about another. On the other hand, there was never anything wrong when it came to rhythm, dance or his specialist subject.

They used to race off to the canteen at Pravda Publishing House, not far from the school. It offered a decent set meal for just fifty kopecks. Cabbage soup or borscht for starters, then some sort of goulash with the usual Soviet side dish of rubbery macaroni or runny mashed potato. You could have meat patties instead but with goulash it was the gravy that mattered. You could go round the tables, gathering up leftover bread and dunk it in your gravy. Sometimes, they might put out a salad of flaccid cabbage in mayonnaise—so what? It was still vitamins. And there was compote with squishy blobs of over-boiled apples and apricots. In short, it was fine, you got by.

And on the day the grants were paid, if you hadn't run up too many debts, your heart would turn somersaults: you could go to the Kebab House on Neglinka or to the *Field Camp*, inevitably dubbed the "*Feel-up Camp*" by the students.

Nor were you left to starve in the hostel. Either Ninka's parents would send a parcel from Vinnitsa containing a huge block of chocolate filched from the local chocolate factory or Nadezhda would sell some bras on the black market (her sister worked in the Minsk Hosiery Factory and helped her little student sister "in kind").

Or you could all pitch in to buy potatoes and fry them to your heart's content. Or whip up a nice rich soup in an enamel pot, throwing in whatever you came across in everyone's cupboards—like the soldier who made soup from an axe. And the whole of both floors, the men on the first and the women on the ground floor, could pack it away for three days or so. Soup like that would bring the actors running too. The Mikhail Shchepkin Theatre School and its hostels shared the courtyard with the circus school.

The evenings were fun. Ninka, Anna's roommate, was always laughing, telling stories, strumming a seven-stringed guitar. She would tickle the strings playfully and sing loudly to drown out the off notes. "Hang on! Hang on!" she would shout in the middle of a song. "I've remembered a joke. So, a Russian, an Armenian and a Jew are on a boat…"

Then there was the beautiful Latvian, Sandra, who left at the end of the first year. People in the same year said it was "on grounds of disability: terrible dropsy". Dropsy or not, her belly had certainly filled out. It could happen if you weren't careful. You couldn't somersault on the trapeze when you were pregnant. But you might say Sandra was lucky. Her suitor—an outsider, not a circus man—upped and proposed. Even she was taken aback: My, what a responsible young man! And so, right out of the blue, Sandra was officially a Moscow resident.

Some ten years or so later, after a show at the old Solomonsky Circus on Tsvetnoy Boulevard, during the last season before it was closed and knocked down, a buxom blonde with two small boys was to burst into Anna and Volodka's dressing room, dart over to kiss them and utter some words of affection…

What a blast from their youthful past!

And Anna would stand and smile in her dazzling costume, the jewels sparkling on the narrow safety belt around her waist, her curly hair still adorned with luxuriant plumes. And how she would suddenly long to run a hand over those two shaggy heads.

***

Right from the start, however, the building of the State School of Circus and Variety Arts on Fifth Street in Yamskoe Pole, was home.

You hurtled into the foyer, handed in your jacket to the cloakroom, quickly checked the post—Was there a letter from your father? Had Khristina scribbled a postcard?—and hurried on. There was an entrance facing the door, open like the wings of a stage. A corridor ran both left and right behind it, stretching half way around the main ring. This was where graduation acts were rehearsed, run-throughs, examinations and performances held, but both Anna and Volodka had a long way to go before any of those.

The staffroom, canteen, changing room, showers, workroom and dressing room were also on the ground floor.

The first two years studied on the first floor in a large rehearsal room in the "square ring." It was a real ring too, almost like being in the circus. A barrier ran around the whole perimeter at ground level and a soft carpet covered the sawdust on the floor. There was a circular gallery up above. And, then, of course, there was all the equipment needed for classes: bars, rings, the trapeze, a track for the acrobats, a low wire…

The first gymnastics class was embarrassing, humiliating. Anna remembered it all her life. A training trapeze, nothing special, but the wretched twisting thing danced beneath you as if it were alive. You barely moved and it swung in all directions. You stood on it and it tried to jump away from your feet. And the more you tried to subdue it, the less it obeyed. And, of course, it had nothing to do with being scared. The safety regulations meant Anna wore a belt round her waist, attached to a safety line. A thin cable ran upwards from Anna, passed over a block fixed to the ceiling and moved freely on a small wheel. The other end of the cable, which ended in a rope, was held by a teacher below, providing safety back up. It was more often called "stabilizing" and it was a great skill in its own right. Holding the safety line required constantly absorbing the slack to keep it taut. Otherwise, the student could be hurt falling from the trapeze. In absorbing the slack, however, it was important not to pull too hard or you'd simply yank the unfortunate student off the trapeze where she was flapping like a flag on a pole in any case.

The trapeze reminded Anna and Volodka of the rope swing on the Southern Bug. Seemingly out of spite it made her feel as if she could take a run up, grab the rope and be carried right up to the huge window, through it and outside.

Anna's course teacher, Lazurin, stood below. From above, the yellow bald patch in his gypsy curls looked like a coin in grass. He tugged on the line attached to her waist and yelled mockingly, "Look at this one! And she's got dreams of becoming an aerialist! Now then, down you come! What did I say? Let go!"

Anna shut her eyes, gritted her teeth and let go. Her whole body plummeted down and to the left. Whey-hey! She could feel she was hanging by the belt but Lazurin was still pulling her up and down, up and down, like a monkey. Just like she used to spin the luckless toy acrobat on his bar when she was little. There she dangled, sagging like a sack, screwing up her eyes and scared to imagine how embarrassing she looked from the side-lines.

"Right," said Valentin Semyonovich, "you do realize you can't go anywhere? So, now, relax… And stand up… That's it… Hold on… Get the feel of it…"

Valentin Semyonovich was a gloomy hard-bitten man but an excellent teacher, tough and demanding. He was forthright, not standing on ceremony or mincing his words. Sometimes, he could swear like a trooper.

Classes were open to the public, whether you liked it or not, whether you were embarrassed or, quite the reverse, longed to show off. Anyone could come along and watch.

More often than not Volodka hung around in the gallery with the older students against the background of the ever-present Leniniana and beneath a poster of a red hammer and sickle. He worried about her and kept an anxious, predatory look out. He was jealous, poor soul.

Anna sometimes looked back and ran a cursory glance over him. Even from there she could see how strongly built he was, what a fine body he had, how recent months had made his biceps and pectoral muscles stand out. The detached professional attitude of everyone around them to the semi-naked body had come as a surprise, a novelty, to them both.

Once you got to school in the morning, you changed into leotard and leggings and spent the rest of the day in them. There was a mixture of classes from nine in the morning until nine at night so no one changed for lectures. They just sat in their leotards, the gymnasts' uniform. They were already used to one another. When the hot weather came, they went to lectures half-naked.

Even the showers had open cubicles like a military barracks. Self-conscious or not, you still wanted to wash the sweat off after class. Especially when the hostel on Pushechnaya Street had no showers, only a toilet at the end of the corridor.

And you slogged your guts out so much in rehearsals that not only did you not look around in the showers, you couldn't care less who was looking at you either. You sluiced the lather away, felt blindly for a freshly-laundered towel, rubbed yourself down as hard as you could and even groaned: That's how sore your muscles were!

Gymnastics drained all your strength. The skin on your hands split, callouses bled. After classes what you longed for most of all was to crawl back to the hostel and hit the sack. The jugglers had it easy. They went off into a corner and practised like automata. And why wouldn't they? They just stood there, waving their mitts. Although even they found that the rings split their palms open.

It was Lazurin who over the three years worked on every detail of her technique so brilliantly that it never once let her down later on. Leg and arm swings, spins, the flag, heel and toe drops—they all became ingrained in her muscles and tendons, could already be felt in the plasticity of her movements. They became her gait, the position of her shoulders, sometimes even her thoughts.

"A trick, any trick," he used to say, "is safe if you follow the rules. Take the toe drop. Open your legs… Feet in the corners… That's it… Now throw your body back! Great! Well done! The main thing is to turn your ankles so that they're facing outwards and your feet are lodged firmly into the angles of the trapeze and you can just hang there and swing… Got it? It's terrifying to go plummeting down headfirst to start with but you get used to it and then you start to enjoy it!"

And she really did start to enjoy it, not so much on the static as on the flying trapeze.

You swing the five-metre trapeze as high as you can so that at its height it's almost horizontal. Just as the trapeze swings back as far as it can, you let go with your hands and continue the movement with your back, maintaining the same trajectory, gripping the corners with your feet. As you hang there, you stretch out your arms as if you want to embrace the whole world. The trapeze bears you away in a long swing, you hear a gasp and applause and you fly and fly, almost melting into weightlessness…

And your body begs to go still higher and still further as if it wants to pierce the invisible membrane of this world and emerge on the other side, in another, mirror universe…

During that first year, Anna and Volodka raced up onto the "square ring" balcony whenever they had a spare moment. Especially if Tanya Manevich, an aerial gymnast and star of her year, was rehearsing her solo trapeze act.

Lazurin himself thought she was absolutely brilliant. Her slight, slim figure twisted and twined around the trapeze bar, down and up, up and down—neatly and precisely, at an unimaginable speed.

Anna sometimes felt that if Tanya let go right then, she would simply fly around the ring, going higher and higher, then dive abruptly back down and, almost at ground level, soar up to the bar again...

***

There were a great many complex individuals—retired performers—among the teachers. Each one was a separate case, with a particular history and a difficult character and quite astonishing ways of behaving.

Take Klavdiya Ivanovna Mastyrkina, for example.

The school relic, a baobab tree in a sacred grove, essentially. She had been teaching since 1926 when the place was founded. Karandash was one of her graduates. She taught dance. An ageless marzipan fairy, with the thin tuneful voice of a cartoon Snow White, her apple cheeks painted red, wearing flannelette knickers under a kilt. Initially, all the first years simply gawped when Klavdiya Ivanovna, unfazed, raised her leg in a lofty attitude, affording them an intimate display of pastel-blue expanses of flannelette. Then they got used to it and stopped paying it any attention.

For many generations of circus school graduates, Klavdiya Ivanovna's pale blue knickers became practically their most poignant recollection of their alma mater.

It was Elina Yakovlevna Podvorskaya who was the universal favourite, however—called Elka behind her back—a short woman, with a refined line in sarcasm, grey curly hair and a neck like a wrestler's.

She taught History of Foreign Theatre and History of the Circus. She remembered the names and even nicknames of all her ex-students and understood them through and through. For the most part, they were the children of performers: ignoramuses and gypsies, on the road their entire lives. Acrobats who only used their brains because they couldn't eat without them.

Elina Yakovlevna drummed Sophocles and Euripides into them with truly classical tenacity. "I have no desire to turn you into intellectuals," she would say, "I just don't want you to embarrass yourselves if you open your mouths somewhere."

"Five percent!" she would exclaim. "If five percent of what I'm telling you sticks in your thick skulls, I can die happy."

She teased what they had learned out of them, like a tax collector demanding payments on a debt that had to be paid. She insisted that they knew the names of the characters in Shakespeare and tedious Ancient Greek tragedies off by heart. She called them up to the front of the class with a cunning little smile. Addressed everyone formally and the more hopeless and slower thinking a student, the more their mouth creaked from disuse, the weightier and more significant the formality became... Later, on the tangled highways and byways of the circus, Anna occasionally encountered graduates of the school, whose poor vocabulary would shock even a circus horse. But no way would they ever confuse Antigone with Elektra. Thanks to Elka's teaching.

***

At the end of the first year, Anna nearly dropped out of school.

Once, after a rehearsal (Lazurin had been yelling and swearing and a couple of times had given each of her knees a painful thwack as if trying to straighten them out), she stood covered in soap under the listless flow from the rusty shower head. The pain in her spent muscles was sweet as they relaxed from the strain under the hot water.

"Hi, Nesterenko!"

Anna didn't even need to open her eyes to recognize Tanya Manevich's voice. It was low, the "r" and "l" sounds pleasantly mispronounced as if she was sucking on a sugary sweet tucked into her cheek, a small tart "sugawy sweet".

"Well, now, I saw you just now... Pwetty good too. Just ho'd the fwag position. Pwess into your arm and ho'd it... It'll come."

Anna flushed, burbled and dived under the water, trying to hurry up and wash the soap off her face and hair to say thank you and that she always watched open-mouthed when ...

Tanya was standing with her back to Anna by the wooden bench, hanging her leotard on a hook. She was tall, too tall even for a gymnast, her physique flawless. Her long back, exquisitely moulded by years of training, rose from her sculpted buttocks as though from a vase. Tanya took a towel and turned around, ready to step into the next cubicle. It was like Ancient Greece. No need for a museum, just stand and admire. Her breasts in particular, small, muscled, widely spaced like all gymnasts'. Her strong chest impressive with its classical Hellenic relationship to the waist, hips and muscular stomach.

Before Tanya went into the cubicle, Anna hastily towelled her face dry in order to tell at last this stunningly beautiful and generous girl that…

Suddenly, behind the physical solidity of the real live person, she saw another, semi-transparent Tanya Manevich, a shapeless heap on the ring carpet, with open, lifeless eyes. High above the ring, just as lifeless and impassive swayed the empty trapeze, the safety line dangling, broken…

Anna gave an otherworldly scream.

Tanya recoiled, slipped on the wet tiles of the shower and went crashing over sideways…

Anna kept screaming in horror. It was the first time, without her wanting it at all, that *the mirrors had shown her a death*. It was a hard blow, painful as a lash.

Doors banged and several people dashed into the showers.

"What is it? What's going on? Is it a fight?" someone asked from the corridor.

"No, no. Doesn't look like it. P'rhaps, she saw a rat…"

Wrapped in a towel, a perplexed Tanya kept on repeating, "She's mental, crazy… yelling like that for no reason."

Wet, shaking and distraught, Anna kept pushing away people's hands as they tried to cover her, to calm her down, and stammered out an entreaty, "Tanya! The safety line's going to snap. Stay away from the trapeze – forever!"

Some of the girls helped her get dressed. They were already pulling her out of the shower but she dug in her heels and shouted, the trembling undiminished, "Don't go in the ring any more, Tanya! Not ever!"

Eventually, they dragged her away.

"I'm telling you, she's sick," Tanya explained to a friend as she examined a long bleeding graze on her thigh. "It's all vewy well, 'Don't go in the wing.' Where am I supposed to go? To sell ice-cweam in a kiosk? Damn it, I've got an exam in a week. And here I am with this lovely little pwesent."

"P'rhaps she's jealous," marvelled her friend.

…The day Tanya Manevich fell to her death in the "round" ring during the last rehearsal before her final exams, someone remembered what had happened in the showers. Of course, a safety line can just rip if the cable gets tangled and on this occasion the entire cable was virtually in ringlets. But how could she have known in advance?

Anna's name came up repeatedly in every class, in the canteen and even in the staffroom. It was repeated blankly and in shock. Did she know? How could she? They do say she was terribly jealous. No, really? No, don't say anything. It might well be superstition but I know one woman back home in Maleevka… So d'you think the damage was deliberate? Why not? I wouldn't be surprised… Girls, she jinxed her, drove her to her grave!

Volodka raced into the hostel and flew into the room where Anna lay on her bed, face to the wall, while three girls from her year sat around her sympathetically but warily.

"I'll kill them all, I will!" he barked, panting. "Fuck off out of here, the lot of you!"

And when the girls tumbled out, getting wedged in the doorway in their fright, he lay beside Anna, pushed a hand beneath her, encircling her tightly, and pressed up hard against her light, barely conscious body.

He didn't know and didn't want to know whether she *had done it* on purpose or not, whether she'd wanted it to happen or not. He loved her so much that if he'd had to go out and slaughter people for the sake of her peace of mind, he would have done it with fateful and religious zeal.

But no matter how closely they lay together, she knew she was on her own, doomed to be alone to face the appalling abyss in which her *mirrors* swung open, always without warning. She knew that the ruthless force that flattened, pummelled and broke her, revelling in the unequal struggle, would not let its toy go again. That mysterious force was either in abeyance for months at a time or would suddenly send her flying with the flick of a giant snake, bending her, tossing her up in the air and catching her, scalding and torturing her until her mouth stretched wide in a soundless cry, a silent scream for mercy.

She was aware every second of the day now that she was being watched with mocking admiration: Oh, what a sight! What a mess! Run, go on, run … let's take a good look at you, puny human… let's enjoy your flailing, the exertions of your immortal—ha!— soul.

No… No! You can kill me, she said, speaking silently to the unknowable and abhorrent force. You can break me, smash me to smithereens. You can crumble me into dust. But that's all.

You are not to toy with me anymore… You are not to use me as entertainment. No, no way.

***

The circus school cancelled its examinations and graduation shows that year.

Volodka and Anna had a contract for a summer tour to Gorky from an organization called the Moscow Circus on Stage.

Anna had been taken on to be Snow White on skates (in an uncomplicated variety show with slight leanings towards the circus). Volodka, a dwarf with a beard, kept trying to escape from Snow White on a unicycle, peddling frantically. A three-minute comedy routine, kids' stuff acrobatics, undemanding stunts—a fun and easy way to make a living, a summer sinecure.

The administrator of the concert team, which was assembled at random within a week, was an ageing performer, or rather, ex-performer, curled into a corkscrew. He walked crabwise, permanently looking over his left shoulder. He was even nicknamed The Corkscrew. At some point in his youth, he had been the top man in a group acrobatic act. The guys arranged to appear in provincial clubs in their free time. At one of these performances, he was in a headstand on the head of the man below him in the pyramid when his big toe went right into a light socket. The current passed through the whole group.

It was after that tour that The Corkscrew got his nickname and with it a disability pension. By nature always on the go, however, he couldn't bear having nothing to do. Every summer, he secured permission from a bosom buddy working at the Culture Ministry to go on tour and put together his latest team of daredevils. In addition to the absolute beginners—circus school students paid a mere pittance while the rest of their earnings went who knew where—more experienced performers also graced the programme—far more inveterate drinkers, in other words.

There was Zheka, for example, a musical novelty artist, so devoid of talent that circus managers preferred to cancel his act and pay him in full rather than have him disgrace them.

Fantastically ignorant—he didn't even see out secondary school—Zheka harboured truly Napoleonic ambitions. He spoke ponderously and liked to insert clever words of his own invention into conversations. If his act flopped, he regarded it as a bad break, a one-off, the perfidy of fate. "Nothing but over-reactions and misunderstandings," he would say. He talked to the cleaners, stable hands and ring staff in a rich, haughty baritone and switched to a thin, bleating tenor with lead performers or management. If a fight was brewing, he immediately shifted his vocal register to an ear-piercing squeal. Demonstrating the range of his own voice, in other words, confirming his speciality: the musical balancing act.

In the circus, the nickname The Wimp stuck.

Semyon Arkadyich, an equilibrist, was the only performer who didn't drink, apart from the youngsters. Meaning, of course that he did drink but not until after the show: He behaved with dignified restraint. He performed his elegant routine to romantic music on a high white pedestal, beautifully picked out in blue-white light. His spare, lean figure contorted in slow pirouettes, posed for half a minute in intricate arabesques, then came back to life again...

The beauty of these frozen statues held the labourers of Gorky spellbound.

There had also been Marina, the rubber girl, but she had to be taken off the programme in the middle of a highly successful run. A rat jumped out right under her nose during a performance, sat down and peered inquisitively into her eyes. The horror made her spine lock up and, still bent into an arc, the poor girl was carried straight off the stage and taken away in an ambulance.

But it was the Latvian, Aleksey Troks, who really put on an astounding act. It was sheer manipulation: a captivating, imperceptible sleight of hand. Tricks using cards, balls, coins, matches.

For example, he would come onto the stage and engage in a prolonged and unsuccessful attempt to light a match against the sole of one elegant patent-leather shoe. Once the jeering murmur of the audience had gathered intensity, a completely different match, held secretly in reserve, would suddenly burst into flame in his left hand.

His appearances ended with a fool-proof number. He would walk along the rows of spectators, distracting their attention and skilfully removing the watches of his simple-minded audience. He would then summon two or three die-hard "sceptics" up onto the stage and, as the credulous audience looked on, would rotate and separate and arrange his volunteers, removing their watches in the process. And all this at a brisk pace, accompanied by banter and some fairly amusing little rhymes of his own invention. So that when, for his grand finale, he started handing out the "stolen" watches, the audience erupted in thunderous applause.

Every day, when they had finished their own kindergarten stuff, they went down into the audience—Anna sometimes still in her skates—to watch Uncle Lyosha, as they called him, and the delicate artistry of his genuinely nimble fingers. They never tired of it.

…By fair means and foul, The Corkscrew arranged for his "gang" to stay in the circus hotel in the well-known Kanavino district. Uncle Lyosha used to say that it was in these very doss houses and drinking dens that the writer Maxim Gorky had found his characters. "Just you smell that, kids," he would say, "and remember that stale reek of alcohol is part of real history. It's what the air's like here."

In actual fact, it was hard to believe that half a century had already passed since Gorky wrote his famous play "The Lower Depths." There were such dreadfully theatrical characters roaming around the hotel and the whole district as if they'd dashed out of the dressing room for five minutes to pop round the corner and down a mug of beer.

Former circus performers could also be encountered in the hotel itself, positively pickled in alcohol.

Everyone knew Katka. A former trapeze artiste, she went around collecting bottles in the morning and cadging a beer off the nearest stand. She lived with her sweetheart, an ex-performer, whom everyone simply called The Hare. He was a fairly sturdy old man, an inveterate alcoholic, who earned a bit of extra cash as the assistant in some act or other. They lived in perfect harmony, plastered for days on end, and when there was nothing to drink The Hare sold Katya to business travellers in that same hotel. Not for much—just for a bottle sometimes.

A handwritten notice hung in the shabby foyer with its pitted tiled floor. It was a desperate howl from the cleaner, Marusya. "Dear Comrades! I humbly beseech you not to piss in the entrance hall. It's hard work cleaning up after you!"

In the evenings, the entire touring coterie traipsed from room to room. Sometimes pulling strings would see the "Muscovites" (civilized people, after all, from the capital) allowed to "relax" in the empty canteen, a room lined with Formica and irredeemably suffused with the ingrained smell of boozed-up belching.

Zheka was having an affair with a local canteen worker, Gerda Ivanovna, a lonely lady with a permanent wave. She used to apply her violet lipstick painstakingly in a cute little heart like the ones seen on cheap postcards… She had a distinctive smell all of her own: The perennial lilac-scented souse of Siren perfume stifled even the mighty stench of the ancient shrimps displayed in the canteen.

She had been given her romantic name by her mother who, as a child, had seen a travelling puppet show at a fair. An enormous foreign Moor from goodness knows where, with a tattooed forehead and a puppet on each hand, told a terribly ethereal love story in a whole variety of voices. The prince and princess, Gerda and Kai, became imprinted in the little girl's febrile imagination. Thirty years later, giving birth to her one and only daughter, she initially wanted to give her both names at once, blending them into an iridescent loop as Kaigerda. When she saw her husband, who had an awful stammer, pulling his face, however, she wrote it off as a bad job and retained just half of her dream.

Gerda wasn't paid much for the refuge she provided. They used to leave her the beer bottles. She never failed to remind them, "Money, mates, does not grow out of my arse!" And, as the fair-minded Corkscrew used to say, she was right in her way.

Having settled into comfort and space and even rustled up some proper glasses from Gerda, the whole circus team sat around the displaced tables that were always covered in viscous oilcloth. Talk would inevitably turn to the virtues of various circus canteens. Not the canteens in the foyer for the audience, of course, but the ones behind the scenes, next to the cloakrooms. There was no getting away from it: They were a very important part of their lives.

"All the same, I tell you," said Semyon Arkadyevich, the equilibrist, pedantically breaking a bar of chocolate and laying the pieces out on a spread handkerchief. "The best circus canteens are in Gomel, Minsk and Alma-Ata…"

"That's right, Sema, the Alma-Ata circus even has its own bakery!" The Corkscrew put in, carefully pouring everyone a glass of beer. He never spilled a drop, even though he had to do it, you could say, behind his own back. The glasses weren't theirs and were treated reverently. "The eclairs they make there. Do you remember?"

"Aha. But then Gorky, Yaroslavl and Tula are horrendous; less to eat than the Leningrad blockade. If you're sent there, stock up on tins, rusks, packet soups. Anything you can."

Zheka the Wimp butted in at this point to say that there was simply no canteen worse than the one at Gorky circus. Nothing but boiled eggs and shrimps.

"On the other hand, there's plenty of alcohol," The Corkscrew rejoined. "The manager likes a drink himself so he keeps an eye out to make sure the working man is properly treated. So, down the hatch!"

The performers drained their glasses, coughed and cleared their throats, politely wiped their mouths with the palms of their hands and reached for the chocolate.

"And there was this time here in Gorky. The performers' canteen is right behind the ring entrance, next to the exit to the foyer … so you get alkies and down-and-outs trickling in. I remember us standing behind the curtain in the ring entrance, warming up in semi-darkness with the show already under way. I look and there's this sack of some kind just lying there. I take a closer look and it's some alkie, completely out of it. He must have crawled out of the canteen and gone the wrong way. Instead of right to the foyer, he'd gone left. And collapsed right beside the holy of holies—the running order."

"And the canteen ladies in Gorky are special too," The Corkscrew added. "So fucking rude! There was one who swore so much our clown—someone you know, Syoma, Kolya Sokolnichy—couldn't take it anymore, grabbed the abacus off the counter and walloped her over the head so hard she hit the floor and the abacus was in smithereens. We got Kolya right out of there and hid him till the police had gone. It did shut her up for a bit though. Afterwards, everyone used to say to Kolya, 'So, you use an abacus to settle your accounts, do you?'"

"On the other hand, there are fights, even stabbings, wherever Sokolnichy is," Zheka recalled. "Don't you think?"

"I do," The Corkscrew agreed. "I'm saying nothing. Kolya's got a temper. He knocked the crap out of you last year or the year before, didn't he, Zheka?"

When he was drunk, Zheka liked to talk about his successes with women.

"Well," he would say in a confiding tone, "I think I'll have another half a glass. There we go. Right, I think I'll make my move!"

The troupe often discussed what each circus had to offer. They were like people really, each with their own reputation and not always a good one. Something always happened at the Kharkov Circus, for example.

"Constant, and I mean constant, issues with the animal trainers," said Uncle Lyosha. "Corkscrew, do you remember the Romanian one? She was killed by a lion."

"I certainly do! There were a lot of fatalities in Kharkov. Like Izhevsk."

"No, Izhevsk was different. It wasn't everyone," Aleksey reminded him. He liked precision in conversation as much as in his work. He wouldn't stand for sloppiness. "The only people flying off are the tightrope walkers. A lot come off and are crippled. Killed too. My brother got himself a sick note twice when he was assigned to Izhevsk. And got pissed to make it real. He pulled it off! And a year after his 'illness', another tightrope walker came off. The place is lethal…"

Anna and Volodka attached themselves to Uncle Lyosha.

He came across as rather pompous in his tail coal and bow tie in front of an audience. He would bow gallantly over ladies' delicate hands, raising one painted eyebrow. In the evenings, in his room with a bottle of beer, the gloss came off and cracked like old face paint. The wrinkles showed through, red thread veins snaked across his nose and cheeks, his eyes became bleary as an old man's. But circus anecdotes and instructive observations fairly poured out of him and never the same one twice.

"Real conjuring is a great art," Uncle Lyosha would say. "If you're the real thing, you should be working every finger on both hands at the same time and leading the audience completely astray with your eyes like a duck away from its nest. Working like a slave every day– that's your lot in life."

He stretched his hands out on the table. The long, sensitive fingers trembled ever so slightly as if listening to the conversation, ready at any minute to snatch a handkerchief from the air, unpick a tightly knotted rope or remove a lit match from someone's ear.

"Your fingers must be honed. The way woodturners work on particularly delicate items. Or an old draftsman sharpens his favourite pencil. The pattern of your skin on the pads of your fingers, the ones the cops use for fingerprints, should be polished like glass. That's when I'll tell you, 'Yes, you've reached the required level of sensitivity. Now you can touch. Touch the petal of a flower, a butterfly's wings, the eyes of a dragonfly and you will do no harm! Piano players call it 'touché'. With us, it's as rare as pearls in shit."

Uncle Lyosha propped his sagging cheek up on his fist, sighed and poured himself the last of the beer.

"In our business, who sticks around the most? Bootlickers of all stripes. Either they've worked up an act in a difficult game and don't fancy leaving the ring that's fed them or they're the offspring of famous parents who've inherited a routine... Then again, what does conjuring amount to in the Soviet circus? Boxes, basically. Different kinds of boxes—big ones using assistants, little ones using animals or feather dusters. The gift that keeps on giving. Anyone off the street can work up an act like that, if I may say so. With boxes, everything happens of its own accord. The main thing is remembering the order of the tricks and not being so drunk that you fall over the props. I had this assistant, Lyolka, who used to say, 'The main thing is that when you clap for the next thing to happen, your hands should actually come together.'"

Aleksey shared a room with Zheka the Wimp but was often there on his own. Zheka would be out stalking the local gardens of Eden, chasing first one then another Eve from Gorky.

Anna and Volodka stayed late in Uncle Lyosha's room almost every evening. Lyosha's head would be drooping, Volodka would already have nodded off at the table and woken up again three times over and still Anna wouldn't let the conjuror go.

"What about Harry Houdini?" she asked. "Is it true that he escaped from chains under water, Uncle Lyosha? For real?"

"What does that mean—for real?" Uncle Lyosha ruffled what was left of a thin head of hair. Carefully combed into a straight parting, it shone with decadent brilliantine on stage but hung down from his forehead like a dull grey dishrag in the evenings. "You're crazy. Forget about 'for real' when you're talking about conjuring, about illusion! About art! Houdini, yes, he was a classic of the genre but he died, when was it now? Back in 1926. Who's going to reveal his secrets now? Incidentally, do you know who Houdini's stage name paid tribute to? He was born Erik Weisz, a Jew from Budapest, and became Houdini in honour of the great French conjuror and illusionist, Robert-Houdin, who lived in Blois, a small town in France, in the nineteenth century. Now there was a magician! A powerful mind and devilish inventiveness. No one has been able to repeat his mirror tricks as yet…"

"Blois?" Anna asked again. "Houdin, with an 'I'?" Free now to do so, she immediately wrote at great length in a notebook, using her feverish left hand and her rapid gobbledegook, her Leonardo's handwriting that no one was monitoring anymore. Volodka sometimes took a peep and immediately looked away again. His head spun when he tried to grasp even the slightest bit of it.

"And," Uncle Lyosha went on, "they all made themselves out to be terribly mysterious!" He might already be slurring his words but he never lost the logical thread of the conversation. He fell silent mid-sentence now and then, as if mentally reviewing what he'd said, nodded in satisfaction and picked up the conversation from the very same words. "Terribly mysterious. I knew the celebrated Messing and I can tell you that in real life Wolf Grigoryevich was a quiet, even reserved individual. But in public? He burbled away, struck fear into his audience. The rules of the genre. Showmanship. Pizzazz? Get it?"

"A-a-nka!" said Volodka, waking up yet again. "Time for bed!"

"Wait!" she said, dismissively. "And this Robert-Houdin. Did he do illusions with boxes?"

Aleksey snorted, lent back in his chair, his already bleary eyes rolling in indignation.

"He invented them. And completely original boxes they were too! What are the ones we work with here like at the end of the day? The secret's either in a double bottom or the sides. I'll show you in more detail some time, when I've got a clear head… In a word, a mirror's fixed at an angle under the bottom of the box, like this." He demonstrated, tilting the palm of his hand. "It reflects the floor, gives an illusion of emptiness. Again, what's most important? Not losing concentration, not getting in your own way, not reflecting your feet or your arse. It has happened. I remember cases…"

"And what if a mirror's added on this side?"

"Which side?"

She took a folded envelope and a ballpoint pen out of her jeans' pocket and drew.

"Here, like this… Or this…"

"I don't get it! What's this doing here?"

"Don't look at it from here. You stand here. Right? And here's the audience. And a blind spot appears in this segment that can be used… Hang on, there isn't enough room…" She turned the envelope, which held a letter from Arisha, over and drew excitedly on the other side.

"Bugger me!" stammered the conjuror. "The girl's got brains!"

They set about discussing and arguing over some details. Volodka went over to Uncle Lyosha's bed, fell asleep and woke up again when their voices rose.

"But where does that come from? Leave science fiction to the writers!"

"It's not science fiction, Uncle Lyosha. It's physics. It's the same effect as a black hole. The pull of gravity is so strong that even objects travelling at the speed of light can't escape. Which means not even light can escape from the hole!"

"Anka! It's morning already!"

"Just wait, you!!!" the two of them yelled as one.

It was at these trivial summer side-gigs that they learnt the rules, superstitions and jargon of circus life. Don't turn your back on the ring that feeds you. Never say the word "last"—it's the worst possible luck. Don't do a routine for "the last time," do it "one more time." Don't eat sunflower seeds in the circus—the show will crash and burn. Indeed, the word "fire" was only ever used in relation to crashing and burning. And then there were the pure circus words, circus tummy and pep, which had long since become common parlance. Circus tummy meant the colly-wobbles but what about pep?

If you never did a trick in rehearsal without a safety line but then the audience seemed to give you wings so that you cast fear and caution to the winds and suddenly pulled off brilliant performances of routines that until then had been a bit iffy, not yet automatic; when you basked in the spotlights, showing nothing but strength and agility with hundreds of pairs of eyes fixed on you, that's what the circus called "working with pep."

"And another thing about pep," Aleksey said. "I'll say this—and I swear on all that's precious, it's the absolute truth. The ring has been a sacred spring for me all my life. It's given me energy, been quite literally healing… You turn up for work sometimes when you're running a temperature or you've been out on the town the day before and you're hurting and smarting, your back's as stiff as a board, your head kills… I wonder how I'll be able to crawl into the ring much less do any work… I drag myself to the entrance and well, now, that's better. My head seems to be clearing up, the back pain's gone… And, when you hear the ring-master announce you and you go out into the spotlight, you suddenly see yourself as if from the outside, sort of, noble, elegant, mysterious. Hah! I'm convinced there's some kind of special force out there in the ring. I can't explain. That really is from the realm of science fiction and yet I've felt it myself many times."

On one of these evenings, Uncle Lyosha said, "Kids, you've got your whole life ahead of you. I'm about to retire. I'm coming to the end of my professional career, so to speak. Why don't you buy my wardrobe trunk? Bear in mind, it's from before the Revolution, real papier-maché. I bought it thirty-five years ago from the famous clown, Mikhal Grig-oryevich Gusakov, and he swore blind he inherited it when Mamont Dalsky, an actor with the Imperial Theatres, died."

"Uncle Lyosha," said Volodka with a grin, "We don't even have any-where to put it. We haven't got a roof over our heads."

Anna was already hovering around the old trunk, however, feeling the metal corners and clasps, and as fixated on it as only a woman can be when something takes her fancy. To be fair, the trunks made in the circus's own workshops were pretty ugly: cheap and nasty with their imitation leather finish and aluminium corners. It was pre-war, German wardrobe trunks that were highly prized. They were made from vulcanized fibre like solid chests. Any self-respecting circus act had one of them, if not two or three. They were an object of pride, of prestige. And cost at least 250 roubles.

And now look what had turned up, what luck. It even had a history. And, when they'd worked another month with The Corkscrew's travelling company, they shelled out the not inconsiderable amount Uncle Lyosha had asked for without further haggling or discussion.

And so quite by chance and without even thinking about a future act, Anna and Volodka had come by a magnificent antique trunk and, what's more, it dated from before the Revolution and was made of real papier-maché that was tougher than plywood.

It was an entire *chiffonier* (unforgettable Panna Ivanovna!)—and had rivets, a hasp lock and brass-trimmed corners. Standing upright, it opened into two halves, nearly as tall as a person: Anna fitted easily inside at any rate. It had shelves, a mirror, little drawers and pegs. It was lined in red, slightly faded silk: the performing life, years on the road. Anna stood between the two halves, arms thrown wide, wearing an otherworldly expression. She was being the Fiery Angel, wings heavy against the crimson lining.

Back in Moscow at the start of their second year, they applied to the capital's Leningrad District Register Office and, pale and tense, they were formally married, Anna clasping a bouquet of daisies. In a photograph, their witness, Arisha—she'd transferred from Kiev that year to the second year of the Moscow Conservatoire and switched from the piano to the organ—stands to the left of Anna, still squinting. It was before her operation but even then the nobility of her fine features was evident, as was her resemblance to her grandmother, the one of a kind Firavelna.

The *wardrobe trunk* was the young couple's only possession—the repository of an as-yet-unknown act. Volodka carried it on his back into the dark, cramped room on Kirov Street, which they rented from the Bluvsteins, a half-crazy couple of old Trotskyists, with what was left of their summer earnings.

***

For many years, Anna heard the deafening roar of helicopters in her dreams and saw the black ripple from their propeller draughts on the water below: Navy Day celebrations.

Already in costume, Anna and Volodka stand on the airfield at Tushino. Everything has been timed to the minute. They will be given the go-ahead at exactly 12:30 (not a thing can be heard over the roar of the engines) and at that point it's crucial to get the timing right. As soon as the flag's waved in front of them and the two giant dragonflies, trapezes suspended from a twenty-five-metre pole, take off, they have to run up from the right-hand side and take their seats on the trapezes. The Mi-8 light helicopter can't hover for long and should anything untoward happen, they have been told to jump smartly to the right so as not to go under the propeller.

They tore off on cue, were on the trapeze in an instant, waved that they were ready, and the bare, patchy field of grass fell steeply away.

For the first few seconds, their hearts dropped away like the ground beneath, but a moment later, their whole bodies were seized by such wild rapture, it took their breath away. And all fear vanished as they gained height.

People below, who had looked up at the roar of the helicopters and spotted the tiny figures of the trapeze artists beneath one yellow belly, waved in delight, stopped their cars, got out and stared after them for a long time.

From this height, blocks of flats looked like little boxes, roads were a confusion of intertwining ribbons… The town was somewhere off to the side, like the circuit of a never-ending radio.

It took them ten minutes to fly by trapeze from Tushino to Khimki. And there, triumphant as gods, they descended from the sky as the festival crowd looked on.

As the trapezes dangled some fifteen metres above the waters of the Khimki Reservoir, Anna and Volodka embarked on their routine. The whole performance took no more than five minutes.

Overall, the tricks were simple, end of first-year exam standard: a stretch here, an arch there, into a hock hang, a lovely arabesque from one hand, into a flag. They wore soft, snugly-fitting kid boots with laces. Nothing was technically difficult if it wasn't for the height. Any kid can walk along the rail of a train track but will there be many volunteers if the rail's slung between balconies on, say, the fourth floor?

Obviously, there was no safety equipment. Asked about it, the officer who had invited them pulled a face and said, "What safety equipment, guys? Just hold on bloody tight, that's all."

And they did. They watched one another and attempted to keep everything in sync.

She remembered the seething, oil-black water right to the end.

A year later, they performed over land in Samara. And oddly enough, it was far pleasanter being suspended high above green grass. Anna's mind understood that water offered at least a chance of survival, unlike that nice green grass. And yet, just imagine…

Many years later the jaunty far-off grass of a Samara meadow would pass before her eyes as she stood on a rocky ledge above the Bay of Naples, just south of Ravello, ready to jump.

The director motioned for action. The engine started up, Anna ran a hundred metres or so through an orange grove—according to the script, she was being chased—and—again according to the script—had to hesitate for about five seconds then dive down, smack-bang into the narrow gap between emerald-black cliffs, their mass flowing down to the water… She was simultaneously composed and on edge: the norm before going into the ring. All she had to do was mentally map out the jump's trajectory.

But, all of a sudden, the sparkling dark blue expanse below glinted to form a deep mirror, revealing the end of the road to her astounded gaze, the final exit, the blessed tunnel into the Mirror World. And it was so unexpected, so arbitrary, like a sort of fall-back option that hadn't yet been earned or sufficiently hard won, a gift of an exit…

She staggered back, both hands hitting a wall of air, turned slowly around … and walked away, drenched in sweat, liberated, set free… Not forever, of course, but just at that moment she thought—And what if? What if?

She walked through the orange grove, oblivious to the shrieks of the highly-strung director and the dazzling cascade of Italian invective that followed as she grabbed the lower branches of the trees, pushing them aside.

The helicopter performance ended in a drop to toe hold. It wasn't the hardest of tricks but still…

The helicopter was pretty rocky. The surrounding air was dense and viscous in the strong airflow. It wouldn't take much just to fly the hell out of there. Softening the drop, they hung from the trapeze bar and, heads down, they waved a greeting to the audience…

They were met with riotous applause. Music was playing apparently but nothing could be heard up there apart from the helicopters' roar. Children squealed and released balloons into the air.

Then the helicopters rose slowly, the performers righted themselves to sit back on their trapezes and they were borne away into the sky.

It was a great little side-gig. The accounts department paid up immediately and crazy money to boot—a hundred roubles apiece. This good fortune came their way two years in succession. After the Samara performance, the chief controller, a former military pilot with the Order of the Red Star, came over to them, shook their hands and looked at Anna admiringly. "I admire your guts!" he said. That was embarrassing—What guts? They had perfected everything in rehearsal, it had become part of their muscles and their marrow. "It wasn't some kind of heroic deed, that's our job."

She was only sorry about one thing: that her father couldn't see her fly or dive headfirst into the abyss, only a centimetre away from soaring away one last time, pure and honourable. He would have appreciated it! Even through his horror and a sedative, with a lump in his throat—he would have appreciated it.

For two years in succession when their tumbling through the clouds came to an end, they spent a week at the seaside in Koktebel, frittering away their easily-earned money on fruit, shashliks and chebureki. They had a blast, pulled out all the stops. Lolled around in the sun, lazily strolled along the embankment, watching the thimble riggers ply their shifty trade.

"There's one who's brilliant," Anna remarked, following the ducking and diving of his nimble hands. "He should go into conjuring. He's brilliant!"

"Who? The dark one?" Volodka asked, embracing her peeling shoulders with their glossy patches of new skin.

"No," she said. "The other one. The redhead."

CHAPTER 13.

If it's practical advice you're after, light of my life, my little mirror, then I'd take the loft even if it is only for a year. It's not horrifically expensive, we're talking about Frankfurt after all and a good area and it would be a nest under the rafters where we could meet, you, my angel, and I, the old grey vulture. I am right, aren't I? It is the loft on Schweitzer Strasse, the one the Tigerpalast usually offers its contract workers, a stone's throw from the Main and its bridges? We spent a whole week there, you and I, a couple of years ago, in a bleak, rainy spring. The kettle was on the blink too, as I recall.

And it's a lovely loft. You open your eyes and up above you there's the sloping white-washed ceiling with ancient sturdy beams, very high on the left-hand side and really low on the right, two semi-circular windows looking on to the river and the bridges.

Something had gone wrong with your act, the factory had sent the wrong mirrors or they hadn't been installed properly, had been welded oh at the wrong angle…You went racing round the loft at night. And the rain muttered dully in an old gutter close at hand, almost above our heads.

Your languid loving at daybreak…

I was waking up at six, raring to go. And while you slept till noon—which meant my bassoon also lay idle—I would go down into the streets and, at a sprightly morning pace, I would head for the old Eifler bakery that had opened at seven. I would spend about fifteen thoroughly enjoyable minutes picking out something to go with our morning coffee. The baking was done right there on site. A small sign hung over the oven: "At 17:00, Eifler's bread rolls are still fresh and still crusty." And it was the absolute truth. The golden rolls hid a soft doughy middle beneath the crust. And the smell! God, the smell! Cinnamon, apple, lemon and cloves and a minty breeze from the half-open door, its bell in the key of B flat.

I used to love watching the shop assistant—a stately lady in the shop's red apron, *Backerei Eifler* in gold letters across her ample bosom, a red kerchief around her plump doughy neck—as she sprinkled sea salt on a baking tray of pretzels—bubliki twisted into crescents—and put them in the oven. Meanwhile, there were pretzels already on the counter, strewn with almonds and poppy seeds, along with vanilla "plunders" (which is what Aunty Frida called these pastries too) and mind-boggling "*Kreppel*," like our doughnuts, generously dredged with icing sugar.

The "*Kreppel*" packed with raspberry jam were the most delicious of all. And the pastries and pies: plum, onion, rhubarb and the house special—Grandma's apple pie!

Three tables and wicker-legged chairs stood deep inside the shop. It served coffee and freshly squeezed juice and any of the bakery's products could be sampled, of course, so that even at that early hour two older ladies, the nails on their porcelain fingers impeccably manicured, were already seated, leisurely enjoying their pastries.

But I couldn't wait to be back with you! I returned to the loft quietly so as not to wake you, laden with heavenly loot in the shop's signature packets, turned the key in the lock, went inside and set about making breakfast. I made coffee, keeping an eye as the froth rose and watching the flow of traffic along the Alte Brucke, the pedestrians trailing like ants onto the Eiserner Steg…

Breathtaking magnolias had already blossomed in the courtyards—do you remember?—And the chestnuts were in bloom: the white, utterly Kievan ones and the foreign lilac ones… Slow-moving clouds circled above them, the river rolled slowly under the bridges and a slow peal of bells sounded from Dreikonigskirche.

As the "eldest" deep-voiced bell rang its last lordly chime, you slowly turned over in bed, revealing a sleepy apricot cheek.

Take it, little one, take the loft, just do it!

It's weird. I grew up by a river and in Ukraine to boot, at my grandfather's. I spent all summer swimming in the Gnivan and the Southern Bug and yet I feel as though I never had my fill of water and have striven to be near it all my life. Why is that?

I used to dream about the holidays, about Zhmerinka, all year long, when I was little and my grandfather was still alive. Coming from Kiev, you simply can't conceive of the powerful call of summer in Ukraine! The summer night in Ukraine! The deep ultramarine of the heavy yet still transparent jumble of the sky, hanging languid over the earth; the meditative glimmer of the Milky Way.

  LEONARDO'S HANDWRITING

I used to sleep in the courtyard on a trestle bed my grandfather knocked up for me out of cast-off planks and mismatched blocks of wood. I would fall asleep late, whereupon the exhaustion of somnolent delight on the brink of sleep would give rise to yet another secret dream in which the stars, the moon and the movement of the Milky Way played out an erotic drama from the life of a Turkish harem.

I loved the Southern Bug so much I trembled, I'd be in it till my lips went blue. The lads and I would be on a Tarzan rope from morning to night.

Do you know what fun that is? Essentially, it's a homemade trapeze. It's named after Tarzan, the hero of an American film you'll never have heard of, with Johnny Weissmuller in the title role. My God, how he flew through those Hollywood jungles, skimming swamps on lianas, in his neatly-made rags, his hair flawlessly parted: the freedom of the wild, American-style.

Anyhow, the Tarzan rope. The bank has to fall steeply away. You grasp the bar with both hands, take a run and fly out over a river that shouldn't be the Dnieper, in the sense that it would be a rare bird that reached the middle, as Gogol put it, but not a stream either. The glorious flight off a sheer drop into icy water, the endless plunge to the bottom and the equally long ascent, up and up, almost out of breath, trained my lungs for my future life. Breathing comes in very handy for woodwind players.

Best of all, I loved the arrival, the station itself, the road to our house.

Zhmerinka has a remarkable station, I can tell you that, exquisite art-nouveau that wouldn't put even Vienna to shame. Every day our neighbour, Uncle Fedya, used to drain a bottle in the station buffet, go out onto the platform and yell after passing trains, "I'm not scared of anyone." He was beaten up once, right there at the station. It didn't put a stop to his sorties, oh no. He carried on drinking in the buffet, going on to the platform and yelling after the passing trains. True, the words changed a little and with them the political sentiment, as is often the case. "I don't owe anyone a thing!" roared Uncle Fedya, swaying in the wind.

My grandfather's house was on Pushkin Street. It's been demolished now, of course, my aunt's dead and I'm the only one who continues to roam the varnished floors in the tremulous dreams of dawn. I still know the layout of the house by heart. You go up a flight of wooden steps from the street straight onto a sun porch where my grandfather's work table always stood, all the tools in perfect order. Seeing him work was a beautiful thing.

My mother used to say that she could sit for hours as a child, watching him repair watches. I liked to creep up on him as well and stand at his shoulder.

"Senchis," he would say, turning to look at me, his face fitted with an eyeglass on an elastic band, "God keep you from coming any nearer than two steps. You're puffing like a steam train. You'll blow the second hand away. Count two steps back, Senchis, and stand there like a good boy."

But, onwards, little one… Next came the living room: the high-backed leather sofa with its strikingly carved ledge holding porcelain figurines (my grandfather knew the detailed history of each one); the book case, the arm chair, all carved antiques. A door led from the dining room into the bedroom with my grandfather's unexpectedly narrow bed and next to it another, huge bookcase. Auntie Frida called them "Masha and the Bear."

Grandma died at forty and my grandfather never remarried. I liked to watch him making his narrow bed in the mornings, neatly smoothing down the creases in the cover from the middle to the sides, as if his hands were caressing the beloved shell of her well-remembered body.

There was the kitchen as well, which my grandfather kept in the same perfect order as his work table. And he was a good cook too, by the way, or rather he could improvise, using whatever was in the house. And he made fabulous *latkes*—potato pancakes.

It goes without saying that the conveniences were outside. Also outside was a shed where chickens lived amid household and garden clutter or rather where they were brief visitors. They weren't there for long, only until the next Saturday meal, at which the little guests were devoured with relish. No matter what, the hen had to be inducted by the butcher. He quickly wrung the noble creature's neck and sliced off her head with a single blow from a sharp knife. It was a ritual. For culinary rather than religious reasons. Shop-bought chickens weren't regarded as chickens at all. But once the butcher had slaughtered the creature, it was smoked— that was left to Auntie Frida, grandfather's youngest daughter—and boiled to make a clear chicken broth, purer than spring water and more fragrant than the fields of heaven.

I almost forgot to add that the whole house was tricked out in my grandmother's embroidery: cross-stitch, Richelieu, open work. With the most idyllic subject matter: landscapes, ladies, gallants, a Gothic cathedral suspiciously reminiscent of Zhmerinka's famous Catholic church—a steeply pitched roof and four finials on the bell-tower amid the thick trunks and pointed tops of pines that appeared to be in a hurry to match it for height.

I remember the streets—Tsentralnaya, parallel to ours, Gorky, Sholom-Aleichem—all crammed with white single-storey straw-and-clay houses, each one, like ours, with a veranda.

People used to promenade along Tsentralnaya on Sundays. Immediately after the war, the cinema club at a textile factory I can't remember the name of used to show looted films: "The Woman of My Dreams," "The Indian Tomb."

You'll laugh but I've carried three postcards in my bassoon case ever since, my talisman, a poor trophy of my luckless childhood. They are pictures of actors from my mother's post-war collection: Marika Rokk, Mary Pickford, Valentino…

Frida had a set of records. Most often, it was Lyalya Chyornaya who performed on our veranda on summer evenings—"Do not leave, my darling"—or Leonid Utyosov's arch and gentle tenor, singing cracklingly of the wide expanse of the sea.

I can still remember the cobbled street being gradually asphalted over. There wasn't much greenery in the centre—maple and linden trees—but there were private houses a little further along, on Proletarskaya, Tolstoy and Shevchenko Streets, each with a garden, filled with the fruit-laden bliss of Eden: apples, pears, cherries… And, of course, flowers. The fragrance of jasmine was everywhere. It's funny—even today the bouquet of any perfume in which I imagine I can detect jasmine moves me to tears. Perhaps because my mother wore that scent. Or because a jasmine bush grew beside our veranda steps.

And at night the scented flowers of *matthiola* burst open and their thick, sweetish smell drifted through the district, permeating even the curtains at the open windows.

Every summer my grandfather and I were bound to pay a visit to my grandmother. The path at the Jewish cemetery ran past apple orchards and Lombardy poplars, their backdrop the deep languor of a dark blue sky. The Catholic or "Polish" cemetery as it was called was opposite the Jewish one. How different these picturesque landscapes were with their rich, contrasting colours to the Russian cemeteries, not to mention the squalid vistas of those in Guryev. And the strong presence of Catholicism conferred a certain something on everything around … a hint of the Adriatic, perhaps.

I used to accompany Aunty Frida to the Big Market twice a week (there was a little one too, undeserving of our attention). We reached it by going down October Revolution Street. And, you know, so many years have passed and it still seems to me that the same men and women are still standing there at their stalls after unloading mountains of sturdy, sweet-smelling Ukrainian tomatoes. Their necks are draped with plaited garlands of onions, straight out of a still-life, as they offer shoppers deep-gold blocks of butter the size of French rolls, wrapped in juicy burdock leaves.

And the purply pink lewdness of the meat stalls? Carcasses, hams, pigs' heads, their little eyes screwed up playfully but drowsily. There always seemed something philosophical about them.

And the stalls of Ukraine's famous pork fat! "Now, then, lady, come see what lovely pork fat, smoked over straw." The straw added a particular savour.

The sauerkraut stalls: "Cabbage, unsalted cabbage, fresh today, lady. Go ahead, have a taste. I've plenty to spare. Shall I take it from the bottom or the top?"

The morose poachers on the fish stalls, who worked the Southern Bug, somewhere downstream from the Sabarov Hydro-Electric Plant. Dairy stalls with the inimitable smell of genuine full-fat cream cheese, lying in a pitted cake in a bowl, its steep flank criss-crossed with gauze. "Only made today. This ain't cheese, it's pure butter."

"Let the little one try it, lady. What d'you say, little lad, isn't that a lovely cheese?"

Not wanting to upset anyone, I just smiled but they would say, "There, see. The child likes it. Take it. I've a long way to go yet."

Frida instantly switched to a strange language at the bazaar, neither Russian nor Ukrainian.

"D'you have any ryazhenka?" she would begin. "You could cut that with a knife! It's standing there like a tin soldier coming to attention for a general. So, how much? No, I'm asking how much this treasure costs."

At the same time, she would try to win the woman over.

"Oy, such lovely eyebrows you have … like they were drawn on. And why are you raising them? You'd be better off bringing the price down!"

She also switched to this language when the loathsome neighbour, Uncle Fedya, sneaked a little something out of our vegetable garden.

"That damned drayman, shikornik, thief!" she would yell to the whole street. "Pulled up another cucumber to soak up his vodka, he has! May he get it stuck up his arse. Devil take it, there's Frida breaking her back and him and his red snout chomping up the pickings."

But I digress.

The famous chocolate, stolen from the Vinnitsa Sweet Factory. A huge chocolate figurine, two hand-breadths in size, a cockerel or fish, shaped in a crude, home-made mould. But most frequently, just a brown wodge on bits of silver paper. Pure, bitter chocolate, like granite.

It was always possible to wangle a painted whistle out of Frida in the crowded, stifling rows of various items amid the second-hand goods, the shiny boots, felt ankle boots, cardigans, shapeless skirts with elastic waists and woven white and red towels.

And often there would be a man with operatically black curls (why operatic? Oh, yes, Aida, Radames's aria) swanning around the bazaar. They called him an "Assur". I don't know what it means but the sheep's curls of his beard and hair would later flash into my mind when I stood looking at the British Museum's reliefs of ancient Assyrian kings.

So anyhow, this Assur, this Yashka, carried a hawker's tray attached to a broad strap around his neck. It contained phials, powders, little boxes, pumice stones and other sundries.

And Yashka would advertise his wares in a fine stentorian baritone. "What do you need a wife or sweetheart for? THIS is what you need." He took out a phial. "Pour it where you need it. Move it up and down and everything will be fine and dandy!"

And my Aunty Frida, all grown-up but mischievous as ever, followed close behind him, doubled up with laughter.

And I mustn't forget that the apples appeared in August: simirenko, antonovka, belyy naliv and another winter variety created by breeders—a huge red-skinned fruit, unusually flavoursome, with a slightly bitter taste. Victory, I think it was called. Then, closer to autumn came the corn and if you cooked it properly, not so long that the seeds popped but just the right amount, and then gnawed the springy, bulbous cob sprinkled with sea salt... Oh, what's the use of picking at old sores!

In a word: summer in Ukraine.

My grandfather, as I now realize, was a real and consistent dissident. So consistent that he utterly failed "to protect me," as Frida used to say. "Ay," she said, "why does the child need to know your *mayses*?"

Grandfather's *mayses*—the various stories his observant mind had accumulated over the years, with their instructive conclusions, prologues and extensive epilogues—were senseless and merciless as a rule. Sometimes I didn't understand why he was telling me how the eye doctor Gurvich, who treated the whole town, was killed. "Why?" I asked, puzzled. "So that you know where you live," he would answer patiently. "So that you don't develop any illusions. You'll be young, passionate, inspired. You will want to turn evil into good and I don't want you wasting years on it. This country, Senchis," he would say, "is a country of bandits and robbers, irrespective of the powers-that-be. Here it's the authorities that will always be bandits, it's the lay of the land. Even the wind here whistles like a robber's signal…"

"Stop pestering the child with your *mayses!*"

"Be quiet, Frida," Grandpa would say. "Be quiet and remember who stole a packet of cigarettes from a German officer… So, then, Senchis… May you never be fooled by anything good on their part. It's just that occasionally the gangster's in a good mood and at that time has no desire to toss you overboard into an oncoming wave… Pick a job that doesn't rake in money, Senchis," he said. "A blameless, unprofitable job so that no one depends on you and no one envies you."

As you can see, little one, I am following my grandfather's guidelines. Have I already told you I've learnt the dulcian over the past couple of weeks? It's an ancestor of the bassoon. An unbelievably beautiful timbre: deep, doleful … sweetly ineffectual…

Sorry. I'm writing nonsense. It's three in the morning already and I simply cannot get to sleep. I can't even play anything: The neighbours will call the police. And somehow I'm not entirely myself today. I'm only complete with you, my mirror girl. That's been true for a long time...

But—my grandfather.

Every morning after waking up and pulling on the slaughtered Italian soldier's legendary boots, he would go to the Soyuzpechat kiosk and buy all the Moscow newspapers in order to compare them and "to read between the lines."

But wait a minute: I promised to tell you the story of those boots and I never did. I'll do it now or I'll forget again.

I need to start, however, not with the boots but with that stolen packet of cigarettes. You see, during the occupation, Grandpa and his two daughters ended up in the Zhmerinka Ghetto and that's where I was born. Logical development of the plot requires that a person born in the ghetto is fated to wander the whole world, fearful of confinement wherever it may be for even a day longer than his soul can bear.

It was a miracle that they survived. A miracle because young Aunty Frida stole a packet of cigarettes from a German officer. She either filched them from a table in an empty room as she passed the commandant's office or took them straight from his pocket—that might well have been the case, I wouldn't put it past her. When I was little, she would borrow a book to read from Grandpa and then use it to heat the stove, without even opening it. He never got those books back… In short, she was caught with that packet of cigarettes and the Gestapo rounded the whole family up into the cellar. They weren't allowed to take me, aged two-months and howling fit to burst, in case I disturbed the commandant's peace and quiet.

The story then becomes almost unbelievable but truth is stranger than fiction, as they say. My mother begged a Romanian guard to release her so that she could go and get her child. "I'm not going to go anywhere in any case," she said. "I'll come back to my father and sister." And he let her go.

En route, she bumped into a neighbour and here comes the twist in the plot. As a young woman, this neighbour had been a circus artist who went on to marry an elderly Armenian. He was a big boss in hides and furs. During the war, however, she'd been openly having an affair with a certain Romanian officer. She was a silly, reckless woman, a proper circus woman, even in retirement, if you'll pardon my saying so.

Anyway, the point is that there was some money in an old mitten of my mother's, hidden away in our shed at home. My grandfather had put it aside for a rainy day. Which, as you will gather, was now upon us.

And my mother, coming across this neighbour, asked her to take the money and ransom us through that very same Romanian officer. And what do you think? She did and I have no idea how but she pleaded with the Romanian and he ransomed the lot of us. The story of such a miraculous rescue, it's like the truncated version of an opera libretto. God keep us from knowing all the details. From knowing all the details of our lives.

Incidentally, later on, that neighbour took herself off to Kiev out of harm's way and my grandfather used to visit her for many years, sometimes taking me along.

So, yes, the boots. Why do they keep running away from me although I only have to close my eyes and I can see the sturdy laces, the buckles on the legs? I often used to look at those boots as a child and wonder where the Italian soldier was who wore them. Now I remember my grandfather and wonder where the Italian soldier's boots are that Grandpa wore for so many years.

A brief history.

Zhmerinka had always been a railway junction. The Germans used to bring in trainloads of butchered soldiers' bodies and force the residents of the ghetto onto the platform to put the corpses in dress uniform and move them into different carriages that were going home to Germany: The soldiers of the Wehrmacht had to depart this world in full dress uniform. And Grandpa found himself doing this work. By that time, he had spent a cold, hungry winter in the ghetto, had buried his wife, had frostbitten feet and could barely limp along on what were practically stumps. As he was putting some slaughtered German into dress uniform, he pulled the man's field boots off. He was supposed to throw them into a pile of dirty footwear, stiff with blood. But they were perfectly good boots. Grandpa thought about it and put them on. A *gefreiter* spotted him and wanted to execute him on the spot but when he forced Grandpa to take the boots off and saw the state of his feet, he suddenly took pity on him. So, he just dealt him a blow to the back with the butt of his gun and led him over to the Italian corpses. "There," he said, "pull some off these. That's allowed. From a German to a Jew," he said, "is sacrilege but from an Italian it's fine."

And, oh, what boots they were, little one. You're not disturbed by my grandfather's looting, are you? I'm not. They couldn't keep that Italian boy warm any longer and they saved Grandpa's feet. And how he used to pull them on in the mornings afterwards—there was no wear-and-tear, no wear-and-tear at all!—lace them up and fasten the clasps and then put his best foot forward and press on, if you'll pardon the terrible pun, to the press kiosk. As a small boy, I used to wonder whether Grandpa's "non-Soviet" boots were the reason for his "non-Soviet" views about life.

Oh, God, it's already after three! And we've a rehearsal with Myatlitsky at ten tomorrow. Did I write that the Professor and I have concocted a programme with a respected baroque orchestra from Boston? It's the Handel and Haydn Society? Sounds quite snug, doesn't it? It's a Baroque orchestra and choir. The musicians play seventeenth- and eighteenth-century instruments. It's a poor orchestra, which doesn't stop it being a local must-see. It was founded in 1815 when Beethoven was still alive. There's a neat myth that a "Boston Overture" was commissioned from the man himself after he'd lost his hearing but he died before he had time to write it. The orchestra performs Handel's "Messiah" at the beginning of every December in the run-up to Christmas and has now done so conscientiously for 200 years in succession. It's the kind of Boston event that every respectable family feels duty bound to take their children to. The tedium goes on for three hours, then the audience graciously applauds and blissfully departs. Not all the musicians who founded the orchestra are still playing. Myatlitsky and I are newcomers and still alive to boot.

By the way, he and I are practically neighbours these days. I have just one proper neighbour, very nice, very quiet and a fool. Unlike lots of people, he doesn't kick up a fuss and damn my bassoon to the underworld. Quite the contrary, he waits for hours until I deign to awake and start tootling away.

I have just one issue with him: When we come across one another by the post boxes, I won't let him kiss my hand.

So, the Professor: I never cease to admire the man. Just think, he's ninety-three and yet such clarity, such a sense of humour, such a brilliant, razor-sharp mind!

After a rehearsal at Symphony Hall yesterday (its acoustics are considered unique, which is nonsense, they're entirely run-of-the-mill), I escorted him home and we talked about Fritz Kreisler.

In his youth, Myatlitsky played for quite a long time with a pianist who had accompanied the great Kreisler. "And Kreisler had taught him a few vaudeville tricks," the Professor said, "*rallentandos, glissando*, soulful *vibrato*, in short, all the hocus-pocus so beloved and treasured by the audience." He paused then went on to say, "Although, believe me, Simon, Kreisler himself couldn't give a shit about the audience. Sure, he wrote salon music but he performed it rigorously and simply, keeping strictly to the rhythm."

He speaks excellent Russian with a slight accent. He spent several years in Russia as a child but he was born in Warsaw. In time for the Revolution! To be fair, he doesn't remember a thing. He was too little. His father, an engineer who built bridges, was invited to work in Russia. After the Revolution, of course, he had to clear off back to Warsaw: The time had come for the gangsters to toss everyone they could get their hands on into the oncoming wave.

I long to introduce you to his family. They're so entertaining. The daughter, Julia, is a famous journalist. She writes about all the scandalous court cases, she's incredibly popular, often pops up on television, sharp as a needle, like her father, but a difficult character. Moreover, as the Professor tells it, she's demonstrated her foul character since early childhood. His wife once rang Myatlitsky during a triumphant European tour and said, "I can't put up with her any more. I can't. Please come home right away." And he cancelled two concerts, paying huge damages, and went. The wretched brat behaved slightly better in his presence.

She has no children and twenty-five years ago she adopted a little girl from China. Do you know, little one, and this is the last thing I'm going to bother your sleepy mirror head with today, that in China care for elderly relatives is the responsibility of their sons?

So that the birth of a daughter a disaster. New-born girls are routinely dumped at the side of the nearest road. Which is how Julia, hoofing around China on her journalistic business, picked up and adopted one of these little girls, who had been abandoned on the roadside. It's a touching story, isn't it?

That's it, everything, go to sleep.

So, I'm expecting you in Amsterdam on 16th. In the *"Do-you-want-to-see-the-lovely-lady?"* hotel. By my calculations, you'll be there by twelve o'clock. You're not coming by motorbike, are you? I've hired a car and we'll travel across Germany to Prague and from there to Karlovy Vary where I'm playing just one concert at the local opera theatre.

Do you remember us, sitting in the pathetic little room of a cheap pension, seven or so years ago—like wandering beggars or street entertainers—looking out of the window at the Grandhotel Pupp, floating slowly in the mist of the ravine, dreaming that maybe one day… So, my mirror girl, I've booked us two nights in that Scheherazade's palace. Relax, it's at a decent discount. Are you pleased? And in Amsterdam, we'll be at the AMS Lairesse as usual. I know it's not your favourite but think about it and say yes: The concert hall's nearby and I, poor wretch, have to go to rehearsals first thing and concerts in the evenings so that I'll be constantly on the go for the whole three days.

And there's that nice Japanese garden you can look at from the breakfast table. And such comfortable big beds! Such big beds! Come to me as soon as you can!

I rang Peter. My bassoon's ready now. I couldn't be happier and I can't wait for the moment I take my future child in my arms. It's a copy of Ludwig Eichentopf's instrument, eighteenth century. Only an incomparable master like Peter de Koenig could have made it.

But you're asleep already… I'm drawing the covers over you gently and also going for a nap. Do you know—and I'm telling you this as you sleep so that you don't hear—what I dream about sometimes? Fairly frequently, in fact. Forgive an earnest old fool: that when I fall into my last sleep, you'll be there beside me.

Good night!

CHAPTER 14.

In the fourth year, her tutor, Lazurin, went on an exchange to Cuba. They'd opened a circus school there. And it was a mischievous old lady, Yelena Pavlovna Krasovitskaya, who saw Anna and her solo trapeze routine through to graduation. In her own wild youth, she'd been a circus rider then worked on the trapezes. And she never had any family, no husband or children. She lived with her sister somewhere in the circus cooperative on Usievich Street.

She always had a cigarette between her teeth in the staffroom. She only acknowledged the ones without filters, making her own by putting cotton wool in the cylinder.

Krasovitskaya was well past sixty back then but she kept a firm grip on the safety line. Anna trusted her arms completely.

And Anna's graduation routine was funny, a "reprise," a piece of light entertainment. Thin and light, wearing a sailor suit with a tiny skirt and a beret at a rakish angle, Anna skipped over to the vertical rope to music by Dunaevsky and, hitching herself up using only her arms, her legs at an angle, she climbed up to the trapeze itself, like a cabin boy on a rope ladder. She climbed quickly and stylishly—her arms were already strong by then—moving her body in time to the music.

Once there, she unclipped the safety line, grasped the bar of the trapeze, swung her whole body two or three times and suddenly let go with her hands so that, after turning through 180 degrees with her legs bent, she could feel for the bar, grip it with her calves then let go and fall.

It was called a half-twist to heel hang. She ended the routine with the same half-twist and came off the trapeze in a long swing to Dunayevsky's fervent music.

Both of them, Anna and Volodka, passed their special subject with flying colours. Now they had to make the long swing through life and its circuses.

Incredibly young, they thirsted for a real ring, the chill of risk, height, spotlights, applause… Fame!

And were a little bit lost.

***

After the final exams, Volodka was taken on as an under-stander acrobat in a good travelling act and was immediately sent to Perm.

Meanwhile, Anna was employed by a youth collective called Circus Revue and settled in Izmaylovo for the "rehearsal period." There was a rehearsal centre there with a cumbersome official name, the All-Union Directorate for Preparing Circus Attractions and Acts. It was presumed that young performers would perfect their skills there by honing their acts. The dismal weeks dragged by one after the other. Not a great deal of ring time was offered for rehearsal—an hour a day. In addition, the directorate compressed the timetable to make savings so that several acts were in there together.

Anna went along, warmed up, rushed through her bends and twists on the trapeze, while at the same time a pair of equilibrists contorted themselves into silent loops down below and a couple of jugglers threw clubs to one another.

She hung around for days on end with nothing to do or kicked her heels at the conservatoire hostel with Arisha. The latter was now crazy about an instrument called a carillon, was writing to some French carillonist and concocting fanciful plans for the future: She must have read too many novels. She knew about all the European cathedrals that housed these carillons and talked about them for hours.

In the evenings, Anna went crazy with boredom in the company of the two Trotskyites who had gone completely nuts about saving electricity. Having spent around twenty years each in Soviet prison camps, they were quite happy with a single dim bulb in the kitchen. Privately, Anna called this "nostalgia for the camps."

"Young lady," Isay Borisovich said in the kitchen one morning, "you had a light burning until three in the morning last night. Why might that be?"

"I was reading a book," Anna replied politely.

His face twisted into a smirk. "I should like to see what kind of books circus people read!"

"By all means," Anna answered meekly and brought a leaflet from her room entitled, "The M-theory of Strings and the Space-Time Lattice in Loop Quantum Cosmology."

Isay Borisovich's cataracts goggled behind the thick lenses of his glasses. He shouted to his wife, "Irina Bogdanovna! She's making fun of us!"

Arisha's boyfriend, Edik Martirosyan, a post-graduate physics student at Moscow State University, sometimes borrowed books and magazines out of the university library for Anna. She had drawn up a list.

Every now and then, she rang her father at work from the main post office. Their conversations were painful—not just because she hated telephone calls and *regarded them as pointless, gratuitous, fake, the sandpapery husk of an eviscerated voice*. But because, even through the crackle and interference, she could hear her father's yearning. She could tell how eagerly he was trying to work out from her voice if she was well and happy. Sometimes he simply asked outright, "Nyuta, are you happy?"

She gave her silvery laugh and said with conviction, "Oh, Daddy, of course."

A silence followed … a rustle … the rattle of a distant teaspoon in his glass.

Suddenly, her father said, "Do you remember our little monkey, Nyuta? She's been moved to Odessa."

"What?" Nyuta asked, raising her voice. "Odessa?"

"That's right… Because of her fractious nature."

And she couldn't understand whether her father was joking or sad. *She could never understand anything on the phone, the mirrors stopped working, grew cloudy.*

After his uncontrollable weeping, they endeavoured not to talk about Mashuta. Anna knew the details from Khristina's secret letters, illiterate and hilariously funny had it not been for their subject.

At that time, Krystina had already moved in with them. There came a time when her "almost widower," demoted from train driver to conductor for drunkenness, failed to return from a long-distance trip. Either he had met an inglorious demise in frenzied haggling with the southern spivs the conductors tried to beat down on every box of tomatoes or persimmons, or he was snuggled up to an unmarried black-eyed bucket of lard in some Erevan or Alma-Ata.

Khristina wrote exactly as she spoke, in Surzhik. Her voice emanated from the awkward words and clumsy sentences. "So, your father's been off doing cholera again."

"So then I has to sit with Mar'Kirilovna and ooh, it's so scary staying with her by myself and what if she takes a turn here without Natol Makarych? If a heap of pills have sent her peacefully off to sleep already then fine but it does sometimes happen that she gets it into her head to spit them all out and then it's so scary with her all by myself, Nyutynka. God forbid! She's smashed all the mirrors everywhere already so that, fine, we've hidden 'em all away at home but she tries knocking the glass out of the windows, she does, specially of an evening when they start reflecting and you have to run ahead, shouting for help and pull the curtains everywhere you can... And your father shelling out more and more at the hospital. She's already smashed up all the mirrors there and they put new ones up and if they're in the bathrooms or the corridor she smashes them up too. What a disaster, Nyutynka. Lord God have mercy. Who could have known that our cultured Mar'kirilovna with that music of hers would become just like a wild beast?"

***

As the new season approached, they took to scurrying round the departments of the Central Administration, looking for an aerial or flying-trapeze act that would take them both. Once again, it seemed unthinkable to be apart: What kind of life is it on your own? Volodka had fairly wasted away that year. But if they were both working, they could travel from one temporary engagement to another without needing resident permits, without becoming attached to the place... Everything could be crammed into the venerable old wardrobe trunk, and they could fly to their hearts' content, wherever they were sent.

It very soon became clear, however, that joining an act as a couple was no easy matter.

Some places needed a boy, others a girl. In addition, a lot of acts were apprehensive about taking on a married couple. They were always an undesirable coalition in the intrigues, scheming and eternal infighting of the circus. They were all slaves on the Central Administration's plantations. Or willing serfs, rather. And the only escape from the serf-owner was into homeless, hungry freedom, onto the streets, into nowhere.

On several occasions, they were offered really third-rate acts. They turned them down and the pen-pushers at the Central Administration began to lose patience at the sight of this self-reliant pair.

 LEONARDO'S HANDWRITING

They frittered the whole summer away like this, already utterly despairing. And on August 26, Soviet Circus Day, they dragged themselves off to the Performance Department for the umpteenth time.

Volodka argued against going, saying there was no point, that everyone in that den of jackals would be whooping it up, celebrating the holiday… But Anna finished her kefir, rinsed the bottle under the tap (glass containers were an extra source of income for the Trotskyites) and said firmly, "Put your going-out trousers on. Let's go."

The Central Administration was indeed in a whirl—some people had already left, others were just about to pack up. Random individuals sat at or on the desks, some smoking, others telling jokes. Albina Konstantinovna, a round bun with a pock-marked face, the person who had shooed them away all these months like scruffy cats off a country veranda, was applying a fresh layer of lipstick to her suggestively protruding lips. She spun the dial on the telephone and yelled at someone on the other end, "Vladimir Ivanych! Get your trousers off for tonight!" Evidently, she had already managed to drink to the holiday.

"But maybe you could find us something on wires or tightropes?"

Why did Anna ask about the tightrope? She had simply picked up a fairly clear mental message that the woman at the next desk was muttering to herself. She was pregnant, her face hidden, her head close to the sheet of paper as she laboriously wrote something out…

When she heard Anna's question, the woman raised her head and looked closely at them both. And she must have taken to them: They were so young and therefore not lost to the bottle, enthusiastic too.

"Guys," she said, "how would you like to take on an act that's ready to go? A wire act with moving ladders?"

She had a fine, freckled face and small pudgy hands that she was constantly lifting into the air as if hoping to find a lost balancing pole.

And right there and then in that office everything tied in, came together, fell into place as only happens at key junctures of fate. "There I go planning a baby right at the end of my career," Lyuba explained. "Well, you have to make your mind up some time. I'm applying for my length of service pension. I ran the act for many years but that's all in the past now. Now, our only props will be muslins and nappies."

"Guys," she said again emotionally and threw up her hands. "Take it. You won't regret it. We had a good act, successful, family-friendly. No one's really come a cropper in a long time, only minor injuries."

And my goodness did that girl ask about tightropes at the right time! Must mean she has determination, a passion for heights…

And I'd so like to sell the props to someone serious, who's worthy of them!

And with the holiday about to begin, Albina Konstantinovna proved to be gracious. She observed the conversation with a maternal smile on her depraved red lips. She even promised "to look into the issue of financial support for the purchase of props."

So in a single day—a day? It was literally a minute—they had become the owners of their own ready-to-go act: equipment, costumes, partners.

***

The equipment was rudimentary: low and very heavy, the costumes antediluvian. They immediately sacked one female performer for drunkenness. The other, Gulnara, aged about thirty-two, already past her prime and lazy too, knew her own modest tricks and had no desire to rehearse anything new. These two Johnny-come-lately aerial tightrope-walkers were mad about height, risk, new tricks—wanted the very rigging in action! To be really aerial—height, gasps, sky, lightness, bottomlessness…

They set about rehearsing zealously with what they had received. The wire itself was a genre as old and traditional as the Pyramid of Cheops. The tricks were all familiar and thoroughly rehearsed. They would get into formation on the platform. The *under-stander* would cross to the opposite platform holding a balancing pole. The others would descend onto suspended ladders, which they could hold on to as they performed trick on the rungs or simply sat there with panache—"striking a pose."

There were complicated tricks as well. Carrying a column of three or even four performers across. But how long could the audience watch these weightlifting feats? All these carryings across were dull and boring, Anna kept saying, had been done a thousand times…

And so, with their dreams of high, wide swings, unexpected tricks, an audience with eyes narrowed and palms sweating with suspense, they made their entry a year later on their tame and earthbound apparatus. At the same time, they both turned out to be naturals on the wire. Volodka especially—his plasticity and balance were extraordinary. The sharks of the genre began trying to entice him over to their troupes. Volzhansky himself issued an invitation.

Volodka declined. They had decided to create their own act. Themselves.

***

In recent months, Anna had been remembering Zhilyansky Park for some reason, where she was taken for walks in early childhood. She remembered the apparatus but not the slow, brooding swingboats that could have been taken to terrifying, tumbling heights, had it not been for Polina's qualms. What kept coming into her mind was very basic: a plank, fixed across a piece of metal tubing. The kids sat themselves on the ends of the plank and, pushing off with their feet, either flew up into the air or plummeted to the ground… The plank bounced and sagged—after all, there might be two or even three on each end—but it never broke. That simple plank in Zhilyansky Park was preying on Anna's mind.

Once, she and Volodka were sitting in the canteen after rehearsal, munching on rubbery cheese sandwiches. Through the window, Anna was silently watching workmen outside the circus unloading a lorry full of construction planks.

"What? What are you thinking? Eh?" Volodka asked. He was always rather afraid when she thought but didn't speak.

"Nothing," she replied. "Listen, there's this thing going round and round in my memory. I can't stand it. I can't get it out of my head at all today. It's a simple design … like a plank. Look, over there, what those guys're unloading."

He followed her glance out of the window. One of the men dropped a plank on another's shoulder and, judging from the hand gestures and energetic lip movements, it was met with lively invective.

"What do you mean?"

"I'm thinking how we could make the horizontal vertical, put it at right angles."

"Wait, what? What horizontal?"

"The old wire… What can we come up for using it? It's so tedious doing just what everyone else has done."

"So were you planning to use it to go into space?" he said, grinning. "All the routines are as old as the world. They were somersaulting on wires thousands of years before you came along. It was all invented ages ago."

"Well, yes, that's true," she agreed. An empty seesaw beneath a huge chestnut tree soared up and came down to earth with a bump. But when there were children sitting on it, they bounced and pushed off with their legs, bounced and pushed off…

"Let's go for a smoke."

The courtyard was baking in the sun. Three workmen were unloading the last planks. One stood in the bed of the lorry, passing them out. Two took them on their shoulders and tossed them to the ground by the wall with a thud. Probably for renovation work.

And at that point, shivers ran up and down Anna's spine. Suddenly she saw her own unique, unconventional routine: a plank across the wire rose and fell at a great height above the ring, a romantic seesaw in an enchanted "snowfall" from a mirror ball. A plank on a wire? What kind of nonsense is that! A lethal routine, two seconds followed by a long-drawn-out official funeral…

She waited for the workmen to finish unloading and leave, went over to the piles of wood and examined them closely. She clambered onto one and jumped up and down, testing it.

Volodka watched her through narrowed eyes, trying to guess what this was all about, what else her restless brain had come up with. Then he flicked the cigarette butt away and went to help.

They chose the longest plank, the smoothest, without any knots, dragged it off to the ring and laid it across the barrier.

Conveniently enough, their friend Ninka from the same year at circus school happened to pop up just then. She was hanging around for rehearsals, practising a nice, easy balancing routine. She and Anna sat on either end of the plank and rocked it like two small girls. The plank bounced and sagged but it bore their weight. They called a ringhand over and he and Volodka sat on the same plank… And still the plank bore their weight. Bless it, it didn't break. Really it didn't.

A minute later they were already talking over one another excitedly, contemplating as they walked how they could adapt the plank, how to balance it across the wire.

"Attach little bits of wood at the centre of gravity on each side." Anna said, "Make a little groove so we're not feeling blindly for the centre in front of an audience but can just lay it straight on the wire."

They began to squabble and to put the details of a routine together.

To begin with, Volodka and Anna experimented on the low-wire. It didn't work. They couldn't find the balance, the fragile equilibrium without which nothing in their line of work could happen.

Then, the juggler, Venya Tarasyuk, who had been minding his own business, quietly juggling balls off to the side, came over and,

   LEONARDO'S HANDWRITING

without interrupting the arc that poured from one hand to the other or its echo in the barely perceptible movement of his chin, he said, "What you need are two female acrobats, the same weight."

And so Ninka joined the act and was to be their loyal partner for years.

They rehearsed recklessly, like crazy, for days at a time. They put the wire up higher and higher, constantly increasing the risk. The newly-minted seesaw rose and fell slowly above the ring, floating beneath the rigging…This was the dangerous flight they'd been dreaming of.

The first performance in Riga was a sensation. They were brought back for five encores, something that never happens in the circus. Igor Petrovich, the manager, a stout man short of breath, ran into the dressing-room, shook their hands and said over and over again, "Good grief! I've never seen anything like it in all my life in the circus!"

And they began to seesaw on that plank of theirs, up and down, up and down, at a crazy height in the void, in an enchanted wheel of light. Non-stop: in towns and villages, circuses and big-tops, thorough different countries and through the skies…

CHAPTER 15

"Genevieve? I've already told you, Robert. She's a great girl. A real friend. And everything …

Anna always used to stay with her when she was in Montreal. And she could spend weeks in Montreal, especially when she had work, the latest commission… And she loved Montreal and felt really at home at Genevieve's. There was a tiny little room up on the roof, completely separate, an illegal extension. City Hall had been sending threats and warnings on official notepaper for years: Take it down or else… But these things move at a snail's pace, as you know… I hope the little roof nest will see Genevieve out…

Anyway, the only way to reach it was to come out of the flat and climb a small spiral staircase from the landing to the attic door. There, another door led right to the little box on the roof. No kidding. It really was a box, eight or nine metres square, but with enough room for a fold-out bed, a little table nailed to the wall, a stool that could be stored underneath… It even had a screened-off bio toilet: complete autonomy. Anna adored that nest. It's what she called it, a nest.

And, as I've already said, she was touchingly besotted with Genevieve's old parrot, Howard. Honestly, he had no peace when Anna showed up. Putting him on her shoulder and stroking him, scratching his head, while he rolled his eyes, lapping it up… He talked with the twang of an old cardsharp… "Anna, boy… Let me give you a kiss!" Why boy? Christ knows who he got it from. Anna was convinced parrots aren't birds but creatures like elves. Especially African greys: they're so crafty, so clever! And, you know, if you listen to the way his answers stick to the subject, you can't help believing him.

And it was Howard who saved Anna. Just imagine how frightened a bird has to be, how much in shock, to attack its owner! It's unbelievable! It doesn't happen. Parrots always defend their owners, better than dogs! And then this… I can imagine him hammering at her head and hands with that iron beak! And I'm sorry but Genevieve had incredibly strong hands. Sculptors don't have weak hands. I've seen her sawing through a plaster body…. Smoothly, all in one go.

And this is a parrot we're talking about, right? Pretty Polly, yeah? He was like a knight in shining armour. She's still got the scar … just here, right by her eye. Like a tear drop, hanging there.

But you know … I don't want to talk about it. Believe me, Genevieve was always skinny but after Anna disappeared she was a shadow of her former self. Even talking to her about Anna is difficult. She just bursts into tears. She's very sensitive, that kid. And you did question Genevieve, didn't you? You've seen her. She's a strong, clear-thinking person, when she's sober, obviously. No, I'm not contradicting myself. Genevieve's a true Breton. They're all made of granite, like the land they come from. And she's not to blame for anything… Not for anything at all.

And this is the subject I least wanted to talk about, Mr. Kerler. Anna really didn't like it and went through too much because of it. It always got her down when some cretin, who happened to find out from somebody … or got a whiff of something… She couldn't always hide it, you see, like when some nosy cretin started asking leading questions, the kind you usually ask fortune-tellers or a palm-reader, for fuck's sake. She could swear, the way we do in the circus, you know. She could be terribly, unexpectedly, or as they say nowadays *gratuitously* blunt.

Sure, I get it, you're here about the case… Although how is it going to help? Anyone can take a jump. After all, I didn't find out myself right away, even though back in the day, as a young teenager, she sometimes played around with her gift, just for fun. She liked blindsiding people, not giving any explanations. And what's to explain? I remember being stunned myself that time in the maize field.

Our watchman, Panas Redko, our pal, our protector, you could say, started boasting about his family one evening. And his wife was "so capable, so hardworking. The minute I get home, I yell"… and there's Anna barking out "Natalya" in his voice right next to my ear.

To start with, the old man was thrilled. "That's it, good guess!" But she was going to frighten him if she didn't stop, wasn't she? But youth, joy, the love we shared. She was like champagne when you've just opened it. She listed every one of them, his son's names, all his girls. To be fair, she got the youngest slightly wrong, Lina instead of Nina… You could see the old guy turn deathly pale. Anna laughed like a drain. "What, Panas Egorovich, did you think witches only flew around in olden times? You just come and visit us at midnight! I'll take you to a coven!"

And she laughed like a madwoman.

Joking apart, though, the old man never came to see us again. True, she left the next day, right out of the blue. She'd had a bad dream about her mother. And I'll say something else now. About myself. I really didn't like all these miracles of miracles either. I might have been a complete idiot but I was an idiot in love. I didn't understand but I could sense what a burden her unique gift was.

Then later when the gymnast died at the circus school and Anna seemed to have told her beforehand, hoping to protect her... Well, it doesn't really matter... What does matter is that everyone lost the plot a little bit, started avoiding her like the plague, being nasty about her behind her back... That's when I realized I would have to protect her all my life ... from all harm... And from herself too.

How can I put it? It's not a job. It's not a well-rehearsed trick. It's a fragile gift, dangerous ... a bit creepy. It doesn't work to order. It all depended on far too much, her mood, her well-being, who was with her... And what's more, even she didn't know everything about herself. Sometimes, she would find something out for the first time. For example, she was taken aback once just before we went on... Basically, she'd lost her comb. We were sitting in the dressing room, getting ready, doing our make-up... And she had a wonderful head of hair then, not styled at all. She sat there, bareheaded, put the tiara to one side and quietly stared at herself in the mirror as if she could find a way in by looking at it. God, how I hated those sessions in front of the mirror. I was in a hurry. "Get a move on," I said, "We're on soon. We need to warm up." Suddenly, the door opens and in comes Kim Devyatkin, the clown, and a comb falls out of his trouser pocket right at her feet. Small, grubby, with three broken teeth.

Anna bent down kind of slowly, picked it up and said, confused, "Thanks, Uncle Kim."

And he's like, "Thanks for what? 'sNot mine. Someone dropped it."

Believe me, at the time I didn't think she should be allowed into the ring. After all, our work hangs on a millimetre. It takes mental as well as physical balance. We had five minutes before we were due on the wire and she's sitting, pulling that comb slowly through her hair. And giving herself such a look in the mirror... I can't describe it ... confused and ... hateful, you know?

That's how it was... Sometimes we'd be taken somewhere and given separate accommodation. Sometimes, we might stay in some friends' empty flat, while some of our performers were on tour... We'd arrive, unpack, have a shower ... and yadda, yadda. Once, she forgot her nail scissors, she was so scatty. So she went to the chest of drawers in the corner of someone else's room and took a pair of scissors from underneath a pile of letters in the third drawer down.

Everything other people saw as flat, she saw in 3-D. Knitting would get muddled, caught up somehow. She could see the thread in the tangle and unravel it right away.

She could get in without a ticket, too, anywhere she fancied. Here's how she explained it to me. As long as there was nothing on her body that could act as an allergen. The scent of perfume, for example, the glint of jewellery... Gemstones were especially dangerous, she said. Especially precious stones. I only remembered later, much later, that we used to steal apples from a palatial garden not far from Pirogovo, Vinnitsa, during our motorbike holidays. The batty old owner used to fire soil from a gun. He'd come over, shout a bit, then fire. She left me outside, climbed over the fence, tore the apples off and threw them over the fence to me. Not really bothering to hide. And there he was shooting at some lads, bellowing and shaking his gun... He couldn't see her! Couldn't see her at all!

You know, I hardly plagued her with questions but sometimes, especially if she was tired or not very well, she would suddenly tell me something. Like a precious little pouch coming undone by accident and a tiny glittering gemstone falling out unnoticed.

She went down with flu once in the middle of a guest tour of Tashkent. Or rather, not flu ... there was a terrible incident. Or rather, not terrible, just the usual circus mayhem. We used to lose so many animals, it hurts to remember. Sometimes I even dream of something from my past life—how the sea lions cried when they were being taken somewhere in their cages in the blazing heat.

And the way animals are moved from town to town on freight trains! Who travels with them at the end of the day? A couple of minor officials, chronically shit faced. The conditions are horrendous, especially in winter. There have been fatalities even, when the hay caught fire or the animals simply froze to death. For example, we went on tour to the States once. The animals travelled by sea. That wasn't much fun either. And again, a couple of officials went with them, plus a guy from the KGB, so that the other blokes didn't wander off in port. No, the real beasts are the trainers not the animals.

I will say this for him, that Guy Légalité at Cirque de la Lune, he's point blank rejected all the antiquated shenanigans of the Durov Animal Theatre and other torturers. They predicted he'd be a complete flop: You can't have a circus without animals And now it's the best circus in the world!

What was I saying? Oh, yes, the incident in Tashkent. There was this illusionist, no talent at all, a real no-hoper, and the act was shit as well. He forgot to take two dogs out of a charged-up box after the show and went off on the town. The dogs spent the whole night crammed into a really narrow pipe. Of course, they suffocated...

Pardon? Charged-up boxes? They're the illusionist's trick boxes. They're "charged up" before a show, ready to work, and then no matter how many buttons you press, everything comes falling, running, flying out... And again, we call preparing our apparatus for a show charging up as well. That's what we say: Come on, guys, let's charge it up—putting the props on the platforms, attaching the safety ropes in the correct places, hanging up fans, carrying the balances up, clipping them to brackets on the platforms. That's what we do, the wire walkers. So that everything's ready for the job, everything's to hand.

And then there are the animals. That myth about humane training, you know... No one anywhere ever saw harsher treatment of animals than in the Soviet circus! I've seen plenty. I could tell a tale or two. When a trainer and his assistants bring a bear out of its cage on strong leashes, stretched out to the side and you can hear the cry of "Hold tight!" even at a distance, everyone gets as far out of the way as they can. A bear is the most dangerous animal, you see, far more dangerous than a lion. It never gives any indication that it's about to attack and if a bear does manage to escape, everyone races off to find somewhere to hide and doesn't stop to look behind them.

Right ... the dogs. I had never seen Anna like it. I tell you, I never saw her like that when we were growing up. The way she went for him. Flew at him. Thumping him relentlessly, frenziedly... We could barely drag her off... And that day she went down with a fever. I lay next to her that evening. She was burning up, tossing and turning, muttering really rapidly, talking about something. I gave her a double dose of aspirin, hot tea and honey and rubbed vodka all over her, trying to bring the fever to a head. We were on tour. You can't go getting sick. Tomorrow you're on the wire, in the ring, even if it kills you.

And then, sobbing away pitifully under my arm, she told me how when she was small she once knocked hell out of a little girl in their courtyard, a scabby little thief she was, called Zoyka. For nicking something off Firavelna, Arisha's blind grandma, from right under her nose in the kitchen. In short, Anna gave the little thief a real drubbing and then she collapsed too, right there in the kitchen. Arisha had to go for Anna's father and he carried her home.

That's how she discovered she mustn't raise her hand to anyone. That some sort of mirrors behind her forehead would break. Shatter into smithereens… And take a very long time to repair.

So it's a pointless question, as you can see. I knew every inch of her body, every tiny mark… There was a round mark behind her right ear. She roared with laughter if I kissed it. It tickled. But I couldn't see inside her head. I just couldn't.

And do you think it was easy for me? Do you think it's comfortable lying next to a woman who can hear everything going on in your head? Although there was something else as well. A sureness of being supported. Just that: held in the most literal sense. I'll tell you about one incident.

Our routine included a virtuoso trick on the oblique wire. The wire was really long so that there could be a serious drop in its height. The upper wire inclined from 12 metres to 17 and even higher…

I went along with a balance pole, stopped, put on a black blindfold, unclipped the safety line and carried on, unable to see. I wasn't completely blind, obviously. I could see the spotlights. I asked for the follow-spot to be trained onto the platform. And at some point, I would pretend to have made a mistake. My foot would slip off, the audience howled… and I just kept going to reach the platform in triumph and at a very great height. Well, during the minutes that took, Anna would stand on the platform and not take her eyes off me for a second, holding me in place with her gaze. I could feel it, physically, with my whole body. As if an extra balance had arisen inside, somewhere near my spine… But once, in Novosibirsk… She always used to say that we shouldn't make such a steep angle but me, stubborn as a mule, I insisted on it being steeper and steeper. It did not end well! Either I hadn't scraped the soles of my boots clean properly or I hadn't rubbed in enough rosin but my foot slipped for real and in a mere second there I was dangling at a crazy height. I'd grabbed the wire with one hand and was holding a heavy balancing pole in the other, an aluminium pipe in a lead sleeve, around 10-12 kilos. I couldn't just drop it. It would hit the audience. Take out a whole heap of spectators. And there was the blindfold too. And even then, I could feel I was being held, I was… Anyway, with my elbow or my shoulder, I don't remember, I tore the blindfold off, threw the balance pole into the middle of the ring and reached the platform using just my hands. You should have seen the audience! But I was looking at Anna on the opposite platform and understood that I had to do the trick again. There was no other way. Otherwise, the pep would be gone and there was nothing worse for a tightrope walker. You can understand that at that moment there was only one thing I wanted and that was to get down. To crawl into the dressing room, lie flat and die like a sick dog… But I could see her face was like stone and her still eyes like green flames. "You're on," she told me wordlessly. "Go on!"

Once again, I stepped onto the wire... There were shouts of "No, don't" from the audience. The ticket lady couldn't bear it. She threw the programmes on the floor and ran out into the foyer... And such a quiet descended that the air reverberated the way it does in the countryside… There was another wire beneath my inclined one. If you fell onto that, it would quite simply slice you in half… That's the way it was... But she was holding me up. I knew she was ... and I got across. It was a triumph! Not mine, ours, understand?

You don't mind if I order something a little stronger? I'm free this evening and it would be good to get off to sleep tonight.

"Monsieur! Monsieur! Cent grammes de whiskey, s'il vous plait."

So, what was I saying? That it wasn't easy being with her and that's putting it mildly. After all, you know, she never told a lie. And her sense of humour was a bit peculiar too. She just blurted out whatever she was thinking to anyone. And I'm sorry, I'm not the soul of tact either but all the same over the years—we were living with other people, after all—I'd learnt to hold my tongue to some extent. Not her! In the generally accepted sense, she wasn't a nice or a *comfortable* person, as they say now. That's what our life together lacked, comfort. And in every meaning of the word too.

And yet, you know, I can't even begin to imagine what it's like to hear the thoughts of the person you're speaking to, to know what someone you work with, or a friend, really thinks about you! What was it like for her? And if anyone knew about her gift, it was really hard for that person to be around her. Even, suppose, someone wished you no harm at all and generally minded their own business still, there aren't many people who would like having someone else rule the roost in their brain.

On the subject of her gift, which was never the slightest use to her in her entire life, it really wasn't…

No, my mistake. She did once make herself use it. But there was no other option at the time. Her father was on his death bed in Kiev and she knew, could tell, that he was dying. And she kept coming up against a nasty official at the Ukrainian Embassy who wouldn't give her a visa. Anna had her own issues with the law because of what happened in the circus in Atlanta…

Anyway, when she realized that her father only had hours left, she went to see that bitch and she did something to her. I can't tell you what exactly but, believe me, when she wanted, those eyes like the sea could draw any conscious being into such deep waters and hold them under till they passed out altogether… And that cow at the Embassy, she signed and stamped everything, good as gold. Anna told me about it a couple of months later when she came back from Kiev after burying her father and I got back from Moscow after making two film clips. Anyhow, she only mentioned *the incident* in passing and her face was so pained that I went easy on the questions.

At any rate, the longer things went on, the more people avoided her. Towards the end, there were days, weeks, even months when being with people made her feel as if she was contagious.

Senya was the only person who was never fazed by anything to do with her. He said to me once, "All that's stored up under these grey hairs," and here he tapped himself on the top of the head, "is love, a commodity that's difficult to shift and isn't subject to tax."

I've already told you. He and I ran into each other once in Las Vegas. About seven years ago.

I was there on a Cirque de la Lune contract to train two new people brought in as understudies for the famous water show, you know, "O." And he was out there with his orchestra on a two-week tour.

And I spotted him in the Bellagio Hotel bar. He was on his own at a table, smiling to himself and getting quietly hammered…

I wasn't scared of running into him any more by then. If I hadn't killed her at the time and I'd certainly tried, aware that I was doing it so that I could kick the bucket afterwards myself… I mean if I hadn't done away with her back then, why would I bother with him after so many years … What would be the point? I had already realized that she had simply chosen him. As she'd chosen me once.

So I went over. We had a drink in the bar then went to his room and partied through the night. I—what? I couldn't accept it, you see. I couldn't and I can't accept that she threw me over, cast me out of her life. Or rather, didn't even cast me out, just forgot me, the way a useless drunk of a mother forgets her baby at the station and is lured on to a random train by her fellow drinkers without even knowing where it's going... She was like that all her life. She cast out, forgot her own parents. Her mother went nuts because of her. Hardly surprising. She went mad! And her father, that fantastic guy, how lost, how wretched he was when he came to Moscow. He was hoping to persuade her, to take her out of the circus school. "Nyuta," he pleaded, "Nyuta, darling, come home for Mashuta's sake! Save Mashuta, darling!" And she … it's impossible to convey to you how she looked at him as if from a long way away, deep in thought, as if she was looking at him across the years, do you understand? As if he was one of a crowd of people scuttling around somewhere far below. And her calm reply, "It won't do anything to help, Daddy. It won't change anything."

Her expression was so resigned… Like she was bowing to her fate. Women in villages have that expression when they've buried three children in a row… Her eyes alone—how their sorrowful green ice flashed beneath her eyelids. You know, I was so spooked by her explanation back then, I actually left the room. Lit a cigarette, went down to the courtyard. Let them sort it out without me, I thought.

And now, when yet again I can't get to sleep until morning, I think, Who knows, who could know even, what she could see before it happened, what kind of sentence she was obliged to serve? And where did she find the strength to shoulder that burden, all the futility of the future, all the worthless jumble of our destinies?

As for me, I would have followed her gladly no matter where. Just tell me: you want to go to Kiev? Kiev, it is. To the North? The North, it is. The desert, a swamp, the sky? Wherever you say...

But what's the point of saying that now?

Right, where was I? That drinking session with Senya in Las Vegas, in 1998...

All the same, I wanted to understand why she dumped me, somebody young, good-looking, strong, who she'd spent years with. And we had everything, she and I: real intimacy and danger and injury and success, an uncanny physical union, our uncanny merging together in both ecstasy and risk… Why did she throw that away, cast it out of her life and become so committed to an old, grey, permanently unshaven, misfit muso who couldn't give her anything except infrequent meetings, sentimental letters and some sort of otherworldly, allegedly everlasting love?

And you know, no matter how much he drank, he never got drunk. He was very resilient when it came to drinking. Musicians are a good match for circus folk in that. And then he had this way of speaking … elegant, sophisticated … and no swearing. As if he was delivering a post-grad lecture. And then, in fucking Las Vegas, a snazzy artificial American city in the desert, we talked about her all night long.

You should have heard how he explained things! It'd blow your mind. For example, he swore she was an angel. You gotta laugh, right? Not an angel-from-heaven kind of angel but, according to him, her nature was similar to some sort of beings that appear as angels and archangels and other celestial beings in folk psychology… That people believe in them because from time to time such beings really do appear on earth among humans… Jesus, for example. Do you believe? I don't really. And I'm sorry for being so blunt but she could do an awful lot that Jesus used to do. I don't know about the resurrection of the dead, I can't say. To be fair, there haven't been any instances… But she could easily pretend to be dead. And so well that you would rush to phone the undertaker in no doubt at all.

Hang on, I've got something mixed up. I started with angels and ended up with dead bodies. May they rest in peace. And for the record, that trick—it's called the "living corpse"—used to be performed at markets and fairs in old Russia. Honestly. We learnt that in History of the Circus with Elka, Elina Yakovlevna Podvorksaya. The performer goes into a state of deep trance, lowers his body temperature, grows stiff, his breathing slows so much it's imperceptible. Obviously, it takes willpower and certain abilities. Do you know who else could do it? Old Longo the Fakir. He came to visit our school when he was already an ancient little old man. So, Longo, he could do an awful lot—put knitting needles through his cheeks, swallow swords. He even used to take his eye ball out and hold it on a spoon near his face. Crazy stuff… And Anna, when he'd shown us that trick, the living corpse, she wasn't herself for days. She sat practising … for hours at a time. And she did it. Was she stubborn?! She really scared me on two occasions. I nearly dropped dead with fright.

It's a shame you didn't hear what a good speech Senya gave. I can't remember his spiel word for word… About what Spinoza said and some Hegel or other and this, that and the other… One thing led to another as if of its own accord when he was speaking and so naturally, convincingly. There are people, he said, and no shortage of them either, who struggle all their lives to become demi… demiurges. Am I saying it right? But it can happen that a demiurge longs with all its might simply to remain a human being. Do you understand what that means? It's telling God Almighty Himself that "I'm giving you your portrait back."

Like it or not, you end up believing you've spent ten years living with an angel. And you can still remember her eyes at dawn when she opened them as if she was still staring at an abandoned horizon … was still in pursuit of her own kind as they flew away … such a clean-washed heavenly green. And suddenly they'd darken from the inside, darken and be filled with such yearning…I sneaked a peak at her waking up like this a few times. I have to say it was awkward embracing such a yearning soul… And she needed to be set free … except how and where to?

But Senya didn't seem all that upset. "What is it about her that bothers you?" he said. "Her detachedness, her otherworldliness? It's because of the vast reach of her vision. For instance, how far does an ant see? And an eagle? That's why the ant carries tiny specks into the anthill while the eagle soars in the cold heights. Can an eagle love an ant?" he said. "It can only pity it because the eagle can see the ant's entire route to the anthill where it will be crushed by the boot of a tourist, bright-eyed and bushy tailed with a cheery song on his lips. 'I love to go a-wandering…'"

And I was drunk. I believed it all. I believed that I'd spent ten years living with an angel, that she'd been sent down to earth to be with me for a while and then recalled, sort of "Right, that's your lot, you bastard, off you go on your own now and ponder what you had, what you've lost…" Sometimes, however bitter it may be, I do think that perhaps she earned her Senya *through me, through the circus waggon, through all that vagabond affliction.* Which guy was it in the Bible, I can't remember, who ploughed fields for seven years and then another seven to win his one true love?

Then sometimes, I think as if I'm coming out of a trance, God, what was it all for, that nightmare of a life? The circus, the strolling gang of permanently drunk partners and travelling companions, making a living at your peril … and finally, my loneliness in Canada…What was it for? After all, she was the one who made me lose my bearings.

Then again, what do you think I would have done otherwise? Drunk myself to death like my dear old dad… But she dragged me by the ears, spun me around, put a balance pole in my hands and sent me off along the wire: to walk above life, above the earth, simply above! Always and only above! Always!

There…

Then Senya looked so sad I thought he'd gone to sleep but all of a sudden he lifted his head and said, crisply and clearly, "You could also ask which of them is happier and the answer would come from the cold, ringing sorrow of the bottomless sky."

That's right. Yes, that's something I do remember: "the cold, ringing sorrow of the bottomless sky."

CHAPTER 16.

They didn't make it to Kiev right away. They travelled the length and breadth of Central Asia, the Urals, the Far East first. Eventually, the Central Administration didn't so much swap indifference for kindness as start to pay occasional attention to requests from various circus managers.

And more and more often these were for the "aerial tightrope walkers, the Streletskys."

And then, in February 1986, they found themselves in Kiev.

The city had changed a great deal. Pioneers' Park, once Merchants' Park, had been rudely disfigured by a grotesque monument to Ukraine's friendship with Russia. A granite group of boyars plus Bogdan Khmelnitsky and a huge metal arch now towered on the site of the promenade that used to direct walkers towards a marvellous belvedere with a view over the Dnieper. The promenade and central spaces had been covered in asphalt, ruining a whole mass of greenery.

Just as before, however, in the Bessarabka district, rosy-cheeked tradeswomen from villages near and far continued to stand in long rows, aprons over their winter jumpers, their heads wrapped in brightly-coloured Ukrainian headscarves. Just as before, they were selling honey, pork fat, sauerkraut. Also just as before, butchers sang the pork fat's praises, demonstrating its soft brown skin, smoked in straw, and saying over and over, "Try a bit of skin. See how soft it is."

The population of the communal flats had long since been scattered across new housing developments. The Girshoviches—Arisha had written about it—had been given a three-room flat in the Obolon district. Borya had long since married a violinist with the orchestra of the State Committee for TV and Radio Broadcasting, had a daughter, and was threatening to go off "to a normal country" where real musicians prospered instead of being left to rot. His parents had grown old, along with

Sonya, the daughter of their late sister Busya, may-her-memory-be-a-blessing-and-all-who-killed-her-burn-in-hell. Firavelna had quietly passed away a couple of years ago in her sleep, as befitted a righteous woman. She had slipped unwittingly from her temporary darkness into permanent night.

"Or maybe into light?" Arisha asked pensively. She had truly blossomed by then and not just because she had undergone successful surgery on her squinting left eye at the Fyodorov Clinic and now gazed triumphantly and straight-eyed out from the new photograph she had immediately sent to her forever friend. She had blossomed as Firavelna would have said "all around": She'd put on weight, had a stylish haircut and overall she'd acquired the look of a well-heeled Westerner. Indeed, she had already spent a good deal of time in either the Belgian city of Mechelen, invited there to teach at the international carillon school, or on tour. Very occasionally she and Anna met up in Moscow when their complicated tour orbits intersected.

Arisha and her husband Marik—who was then in the process of moving, or rather being passed on like a Red Banner award from one family to another—lived in a two-room Khrushchev-era flat on Presnensky Val. Whenever Anna turned up, Marik was driven out for the whole day so as not to be underfoot or to butt into their Kiev conversations (he wasn't the sharpest knife in the drawer, as it was).

Arisha would cancel her teaching and any meetings, unplug the phone.

Anna would appear in the doorway and gasp every time—Arisha just got prettier and prettier.

"Am I pretty?" Arisha would asked plaintively as she did as a child and Anna would sigh with feeling as she did as a child, "Awfully pretty."

And they would spend a long, blissfully unhurried day, putting Firavelna's trademark mushroom pie in the oven, the recipe for which she had brought from the Czech colony. They would bustle about in the kitchen, smoking and, to begin with, interrupting one another in heated discussions of everything under the sun, then lolling on the sofa, drowsily finishing off the conversation. Falling asleep … waking up again…

"D'you know who else met an easy death?" Arisha said during one of these meetings. "Old Fayushchenko. You won't believe this. He went into the bathroom to wash his brushes after a sitting, fell and was dead. The model ran out, wrapped up in a sheet or something, a nipple hanging out at the side... And the thing is he really didn't want to move out of his room. He used to wave his arms about and say he'd hold a sit-down strike outside the City Executive Committee … well, he's on permanent strike now. Do you remember his astrakhan hat? The neighbours divvied up the pictures. Even Major Petya. Such a little old man now and he's stopped drinking. He sneaked out a nude without telling Lyubov Kazimirovna. She found it, created merry hell, took it outside and threw it away. The yard keeper picked it up. And I chose two portraits on card. They're not finished … but there's something about them. Wait, I'll show you them right now."

She brought two small, unframed cards out of the box room. Set them each on a chair.

"I just can't get round to having them framed," Arisha said. "Life's so hectic."

"But who are they?" Anna asked, closely inspecting the two portraits, an old man and a boy. The old man was drawn in a range of ochres, the background unfinished. Even so, the expressive face with a large, characterful nose, strong chin and calm eyes had come out well. The boy wasn't finished either, just a few broad blue strokes instead of a shirt. Generally speaking, the boy was painted as if he had just sat down for a minute and was about to dash off at any second. It was a fine face. A small forelock stuck out on a shaven head, grey eyes canted cunningly sideways, a faint smile on the lips.

"I haven't the faintest idea," Arisha said, plonking herself down on the sofa next to Anna. And they were both silent, contemplating the portraits. "It says 'Arnautkin' on the back of the old man's for some reason. His surname maybe? The person who would have been able to say was Panna Ivanna. She's dead now. She remembered everybody."

"The boy," Anna mused. "I know him."

Arisha roared with laughter and hugged her, pulling her close and planting a kiss on her cheek.

"Get a grip!" she said. "He's not a little boy any more. He's an old man. The year's written on the back: 1952."

∗∗∗

Anna's father attended the performance on the very first evening although she was still plucking up courage to ring and invite him. Touchingly, he purchased the most expensive ticket and sat in the second row across from the ring entrance. And, running in after the usual introduction—"the aerial tightrope walkers, the Streletskys!!!"—Anna saw him right away. The lenses of his glasses shone in the spotlights and her heart tugged her in his direction in any case. He sat wearing his unmoving, official, "doctor's" expression, meaning he was horribly worked up.

She threw her arms wide in a fixed bow, to wait out for a few seconds the roar of applause with which the audience always greeted their dazzling entrance. And then she cast a fleeting glance to where his glasses shone. His sight must have deteriorated if he was wearing them all the time…

And she knew that he would enjoy, really enjoy their routine. It was sterling work and her father had always been a good judge of that sort of thing, had always loved risk and courage and the beauty of physical effort, had always respected, even venerated, any physical achievement or artistry.

After the show, she asked the ringhand Slava to run over and bring her father into the dressing room. She deliberately didn't get changed. Let him see her in makeup, in costume, close up. And when he came in, as imposing as ever, stooping slightly in the rather cramped space of the dressing room cluttered with wardrobe trunks, he actually froze in the doorway, hesitating to approach his daughter.

"Oh, look at you," her father said and, with a grimace, she launched herself at him and they hugged each other firmly as they did when she was little. "No piggy backs for you anymore," he said.

And then they talked quickly, both at the same time, happily. For some reason he went through her whole routine, probably because he wanted to show that he'd noticed and appreciated and was thrilled… Volodka, he was a sensitive chap at the end of the day, went out and left them alone… And they kept on interrupting one another and reminiscing and simply couldn't get enough of it…

But not a word about Mashuta, not one single word, until eventually Anna said, "You know, Daddy, I'd like to see her."

He faltered, his smile vanished. He grew thoughtful, evidently looking for the right words. Then he remembered that this was Nyuta … that with her there was no need to find the right words…

With some effort, he said, "You see, my darling… She's at home now, after a long time in hospital…" Then abruptly, he slapped his knee as if angry at himself. "You know, what? Come. Just come… I'll prepare the way, make an effort… She's in remission just now. She is, really!"

Once his mind was made up, he cheered up again and starting telling tales of the hospital. They were refusing outright to let him retire!

"Why do you need to retire?" Anna asked in surprise. "You're far too young, Daddy."

Volodka appeared. He'd brought coffee and sweets from the canteen and the three of them sat for quite some time until her father suddenly came to himself, checked the time and let out a gasp. "Will you look at that?" he said. "How time flies! And I feel as if I've only been here a minute. Khristina's keeping an eye on Mashuta, such a kind soul. She was longing to see the show but let me come first."

"Never mind," Anna replied, "she'll still get to see it."

As he prepared to leave, her father took a hospital envelope out of his coat pocket, with a smaller envelope sticking out and she recognized the handwriting immediately, while he was still holding it.

Only one person in the world could have written her a letter in *that* handwriting. She darted across and snatched it out of his hand. While her father hurriedly explained that it had reached them three years ago and he'd hidden it so that Mashuta didn't … and then, silly old clot that he was, he'd forgotten about it, Anna was already reading, her eyes skimming the lines avidly, soaking up the elegant turn of thought, the beautiful mirror writing, inexplicably reflecting the way her own progressed, spooling away in tiny spirals, fitting precisely into the available space, inscribing the coils of her mind's momentum.

"Nyuta, my angel!" Eliezer wrote and each word resounded within her with sweet longing for her real self, for the self so oddly reflected by this physically very different person, who nevertheless was her secret twin, the mirror of her soul. "I don't know whether you will read this letter. I hope some day you will…"

When her father had gone, she reread the letter more calmly, over and over again, taking little sips from what was already her third cup of coffee. She maintained a strange, profound silence … wiping her eyes with her forearm a couple of times.

Volodka, already out of makeup and costume, sat in the armchair, patiently leafing through a year-old copy of "Variety and Circus" magazine, waiting for her to come round and tell him about that weirdo, who had popped up like a jack in the box, for goodness sake! He wondered what he was up to, what he was doing for a living.

∗∗∗

The following day, a day off, Anna went up to the second floor, up the stairs she knew even by feel, carrying a bunch of purple asters and a big box of chocolates.

The entrance hall had recently been painted. The "Anya's stupid" carved into the banister in desperation by one Volodka Streletsky in Grade Seven had been painted over in brown but could still be made out by touch.

And as she climbed, she could see herself desperately running away again more and more clearly. Already knowing how it would go, she strove wholeheartedly to hold back the avalanche. She stood, just outside the door, shifting from one foot to the other... She turned round a couple of times, went down a few steps and then back up again. It's just to see, she told herself. She made up her mind and breathed a heavy sigh the way she did before going out onto the tightrope and rang the bell.

Her father opened the door, dressed formally and uncomfortably as if going out. He stepped outside towards her, pulling the door behind him and said in a hushed voice, "Wait here just a minute... I'm optimistic... I've worked at it and... I'm hopeful!"

He went inside and Anna heard the stupidly, awkwardly cheerful voice he'd used as Grandfather Frost when she was little, "And who's been to see little Nyuta? Who's left some lovely little presents?"

"Mashuta! Masha, darling ... do you know who's come to see us?" Silence. Or perhaps an impossibly quiet voice.

Khristina, however, gasped and with a shout of delight said, "What? Is our little Nyuta really here?"

She ruined everything, damn her! There was silence, a strained silence... But her father continued, cheerfully, "That's right, our Nyuta's here, Mashenka. Your daughter's here to see you."

Alas, he was no actor and no diplomat, poor soul...

Anna shoved the door open, went in, took her jacket off and threw it onto a chair.

She could see Masha in an armchair through an open door. She was terribly changed: greyer, shrunken and yet at the same time heavier somehow. Later on, rifling through her memories of the meeting, Anna realized what had given the impression of heaviness—Masha's swollen, impassive face and the lethargic movement of her once quick, deep-set eyes.

She went over and squatted down in front of Mashuta, stroked a limp hand and said, "Ma, I've been so longing to see you."

Mashuta looked helplessly at her husband. He gave a tender smile. There was so much suffering in it.

"What is it, love, don't you recognize Nyuta?"

And then Masha spoke in a dull, cracked voice, "But this isn't her."

And suddenly got to her feet. Anna did the same. She could see Mashuta's face slowly changing, her agitation growing, red blotches spreading across her cheeks.

"Tolya!" Masha said to her husband. "For goodness sake, you are so gullible … I knew you'd fall for it. It's not her!"

"So who is it then?" cried Khristina. "A fine mess this is!" And, irritated, Nyuta's father gestured at her behind her back: Shut up, for God's sake, you blithering idiot.

"Mashuta," he began patiently. "We agreed you and I … We talked it all over… You promised me…"

"I promised about Nyuta!" Masha exclaimed with some force. "But it's not her. I can tell! Nyuta may have passed away long since! This is that damned wretch from the mirror, it is, I tell you!"

Recoiling, Anna backed away.

Her father strode over and put an arm firmly around his daughter's shoulders.

"Masha, Masha!" he entreated. "For the love of God! Get a grip. It's Nyuta, our little girl! She's an amazing artiste nowadays! If you had seen the audience applauding her, how much pleasure, how much delight…"

Dear God, why was he…? Could he really not see how firmly ensconced the madness was in those pasty features?

In desperation, she said "Ma," and then, for the first time in her life, "Mama!"

Mashuta suddenly sprang back to life. A subtle and insatiable idea appeared in her eyes.

"There, you see!" she told her husband in triumph. "See? Nyuta never called me 'Mama'. That's not Nyuta. It's her blasted reflection! She's destroyed Nyuta, devoured her and now she's come for me! Tolya! Quick, smash her to pieces. Go on!"

She was shouting now, spraying spittle. Khristina grabbed her elbows from behind in an attempt to gain control of the trembling, flailing arms. And Tolya bent towards the sick woman, firmly embracing the writhing body.

Anna bolted into the entrance hall, grabbed her jacket and her hat, tumbled down the stairs and ran almost the length of Zhilyanskaya Street as she was, still holding her jacket.

In the end, she began to slow down … to slow down and then to stop. She put her jacket on, struggling for ages to get her arms in the sleeves, crammed her hat on her head and took a deep breath of the frosty fumes of the railway district she grew up in.

The dull cloudy sky of the winter's day was implacably locked and bolted.

Not the slightest movement met the eye.

****

If they had struck lucky with anyone, it was their partner Ninka, Nyuta's fun-loving roommate from the student hostel. What a resourceful woman she turned out to be. It came as a surprise every time. And her eye was designed in such a way that she could fish just the right speck of glitter, some glass beads or a few links of a chain from any pile of jumble on the counter of any village shop or from boxes of broken kaleidoscopes. And she already knew where they would go, on which bra or safety belt, so that they would sparkle like precious stones under the spotlights. Costumes are a not-insignificant part of any routine.

In general, costumes were run up in the circus's sewing unit but obtaining permission to have one made required a slog around the offices of the Central Administration. It gave you more corns than training did.

Nor was it easy to cadge material, and costumes were different for the upper crust and for ordinary performers. In the circus, connections were needed everywhere.

And then there was Ninka. She thought up all her own costumes and she made them too. What a fringe she trimmed her cloak with! She went to a poultry farm somewhere in Moscow Region where, for five roubles, they raked together a vast cloud-like sack of white chicken feathers for her.

Then she and Anna spent two days sorting through them, picking out downy feathers in the circus hotel… They sat naked, down stuck all over them, amid clouds of feather-light snow, sneezing, swearing, cursing their existence, occasionally jumping up and rushing into the shower… Then, they washed them all and dried them with a hair dryer. Anna came up with the idea of fixing the tiny feathers, as light as breath, to a strip of sticking plaster and winding it around a pencil. It produced luxurious little boas that Nina then stitched all around the edge of her cloak.

And such white plumes towered above their heads on willowy strips of metal and they were made of chicken feathers too. They fluttered and quivered as soon as the performer tilted her head towards her shoulder… If only those hens, now long since eaten, had known what a dazzling stage career was in store for their feathers!

***

A city premiere always meant rapid breathing and trembling hands but also a flash, a paroxysm of delight in the pit of your stomach, a cranked-up physical weightlessness. Lights! Music! Applause closing over your head like a giant wave in a mighty gale...

Before going on, you warm up backstage near the entrance to the arena. There's bound to be a large mirror there. And, as a ritual, before going into the ring, everyone has to examine themselves in it from all sides, adopt a couple of poses. After all, in a minute, hundreds of demanding eyes will be seeing you exactly like that.

Anna did not like these mirrors. They were cloudy, fit to be thrown away. A fake life, shapeshifter faces curled in their depths. These circus mirrors at the entry to the ring had taken in and digested so much falsehood, baseness, gossip, betrayal and flattery, had reflected so many wigs and false noses, tail coats and tuxedos, starched shirt fronts, fans, frippery, the sparkle of cheap bits of glass… so many powdered cheeks, pasted on beauty spots, arched eyebrows and bright red, bloodsucking lips that they could no longer provide a true reflection of people or things and everything was featureless, depleted and dull.

It took extreme care not to break them by accident with a blow from an arm or a leg. It was very bad luck to see yourself in a mirror fragment. Best go off sick if you did.

And yet those mirrors contained the most important thing: the final glance before going out to face the many-headed, many-eyed bellowing maw that was the audience. The audience! God and Caesar, judge and executioner. The audience! Is that how they'll see you? Is that how they'll judge you?

Oh, Lord, have mercy upon us! Good Lord, deliver us!

A premiere in town! You've got the heebie-jeebies from early in the morning but by the time the show starts you can't feel your body at all… You rub your hands with eau de cologne so that they don't sweat or dip them in chalk—and you're on! You stand *on the apparatus*. Your legs are weak. Your chest's tight. It's normal. And now it's nearly your turn: a deep breath in and out. You vigorously clench and unclench your fists three or four times. Give the inner command: Focus! And as you head into the routine, you're already calm and centred. Except that you can't see anything around you, the world is blurry, fuzzy, a listless plash in the distance.

And the ecstatic roar is barely a flicker. It doesn't reach your heart.

But when a trick's already tried and tested, familiar from daily runthroughs, when you control your body the way an experienced spoken-word artist does their voice, you don't switch off any longer, you can make out individual faces: there's a little girl with one lens of her glasses covered over; there's an old chap with a moustache who's still got his hat on. And you can hear every sound, all the *familiar sounds of the circus*, albeit a bit muffled…

And once you've got the trick off pat, the first half hour is just like flying. Then, of course, tiredness kicks in, especially on Sundays after the third performance… You shuffle off to the hotel, dragging your feet, the makeup washed off somehow. The huge expenditure of energy saps your lifeblood. You're drained … the soughing silence of muscle… But bodies are revived one way or another. One person doesn't get out of bed until the following evening. Another grabs a bottle like a life belt and drinks until they collapse. A third, like Volodka, simply sleeps like a dormouse and then, on waking, whips up a twelve-egg omelette, tucks in like a coachman at an inn and there he is—fresh as a daisy.

***

Anna's habit of flying straight from the dressing room to the ring entrance at almost the very last moment had always driven Volodka crazy. He, by contrast, had a preternatural sense of time. You could ask him the time sometimes and he would give the right answer to within a couple of minutes without even looking at his wrist. He was always irritated when Anna had her head in the clouds. What was she doing, dawdling about like that till the last possible minute when the guys had already warmed up and Sokolnichy's clown trio could be heard finishing off their "wicket gate" routine?

They always went to watch this reprise if they weren't working. The trio would come out to the music of a well-known soulful romance— tall, lanky Egor, playing a young and seductive Gypsy girl, stumpy Sokolnichy himself made up and dressed as an old Gypsy with a curling Assyrian beard and Vityok, a young guitar-playing Gypsy. All three of them sang the romance, swaying, tuneful to start with, heartrending …

gradually they upped the tempo and started to dance… And soon they were dancing fit to burst heart and heels, smashing a pretend bench and wicket gate in their enthusiasm.

Most importantly, though, it was all done with such rapturous, inspired, earnest faces! The audience fell off their chairs, wiping away the tears…

"Right, let's go!" Volodka said and left the dressing room. It was a few steps away from the entrance to the arena.

Anna finished cleaning her boots with a metal comb, put them on with slippers over the top, threw a dressing gown over her costume and headed for the entrance. And there by the red velvet curtain, already warmed up and out of their slippers and dressing gowns, they waited for their act to be announced.

When you stand at the entrance and you know that you're on in a moment, it's as if the flick of a switch takes you to a different energy level.

"There. You can hear the racket of Sokolnichy's boneheads finishing off their gate."

Right then, two musicians appeared at either end of the half-dark corridor. One was holding a case. He'd obviously done his bit and was heading off to the canteen. The other, by contrast, was coming from the canteen and yelled from a distance that the sausages were perfectly acceptable today and to hurry up or they'd scoff the lot, those cavemen… To which, the other, drawing nearer…

Why did her heart start to flutter? Something about Dad? Why Dad? When's his birthday? … *He's like Daddy.*

"The aerial tightrope walkers…" It was the hoarse bass voice of the ringmaster, Grigory Lvovich. "… The Streletskys!!!"

On came the music for their act: a smooth rolling river, lashings of romance… Spotlights swivelled towards the ring entrance. The young assistants drew back the curtain and Anna and Nina were the first to sweep through a line of ring attendants. The men followed.

The ringmaster bowed his head respectfully as he admitted the group of performers. Everything just as usual—a most august family's triumphal walkabout among the people…

The morning after the rehearsal she went over to the musicians. Her pulse was pounding in her temples like an incoming wave, deafening then fading away to the utmost inner peace.

And she saw him, recognized him instantly from behind.

He was stowing an instrument into its case—some sort of wood-wind, she always got them mixed up—with careful, almost unthinking movements, like a mother tucking a baby into its cradle. The fine, strong wrists…

Yes, it was the very same person, their long-ago visitor, just with hair now completely grey and cut very short. It was how Mashuta's father looked in photos taken in exile in Kazakhstan.

He turned and said a few words to the drummer who laughed.

This musician had something of the child about him, something arch, *something out to defy destiny*. Just like her.

… And I know him and I always have…

He was the boy… her boy, the one she was supposed to have run around with, hand in hand… The one who had been appointed… this was who she was meant to be with, to run to, to inspire, to be worthy of … This was who should have been beside her all her life but who, because of some sort of error in the calculations, had slipped by until now. And he'd turned up out of the blue—and this hurt—almost at the end of the road…

At this point, the musician turned round, still suppressing an ironic smile: hollow, grey temples, a two-day beard, a network of wrinkles at the corners of his grey eyes.

They both recoiled slightly, embarrassed. As if about to go their separate ways. It hadn't happened and quite right too.

"No, You are not to use me as entertainment. Break me, if You like. Trample on me, wring my neck, put me on the rack. Just not that!"

He was reflected in the dull white mirrors of early autumn. His woodwind instrument sang, soft and sombre, in a snowstorm.

And it was already late. Too late.

***

When she left Senya and went back to the circus hotel, Volodka was lying on his bed watching Spartak Moscow playing Dynamo Kiev on the transistor TV set he'd placed on his stomach.

They had amassed some clutter over their travelling years. Volodka was a "things" person. He liked his comforts, even on the road.

And for the sake of those comforts, their baggage included a table lamp, an alarm clock, bedspreads, a tablecloth, pieces of crockery, a Morozko fridge and even a Malyutka washing machine. While Anna wouldn't part with a pile of her books that normal people simply didn't read. They were tattered and falling apart from their lengthy journeys: Anna occasionally rebound them, bandaging them with broad strips of sticking plaster.

"Where've you been?" he asked automatically. No answer was needed, especially since Kiev finally had the ball ("…and Prikhodko's got the ball. On to Sidorov, Sidorov moves infield, it's taken up by Bezborody. He's going all the way, he goes past one defender, and another…")

"Volodya," she said, standing in the doorway. "I'm leaving."

"Now where?" he asked, irritated, eyes fixed on the screen. "You've only just got in. What's bugging you? Here I am, waiting for her, haven't even had a bite to eat…"

She said nothing. As the silence built up against the background of the commentator's fast-paced mumbling, Volodka grew more and more uncomfortable, cold even, although it was a very hot evening. Suddenly, he turned abruptly towards Anna.

She carried on standing there, like a casual visitor, like a stranger who'd popped in for a minute just to let him know that…

Why and how did he grasp everything right away? For many years afterwards, he was unable to give an answer. Or rather, he suspected that she'd said everything right there and then but *by other means*. He simply understood it *all*, saw it all—in an instant. Perhaps because, like the day he fell off the wire, she was holding him up with her gaze. And with all her strength.

He took the television off his stomach. Sat on the bed.

"You… what…" he said, his strength draining away in an instant. "Anna, Anna, sweetheart?! What are you on about?"

"I'm leaving for good, Volodya, for good." Her gaze was level, concerned, direct. She was holding him up with all the strength she had left. "Take someone on to replace me in the act… Spend some time in rehearsals. It will all come right in the end, Volodya…"

And she wouldn't stop.

He stood. A chill rose from the pit of his stomach, spread through his chest and turned his heart to ice. His throat was so frozen, he couldn't get a word out.

He strode towards her. He wanted to say something pitiful and tender: No, my darling, my beloved, my one and only. Get a grip. No, you won't do it. You won't do this terrible thing, this nightmare, this dark delusion… Nothing means a thing without you… not this fucking circus, not life, not a single day, my love… love… love… and he felt himself plummeting from such heights that he would inevitably plunge to his death.

He had been beating her up for five minutes when the indefatigable Ninka happened to put her head round the door. Seeing blood on the floor and the walls and Anna, face down by the wall, looking to all the world as if she was dead, she started shrieking like she'd lost her mind.

Some guys rushed in, pinned Volodka's arms to his sides, someone rang the police, an ambulance …

And then for an hour and a half or so everyone hung around in the hotel lobby in excitement, discussing what had happened.

It was unexpected and inexplicable. "They were such a solid couple! Glued at the hip! Such great guys and talented… Up for state recognition, weren't they?"

"Yeah, yeah, guys, maybe she was seeing someone else? Just imagine, killing someone for that…"

"Idiot! You're such a slut, Duska, a guy's hands would fall off trying to kill you every day. But they were in love, these two! Why did Hamlet polish off Ophelia?"

"Not Ophelia, you great oaf, Juliet."

One of the men said he was sorry for Volodka. They should write a collective letter or something, a statement but to whom? The police? The court?

When she got back from the emergency room at the hospital some three hours later, a tear-stained Ninka spent nearly all night washing the blood off the room. What would happen to their act? The assistants? Where could the equipment go? Volodka would definitely be going to jail. Where was Anna going to go if they put her back together again? And where was she, Ninka herself, going to go? All these miserable questions were going round in her head like smalls in the Malyutka washing machine.

Crawling along the floor with a rag she moved beds, chairs, stools out of the way then put them back again…

Behind one little stool, two already opened letters lay on the floor. One was kind of crazy, in that backward writing only Anna could read.

Must be from that bloke abroad. It was a long letter: copperplate handwriting, six pages. Even the numbers of the pages were the wrong way round. Honestly! It takes all sorts. Only a few words on some kind of diagram were written in Latin script that went in the right direction.

Ninka read "Blois" above an arrow.

The other letter was from Anna's friend, the organ player or bell ringer or bell something or other. And Ninka set to reading it avidly in the hope that something might become clear as a result.

Nothing did. It was an ordinary boring letter. And old, too, as Ninka found out later. From 1984. The bell ringer wrote that she'd been given an excellent reception in Belgium, that before her concert, there was a meeting with the burgomaster, cheese tasting and sampling of other delicacies, and only then the concert. And that she'd been really nervous because before the concert she had to go up into the bell tower to warm up, psych herself up but they were still at the reception. But then everything was fine. Some spectators went up to watch her play and a big screen was set up down below for the audience. A camera was installed in the bell tower itself.

And now she had been invited to go straight from Belgium to France to give a series of concerts in Lyon, Dijon and Meribel.

"And something else, Nyutochka," the bell ringer wrote, "my Auntie Ida died suddenly of a stroke, the middle daughter of your beloved Firavelna. I happened to be at my parents' in Kiev. Nobody knew how to tell Grandma. But she sensed something. Her eldest son flew in from Moscow on the day of the funeral and he and my mother decided to prepare her. They were barely through the door when Grandma looked up and asked, 'Is my Ida dead?' They started crying and so did I but she didn't shed a single tear. She slowly got up, went over to the chest of drawers, and felt around for her black lace scarf, put it on, and off we went. And there was already a crowd of people outside the house, neighbours, people she worked with. You know, Aunty Ida was an accountant at the Arsenal for twenty years and they had so much respect for her… Everyone saw her blind mother being led along and they howled but Grandma was hard as flint. They took her into the house. She stretched her arms out, feeling her way to the coffin. They sat her by the coffin. She ran her hands over Ida's face and just whispered something but she didn't cry. And there was groaning all around, like a Greek tragedy, but when the coffin had to be taken out, they struggled to pull her hands away from her daughter. Of course, she wasn't taken to the cemetery. She stayed with me. She asked me to take her to the window. I'll never forget her standing at the window as the coffin was carried out. She asked which way to look and she stood … and *looked* … not with her eyes, obviously … with her heart.

And a couple of days after the funeral, she fell and broke her arm. And it was one thing after another. Something didn't set right. It had to be broken and set all over again. Can you imagine the pain? Unthinkable. I went to the hospital with her. And we had such a lovely doctor. He was so kind, although he was really young. He set it and said: "Is it painful, dear?" She shook her head. "Do you call this painful? I buried my daughter a couple of days ago – now that hurts." The doctor's face fell and he leant down and kissed her hand...

In short, Ninka couldn't deduce anything meaningful from the letters and she threw them both into Anna's backpack.

When she was wiping the floor with the rag she'd squeezed dry, the floor manager knocked on the door.

"Listen," she said, "what do we do? This came from Kiev for one of your lot, Anna Nesterenko… She's got to go to Kiev."

"What d'you mean, Kiev?" Ninka said with a sob. "She's got two broken ribs, a broken right collarbone and a bloody mess where her face used to be. Her darling husband tried to… Give it to me."

She took the telegram, turned it over and absorbed the information. What a day!

Pasted onto the telegram in small, widely spaced, cheery letters were the words:

"Mashuta Dead Stop Fly Back ASAP Comma Funeral Tomorrow."

CHAPTER 17

She had a much-loved harmonica—a performer's trophy. Once when she was young on tour in Hamburg or Berlin, a little Chinese girl ran over to her in the ring and, all smiles, squealing with excess emotion, thrust her own harmonica into her hand. Anna kept it all her life. She regarded the gift as the ultimate accolade.

Incidentally, the harmonica was a genuine German one. The words "*Unsere Lieblinge M. Hohner*" were written in gold on the small oblong box that was covered in blue goatskin and slightly raised like a part-baked pretzel. A white-toothed lovely flaunted her charms in a medallion on either side. A brunette wearing large beads and a slightly fuzzy blonde of the Marlene Dietrich kind—it might even have been her.

And for fun, I taught Anna to play "Lili Marlene" and used to play along on the bassoon. She would put the harmonica to her lips, give it a trial blow, and start, eyes protruding, face stretched.

> "You wait where that lantern softly gleamed,
> Your sweet face seems
> To haunt my dreams…"

At that point, I would come in on the bassoon, softly so as not to drown her out.

"There is nothing rounder than your lovely knees…"

It was a peculiar kind of duet, I can tell you, especially if you take into account that the players didn't usually bother to put even a dressing gown over their naked bodies…

She was inescapably bad at music and that despite being so utterly talented, with fabulous coordination and a quick, bright, versatile mind.

…About five years ago, I dragged her off to Rudesheim which I was in the habit of going to visit whenever I was playing concerts in Germany. And our version of Lili Marlene shed all her inhibitions to mingle freely with a restaurant trio up above the trees, the tin-pan jingle of a doddery hurdy-gurdy blending seamlessly with the tavern songs of evening revellers, soaring up, up and away to the vineyards, above which lay the small half-timbered houses of the town's outer heights, a blur of white.

And she was happy. I could see that.

Only once did her mood turn sour for some reason.

We happened upon the cable cars when we were out for a stroll and, on a sudden impulse, we bought tickets and ran over to take our seats in the metal gondola.

It was a pretty stupid plan if you consider that the entire town was plunged into a light but unremitting fog that you felt you could touch with a hand or even sink your teeth into.

Anyway, the other gondolas, both the ones behind ours and those coming towards us, bursting unexpectedly out of the fog's milky silence, were empty and forlorn. Naturally enough. The Germans are thrifty and rational and presumably there were no tourists about at that time of year.

And so we ascended blindly into the unknown and empty metal gondolas sailed one after the other out of the damp fog like diminutive versions of the Flying Dutchman. We grew quiet, exchanging the odd sentence in a whisper.

I took her in my arms. I felt this was an image of my life with her: only an arm and a metal pole visible and an occasional gondola approaching and going on by, not a soul on board…

Suddenly, the next gondola emerged towards us and in it, stunned by the silence, sat a fat goggle-eyed albino wearing a suede jacket and a red Tyrolean hat with a black feather. We both gasped at the same time. He seemed horribly insubstantial, white in the white fog. And that red Tyrolean hat, crammed grotesquely onto his head by somebody else and seemingly with some force as if someone had hastily dressed him backstage while he was unconscious, plonked him in the cable car and hightailed it out of there. Motionless, he floated past us. Nothing stirred, not even the feather in his hat.

Anna went so white it was obvious even in the fog.

"Who is he?" she asked sharply. "What does he want? Where is he going?"

I burst out laughing and held her closer.

"Little one," I said, "Can't you allow that he's as big an idiot as we are and a lonely one to boot and that he simply has nowhere to go, so he…?"

"No," she said, flustered. "No, that's not… He's too much like… And that mocking black feather. Did you see? It's no accident…"

I made fun of her, telling her some devil of the German countryside, a petty malefactor, a disseminator of influenza, had decided to explore the locality, bumped into us and been scared witless.

I did manage to distract her. We had lunch in a deep, white-washed medieval basement, its walls steeped in the smell of the wine and beer that had been locked in there for centuries, and on the way back to the hotel we also popped into a couple of stores to sample the area's famous *Eiswein*. And in the end I was so hammered that, in full view of two respectable ladies, I started groping Anna in the lift—"Is everything in its proper place?" I said—and asking loudly in German whether she would mind if I made a pass at her today.

… And that evening I had pains in my chest that were so strong they left me speechless. There, I thought, your dream's coming true: You're going to peg it right here in her arms.

But she was utterly composed. She massaged my chest in large, firm circles with the palms of her hands. She comforted me, saying repeatedly, "Don't be frightened. You won't die now. This isn't how you're going to die, Senya."

And I believed her and I really did feel my usual self again before long. I lay, letting a sedative dissolve, and watched her comb her hair and get ready for bed, the window in the background lit up by the lights of the restaurants. How languorously her nightdress glided over her slender naked back…

"And how am I going to die?" I asked.

She smiled, removing hairs from the comb, blew on it and, looking at me from the mirror, said, "You, Senya, will take your leave in a mighty snowstorm. With music playing…"

Her frankness bewildered me and I burst out laughing. "Isn't that too romantic, my little one?" I leant across the bed, took her hand and kissed it.

… She was not a great talker, surprisingly enough. Sometimes she would go a whole day saying only a few sentences and, to be honest, it would be hard to say she used sophisticated language. I presume it was the effect of her many years in the circus and her marriage to that lad who had been essentially decent but as simple as they come.

I sometimes felt that no one had ever taught her anything, that she'd taken from the people around her only what she needed—like a bird on the wing catching a fly. Or that she had come into this world with a small but secure store of knowledge that only she needed, that had been instilled in her somewhere … I don't know where.

There were occasions that left me simply flabbergasted. I remember when we first went to see the Professor together. We were waiting for him in the living room of his house in Newtonville, walking from one personally dedicated photograph on the wall to another. We stopped at one in which a young, laughing Professor and an even younger Isaac Stern, stood in a gondola, arms around each other, the dome of Santa Maria della Salute in the background. Then I led her over to a small, brownish photo, beneath which in a sprawling hand were the words: "To my dear friend…"

"And that, my light, my little mirror, is Gershwin…"

She looked at me, utterly serious, and asked, "Is Beethoven in it?" And I'm sure she wasn't joking.

To be frank, all these endearing female clichés about kindred souls—or, what do they call it? Spiritual affinity?—had nothing whatsoever to do with the sweet agitation that stirred my heart when her boyish little figure appeared in a crowd of airline passengers or as I waited for a sight of her motorcycle from early morning on the balcony of yet another hotel room. And there it was! The smooth lift of her thigh as she jumped off, like the rise of a bow over a viola.

This sweet agitation was completely unlike the physical agitation that gripped me every time I *left* her. That was different and I have no intention of putting *that* into words of any kind nowadays, not even to myself.

She always reacted with striking clarity, dividing the world inviolably into good and evil as if she was the first person not yet touched by the vile and tragic history of human morality.

Sometimes she would become so inarticulate she seemed like a foreigner who had learnt my language in a hurry so that she could talk to me. All the more so since I had observed her on many occasions as she proceeded to speak various foreign languages. Slowly building momentum, initially probing the sounds with the tip of her tongue, rolling the unfamiliar combinations of syllables … individual words … around the roof of her mouth, then gluing them together in sentences … and about ten minutes later already chattering away to someone in a completely new language. And even though I became used to everything about her and seemingly nothing could shock me, I really was stunned when I left her for five minutes in the Orangerie in Paris and came back from the bathroom to find her chatting demurely to a Japanese couple—in Japanese! They didn't know English or French. Why bother travelling in that case, one might ask?

I took her hand and pulled her away.

"So what, did you just start talking to them in Japanese?" I asked. And she replied, "No, of course, not. I don't know any Japanese. No, I do know one word: Kama sutra!"

She impressed me several times by drawing conclusions that were set out as precisely as mathematical proof. And her memory was always disconcerting. I'm not talking about her lethal *computer database* in her head, which stored an endless number of figures, objects, names and faces. She kept *that* memory to herself, never frightening me with it. I'm talking about the other, focused human memory. Sometimes she would say all of a sudden, "Let's go to that food place opposite the station. Remember, we talked to an old man playing the piano there in April 1995. He's dead now, obviously. Do you remember how quickly and unevenly he played a timid little sparrow of a foxtrot? He was missing the tip of his right little finger."

At a café table once in Jerusalem, looking at an Orthodox family with lots of children, she suddenly said, open as a child, "And you know, I can remember my Mum really well…"

And when she saw that I was puzzled, she said quickly, "No, not Mashuta. My real Mum. She used to work somewhere that involved doing night shifts. And I stayed home by myself. I was so little. And to stop me from being scared she used to say, 'I'm not going far and not for very long, just here into the mirror. I'll sit there for a bit and then I'll come back.' We had a round mirror hanging in the hall, you see, just opposite the door. My Mum used to turn me to face it and I could see her walk away into it and shut the door. So, when she wasn't at home, I knew for certain that she was in the mirror. Sometimes I would stand in front of it for hours, calling, 'Mama, that's enough. Come out now!' And on many occasions, that's what happened. In the end, a door would open inside the mirror and my mother would appear…"

So, quite by accident, I learnt from that slip of the tongue that she wasn't really the daughter of that wonderful loving couple to whose house fate had led me—For good? For ill? For my own sweet torment—many years ago…

And she never mentioned it again.

I am afraid to suggest it but might it not have been these childhood looking-glass adventures, as well as her suppressed left-handedness, transformed into a breath-taking virtuoso ambidextrousness like the frog into the Swan Princess, that produced such mighty oaks—her lifelong fascination with mirrors?

Even I, eternal wanderer that I am, was stumped by her asceticism when it came to clothes and everything basically to do with the captivating world of human attachments, the frippery and trinkets designed to gladden the heart. All her belongings fitted into a small backpack: a bit of underwear, a pair of jeans, socks… Naturally, she received fairly frequent invitations to receptions of various kinds—noblesse oblige. Then she would pop into a shop and within twenty minutes had bought a dress, shoes and a bag—all pretty expensive—she made plenty of money—simply to leave them somewhere for someone else later on.

This annoyed me. Several times I towed her into designer boutiques, forcing her to try first one evening gown then another on her sylphlike figure. I literally fell in love with one of them, dark green, with a classy silver sparkle. Set off by the colour of the dress, her eyes took on such a deep shade of azure, I couldn't look anywhere else.

"Please," I said, not in the least bit bothered by the shop assistant who was looking at us, not sure what was going on, so much did the scene not fit her picture of the world, of men and women. "I'm begging you, let's buy this dress. You'll be radiant in it!"

She grinned and said, "I've already been radiant in the spotlights."

It was as if things, attachment via things to whatsoever it might be, weighed her down. Not a ring, not a necklace, not a single knickknack worth remembering. An eternal biker—jacket, gloves, helmet. She was like someone ready to head out at any moment. Where to? God knows. To head out, as people do who have a long road ahead: into exile and hard labour, for example. Or to heaven.

I never paid much attention to the rides, illusions and tricks she invented, although over time she became one of the few experts in the field. And if I had? What would I have grasped from all those drawings and jottings, especially in the hieroglyphics of her crazy handwriting?

Incidentally, when I first saw a page of her notebook covered in those loops and dashes—a swift's breakneck line of flight—I suddenly remembered Genka's illiterate grandmother, Kapitolina Timofeevna. I remembered the four pages from school exercise books she'd begged off her grandsons before she died and then covered in just such curling, partly joined-up spirals. Needless to say, her grandsons gathered up the sheets of paper and threw them away: Why on earth would you keep the scribbles of an illiterate old woman?

So there you go, I thought back then, that's the kind of weird illiteracy the late Kapitolina Timofeevna had… That's why, when she checked Genka's maths in his exercise book, she would pull his hair and keep saying, "So what's left over when you divide it, you bastard, well?" Whereas she never so much as touched his stories and compositions. She must also have been burdened by the exquisite curse of that diabolical handwriting.

I saw her shows several times—they were spectacular. Particularly when she staged her mind-blowing "Ring of Fire," at the Auditorium Theatre in Chicago. Apparently, it's still pulling in the crowds.

She would try to explain the technical details to me. I'd pretend to listen closely, nodding my head… Obviously, I didn't have a clue. Something to do with tinted mirrors, shaped into a thin hoop. Fine, I didn't need the technical details but the routine itself was as follows. A dancer holding a single candle appeared on stage, the auditorium was in absolute darkness. The feeble flame flickered for a couple of minutes, pulsing erratically as it appeared suspended here and there to the accompaniment of elegiac music. Then the dancer ran up a black deck to the outlandish *apparatus*, as Anna called her construction—circus-style.

Meanwhile, mirrors were slowly lowered on three sides as she ran, enclosing her in a trap. When the dancer brought the candle up to the tip of a cone-shaped mirror, the whole ring of mirrors, further reflected in other, surrounding mirrors, burst into fierce flames! She moved the candle around the ring and waves of flame followed its progress, becoming a wild dance of fire. And so she fluttered there on the platform, a slim figure in a ring of fire or rather lit by a single candle, cunningly reflected in the mirrors, struggling amid the mirrors, unable to escape from the burning hoop.

It was a ferocious battle to the death. The maddened flames pranced around the dancer, fanning her despair to the point of pagan triumph, insanity even, growing more and more intense until it became unbearable: pressing down on her head, blazing in front of her eyes. You wanted to start shouting, "Enough now. That's enough. Have mercy!"

Eventually, the mirrors were lifted up, the music faded… And in the pitch blackness, in a silence more deafening than the music, a solitary woman on the black platform that was life held the dull spark of her tortured soul in her hand.

In point of fact, I don't like all these spectacles.

I don't like sleights of hand, the bare-legged, bare-arsed corps-de-ballet… Let it lie, I'm long since done with the Circus.

Although I did experience genuine shock on one occasion when she and I visited the hereafter.

It was in Frankfurt after she'd decided to take that wonderful loft on Schweizer Strasse in Sachsenhausen. She was working for the famous Tigerpalast Varieté again and had disappeared for a few days from dawn till dusk to spend the whole time at a little factory somewhere in Rudesheim. They were making equipment to her designs.

I regretted those lost days—five days, each of them precious. I'd clawed them off the orchestra so that I could be with her at Christmas which Germany celebrates with greater cheer and better food than anywhere else.

Everywhere, holiday merry-go-rounds were already turning. A Christmas tree the height of the city hall had been raised on the Romer. Almost all of it could be seen from the loft window and its warm sparks twinkled as dusk fell, generating an utterly childish blend of delight and melancholy in me. Stalls and booths thronged the main square and central streets. Crowds hastened to indulge in Christmas comforts. Magical aromas streamed from every stall: the sputtering of fried sausages of every sort and shape; the sweet smell of toasted almonds, hazelnuts and peanuts.

And above it all hung a spicy, chocolatey smell. Pick any fruit—a strawberry, banana, kiwi, plum—and it would be dipped into hot chocolate before your very eyes and a gigantic sweet handed back to you. And so that no one went thirsty, the food stalls mixed with drink stalls offering gluhwein, hot cider, beer and Rhenish wines. And—depending on the weather, depending on what the frozen individual fancied—some opted for the gluhwein, some for a tart Rhenish wine, and others for a distinctive Bavarian beer, wonderfully named Blue Goat and specially brewed for Christmas.

Easily assembled wooden booths were already selling every possible sort of handcrafted item made of stone, wood, leather or ceramics. Glittering Christmas-tree decorations, hanging from threads, spun gently. A stall selling scented candles gave off perfumes of lavender, jasmine, clove and mint as if linked by a bridge to the stall opposite that sold soap, carved into figurines and imbued with the same scents. Little children whirled round and round on a merry-go-round to the sound of Jingle Bells… And there was no way of elbowing your way through that festival of life.

I tried to slip away into the quiet lanes. I turned off Schweizer Strasse onto the Museum Embankment, walked past ancient gingerbread mansions, tastefully lit by candles, and admired the succession of lights on the bridges… I crossed the Iron Bridge to the other bank where the culinary mayhem continued. There were king prawns sizzling in enormous frying pans, Alsace pies puffing up in the ovens. And it was on the embankment that I came across the best gluhwein, at an unassuming stall romantically named Gluhwein Cottage. I sat there, looking at the bridge…

Snow in Frankfurt could only be dreamt of. Not a flake in sight. Every year, people try to guess whether it will be a "white" Christmas.

I sat in the cottage to which I had taken a shine and thought back to snowy winters in Moscow and Leningrad … and my teacher, Dmitry Fyodorovich Eryomin. A fat, kind-hearted man, first bassoon under Mravinsky, he installed himself in Auer's chair—the legendary Leopold Auer had taught in Lecture Hall No. 24—a soft, deep leather chair with high armrests. He would sink into it and go to sleep. He didn't wake up no matter how the students played. There's an interminable note in a cadence in a Weber concerto. I held it until my breath ran out. Even then, he didn't wake up, just kept on snoring and sighing snugly.

I sat in Gluhwein Cottage on the bank of the Main and recalled my conservatoire girlfriends, the ice-sugar dusting of snow on the ski track into Komarovo, the first gulp of hot wine made by a girl on my course. It smelt of cinnamon and cloves, whatever spices could be found on the shelf.

Now I knew it was called gluhwein.

In short, I missed her dreadfully.

One evening she came back, tired. She didn't want dinner although I was hoping to drag her out to some decent restaurant or other.

"I'll show you … tomorrow…" she muttered and fell asleep right away like a small child. Generally speaking, she did fall asleep quickly.

The following day, she took me to the factory.

We went down into the workshops via welded metal stairs, passing three vast underground rooms and the workers, all of whom she knew by name. Some Helmuth or other led us behind a protective folding screen where the *apparatus* had been set up on a metal cube: an enormous many-sided box on a vertical axis. And there was an oval aperture in each side.

"Here," she said. "Go and put your face up close to any of them … nearer … stick your chin out a bit … that's it…"

I pressed my face up against the aperture in one side and Anna did the same in another. And I saw.

An endless forest of columns stretched out inside, a small oval mirror window visible on each one. In that, I could see a face, either mine or Anna's, in an incomprehensible sequence, and our faces, alternating, shuffled like cards and nodding at one another, went off into the boundless distance—the inner space was quite simply limitless.

I was amazed, thrilled to begin with. It seemed entertaining and inventive… Then I felt unable to tear myself away, I couldn't leave… I kept on staring at our solitary faces multiplying in a desert of mirrors, utterly unable to draw closer to one another, to come together in a kiss or in destiny…

I was terrified. Bitter longing gripped my heart. This endless desert plain, planted with columns that seemed to dance as they vanished into the limitless distance—and our faces, silent, staring out at me fixedly from the dizzying expanse. That, I thought suddenly, is how the world to come might look: your soul and the soul of the person dearest to you, locked in mirrored columns. And all you can do is silently—and eternally!—gaze upon your unreachable reflections, repeated a thousand fold.

To shake off the illusion, just to say something, I asked, still looking at her face in its halo of mirrors, "What holds the walls of the box together? Screws?"

"Bayonet locks," replied her unreachable face in the mirror. "Well, and spring-loaded locks, too. The whole construction can be assembled or dismantled in ten minutes."

On the way home, she asked, "Did you like it then? Did you?" She was unusually animated.

I did not want to say, "My little one, my dear little one, what's going on in your head if it gives you such blissful pleasure?"

At night I dreamt about that endless forest of dancing columns. I woke in a cold sweat and woke her up.

"Did you think that up yourself?" I asked.

"What?" she mumbled, baffled.

"The mirror freakery in the box?"

"No… Robert-Houdin did."

"Who?"

"A French conjuror … Jean Eugene Robert-Houdin. He lived in Blois in France … in the 1800s… What's the matter? What time is it? Give me a cigarette…"

Then she deigned to explain. Eliezer (Oh, that wretched, mysterious Eliezer from her childhood, with whom she corresponded in mirror writing—wouldn't I like to set eyes on him?) had tracked down accounts of some of Robert-Houdin's inventions through people he knew from Kiev, who worked in the Library of Congress, and he'd puzzled them out.

And she'd decided to try and create one here in the "Magic Mirrors" show but had made it more complex by increasing the number of sides... And so on and so forth.

"I see," I said, sinking back onto the pillow.

Incidentally, that night, since we weren't getting any more sleep, she told me the story of how Eliezer and his deadly twin were saved. It was as improbable as only the truth can be.

They were born prematurely at home to their startled mother and delivered by her ancient Ukrainian nanny. That night, the Germans pasted leaflets all over town, the ones that said on grey wrapping paper, "To all Jews of the City of Kiev"… When the babies had been bathed and their mother had groaned out their names—their grandfathers'— the nanny said, "Now you give them sickly little mites to me, Riva. You'll not make it with them."

At the time, it wasn't death they had in mind but a long journey. The next morning, her husband carried the new mother to the set assembly point.

It then became clear to the old lady, and very quickly, that no one would be coming back and she took the children to her sister-in-law in a village. And what did she come up with, that old lady? She swaddled those two tiny wrinkled little maggots up tight like a single child but with both heads sticking out. And that's how she made it past every patrol and through every barrier. "See," she wept, "my granddaughter's gone and given birth to a monster with two heads… And here I am, going to the village. We've got this woman lives there, a wise women. She has this herb and it will make one head fall off."

She had worked it out better than any psychologist. No one could bear to look at the monster-baby. Everyone turned away in horror and waved as if to say, "Away with you, you and your monster. Out of my sight…" She raised them and looked after them in the village and then the three of them lived together after the war and until she died in a tiny room in a communal flat in the Podol area of Kiev. They called her Granny Liza and that's the kind of granny she was. Let's not get involved in reflections on the selflessness of the common man. Forget the common man—he comes in all shapes and sizes. The main thing is that she didn't change their names. How on earth did those children manage with names like that in anti-Semitic Soviet Kiev?

She didn't change them, saying, "Those are the names their mother gave them. Who am I to argue with her now she's dead?"

Later on, the brothers turned their granny's tale into a family saying. "No chance," the Albino would say, "it won't fall off." And, as Anna told it, that white head of his not only failed to fall off, it was quite content to rule over his brother as well.

After that night, unexpectedly brightened by this monologue—unlike our other nights—I abandoned any attempts to understand the workings of her mind. I didn't need to.

That's a lie! The need did arise once and I decided to stir her up a bit. She was very keen to help the Professor in his hour of need. The old man had simply driven himself crazy over the "theft of the century." It had certainly been stolen, an original Stradivarius, and with such elegant simplicity. Myatlitsky said several times that he knew who'd stolen it… Maybe, he'd worked it out. Then why was he so excited about accepting Anna's help?

PART FOUR

...the mirrors were quite reluctant to return one's visage, out of either greed or impotence, and when they tried, one's features would come back incomplete.

Joseph Brodsky, *Watermark: An Essay on Venice*

CHAPTER 18.

She turned off onto Rue Iberville and drove for several blocks. At the lights—they were always particularly slow there—she darted past a Peugeot, with the sullen inscription "Je me souviens," "I remember," under the number plate, like any Quebec car. She crawled cheekily onto the crosswalk and looked round. "Let me through, mate, okay?" He nodded, disgruntled.

And that was the clear advantage of a motorbike, especially if it was a high-speed beast like this baby, a four-tonne Kawasaki ZZ-R1200. It was the latest model and Anna had spent twenty minutes breaking it in like a horse to gain the familiar sensation that her thighs and back had been grafted onto the seat. And it was a good thing she'd let that kid at the rental store talk her into taking this precise model. He was right. The bike was pretty handy even in heavy traffic and could slip into any gap to worm a way through. And it was a comfortable ride with a smooth saddle and it was easy to change position during a long trip. And it was stable at cruising speed.

One of the two-storey cookie-cutter houses lining the right-hand side of the road had a large balcony jutting out on stilts and studded with plant pots. The ornate railings were wreathed in equally ornate clusters of small green tomatoes, amid which a man in shorts sat in state, blinking in the sun, his stomach spilling out, as green as the tomatoes.

She loved Montreal—a light, bright city, Montreal city of churches and circuses. The downward spirals of its coquettish outdoor staircases, like a woman lifting the hem of her skirt slightly to reveal the curve of her thigh; the little balconies, the decorative railings, the light grey stones of cathedrals and churches, the sharp-eared ivy subjugating the columns of the castle-like villas in the English suburb of Westmount; the menacing fairy-tale mass of the Royal Victoria Hospital, the dome of Saint Joseph's Oratory, and the unobtrusive intermingling of French levity and English politeness…

The light changed to green. She turned onto Second Avenue, let two yellow school buses go by, most probably carrying performers, and drove into the spacious parking space outside the Cirque de la Lune's huge rehearsal and office building.

Leaving the motorbike close to Guy's personal covered and screened-off parking spot, she removed her helmet and gloves and stuffed them in the pannier. Right, then: backpack on her shoulder, her rag of a bandana—a headscarf she wore round her neck when she was out on the bike—in her jacket pocket. She was ready to negotiate.

A giant metal shoe stood on a plinth at the entrance, the tongue tumbling out, the laces untied. Rumour had it that it was a copy of some well-worn shoe from the former life of Guy Légalité, heavenly father, great man, one-time street performer and fire eater and now absolute sovereign of the mightiest circus empire in the world. There were five permanent shows in different hotels and casinos in Las Vegas alone.

Lucy, a smiling mixed-race woman, tiny Shan-Shan, a Chinese woman dwarfed by her double-barrelled name, and the prim and proper Esther in her glasses sat downstairs on reception in a cavernous hall beneath a slanting dome.

At the sight of Anna, all three revealed teeth of varying degrees of white.

She could see through the glass wall that the canteen was full of people. These were always the busiest months at De la Lune, "formation" time when the athletes and circus performers from all over the world, selected by casting, turned up for try outs, rehearsals and the signing of contracts.

The tables were all full. There was a good-sized queue at the till: performers in training gear, people from administration, two translators, Ronan, the massage therapist… It would be good to get a bite to eat before meeting Philippe, she thought.

Anna had had several meetings over the past year with the production director of her forthcoming show—a tremendous new project and a new direction for Cirque de la Lune (the basic conceit was small box, ordinary box, gigantic box). They had not gone as well as she would have liked. Philippe was in two minds. He kept saying they had to see about insurance and safety. "Mirrors, Ann, are a delicate matter," he said, grinning at the double meaning. She demurred, suggesting safeguard options involving extremely fine safety nets that would be invisible from the auditorium in a bid to persuade him but… Alas, what was true was that the concept she had devised—and this was the constant fly in the ointment during all their talks—cost a good deal of money.

Moreover, she knew that the creative team behind the show was still considering several other options. It was all routine but, on this occasion, it was dragging on for too long.

She preferred just to wait in these kinds of situation. Eventually, the moment always came when the time was right for the heavily laden barge of joint work to pull quietly out into the current.

Grabbing a coffee and some strawberry waffles, she sat at a separate table she found in a corner, next to a rubber plant that came as a surprise in this setting. A young gymnast immediately joined her—is this seat free? A rider, she decided from his physique, from the muscles. He turned out to be "Seryoga from Ukraine" and to be unbearably chatty. Just as well he was young. In the time she drank her coffee, he managed to recount his entire life story from Dnepropetrovsk school football team to Ukraine's junior national gymnastics team.

Genevieve had said that Cirque de la Lune had taken on more "Russians" that year, which included Armenians and Azerbaijanis and Ukrainians. She reckoned they accounted for about seventy per cent these days. "The Russians," as they always do everywhere, did everything no one else did.

"So, do you work here too?" Seryoga asked.

"Sometimes," she replied.

There was plenty of time left until her meeting. She roamed the familiar pathways, spent twenty minutes or so at a computer in the library browsing the Internet, looked in on the massage therapists, even took a brief turn on an exercise bike… Then she wandered into the rehearsal hall.

Two people were training there: an aerialist on the trapeze, another Russian Anna didn't know, and someone else on pull-up bars—Jerome from the French national team. He'd recently torn his Achilles tendon and was now gingerly getting back to par. His leg was still bandaged up. Both gymnasts were rehearsing in "*chevilleres*," lace-up leather boots with no soles, a Cirque de la Lune invention.

The Russian was being trained by acrobatics coach Roman Petrovich, rangy and loping in middle age and wearing a huge silver cross on his exposed chest. He held the safety line, patiently casting an occasional glance at the gymnast who was swinging reluctantly as if pondering what to do next. A long listless swing, an ankle hang, another long swing… Evidently, it was the very beginning of the work before the artistic component, before the choreography was added.

Anna sat down on a long low bench, the kind that have always been and still are present in all sports halls.

A big top could fit into the studio, the tallest in the world. The lights hung high up under the ceiling. A balcony at first-floor height circled the entire perimeter of the hall.

And there was a lot in the hall: two enormous trampoline beds pushed over against the wall in the far corner, thick blue mats on the floor, two deep safety pits filled with cubes of yellow foam to the left of the entrance and along the whole length of the wall. To the right hung a structure that looked like a huge metal glass and was commonly known as the haemorrhoid-maker: It was where the catchers, the under-standers who caught and threw the riders, trained.

There really was everything here and all of it beyond ordinary human ability.

Slowly, seemingly reluctantly, the Russian aerialist sailed above the floor… Roman Petrovich looked round, spotted Anna, nodded and started to winch the trapeze higher.

It was time to go and meet Philippe.

✳✳✳

Genevieve was working her magic on a plaster torso. She was leaning over a table, her bony back to Anna. She cut a quaint figure: dragonfly legs touchingly protruding from her shorts, a leather apron tied in a bow at the back.

Anna lingered a little in the doorway. Glass jars of various colours full of plaster ears were arrayed on shelves all over the room while the wall to the left of the door was covered in plaster earflaps. A comical collection, a whim of Genevieve's. Many years ago, she used to collect production waste—ears from plaster heads, of no use to costume designers, makeup artists or wigmakers. A miscellany of performers' ears—jug ears and ears that sat close to the skull, big ears and little ears, cauliflower ears, wedge-shaped ears, tight little whorls and sophisticated elongated shells—sundry different ears, little plaster receptacles for all the words in the world...

Two of the room's adjoining walls were mirrored and, above Genevieve's bent back, Anna could see herself in these dazed twin shutters, already dazzled by their visions of insensate plaster.

She gave a soft whistle. Genevieve looked round, squeaked, pushed her large plastic goggles onto her forehead, ran over and used her elbows to give Anna a big hug round the neck. Both arms were white to the elbows with plaster dust.

"Have you been home?" she asked. "I left your lunch in the kitchen."

"I didn't make it … the traffic was really heavy and a trailer had turned over on Twenty Fifth Street. Will you be done soon?"

"About forty minutes. Wait for me, okay? You know, Howard's been so excited today. He's crazily aware of you. Mind you, this morning I said to him, 'Anna's coming!' and he opened his beak, fluffed his feathers up. 'Anna, boy! Let me give you a kiss!'"

"My old pal…"

"Crazy. Listen… I still have to make heads for two Spaniards. Will you help? Really great guys, tightrope walkers, strongmen. They're here for 'formation.'"

"Sure. Of course."

All new contract staff underwent the same procedure here. It was mysterious and not especially pleasant for them. By analogy with death masks, their whole head was moulded in plaster and the result kept in storage by the circus even when their contracts had expired.

Rows of these silent heads, eyes closed, mouths tightly sealed, nostrils cut into the plaster, stood on long shelves in storage, close at hand, just round the corner from Genevieve's studio.

Anna used to drop into the long cramped warehouse fairly often, turning almost sideways to thread herself between the wooden stacks.

It was possible to determine a performer's character and nationality from their plaster mask. The Russians could be distinguished by tension in the eyebrows and particularly tight jaws.

Performers' attitudes to the unnatural procedure varied. Some found it hard to take, having to sit completely still in a plaster cast that registered every pore in your face for half an hour, unseeing and unspeaking, breathing through the two tiny holes Genevieve had kindly made in the plaster nose with the end of her brush...

Anna once saw an Italian clown leap up from the chair, unable to tolerate this brief, chalky death, and start smashing the place up unseeing, bellowing and shaking his plaster Minotaur's head.

***

Anna and Genevieve had met some eight years before at a gargantuan reception, one of those Guy occasionally held, with dubious delights, like the naked girl who arrived on an enormous serving trolley the size of a hospital stretcher, strewn from head to foot with tiny portions of sushi—Please, help yourselves.

Anna was at the banquet because she had an invitation from George, someone she knew in casting, exquisitely gay and the lover of the man who was all but minister of culture. He'd seen her show in Berlin "Ghosts in the Mirrors," the one where the mirrors responded to one another, where a figure captured in two ingeniously placed mirrors was passed on to the next pair and slowly dwindled in the distance as it dimmed and departed, although the performer stayed put, waving farewell to their own retreating hat.

George sought her out himself and enthusiastically offered to introduce her to the artistic director of Dralion, a show that went on to become famous, like everything put on by Cirque de la Lune but still only under discussion back then … George was sure her "mirror ideas" would go down well with the creative team.

At the time, however, she didn't make the acquaintance of that cheerful, dissolute community, that den of iniquity even. Anna was already on the point of leaving and, as a shout of "Have you forgotten who your daddy is?" from Guy himself reached her from somewhere or other, she was setting off to find her way out of a sequence of shorn and tufty Japanese gardens, paper houses, glass waterfalls...

It was then that an embarrassed George caught up with her and not on his own but with a quaint little woman with a sharp profile, a child's hollow chest, dragonfly legs. "Anna," he said, out of breath, "Anna, I'm sorry that's how it went. We'll definitely bring your idea to life, it's just that they're all drunken beasts right now and all they want is a good time… In the meantime, it occurred to me that you don't have anywhere to stay, do you? So, Genevieve has offered…"

Genevieve's handshake was surprisingly strong. She turned out to be a Cirque de la Lune sculptor and was pleased to meet Anna, very pleased actually and prepared to offer her a "refuge from that nightmare world."

They sat in the bar for a while, drinking the cider served in bowls that reminded Anna of Uzbek tea bowls. George had gone off somewhere and Genevieve was vivacious as she talked of growing up in Brittany. It arose naturally. Cider's the national drink there, like the rum brought in by pirates, or calvados...

Cider's not the only thing she's on today, Anna thought. Does pot grow in Brittany, I wonder?

They were stuck for ages in that bar with seafood on the menu, including oysters, Huitres de Belon, the one thing Anna couldn't stand. Genevieve ate them with relish one after the other, eyes rolling, her fingers quivering in sheer bliss, inviting Anna to help herself.

"You don't like them? No! I don't believe it!"

"Sometime," she said, "I'll treat you to a real Breton pound cake, the *guatre guarts*, the four quarters, equal amounts of flour, butter, eggs and sugar and I'm definitely going to make a Far Breton cake, the way my Grandmother did. She cooked them in such a very hot oven, the upper crust was black!"

Then they got into a small elderly Renault Clio and set off for Le Plateau.

"It's a fun kind of place, bohemian," she chirruped like a small, intoxicated bird. "All kinds of delightful riffraff... I've been renting a flat there for eight years or so but the owner passed away a while back and the kids—they're from Brittany too—sold it to me cheap. Oh, when you see my pad, it'll blow you away."

Anna had realized back in the bar that Genevieve was unusually hyped up but there had been noise and music everywhere and she'd put the tension down to alcohol and trying to battle the "environment," as Genevieve had said. Now, in the car, she suddenly saw the real reason for the excessive attempt to be alluring, to wrap herself in a tentative hope ... and her heart sank. She decided to dump the poor little thing and rent a room somewhere... After all, Montreal has plenty of...

"Genevieve," she said softly. "I'd better get out somewhere round here... I'm sorry, it's just I..."

"Don't worry," came the reply. Genevieve didn't look at Anna, her profile birdlike in the flashing lights of the neon signs. "Forget it! I knew right off you weren't one of ours. It's a crazy shame but what can you do? It's just ... I really enjoy looking at you... You're like a boy, like Verrocchio's David... I'm happy to put you up. I have this funny little place up on the roof... No one will bother you there."

They sat up all night in the kitchen on the day that they made one another's acquaintance. The sight of the visitor sent Howard, a hunch-backed African grey parrot, into a great but extremely affectionate flurry. He pecked at the bars of his cage, squawked "Spare the parrot!" in French, interrupted his owner's every word with a languorous sigh of "*Horreur! Horreur!*" memorized Anna's name in an instant and repeated it every which way, even in song... In short, all the signs were that the poor creature was in love…

Laughing, Genevieve said, "We both fell in love with you at first sight."

And it was only towards morning that Anna, encumbered by a throw and an armful of bedding, went up to the roof and the small room that she immediately dubbed a "nest" and that became her home that very night whenever she happened to find herself in Montreal.

…The Spaniards arrived—two sturdy dark-skinned men—using gestures to make themselves understood. Anna identified them both at a glance as bearers, "under-standers," powerful guys.

As usual, she soon began to grasp the meaning of individual words in their lively exchanges and five minutes on could already understand a fair amount. In everything to do with mastering someone else's lexicon, she used the binoculars approach. She focused on the lip movements, mentally bringing the bubbling substance closer as if enhancing its definition. And as with a pair of binoculars, the stream of words grew clearer and clearer until the outlines could be recognised and the *whole shape* of the language became clearly visible.

She knew, however, that as soon as the men went, they would take the *words' outline clarity* with them. And no book in Spanish would awaken the slightest meaning in her mirrors after that, only the spoken word...

While Genevieve, chirruping a welcome in French, stirred a small tub of liquid plaster, the Spaniards talked between themselves, naturally enough, about the two women. One said: "Good-looking old birds. You wouldn't say no to the redhead, eh, Francisco?" And Francisco answered along the lines that the "redhead isn't as young as she seems but she's still just the ticket. A cracking figure. Except I have the feeling the two of them can manage quite nicely without any help from us…"

"Who's first, please?" asked Genevieve. She pointed to the swivel chair, specially moved to the centre of the room for the procedure to be carried out. The young men exchanged glances and the one the other had called Francisco took his seat, rolling his eyes in comical fright.

They kept up their patter for a few moments while Anna soaked strips of gauze over the sink and Genevieve put a tight-fitting rubber cap on the Spaniard's head and smeared Vaseline onto his eyebrows, eyelashes, neck and chest. They still didn't know what was to come.

"Here goes," said Genevieve with a nod, pouring the liquid plaster over the back of the Spaniard's head, neck and shoulders. Then, she and Anna together deftly packed cotton wool around his head and began wrapping it tightly from the top down.

The sitting *bearer*'s swarthy face still bore traces of a fading smile in the corners of the full, mobile lips. His friend instantly became serious, however.

"Hey," he cried. "How's Francisco going to breathe?"

"Everything will be fine," Anna told him in Spanish. "Tell him not to be frightened. Half an hour. Men!"

"What? Are they fretting?" asked Genevieve, applying bandages in wet layers from the tub. "It's their own fault. If they'd spoken French or English, I would have explained everything."

She showed the gymnast the end of her brush, brought it to her own sharp nose. "He'll breathe. Don't worry!"

She began to clear crumbs out of the holes in the Spaniards' nostrils.

She was used to Anna's weird ability to understand any language that might be passing through although the first explanation of this *quirk* had been painful.

"Imagine, what that bitch Tina, the decorator from the arts department, has been saying?" Genevieve said, grinning, some five days after Anna had moved into the nest. They had already talked about a whole heap of topics, discussed Brittany, Russia, the enigmatic city of Kiev, the difference between light and heavy motorcycles… Genevieve had already sobbed out the story of her first love, telling Anna of the actress who came from Lyon to stay in their small town, the actress Genevieve's older brother found her with, after which all ties with her family were severed once and for all; she also sobbed out her second love for a long-legged mercurial Italian student in a Slavonic studies department—in short when Genevieve felt as if she'd known Anna for many years…

"….so that bitch Tina goes and says today, 'What are you doing letting that woman come and live with you? She's a witch!'"

They were sitting in what they called the dining room.

Basically, Genevieve's flat had been fashioned from the remnants of two other good-sized, comfortable apartments, located to its right and left, and consisted of two cubbyholes linked by a corridor. There was also a small and fantastically impractical triangular kitchen and a toilet and shower room where you could only take a wash if you stood to attention.

But one of the cubbyholes, about twelve square metres, was enchanting. It had a semi-circular wall with a glass bay-window full of pots of geraniums, jutting out to form an extra pocket of space. And the window gave on to a serene and utterly Dickensian view: the corner of a quiet street and an old greystone house, scabbed with dark-green ivy.

Anna was twirling a broken set of bagpipes. She tried to blow into them the way she used to blow her harmonica but the old goatskin wheezed at her unsuccessful attempts to invigorate the deflated udder. The most logical thing of all would have been to discard it as junk but Genevieve considered the bagpipes the best instrument in the world since they were played in Brittany.

"So, I said, what nonsense is this you're churning out?" When Genevieve set about recounting a scene or dialogue, she would always relive the whole story, replaying the action, becoming each of the characters in turn. And now her cheeks burned with indignant heat. "'What has Anna ever done to you?' 'Nothing,' she says with this snide grin. 'It's just that she's a witch!'"

Anna set the bagpipes aside and said, "If you really want to have the instrument checked out, I'll take it to Senya and he'll find an expert."

And she looked up at Genevieve sitting astride a chair. Genevieve already had her heart set on a proper dissection of that "bitch Tina" and had probably expected an equally indignant response from Anna.

But Anna said nothing.

"Did you fall out then?"

"We're not friends. I've bumped into her a few times in the corridors."

"But what the hell's she going on about? And why?"

Anna gave a hopeless smile and said softly with a dismissive gesture, "Because I am a witch."

Howard pecked the bars of his cage and sighed. "*L'horreur!*"

Genevieve roared with laughter but suddenly broke off. For about a minute, she stared at Anna.

"What does that mean?" she said with a grin. "Can you do magic?"

"No." Anna shrugged her shoulders.

"Can you heal people?"

"I don't know… I haven't tried."

"So what can you do?" Genevieve looked at her new friend with baffled misgivings.

"How can I tell you?" Anna said reluctantly, looking out of the window. The owner of the idyllic house opposite was leaning over the wide windowsill, using shears to trim the shoots of ivy that had boldly emerged from the ruffles of the overall cover. "I just see things."

"What?" Genevieve pulled a face. "What do you mean—see?"

"Well, sometimes I see a kind of cinema. I can wind it forward or backward."

"You're lying," Genevieve gasped like a child. "You're pulling my leg! What about me and my family … can you see them?"

Anna sighed. It was getting boring. It was always the same. And now this sweet little Genevieve. After all, none of this was her fault. And she was so tense! It wasn't very nice for her, poor thing.

"I can. Your grandmother had a bad limp, didn't she? Your older brother condemned you although he loved another man's wife for many years. And you used to have a favourite dress, dark blue flannel with small white dots… And a little white collar… And when you were ten, you stole ten francs from your grandmother's purse to buy a ticket to see the circus and it still bothers you." Stop, she thought with a familiar wistfulness but pushed on to the end even so. "Sometimes, I can see your thoughts. But that's because your thoughts are clear and articulate. Almost like the way you speak: in sentences."

Genevieve leapt from her chair, stunned. She threw up her hands at a loss, as if trying but unable to bring them back down. She charged up and down the little room.

"No!" she managed at last. "My thoughts? No way. How is that even possible? Does that mean that to you it's like everyone's naked? Worse even! What are our bodies compared to our thoughts?" She stopped in front of Anna with a strained, distrustful smile. "You're joking… So, tell me what … what I'm thinking right now?"

You've done it now with this wretched truth of yours, Anna said to herself. Aloud she said serenely, "You're thinking that you've really got yourself into a dodgy situation, about the least unseemly way to turf me out, plus a truckload of swearing."

Genevieve staggered back as if someone had hit her, flushed a deep red and buried her face in her hands.

"I'm sorry," she said in a dull mutter.

...As Anna came down the spiral staircase from the nest carrying her backpack, Genevieve darted over, threw the flat door wide open, stood in her way and said forcefully, "You're not going anywhere! I won't let you. Damn them all, the two-faced lot! There you go, those are all my thoughts!"

***

… It wasn't long until the Spaniard in his Roman-headed lump of plaster went still in the chair. A couple of minutes later and shudders ran in perceptible waves across his muscular shoulders, chest and belly. For a few moments, the captive Francisco gripped the arms of the old leather chair tightly, then spread his fingers compulsively as if trying to feel at least something alive in the sealed black darkness.

His friend gazed in silent horror at how Francisco had been so precipitously transformed from a human being into a plaster-headed monster. Yes … the procedure's surprisingly weird—ruthless, too, Anna thought. As if you're being bricked up from the head down. And you're not much bothered any more about where your backside's sticking out or what it's up to… But hey, it's really handy for work. Now, no matter what far-flung branches of the circus the performers might work in, their exact measurements will also be to hand for artists, tailors, wardrobe managers and wigmakers.

Suddenly, the Spaniard in his plaster restraints let out a bloodcurdling howl. There was such suffering in the desolate nasal sound. Anna placed a hand on the Spanish tightrope-walker's wrist—so very like Volodka's—and gripped it tightly… And he, like a child, grabbed her hand gratefully and fitfully and crushed it and squeezed it and didn't let go until it was all over, until Genevieve broke the hardened form in two and began to wipe the dirt, Vaseline and bits of plaster off his pale face, neck and powerful shoulders...

That night Anna dreamt of never-ending rows of plaster heads that were reflected in mirrors and nodded out of them, endeavouring to flirt, to engage in small talk in various languages—unlike the real ones which were frozen in stupid silence, motionless and censorious, on their shelves. Quite right too, she thought in the dream. All objects come to life in the Mirror World.

And once again she was riding her motorbike at top speed, took off and flew up and up until she pierced the thin mirror membrane of the heavens, a rainbow like a ripple of petrol in a spring puddle.

And when she woke up—after five in the morning—her thoughts turned to Mashuta once again.

She had been thinking of her more and more often in recent years. It was strange: She thought about her far more than about her father whom she continued to love passionately and loyally as she had as a child, giving him a proper burial and mourning him as anyone would, although a distraught Khristina hadn't even wanted to let her in or "anywhere near that pine box."

Indeed, when Anna rang the flat after flying in at dawn, Khristina was already up and dressed or perhaps hadn't been to bed at all and when she saw her former charge, frozen in clouds of breath, she yelled not in her usual Surzhik for some reason but in Ukrainian, "Well, lookie here, good people. Look at this slut from the circus!"

They were alone in the flat, unless, of course, you counted her father, lying in his coffin in the living room with a face that was inaccessible and unfamiliar to Anna.

"You bitch, you goddamned bitch! You didn't come to bury your own mother but you show up for the inheritance!"

Anna went over to her and put an arm round her neck in silence, drawing her towards her.

"Now then, that's enough," she said, pained. "Put a sock in it! What's made you come all over Ukrainian?"

And Khristina obediently broke off her theatrical shrieking and let Anna take her full weight.

"Fuck, Nyuta!" she gave a loud and truly dreadful wail. "Fuck!"

"That's better," Anna said.

She had a fleeting thought that she would still have to answer for what she had done at the Ukrainian Embassy. She recalled the glassy dilated pupils of the woman at the visa section—what did they call her, a consul?—and her own cold fury, insurmountable because her father was dying even as they spoke. "Fine … Come for your passport at nine tomorrow." "No," she said, expressionless, trapping the woman *between her mirrors*, "you will do it right now as a matter of urgency. Get the stamp. It's in the second drawer of the desk…"

For the first time it occurred to her that Khristina must have loved her father. It wasn't for nothing that she moved into the flat after Mashuta's death and did Doctor Nesterenko's washing with all the fervour she'd brought with her from the village and been able to retain amid the hectic life of the big city.

The day after the funeral, on lined paper from the pile that was always on her father's desk and in the proper *shapeshifted* script so appropriate to the circumstances, Anna wrote a will in Khristina's favour. And for safety's sake, a sort of gift deed of *inheritance*. She lost a whole week drawing it up properly with a notary and a lawyer. Ridiculous!

And in an instant Khristina became an old woman. A silly, solitary old woman with a red tear-stained face, marooned in her mansion for good.

"Nyu-u-ta!" she would call across the room every now and then as she had when Anna was a child.

And when Anna appeared in the doorway with her quiet, "So, what are you roaring about?" she would say, "Coz when you go, I won't have anyone I can call."

She talked incessantly about Anna's father, what he ate, what he drank, who visited him during the months he was ill and how kind they had been to him at the hospital and what a beautiful funeral he was given, wasn't he, Nyutochka? How many flowers, the things that were said. She must have found these oft-repeated conjurations needful, therapeutic. Anna, meanwhile, had no hope of escaping from the grip of the house, which reeked of madness and calamity and was no longer her home and had not been for a long time.

"And how he cried before he died," Khristina half said, half sang to herself, rocking to and fro on the sofa. Now she went from Surzhik to Ukrainian and then back to Surzhik as she talked. "Poor soul, how he cried."

"Over Mashuta?" asked Anna glumly.

"No." Khristina raised her greying eyebrows. "Over you … the tears that poured and poured… And always saying, 'Khristina, she has been given so much! So very much.' Made me go cold all over, it did. So, I thinks, what is all this? Crying over her like she's dead."

And all of a sudden, she checked herself, remembering that she was now the owner of such abundant riches.

"I'll bring that mirror out of the pantry," she said talking herself into it. "It's been standing in there for a bloody long time. It's all covered in dust."

"Later," Anna pleaded. "Later, when I'm gone."

***

Once dressed, she sat at the fold-out table and spent a couple of hours working on Genevieve's computer which she always took up to the nest during her visits.

A series of Cirque de la Lune characters appeared on the screen.

Photography was Genevieve's selfless passion. This world, none too welcoming of her in real time, was transformed when seen through a viewfinder. It became meaningful, moving, magnificent and wrenchingly transient. Her particularly successful photos were used as Cirque de la Lune postcards in promotional material and albums and hung in the managers' offices.

There are the sharp whirls of the big top's blue and yellow striped domes like sand dunes swirling in the wind. The white spotlights on their tips, the pennants rumpled by the wind. It's even possible to imagine a faint sound of music.

And there's the photograph of the Alegria house troupe: all in a huddle after the show, all still keyed up, in greasepaint and costume. Their convex breast plates still rising with their shallow breathing.

The tiniest details of the sophisticated makeup with its spattering of coloured glass, gold and silver sequins are visible in the spotlights. And the masks of the monsters and dwarfs are both scary and comical to look at: incarnations by skilful artists of the dazed and baleful, grotesque and doleful devils of fairy tale.

Unbelievable, fantastical costumes, each one a designer's masterpiece, planned to the very last sequin placed between the eyebrows. Each one painted with rainbow patterns like Venetian glass. Every detail of the costume—the trousers, the boots with turned-up toes, the stunning clasps, fasteners, buttons, epaulets—unrepeatable and exorbitantly expensive. One person wears a plume of feathers, another a tall stove hat, a third a wild wig like something from a nightmare. Together, this small troupe of performers appears to have tumbled out of a wonderful, gleeful, spine-tingling dream…

In the foreground is a melancholy clown, the famous Lyonya Katkov: white pancake lips, a red ball on his nose, an elongated black tear below his left eye. And the eyebrow above it much higher than the other, like a small parachute descending, surprised and sad…

Snake Woman. She's from China and without equal in her field. Fiery peacock eyes and green snake scales all over her body. Not a single crease, it looks like a second skin. Taken at the very moment her buttocks came down on the back of her neck. An enigmatic, closed face, propped up by her chin on the floor; extended legs stretched out like little logs.

And there she is: her body a jumble, an inconceivable bundle of limbs… Her legs a yoke around her neck.

And this is new: a silvery white acrobat on a trampoline cross, caught in mid-somersault by the predatory lens, arms stretched wide, her face blurred, retaining only one great eye and an astonished eyebrow…

When Anna came downstairs, Genevieve was already standing over the frying pan, flipping her trademark *galettes bretonnes*, buckwheat flour crepes made with egg.

Khristina had made them for breakfast all her life without the slightest suspicion that they were practically the main dish in Breton cuisine.

Genevieve remained a Breton in everything she did. And a Catholic in spite of it all. A crucifix hung above her bed and every morning, eyes barely open, she muttered a prayer in an urgent, passionate whisper and only then poured herself the first little whisky or brandy pick-me-up.

She went to Brittany every August, roaming around with her camera from dawn to dusk, doing odd jobs in search of characters, pretending to be a student, and taking photographs like one possessed. Each time, she came home with an entire exhibition of new pictures, completely replacing the display on her walls.

Anna knew the ones currently on show by heart. The three fishermen in startling pink shirts taken against equally pink waves at dawn as they haul in their nets. The rhythm of their joint effort merges with the even swell of the waves. It's like a trendy modern ballet—the invisible spotlight of the rising sun seeming to light up a stage…

And here's another photo. Two women in black dresses and very odd headdresses, tall and white like chef's hats, are strolling along a coastline at twilight. And in the background a row of hunched menhirs, rough, unhewn standing stones, echo their route, retreating and fading into the fine autumn drizzle. A lighthouse can just be made out on a jutting cliff far, far away. There's even a smell of iodine from the frozen seaweed left on the shore after high tide.

Several more photographs of a rough, wild sea hang in the "dining room." Nothing but the raging water, wisps of spindrift atop waves that bulge like tensed muscles…

Howard was strutting silently and haughtily about on the top of his cage. He was not very talkative in the mornings. When he saw Anna though, he shook his wings and immediately flew to her shoulder. He nipped her earlobe and posed his personal question in a cantankerous voice, "Anna-boy, let me give you a kiss?"

"Go on then." Anna gave permission, scratching him on the back of his neck.

The video-recorder was playing a tape of Alegria: Genevieve couldn't go an hour without her beloved circus.

On the screen, the White Singer, one of the symbols of the Cirque de la Lune empire (the souvenir doll in a white dress was sold in a stall in the administration building, along with branded tee-shirts, cups and other clutter) was singing slowly in the deep quavering drone of the bagpipes.

"Did you know that was my idea?" Genevieve asked, nodding towards the screen. "I told Guy and the gang that the bagpipes, the real guttural drone of the bagpipes, that's what should break up the show. We always have something so ridiculously intense... The music in the shows, I said, should be Celtic, erotic and original."

"You've got some new photos there," Anna said. "On the computer. Some of them are people I don't know."

"That's right. There are two new Chinese. Have you seen the Ring of Fire? Such dab hands. The pace is out of this world. And..." She took a deep breath in and, after a brief pause, she let it out again... "There's this unusual Russian gymnast... She's so delicate, Anna... Gymnasts can sometimes be a bit coarse, you know, but this one... Her name's E-le-na. Is that how you say it in Russian? Is it really prettier than plain Helene? There's a sort of infiniteness about it, it's not restricted by consonants..."

Ha! Looks like she fancies someone else now, thought Anna, glancing at Genevieve's pointed little face.

A thin-armed, long-legged pupil of a rural Catholic school, a long neck in the collar of a black wool dress. She sits watching a circus performance, open-mouthed, amazed. Her thin, red chapped hands incessantly adjusting her hem on her knees. Her shining black eyes devour a gymnast in an antiquated pink leotard, the star of this unknown and mediocre troupe that had ventured as far as their coastal isolation. The name of the circus? It seems to be Italian, barely decipherable on the rain-soaked canvas of the big top.

"I'm leaving the day after tomorrow," said Anna, finishing off a galette. On the television, an enormous Mongolian and his spitting image, a

Mongolian child in identical makeup, a red apple blush on their whitened faces, performed one trick after another. Fire sticks flew up to embroider fantastical patterns in the air, fiery tails scrolling into figures and flourishes. Oh, bravo! Say what you like, it's top class.

"So soon?" Genevieve marvelled and Anna realized she was right, her friend had got it really badly. Otherwise, she'd never have spoken so calmly about Anna's imminent departure.

"I have to go to Boston to see Senya. This awful thing's happened over there. A really valuable violin's been stolen from an old friend of his."

"Oh, God," sighed Genevieve, "everyone has their own passions."

You're not kidding, Anna agreed silently.

"Are you still going to meet Philippe?"

"Not right now. To be honest, I'm cross after yesterday. Philippe's a bright guy, a visionary but with absolutely no principles. Plus, he has a personal interest. He's trying to pull strings for his own favourite and hoping to win Guy over. I have to let it go, basically... Let it sort itself out and come to a head. I like getting involved in things once they can't do without me. Pour me another coffee, please. Thanks! And a drop of milk... I've come up with something for the lighting, you know... It could make an incredible impact. It hasn't been done before. We take rotating prisms, a light scanner and four mirrors, okay, and I put one of them behind a transparent curtain."

… In fact, she wasn't happy with herself and how passionately she'd set out the attractions of her project for Philippe the previous day: the giant mirrored box on wheels with fall-away sides that could be moved, dismantled or assembled in a matter of moments—a whole heap of possibilities for utterly paradoxical productions. Why did she have to reveal so much of herself to that devious guy? she wondered. It *served no purpose...*

"Philippe," she'd said, "I'm really very interested in your space. I've never worked on that scale before. Imagine, what will happen on stage and in the auditorium when your house troupe—quite a few people, essentially—appear in my mirrors! We'll make the back rows bigger... An infinite horde of fairy-tale beings! Just imagine them, crowding in from all directions, no matter where you look, they're everywhere, even on the ceiling! The inhabitants of a whole dream plant! A gigantic mirage! Another, mirror universe!"

Philippe sat, smiling, nodding, one leg laid across the other's sharp knee, wiggling the toe of his loafer ever so slightly now and then. He kept smoothing his grey-streaked chestnut beard lovingly with two fingers.

… They left the house together. A disgruntled Howard had been rein-stalled in his cage and they could hear his indignant squawk, "Spare the parrot!"

***

Before she left, she asked Genevieve as usual to go for a meal at one of the gay bars on Sainte-Catherine Street.

It played rave music in the evenings. Young men danced along, stripping off shirts and tee-shirts as the dance went on, showing off beautiful bodies.

For some reason, Genevieve liked these hard-core, noisy hangouts. It had been a long time since Anna herself, worn down by the circus drums, had been able to tolerate any loud noise. Howard's screeching was the only thing that didn't irritate her.

But in the day time you could just have a meal and a pretty good one at that.

"You won't mind if Elena comes too?" Genevieve had asked care-fully in the morning.

Anna smiled and said, "Why would I mind?"

"And I will sit and listen to you speaking Russian," Genevieve con-tinued, thrilled.

Elena turned out to be a somewhat chilly blonde with high plucked eyebrows that gave her face a permanent expression of slightly fastid-ious surprise. As if she had just heard something she found extreme-ly distasteful… In the end, it's the eyebrows that determine the over-all expression of a face, Anna thought. So what? If Genevieve's crazy about her, if she's capable of returning a modicum of feeling… And really, it's time the poor girl had someone to relieve the monotony of Howard's company for a while.

As Genevieve looked on fondly, they began to speak Russian half-heartedly, exchanging views about local circus procedures, at-tempting but failing to find friends in common—Elena had gone to Cirque de la Lune from sport, not the circus. Then they switched to the kind of wooden English Genevieve's new love interest knew from school. How on earth did they communicate in such impoverished language? Then again, who needed language?

After about forty minutes when they'd just served the fish, Elena went off to the toilet and Genevieve leant across the table and asked excitedly, her hand on Anna's elbow, "Do you like her? She's very sophisticated, isn't she?"

"Awfully," Anna confirmed, remembering what women like that were called in circus lingo: "a cunt on tiptoe."

"I think she's a bit jealous when you're around," Genevieve said, giggling.

Anna was beginning to feel bored. It had happened a lot in recent months. A deadly desolate spiritual rather than physical weakness enveloped her although it should long since have been given some other name—"*Ennui, the mangy cur, comes right out of the blue, Nyuta, my angel...*"

Ever more frequently, she was gripped by a sudden longing to be somewhere else immediately. Where? It didn't matter. To be on her bike and away as soon as possible… And to ride … until her abused muscles began to groan as they did when she was young, until they begged for a break…

Now too she suddenly wanted to stand and go out into the fresh air, saddle up her ride… She even felt for the bandana in her pocket.

No, she had to finish her dinner, pay the bill and say goodbye to Genevieve properly.

She looked around at the bar, empty in the afternoon, ran an indifferent glance over the wall opposite where a mirror, sick and crusted with white, hung between two over-the-top red and blue posters of semi-naked young men. The mirror reflected the door to the ladies' room. It opened slightly…

In the very next moment, stretched out like a mouth yelling in great pain, she saw Elena hanging in the doorway, dangling from a safety-line noose and looking at Anna out of glassy red eyes in an astonished dead face…

Anna gagged and coughed… She slumped back in her chair and groaned.

"What is it?" Genevieve asked in alarm. "What's the matter?"

"Nothing," Anna muttered thickly, covering her face with her hands. "Cramp … the weather, maybe … migraine…"

Elena was already nearing the table, her smooth thin lips freshly touched up.

Shortly after that she made her apologies and left, despite Genevieve's evident dismay.

The ringing headache that had descended upon Anna with the picture she had seen in the mirror was still throbbing behind her eyes and experience warned that God alone knew how long it would last.

She asked the waiter for the bill, hesitating…

Through the window she could see her motorbike in its outside parking spot. Now, she said to herself, kiss goodbye and go… Forget it all…

No, You will not drag me in! Damn You! You are not to use me for entertainment!

Get up and go, she told herself. You're a passer-by who just happened to see a highly intimate picture not meant for your eyes.

"Genevieve," she forced out, still seated. "Listen to me. For the love of God, listen to me and don't ask any questions. Just believe me. That's all. It's not worth getting too attached to that girl."

And she raised reddened eyes to her friend. Genevieve stared at Anna, surprised and offended.

"Why do you say that?" she stammered. "It's weird and … hurtful!"

Anna understood but could never tell her. Never.

"Please, I'm begging you!" she said with force, grabbing Genevieve's hand. "Don't get attached to her."

"But why not?" Genevieve cried, wounded, snatching back her hand. Her bewildered face had paled, her lips twitched as though feeling and holding back words that were ready to slip out irretrievably.

Anna said nothing, eyelids lowered. Pain was boring holes *in the mirrors* with especially fine inquisitorial drills…

Genevieve started to speak, taking in a noisy breath, punctuating her speech with brusque gestures.

"You! For many years you were my … but I'm only flesh and blood, do you see? Flesh and blood, pathetic, maybe, criminal even, as my brothers say, but I want some affection too!"

Her hands seemed to be trying, ineffectually, to stem the flow of words and dropped helplessly onto the table before flying back up to her face. Such skilful, talented hands, more imposing than her sharp-profiled little face like some outlandish bird's. "I'm only human. You could never … I mean, sorry, I didn't mean, we're friends, okay, but you have to understand me too… And it's very selfish if you… Maybe you're worried about the practicalities? Please don't, your room will always be there…"

They brought the bill. Anna put some notes between the flat leather folds, scattered the tip in coins on the top. She stood, took her leather jacket off the back of the chair and put it on, tied her bandana round her neck…

Genevieve remained seated, her face unhappy, already cursing herself for having said too much.

Anna leant forward and, placing both hands on Genevieve's stick-thin shoulders, planted a kiss on the top of a head as tousled as a parrot's crest. She said, "Right, the room… The room's really convenient."

She went outside and inspected her bike for a couple of minutes out of habit. Then she took her seat, put her helmet on and checked that everything was in order, her fingers automatically running over the fasteners.

Pain flooded her eyes, flickered across her forehead, pounded her temples in an endless wave.

Even through the window, it was clear how crushed Genevieve felt.

Her lonely, slightly stooped figure remained motionless at the table and a moment later as Anna kicked away the stand, it veered to the side and dropped behind along with the café and the petrol station, along with the fun, bohemian Le Plateau district, dragging with it the whole of Montreal, city of circuses and churches.

＊

"No, little one, let me drive … This is a city of particularly crazy junctions and no road signs at all. But you'll go racing off as usual, taking the trees on the side of the roads down in the process. You know, there's this fantastic local guide, divided into chapters: "How to Shop in Boston," "How to Visit Restaurants in Boston,"… Anyway, the "How to Drive in Boston" section has only one sentence: "In Boston, it's better not to drive."

"Tell me about Myatlitsky," Anna asked.

"I wrote to you that he's having a hard time. His Stradivarius has vanished. And it was a really good one, too."

"Obviously," she replied.

"Not as obvious as all that!" Senya objected.

He had met her at the airport that morning, persuaded her not to take the motorbike (he hated her motorbikes, the stupid biker's gear—the leather jacket, the helmet, the horrendous gloves) and, as a result, he was in an excellent mood.

"Not obvious at all, actually! He made around two thousand instruments in his lifetime and didn't destroy or remake the less successful ones, just left them as they were. And in addition, you can never tell whether an instrument was made by Stradivarius himself or his pupils."

"Is that right?" Anna remarked, distractedly. But Senya knew that his every word was instantly stored away in compartments he couldn't really understand, to be brought out whenever it was needed, preserved intact, up to and including the intonation with which it was pronounced.

"Guarneri's are the best violins," he went on. "He didn't make many in his lifetime and each one is worth its weight in diamonds, let alone gold... See that lunatic? He's not even indicating. It's utter chaos, I tell you. Almost like Russia. Sorry, Myatlitsky's Stradivarius. It really was out of this world and now it's been stolen."

"How?"

"Lifted from the green room. There are two rooms next to one another and the second one has a door leading into the corridor. While the Professor was receiving compliments back stage after the concert, they just walked away with his violin. Darling..." he glanced at her apologetically. "I'm sorry to bother you. I just thought perhaps you'd be able to..."

"We'll see," she interrupted. "And keep your eyes on the road. Tell me more about him. You're fond of him."

"I am," Senya said. "He means a lot to me, you know. I mean, I'm an inveterate, a confirmed orphan, but there's something about him that reminds me of my grandfather. Some natural, innate gravitas... It's hard to explain. I've written to you about it and talked about it too. He was born in Warsaw but lived in Russia as a child and speaks good Russian, even insists I speak Russian to him, to 'exercise the muscle.' Crazy! A man of ninety-three! It's people like that who are the backbone of the world. 'To exercise the muscle,' right. So, when he was sixteen in the mid-1920s Andrzej Myatlitsky went to Germany and studied under the famous Carl Flesch. And since he was already pretty much a virtuoso, it wasn't long before the maestro made him his assistant. At all events, when Flesch was approached by a little girl, eight-year-old Ida Grendel—and Flesch didn't accept children in his class—Myatlitsky took pity on her and started working with her himself... She's still performing, not letting on about her age, turning up everywhere with her poodle, which gets under everyone's feet and is comparable only to its owner in terms of its shrewish nature. Myatlitsky's the only one who remembers how old she really is..."

...They drove along orderly, ultra-quiet streets for around fifteen minutes. Judging by the mighty plane and linden trees, this had been an old and respectable area a century ago. The immaculate green nap of the lawns sloped away from the road, each with its own palatial residence. Each detached home was in a different style—windows with stained-glass inserts, carved columns, spacious wooden verandas, the morning breeze stirring the empty string hammocks and lightweight swing seats. The chatter of the birds was as deafening as in a forest.

Eventually, they pulled up outside one of the houses: yet another hammock, yet another swing, this one with a squirrel, unperturbed, examining some find in its vice-like paws.

"It's quiet…" Senya said, looking around and closing the door. "We're about ten minutes early. Maybe, the Professor's not ready yet. Right, come on…"

"Won't anyone mind?"

"Come on. I'm as familiar here as the home help. I played nearby once. I couldn't get my old banger started so I walked here. It took some skill to get into the house. It was already late. I didn't want to wake the old man up. I lay on the living room sofa and had an excellent night's sleep. In the morning, they fed me without so much as batting an eyelid."

They dislodged the squirrel and went up wooden steps that could have done with a lick of paint. Senya pushed the door open—it wasn't locked—and they entered a small hall, chock full of very old and well-worn furniture. There was a coat rack with curved pegs, exactly like the ones that had stood in the waiting room of any official building in Kiev when Anna was a child.

The wide gap created when the double door was opened revealed part of a spacious living room with a fireplace. It was full of small carved and inlaid tables, armchairs, writing desks and sofas, the floor spread with an abundance of carpets of different sizes, styles and colours, and the walls hung with pictures, drawings and photographs. No one had bothered about style here at all. And quite right too.

"Professor, hello!" Senya yelled. "Andrzej Vladislavovich!"

No one answered although there was a sound of water somewhere.

"This is awkward," Anna said. "And how come the door's open…"

"You could leave your own skull open here and no one would steal anything."

"What about the Guarneri? Does he take it into the bathroom?"

Senya guffawed although Anna hadn't really been joking. Not infrequently, he had a peculiar way of understanding many of her questions, smiling or even laughing at who knew what.

"Let me show you something," Senya said. He put an arm round her shoulder and began to lead her along the walls, bumping into tables and writing desks now and then, nearly knocking off their candelabra, jewellery-boxes and silver cups. He wanted to show Anna a whole host of photographs, depicting Myatlitsky with such an array of celebrities it made their eyes spin.

Old photos, turning brown or green. And new coloured ones: portraits, posed and casual … taken in passing on flights of stairs or in concert hall foyers, on stage with the orchestra or in green rooms among bouquets of flowers. Carefree snaps on boats, in deckchairs with a cigar between his teeth; at the wheel of a car that looked unbelievably like a museum exhibit—it even had a bulb horn; in restaurants and bars, at tables on the terraces of cafés in Paris, Madrid and London; in pompous hotel lobbies, amid the gilded condescension of enormous mirrors, in baroque armchairs with lion-headed armrests, in recording studios… And on the steps of antiquated aeroplanes and even at the open door of a helicopter, all ready to dip inside: there stood the virtuoso, Andrzej Myatlitsky, elegant in his long grey coat and soft felt hat, holding his violin case.

"He's 93," Senya commented. "He's had plenty of time to take pictures…"

Slow steps were heard and feet in slippers appeared on the stairs as pyjama-bottomed legs made their unhurried descent. A dressing gown followed, loosely belted at the waist … a tee-shirt under the dressing gown … and then the whole of Professor Myatlitsky hove into view.

"Yes, well, you could have put on something a little more decent than a dressing gown when you were expecting guests."

But the elderly, shrunken, stooping figure with a shock of grey hair evidently felt both comfortable and extremely well.

"Oh," he said, immediately heading towards and addressing Anna and extending a hand, "Simon, you've talked about her and even boasted about her but you gave me no warning that she would be so…"

"What?" Anna inquired seriously. She had taken an immediately liking to Myatlitsky.

"Such eyes, my dear, are no everyday matter! Eyes like that are not every day wear!"

In short, the old man was still a smoothie.

It turned out that Julia, Myatlitsky's daughter, was due to put in an appearance before long—she wanted to meet Anna too—as was his granddaughter ("Oh, you'll see, such a little beauty. I adore her!").

That's right, Anna recalled, Senya had written about a little girl being adopted from China.

"In the meantime, though, there's no objection to us having coffee, is there?" Senya asked.

"Of course not, as long as you can be bothered to make it your-selves," the Professor replied, quick as a flash.

"I knew it: I'm destined to wait on the entire company."

Anna immediately relaxed. It was a long time since she had felt as comfortable as she did in this house, packed with well-loved belongings, surrounded and warmed by a long, long life...

Senya went off to the kitchen. It was right alongside, next to the living room, on the ground floor, and from there, he kept up the exchange of barbed but utterly homely remarks with the Professor, as if they were playing ping pong. Finally, he was back with a tray: cups, a sugar bowl, a dish of some kind of biscuits.

"Listen, Simon!" exclaimed a contented Myatlitsky. "I suspected you knew your way around my kitchen better than I do but you've achieved the impossible. Where did you find these super-bad-for-you, utterly delicious biscuits? Julia has been hiding them for two weeks now!"

"I just reached up to the top shelf."

"Give up the bassoon. Dear God, you'd earn far more as my home help. And I'd arrange a pension for you later on. I, of course, am eternal, like an old parrot."

At the word parrot, Anna began to recount the story of Howard. The Professor laughed, asked questions, exclaimed, "What? Come again? 'Spare the parrot?' Very smart..."

It was nice there ... so nice... A light, smiling house that cared about its inhabitants. No mirrors. No, that's wrong! It needed a large square mirror above the fireplace, diverting and absorbing...

Without noticing, Anna stood and began wandering around the living room. Nice... so nice...

Some kind of trepidation, even terror, connected to the inhabitants of this house, existed not in it but outside. Both the trepidation and the terror were lacquered over like the elegantly cut, reddish string-plates on a new made-in-China violin.

"No, in Warsaw, we lived at No. 10 Medovaya Street. It's more legato in Polish – 'Miodowa,'" Myatlitsky said. "The house was what's called a 'kamienica', impressive with a square paved inner courtyard. And the façade was the ochre colour so much loved in Warsaw. I have an excellent memory of it all. Do you understand how well people were put together in the past, Simon? It was a labour of heart and soul. I remember Russia very well too. After the Revolution, my father moved to Samara and then to Saratov… And that's where I kept up my studies with Professor Ziskind. I was a virtuoso little wunderkind… But those days, just imagine, the hunger, the cold… My teacher's wife was a ladies' footwear designer. She made me some boots but on a woman's last. With little heels. So that, aged eight, there I was trotting around in boots with heels."

"Nowadays, the psychologists would say that was playing with fire," Senya commented. "More cream?"

"Just a drop! Easy now, don't just slosh it in! Maybe so but nothing bad came of it as the endless list of the women I've loved can confirm. Anna," the Professor said to Anna's back, "ten years or so earlier, you wouldn't have got away from me!"

"And I wouldn't have made any particular effort to," Anna replied amiably and Senya, moved, thought how she always precisely matched whoever she was talking to, as if she reflected them and was herself reflected with them in invisible mirrors.

"Whereas this," she said all of a sudden, pointing to one of the photographs, "is a circus dressing room. There's the brass rivet at the corner of the trunk."

In the photograph, a young Myatlitsky stood next to a smiling young man with curly hair.

"Quite right!" the Professor replied. "The Warsaw Circus in the 1920s."
"So who's this?"
Myatlitsky narrowed his eyes and paused.

"The name probably won't mean anything to you … Although he must still be remembered in Russia. And every man and his dog knew him in Europe before the war… But when we had our photo taken together … I was already famous, had performed a lot whereas he wasn't widely known although he could electrify an audience. He was a corpse … in the circus."

"He was what?" laughed Senya.

"A corpse," the Professor said again with a ready smile. "He used to die in front of the audience, go absolutely stiff, anyone could go up and touch him. I did myself. Then he would come back to life."

"But you haven't said his name."

"Really? That's old age for you. He knew my name, mind, before I even went into his green room. He was sitting there, removing his makeup. He glanced at me in the mirror and said, 'And here comes Jedrek!' I was speechless."

"He could have known you from the posters."

"But he said, 'Jedrek.' My name, Andrzej, was only ever shortened at home, by my sisters. 'And here comes Jedrek!' In my mother's voice… It was the legendary Wolf Messing, who predicted the death of Hitler and as a result was forced to flee to the Soviet Union where he died."

"Why died?" Senya objected. "He was performing in clubs of some kind until he was really old."

"Per-for-ming?!" Myatlitsky exclaimed disdainfully. "A man who could see the future, who could easily read the thoughts of the person he was talking to and was capable of God only knows what else, per-for-ming? And that's what I'm saying: He died."

A car door slammed shut outside. Someone ran up the stairs and an imperious female voice shouted in English, "Daddy! You've left the garage open again!"

"And here's Julia. She isn't even in the house and she has to give me instructions on how to lead my life!" The Professor also switched to English and his daughter, tall and thin with her father's features in a plain, angular, beaky face, instantly took up the thread, removing her raincoat as she advanced and hanging it on an old-fashioned curved peg.

"Because if I don't give you instructions, you'll do whatever you like."

"At the unhappy age of ninety-three," her father added.

"At the magnificent age of ninety-three!"

Anna glanced at Senya who smiled, saying nothing. The well-established duo, their repertoire tried and tested over the years, performed for the public so smoothly that no rehearsals were required. They could pick up anywhere in the score.

Julia came in. Anna was introduced and subjected almost blatantly, uninhibitedly, to a close and critical examination and assessment. Practically asking her to take her shoes off to check her nails were clean, like they did at school. No, no trepidation or terror emanated from this straight-talking woman with lightning-quick reactions. She belonged to the house, had grown up there and loved her father and everything to do with him.

"So where's Edna?" the Professor asked.

"Edna dug her heels in for some reason, swearing that she was frightfully busy. But I insisted. She'll be along, a little later. Well, have you been famished without me? I've brought a whole heap of goodies…"

She took the bag off into the kitchen. Her father followed her so that he could supervise. Their voices could still be heard, cheerful and cutting, now louder, now tailing off slightly. Once or twice they burst into identical laughter at the very same time. And, quivering with tension, above these family voices that spoke in the same key, hung the name *Edna*.

At lunch, father and daughter kept up their repartee as they talked to one another and their guests. One would begin a sentence, the other complete it. It was evident that the two of them adored one another even though the needling never stopped.

"Julia is just like me from her big-bird beaky nose to her incredible staying power when she's working…"

"And ending in her dreadful character," his daughter continued.

"Oh, yes, she's had the sweetest character since childhood. I remember when she was seven, her mother was set on getting her into a particularly prestigious school. Very expensive and very prestigious! She even had to go in for a chat. Well, we arrayed her in her finery first thing in the morning, curled her hair, put her in her nice white coat and little white boots…"

"And a big red bow that went so well with my chestnut curls…"

"Indeed. And a big red bow. But during the whole of the so-called chat…

"…when I was supposed to be as docile as a lamb to win over three old sticks who were past their sell-by dates…

"…basically, the little brat sat through the whole of it, lips pursed, without uttering a single word! On the way home, I asked, 'Why didn't you say anything when they asked you a question, Julia?' She said portentously, 'I did not feel so inclined.' To which I said nothing but when…"

"…when we were passing the next enormous puddle, he suddenly shoved me right into the middle of the stinking sludge! And there I sat, absolutely stunned, up to my ears in dirt!"

"That's right. 'What have you done?!' she wailed from the puddle. 'What for?'"

The Professor gave a real wail as he told the story, his blue eyes round in their deep wrinkles. He was clearly enjoying reliving the long-ago incident. At the same time, he did not rob Julia of her rejoinders, the ones that, according to the score, were meant to be hers and hers alone. So, now too, after his yell, he fell silent and Julia finished the tale.

"My father shrugged his shoulders and replied regally, 'I felt so inclined'…"

Meanwhile, the oppressive weight in the space behind Anna's forehead was constantly increasing.

Malice streamed from the name *Edna* in pulsating circles.

Julia rang her tardy daughter: She was already on her way.

Anna looked up at Senya. He was sitting opposite her in an armchair, barely speaking, watching her with quiet concern, and when the Professor and Julia began a fiercely enthusiastic argument as to whether or not a cactus on the veranda should be watered in the winter months ("Why are you so upset, in summer, about the sodding cactus's well-being in the winter?"—"Sodding?! An excellent endorsement of a rare plant I brought you from Guatemala in my own bosom, you might say!!!"—"Forgive me, I ought to have remembered that only your determined bosom is capable of tolerating the dreadful spines that have twice stuck in my precious fingers!") Senya furtively blew her a pleading kiss, as if asking forgiveness in advance. For what?

The Professor had time to pass on one more piece of gossip, about Phyllis Lane, who was old and fat and never left her chair but was forever crisscrossing countries and continents, giving master classes here, there and everywhere. She would bang her stick and yell, hammering out the rhythm. She had so many pupils that countries and cities had become completely mixed up in her head. People said that she had recently found herself on a train, next to a girl holding a violin case.

"Oh!" said Phyllis. "You have a violin too. Who's your teacher?"

"You are, Madame," the young pupil replied.

From Phyllis Lane, they turned to violins in general. Julia mentioned the disappearance in passing. Eventually, the name *Stradivarius* came up. The laughter stopped. The Professor's mood darkened.

"I would be incredibly grateful to you, Anna," he said. "Semyon Aleksandrovich did mention… I know you are categorically opposed to acting as an oracle but, believe me, my despair…"

"I understand," Anna said, interrupting. "I'll try."

She wanted to ask to be left in peace for a minute. The malice was drawing nearer, acquiring ever more specific outlines, breathing down her neck with such venomous force that she wanted to leave there and then. Anna was afraid to look into the glittering vault of the mirrors to be certain. What then? How could she tell them everything, poor things?

In recent months, she had been finding it harder and harder to control the intractable force of the mirrors in her head, recoiling ever more frequently from dazzling flares that stung like slaps across the face as if she was being *punished for disobedience.*

A bell rang in the hall. The Professor and Julia barked as one, "It's open, for goodness sake, as if you didn't know." The door slammed and a light musical voice was heard, stuffed full as a bun with the pungent, fetid terror of a frightened skunk...

And suddenly into the room came an enormous violin. Anna's first thought was that the girl had swallowed a violin in some grotesque fashion and it had expanded within her and was vibrating, desperate to escape.

And suddenly she could see it all: a scrawny figure, with a nasty little moustache, eyes distinctively set—Latino, maybe? There was a glimpse of him in the corridor as he hastily received an uncovered violin from Edna, wrapped it in his jacket and hurtled past a drowsy black doorman to the concert hall's service entrance.

And now all that remained was to tear this happy home apart, confound its boundlessly loving father and daughter duo and bring even more misfortune into the life of an abandoned baby, the fragile and improbably womanly young Chinese girl, found at the side of a road, her eyes flooded with fear while her womb already carried the tiny fleck of an embryo.

Anna closed her eyes and everyone fell silent. Several brass seconds dropped weightlessly one after the other on the antique wall clock in the corner of the living room.

The two foundlings in the room gazed at one another in silence... And the utterly blameless little fish in the still small but already taut uterus kept on spinning the thread of forlorn lust.

No!

No, You are not to use me as entertainment!

"I can't see!" Anna declared hoarsely and curtly. "I'm sorry. I can't see anything."

CHAPTER 19

I'm up to my ears in work right now. B-movies, one stunt after the other. Means I'm in great demand. I don't do the stunts anymore but I stage manage a lot... No, experience of sport or the circus doesn't help at all. Just the opposite, you have to do some serious retraining. For example, if your stunt is falling from a height, a cliff, say, or a fourth-floor window, you're in free fall. If you stick to all the rules of gymnastics when you do it, you'll end up disabled if not actually dead.

Plus, situations occur on shoots where you don't know what's hit you and they have nothing to do with sport. I did this film, right—"The Lieutenant." It started with shots of a burning tank on a battlefield, a Red Army soldier jumping out in flames. It was filmed at a military training centre near Saint Petersburg. So, the reality's an old T-34 tank from the LenFilm Studios. On the back of the tank, there are trays of rags soaked in napalm and set on fire.

But the tank's an old one, the sides are full of holes. The cooling system's fuelled with diesel to stop the water freezing. You can imagine, yeah? So, there are two stunt performers in the turret and I'm underneath at the controls. And they kick me either on the left or the right arm to tell me which way to go. The tank's on fire. You can't see a damn thing. And it rumbles over the ruts and pot holes in no particular hurry. To cut a long story short, the napalm seeps into the engine compartment, the hoses burn through and the diesel catches fire.

The order comes to halt. I stop and turn off the engine. And then? When the engine stops, the flame bursts into the driver's section and there I am inside taking a rest, enjoying the moment. Okay? Oh and by the way, the hatch weighs around twenty-five kilos, no less. Anyway, the people watching said that at the very moment the tank went up in flames, the hatch went back, light as a feather, and I shot out like a torpedo, head-first... The tank was burnt to a cinder. Go figure...

Anyway, I was forced to change my job. And not because I could see so far ahead that I guessed the Soviet circus would collapse. The real collapse came at the start of the 90s. We stopped being serfs, could enter into contracts, negotiate rates ourselves. Those who felt they had something to offer told the Central Administration and its bloodsuckers where to go and scattered in all directions. There aren't many places our guys don't work. There are a lot of Russians in China now. They love the circus there, think of it as an academic art. In Shanghai, you're given a contract, a residence permit, a flat... Only the measly dregs have stayed behind in Russia, infighting, murders, nonentity... Do you know how many flying acts there used to be? Forty! Now, there are three or four. Yet another roof of yet another circus collapsed recently in Novosibirsk. The only reason no one was killed was because the circus hasn't been working for many years. It's going to court.

To be fair, we always had a great circus school and we still do. Even now Italian street performers, brilliant people, come to Russia in the winter to study and to keep warm...

Then again, the circus had been a putrid, stagnant swamp for a long time: bribes, bastarding arselickers of all kinds, real criminals in every department of the Central Administration...

But that's by the by. You see, when it all happened to us, to her and me ... when we were torn away from one another...

By the way, here's a puzzle for you. Do you know where she snuck off to lie low after the hospital? After all, these very hands ... these thwacking great fists ... had virtually crippled her.

Not to her father. Not to Arisha, who had already moved to Belgium and was teaching at Mechelen's famous carillon academy and only popped into Russia for competitions... She went crawling off to the Bluvsteins, the Trotskyists! The very people who had showered us with Bolshevik swearing, followed us around, switched the lights off after us, cursed our motley crew of bohemian clowns and accused us of stealing matches... Irina Bogdanovna had full-blown Alzheimer's by then and was cracking her fleas in a nightmare of an old-folks' home somewhere on Shchelkovskoe Highway, while Isay Borisych still walked with a stick to fetch his kefir and a nice soft bun... So, just imagine, she crawled off to his place straight from hospital and spent three months laid up there as if she'd gone to earth... Forsaken idiot that he was, Senya sent cables from Leningrad and used to come over on his days off and snoop around trying to find her. He still didn't get it, that she'd turn up when it suited her. Meanwhile, the Trotskyist Bluvstein was practically spoon feeding her.

He told me himself later, "We had an agreed signal, two short rings, one long. I open up and there's Anna as if she's back from the dead, pale, all doubled up, leaning on the wall. And in such an unfamiliar voice, she says, 'Isay Borisych, I've nowhere to go.'"

There you go... For my part, when I got out of the holiday camp of prison six months later and realized that I couldn't stand seeing the circus anymore—it hit me like an electric current as the trolleybus was turning onto Tsvetnoy Boulevard—I hung out at a friend's, lolling on the sofa for days on end, watching illegally-sourced Hollywood drivel. One day it dawned on me. I realized what I had to do. I should open a stunt school. For our Russian stunt performers. Several groups were already working at the time. But their lack of rights was unique: no insurance, length of time in the job not taken into account. The guys were doing whatever work they could find, some as yard keepers, some as watchmen... The situation needed changing somehow.

I won over a couple of horseback jugglers, Seryoga and Petka Nestroev. They had already been wailing about our neglected circus business. We hired a sports hall in a school near Vodnyy Stadion Metro Station, came to arrangements about training sessions at the race track on Begovaya Street and put an announcement in the paper about setting the group up. At the time, for-profits were all the rage everywhere. And people flooded in. Some came from sport, others straight off the street. And here's the paradox: quite often it's screwed-up people, desperate to boost their self-esteem, who come into this business that calls for a strong nervous system.

So we selected about fifteen people, four of them girls, and started really pushing them: motorbikes, martial arts, heights, underwater stuff, pyrotechnics. And people would turn up out of the blue. We had some funny situations. And at the time the whole thing simply got me back on my feet. I didn't have time to moan or weep about my life being ruined, you see. And that's how we got things off the ground.

One or two of the guys soon found themselves in pictures. I was filming all out too...

And one time, Anna turned up...

Claiming to have seen the ad, but I don't believe that. I think she came to save me from myself. To heal me and to let me go. Somehow she wasn't surprised to see me. She knew where she was going and why.

And I will remember that day till my dying breath, as they say. It was April, a Sunday... Such a blue sky, the sun beating down on the windows. And there I was, sweating, knackered and frazzled after training, sitting on a chair in the middle of the sports hall, taking a break … assuming you can take a break from yourself, right? And then, just like in a film, and God, I always take the mickey out of that kind of crap, the door opens and Anna comes in. She stands in the doorway, looking straight ahead, imperiously, as if we were up on the wire again. And the sports hall is positively boiling in the sunlight, bright enough to dazzle you.

So there I am, sitting on my stool, nailed to the spot by the sun. I can't stand up. She comes closer and closer … and suddenly hauls me to my feet. And gives me such a hug. And I realize straight away—my body realizes—that she's not there to come back but on the contrary to set me free… And I stand there with her in that blaze of sunlight just as we did back in Grade Nine, hugging each other tightly like brother and sister… As if we hadn't spent a lifetime together, had not had love, the circus, the homelessness … nor that terrible evening … or rather we had … but it had all merged into this blessed love between kith and kin.

It's beyond me … expressing such yearning, such bliss. I can't do it. I don't have the words.

Anyway… She joined in the training sessions, was back up to par fairly soon and we started working in the same team. It was an interesting time. Short but interesting. Once she simply pulled me, dragged me back from the hereafter… It was in Saint Petersburg, 1992… We were filming "Special Assault Force." According to the script, there's a fire, a makeshift building about ten metres long goes up in flames. The hero has to run in, grab a Spidola radio and save national property. It's that kind of heroism. The famous Makarsky's the stunt coordinator. Pyrotechnics reckoned they could do all this fire action themselves but back then Soviet fire safety rules were still in force and they weren't given permission. They dug in their heels… Industrial action, in short. Anyway, pyrotechnics were supposed to coat the inside of the building with napalm, just the door and window frames, but to spite the bosses they daubed the whole thing. And then they were told to "Set it alight!" "Do it yourselves," they replied. And walked off.

When I dived into the burning truck, I realized right away that I was in a blast furnace. I was wearing a hat with ear flaps but my hands were bare and my face exposed. I ran into a wall instead of the door—I couldn't even find the door—knocked a bucket of petrol over and bang! What saved my face was that before the take, as if I'd sensed it, I'd piled snow up outside the door and I fell, face first, into it... In a nutshell, an ambulance, a lot of racing around, a hell of a lot of swearing ... a hospital in Vyborg... I was like a charred log... So, naturally, the head of pyrotechnics was sacked. Which was no help to me! And that's when Anna flew straight away into Vyborg and sat with me for several days. I don't know what she did. I couldn't see a bloody thing but that first dreadful pain was already gone by the end of the second day...

And a week later she flew out to the US with the TromBon Circus, a mickey-mouse outfit that had been cobbled together quickly. Maybe you know the story? It certainly hit the headlines. A collection of acts. They stayed in Atlanta. They were robbed blind, left without a penny, taken to the cleaners, as they say...

It was a risky business from the start. A con. The guys signed private contracts with some dodgy types who knew there was no big money to be made in the Soviet circus. The times weren't right and they scarpered, taking all the money they'd managed to raise from advance ticket sales. They dumped the performers in the scary jungles of America. Not bad as a survival trial, I can tell you. Just imagine. Soviet circus guys: good at their job but completely unprotected, used to going around in formation, being paid their small guaranteed salaries, doing what they're told, going wherever they were bought a ticket for. And now there was freedom of choice, without the language.

They couldn't even scrape the money together for the return flight. They lived under bridges, under some kind of flyover, in tents, with their little monkeys, dogs and doves...

And, do you know, the whole town rushed to their assistance. The grapevine: local "Russians"— still in tatters themselves, still on skid row—collected money and food for the performers. Some Russian émigré had opened a food store in his garage—gobies in tomato sauce, sprats in spicy sauce—and he let some of them bed down there for the night. And Americans helped too, the general public. Then everything was sorted out somehow. Everyone scattered, drifted away... The monkeys were given to the zoo, the snakes slithered off somewhere, the performers found jobs as waiters, mopped floors. Most didn't want to go back. And as always happens in life everywhere, each person's lot matched the hand they'd been dealt, their character and luck in other words. Some adapted, settled in. Others had help with contracts and have been working for years with Cirque de la Lune or the Ringling Brothers. And others sat it out notwithstanding until the Ministry of

Culture bought them return tickets and off they went to their native hearths...

Senya was already playing in some orchestra in either Baltimore or Chicago by then... So Anna knew where she was going and why. And she immediately looked up Eliezer. After all, they'd been writing to one another for ages. I can remember how furious I used to be when my eyes fell on his letters with those crazy patterns: you look and feel like such a moron...

So, I come out of hospital... My face is still the same, scars not healed, like leaches on my forehead... And I find out—I don't remember from who—about our guys' American epic. And I realize that Anna's gone again and this time it's probably for good.

She had a habit of disappearing in general. You know, there's a saying, to vanish off the face of the earth... Well, in the end, she did ... right off the face of the earth…

So one month goes by, then another… After the injury, with these bumps on my skin like some kind of convict, I'm down to my last bit of money and too shattered to get involved in any more cooperative nonsense. I'm wallowing around feeling so low, so fucked that even I start to wonder if now's the time to hang myself or whether I should wait a bit…

And suddenly, the phone rings. How did I know it was her? I don't know. I could sense it like a dog that's lost its owner. The main thing is she hated all these phone calls, letters, telegrams… All her life, she just turned up when she felt like it. And now, there's a phone call. I practically flew over to the phone, I nearly fell. And I hear her voice, kind of unhurried, calm.

"You will soon receive an official invitation," she said.

"What sort of invitation? What to? Where are you?"

"I've arranged for you to perform in Vancouver," she says. "There are these festivals there every year, kind of fairs, in the open air. You'll be heading the bill..."

"What bill?" I yell and such rushing winds rise in my chest, you know, like before when she suddenly announced that we were off somewhere or other and I always wanted to shout: Wherever you say!

Her reply? "What difference does it make? You'll be walking along a wire three times a day. True, it's thirty metres off the ground, over tarmac, and the wire's slack rather than tight… And you'll do it."

"I will…" I just mouthed that.

"And no safety line."

"And no safety line."

"And you'll do it. And everything will be fine."

And her voice was sort of calm, glum. She wasn't one to ask, "How are you doing? You okay?" She muttered, "See you" and put the receiver down.

That was just like her, though: a slack wire thirty metres over tarmac. No safety line.

I nearly cried, d'you hear me? I nearly cried with happiness…

CHAPTER 20.

Imagine, pressed caviar had been 'dropped off' at the Russian shop here. I saw it and was lost in admiration. Do you even know what it is, light of my life, my little mirror?

It's a delicacy that was the daily accompaniment to my Guryev childhood. The caviar eaten in restaurants and purchased in tins is fresh-grain caviar, you see. It can be a bit too runny or a bit too thick.

Whereas pressed caviar, as the name tells you, is pressed then shaped into fairly solid rounds like cheeses. And cut with a knife. It keeps perfectly well in the fridge until New Year. Even though the fishing season, I ought to say, is in May...

Guryev itself stands on the Ural River estuary so that sevruga and white sturgeon, ready for spawning, used to swim right past the town at the end of May. Terrible poaching flourished, with people being maimed and murdered. Zhilgorodok didn't sleep for about a fortnight because a knock at the door might come at any time of night and an offer of caviar or gutted or gravid fish.

All the women in the neighbourhood were dab hands at lightly salting caviar. It had to be eaten the way it was in the olden days, spread thickly on buttered brown bread and chased down by a boiled egg, radish and spring onion.

Anyway, when you've stuffed yourself with fresh, lightly salted caviar in May, you lose all interest in it. Home-made fresh-grain caviar goes off quickly. It becomes rancid. But pressed caviar is quite another matter. The taste is concentrated. It's designed to be chewed and to stick to your teeth. It goes solely with vodka and hard-boiled eggs. Such profligacy was possible only in Guryev.

Our neighbours, the Solodovs, made salted caviar in industrial quantities. And it was a magnificent sight—circles of black caviar half a metre in diameter...

Aunty Lyolya's relatives descended on the Solodovs for the fishing season. The most colourful was her sister, Shura from Makeevka, a deputy in the USSR Supreme Soviet. A generously proportioned, big-hearted woman, she had her own way of strolling around the courtyard in navy-blue knickers and a pristine white silk bra she referred to either as a tit wrap or as booby holders. Guryev's residents were overwhelmed by such beauty. Our women didn't allow themselves such things. Also, Aunty Shura swore like a trooper—she had once been the gaffer of an iron and steel gang, "shovelling coke"—and when her older sister ticked her off retorted, "Lyolka, that's not swearing, it's the people's language! And I represent the people!"

Talking of the people, it's just occurred to me that you probably don't know what they wore back then. The men cut a dash in white silk jackets and thick, heavy trousers with immensely wide legs. Women wore knitted dresses with tiny roses embroidered on the bodices in such intense bright un-Soviet shades. The word "Druzhba" was written on silken labels sewn onto the underside with some sort of Olympic-type rings as their logo. And women twirled Chinese parasols with wooden spokes...

Mind you, these silk and knitwear reminiscences can hardly be of interest to you with your everlasting sweatshirts and tee-shirts.

But—the month of May, oh, the month of May.

Do you know how hard it is to have a wash when the bath contains a pearl and silver sturgeon in its death throes, with its dark grey spine, like a German Shepherd's, a sharp snout and a tail lifted in ladylike fashion?

In the daytime, the Solodovs' courtyard was a hive of production activity. Basins clattered, the caviar was washed in sieves the way prospectors apparently washed gold. The wind blew the pieces of gauze off the cured fillets into the neighbours'. Caspian roaches were threaded onto wires, the courtyard decked out in these aluminium garlands. The sisters bustled about, sending the children off on errands. Uncle Vasya in his sagging chair, crutch at the ready, was in charge of caviar production, incredibly excited at having so many women temporarily doing his bidding. We children pestered him to give us nails to knock into the mailing box (the caviar was smuggled out in parcels allegedly containing jam) and when Uncle Vasya's patience reached its limits, he skilfully tossed his crutch at us. He was always right on target!

...So, I can see Aunty Shura standing before me in her silk bra, a people's deputy, master of the saltiest speech. The wind is carrying wisps of gauze up into the clouds and Genka, the future monk, and I are gazing proudly down at everyone from high up in a mulberry tree because the moment is approaching for dispatching the goods, when we would be more important than the adults.

We were friends with Guzelka and Rozka, the daughters of Batima who ran the post office, and they were our protection really when it came to dispatching the parcels, since legally parcels had to be open when they were handed over...

And what close family evenings those were! Uncle Vasya and Aunty Lyolya, who struggled to put up with one another in the normal run of things, even coming to blows on occasion, would down a bottle, give one another a hug and sing,

> "On the old porch with you
> Every evening we two
> Linger dreaming, dear heart,
> And regret that the time's come to part."

And, dear God, what voices they both had! Their singing was sonorous, full of emotion, climbing into the high range, dividing into two parts, coming together again… The rest joined in—everyone was constantly fired up and frighteningly talented. And the air was infused with the goodness of May, an all-inclusive love hung over the garden Uncle Vasya planted and tended in Guryev's clay.

I remember the romances and soulful popular ballads from those days.

> "So crimson the moon did seem painted...
> My beauty, so long have I waited
> For you to come sailing once more...
> Next morning two corpses were floating"

Or

> "I must bid my homeland farewell now
> Take leave of my children, my kin,
> But then eternal watcher in your tower
> I'll return and I'll hand myself in."

Oh yes, I know more popular songs from those days than there were Kazakhs in Guryev!

Then the fishing season came to an end, ordinary days returned and Aunty Lyolya went back to yelling at her husband, "You useless animal! One leg and you can't even wash that!"

One of the letters my mother used to send to me regularly in Leningrad when I was studying at the Conservatoire—and it may very well have been the most regular thing she did for me in my entire life—describes Uncle Vasya's death and subsequent events in the Solodov family. Uncle Vasya died after losing his marbles altogether. He would sit on his bed, trying to pull the sheet over his missing leg, staring wildly at the wall and, gulping back tears, would mumble, "Esteemed members of the Party Commission… Esteemed members of the Party Commission…" Evidently, the CPSU was present even in other dimensions...

Right before he died, Uncle Vasya, gaga, told his son Genka a terrible secret: He had buried 47,000 roubles under a tree in the garden and, for several weeks after his father's funeral, Genka dug like one possessed, just as his father had when he planted the trees. He cut through all the roots, completely ruined the garden... He found nothing, of course. And immediately left Guryev.

Could it be forgiveness for destroying that garden that he's praying for in that monastery of his?

And that's it. I'm not going to bother you any more with my Guryev ghosts. Now I'm going to live for August and our meeting in Rawdon. Like last time? By the waterfall? You'll have to switch your mobile on though all the same, so that I can track you through the tangle of Canada's highways…

Do you know who I almost ran into in Middlebury? Your Arisha. She's teaching carillon, although she was away the week I was there with Myatlitsky.

He, however, was giving a masterclass comparing the functions and usage of baroque and modern bows. As an illustration, he and I played one of Francois Couperin's four "*Concerts royaux*" for violin and harpsichord with a bass instrument, me, for example, on the bassoon.

They are actually dance suites, written to entertain Louis XIV, the Sun King. That Sun Prick used to spend up to five hours or so a day standing in front of the mirror, rehearsing beautiful poses. More than that, he used to paint his cheeks with brightly-coloured rouge, stick on beauty spots and curl his moustaches. Any gay club nowadays would welcome him with open arms.

Anyway, all Couperin's style is drowned in a multitude of trills and mordents. That, little one, is when the music is so flowery it makes you feel sick. Only Couperin drags things out with all these affectations: beauty spots, curled moustaches, lacquered gonads. Studying the music's

   LEONARDO'S HANDWRITING

tiresome but once you make your way through the jungle of frills, playing it starts to be interesting, considerably more interesting than listening. It lacks all real melodic beauty and naturalness. Everything's artificial and contrived, three-four time or six-eight time predominate. That's because, for the French, everything comes from dance rather than singing. And there's no suffering whatsoever! My lectures haven't killed you yet, have they? Listen a bit longer, my little one, no one else is going to…

So, as a contrast to the flighty Couperin, the Professor and I would play something by the tragic Ivan Khandoshkin. Ignore the unaesthetic surname. He was the first Russian violinist, the son of serf musicians. He secured a place at the first "music school," dreamt up by Peter III—can you imagine?—but not shut down, strange as it seems, by that slut and murderess, Catherine the Great. The school was attached to the tsar's orchestra. Obviously, the teachers were Italians and the students, children of domestic serfs, who had, quite literally, "not unpleasant features." I wouldn't have got in. And so this school, which had eleven pupils, produced the first two Russian musicians, Khandoshkin and Maksim Berezovsky. The century outside was very much a Russian one, the middle of the eighteenth, in fact.

So, then, Khandoshkin. Ivan Khandoshkin. He wrote in the Italian style, of course, but about Russian topics. The music was guaranteed to have yearning in full spate. Virtuoso yearning, protracted and heart-rending—business as usual. No matter what the century outside. The Professor and I played variations on the Russian song "All that I love, I lose." Let's spit it out together, shall we, that tune?

Afterwards, Andrzej Vladislavovich gave an entire lecture on the bassoon's role in the orchestra and, just imagine, he made me play for "these dummies since I have invited you, Simon, for the whole week."

As a teacher, Myatlitsky is in a class of his own, artistic and relentless.

"Who understood and embodied the beauty of the clarinet blending with the bassoon better than anyone else?" this lion roared in such a way that the "dummies"—one Indian, two Chinese women, a mixed-race woman and three American boys, whose great-grandfathers were probably making boots or sewing trousers with mine in the filthy alleyways of some Uman or Bershad only a hundred years ago—the dummies just goggled in fright. "Who embodied beauty that could kill? Tchaikovsky. To whom did he entrust the theme of the main part of his Fifth Symphony? After playing the intimidating introduction, the clarinet and bassoon come in in unison. You haven't heard it? I envy you! Simon, please give them a bit of a fright…"

And I did, I frightened "those dummies" and all the more so because I love that bit in the key part of Tchaikovsky's Fifth myself, where the soul goes round in never ending circles and there is no salvation…

Oh, those old American universities, the lichened campuses in two-hundred-year-old buildings. Oh, those bathrooms with the showerhead welded tightly to the pipe back in the 1930s! Oh, the inevitable impossibility of swilling the soap off your bits!

…Incidentally, and I'll end here, about those bits. I think I've told you that I lost my virginity when I was still in Guryev, with my friends, Guzelka and Rozka, the sisters. Enchanting, quick-eyed flirts, they bestowed their favours in a friendly fashion and without ceremony either on me or on Genka. We had this little hut on the banks of the Ural River, which he and I put up together in record time during the holidays between Grade Eight and Grade Nine—it took barely an hour—impelled by the violent beat of our impact tools. The girls were happy to lend a hand, dragging branches over from the nearest elm tree... Both were clearly intrigued by my bassoon. I had already started playing in school concerts by then. Perhaps, in their imagination, they linked that mysterious instrument of mine to my other instrument which at that time they still found just as mysterious.

They were mix of Tartar (dad) and Chechen (mum). Both later became unbelievably beautiful without being at all alike. Guzelka was small, tempting and curvy, with prominent cheekbones. By contrast, Rozka, when she was a little older, lengthened somehow, became slow and languid. They both had innumerable suitors. Each lasted a couple of weeks then was sent packing and not only that but covered in confusion as well. It was called: "I treated him like shit." The boyfriends included lads from other towns who penned passionate missives to our beauties.

But their dear dad, an ugly mug of a Tartar (as his wife, Batima, called him) got into the habit of taking the letters out of the post box and reading them. Eventually, of course, he was caught and shamed while the girls transferred their suitors to poste restante.

The ugly mug of a Tartar was bored ... but he came up with a solution. I was going to see them once. I was already a student by then and on vacation (the girls were being kind to me for the sake of the old childhood days) but their father was sitting in the kitchen wearing his glasses and reading a Literary Monument edition of "The Letters of Thomas Mann."

By the way, on the subject of Thomas Mann. Bring your harmonica, little one. It's a long time since we played "Lili Marlene" together.

CHAPTER 21.

She increasingly suffered from headaches, was exhausted by a noise in her ears. It all started as a rustle, someone's worried whisper … and grew to an indistinct roar, in which words came in bursts. As a teenager, she had been able to block out other people's voices that she heard inside herself, pull a cloud of sound over her head, mentally *wipe the mirrors…* She had no strength left now after the roiling groundswells of melancholy, and clouds of other people's thoughts and plans circled, bugged and bit her like gnats. It was pointless trying to fight them off.

She built a corridor of mirrors and swept along it, trying to leap-frog the congested zones...

It was easiest on the move, on the motorbike, in a car, on trains and planes… As if speed could carry her away from the chase. More and more often she caught herself wishing she could "leg it," as Khristina used to say. Altogether. For good.

There were days when she would suddenly pack her backpack and take off—it didn't matter where—sometimes not far at all, although the previous evening she had planned to spend the whole day working... But night would come, pressuring her, driving her on and on… Anna was racing away from someone, they were gaining on her … someone she couldn't see grabbed her from behind, forcing her arms to her side in a furious battle of love … and she fought with him until the breaking of the day—*No, You will not use me for entertainment!*—and suddenly set free by someone's most sublime mercy, afraid to believe, she flew around the edge of the sky on her motorbike in the obsessive hope that this time she would tear through the mirror membrane of the heavens.

...So, in March, missing Senya, she suddenly decided to go to Rudesheim where, as if to order, she was once again caught up in a steaming fog that wreathed and swathed the little mountain town in a thick cotton blanket. Nevertheless, it was easier for her there, as if the fog swathed her poor head as well, offering warmth and protection, even loosening the encircling band of noise...

Until midday she wandered the little streets alone and then ate in her and Senya's deep white basement. She had some simple dish, sauerkraut and sausages, perhaps, and pushing it onto the fork with a crust of bread, she ate the lot, something she hadn't done often in recent months.

Then, when she'd drunk her coffee, she set off to wander around again and, finding herself at the cable-car ticket office, she suddenly bought a ticket and sat in the gondola that had arrived as it made its way round.

As the gondola broke the surface, gripping the cable with a gnarled iron hand, the waltzes played by the little orchestra in the nearest restaurants could still be heard, people's voices, the hurdy-gurdy's measured stumble, the tapped-out conversation of the small commuter train's wheels, a mere five coaches in all... The barrier opened both arms in astonishment and dropped beneath the surface...

As the iron gondolas sailed above the little town, the dragon scales of wet slate roofs could still be seen below: the museum of musical instruments (four finials, each topped by a human-figure wind gauge), the square brown-stone monastery tower of the Rheingau wine museum... Also visible was the broad ribbon of the Rhein, a flat-bottomed barge dragging itself along, being overtaken by the St. Nikolaus I, a tiny double-decker steamboat. Only the outline of the "witch's castle" could be discerned on the opposite bank. Then that too was engulfed in the fog and all that remained were the furrows of low, curling vines beneath the ascending gondola, rows of never-ending vines, inscribed in different directions this way and that on the mountain slopes...

In the end, they disappeared as well. Everything around was submerged in the fog's white silence. There was nothing but a soft hum and a slight judder.

The gondola hung at a standstill in the cloud between times, as if time had leapt out of its groove and was spinning wildly: tower, castle, train, fog ... tower ... fog ... vines ... castle ... fog...

All of a sudden, she was assailed by an oppressive sense of déja vu.

Time had cut loose to make this fogbound ascent just for her. The only thing missing, she thought in vague terror, is for that ... that bug-eyed albino to come sailing out of the fog towards her, the one like...

And thereupon he did just that, the albino in the red Tyrolean hat. As if he hadn't moved a muscle since the last time but had been constantly ascending and sailing along the set route, sailing and ascending

     LEONARDO'S HANDWRITING

on the cables, tracing the ruled lines of the vineyards on the slopes, his pink eyes goggling in the soft, cotton-wool fog… Only the diabolical opera feather in his hat quivered in time to the humming wires.

Five minutes went by and she sat, utterly debilitated, a thick film blinding her mirrors. Movement of any kind was beyond her…

And when she changed gondola to come down, she kept telling herself that Germany had thousands of bug-eyed fat men in Tyrolean hats, it might just be the local postman who lived in some little mountain village and took the cable car down to work every day…

It was hopeless. She felt as if both her inner debate and the illusory Tyrolean had happened before, more than once, and the glint of time past reflected in the mirror of her compact had bowled through the mountain vineyards and had now returned, revealing the fat albino's reflection…

The fog was less thick below, however. The street lights had come on. People were out and about.

She recovered from the fright somewhat and decided she would leave immediately for lively Heidelberg and its students. She might spend the night there, in a cosy and familiar hotel… Turning onto the central street, however, she came up against the gates of the castle to which Senya had unsuccessfully attempted to drag her. Okay, she thought, if that's the way it is, I'll take in the musical collection this time. Senya will be thrilled…

The young man in the crumpled organ-grinder's hat, the cuffs on his frockcoat sleeves threadbare, was not distracted by discussions with a translator now. It was a German group and he sang like a nightingale, albeit one with a guttural burr, as he explained in detail the manufacturing processes of the antique violins, the music boxes, the singing lamps and the chairs that played when sat on…

In the room with a pianola, one of the first, dating back to the mid-nineteenth century, he even sketched the opening bars of the immortal Lili Marlene in passing…

Eventually—and this was evidently the height of the visit—they went into a room where, the tour guide explained, the eleventh-century floor tiles were older than the castle itself. It contained only an enormous and peculiar apparatus with two vertical drums in its upper section, in which five violins went round in circles. In the lower section, meanwhile, dolls emerged from the wings and each one performed its own routine: stamping, nodding, jerking a hand or foot, opening its mouth or turning its head and all this mechanical magnificence sang tunefully, played, plinked rhythmically, twanged and lifelessly kept time...

And once again a wave of *mangy ennui* that nothing could beat back washed over her.

She turned away from the mechanical marvel and stared at the room's floor-to-ceiling window that gave straight onto the mountainside vineyards, intercepted at an angle by the cable-car wires.

Empty gondolas sailed noiselessly by, emerging in the window's top corner and drifting into the bottom corner on the current of the sky or arising there and ascending to the top. In the foggy evening, they were just as empty and transparent as the ferry at Charon's crossing.

As a result, she was not surprised, merely transfixed, when she made out a red Tyrolean hat in the next gondola to descend and saw a slow smile of triumph on a bug-eyed face.

The fat man was holding a rolled-up newspaper. He waved it as if conducting the lifeless music of the mechanical apparatus in the room where she stood...

*****

The setting sun's last lightshow bled from beneath the sharp-edged wing of a deep-blue cloud.

Dark smoky jelly-fish clouds were swept into a torturously slow dance.

Once again she was shown to the window seat, up close to the aircraft window, a hellish aperture, the Mirror World's urgent ravenous maw.

A huge black woman was sitting next to her with an infernally strong bladder. It must have been made of tarpaulin. At any rate, she didn't get up once during the whole flight and so Anna couldn't take a break. Making her get up, apologizing, even just talking to someone was a depressingly tiresome burden for her. Sometimes she was sure that a moment before she had just asked or said something ... and every time she realized she had stayed silent, saying in her head what she'd wanted to say out loud. I am going away, inwards, she thought. Mashuta watched her more and more often out of mirrors—not the one with the heavy pasty face but the young Mashuta, all dotted with the charming freckles that went so well with her quick hazel eyes... She was there now, watching even from the window.

"Nyutochka, why are you always in jeans? You're a girl, not a boy!"

It went without saying that she could expect no respite on the plane.

Moreover, behind her sat the usual youthful looking Humbert-Humbert and his chestnut fawn who in this case, seemingly, was in fact his daughter. They solved crosswords, giggled and played cards for the whole journey and the young lady kept kicking Anna's seat with her pubescent jailbait weapons in their little white socks…

In days gone by, Anna had enjoyed scrutinizing her fellow travellers. She found the variety of faces and destinies moving.

There was someone whose squint gave their face a wonderstruck dreaminess…

The two-metre tall black woman was magnificently proportioned: sculpted buttocks, a neck that was a column of sturdy folds and multiple stacks of tiny, delicate plaits, laboriously braided and beaded—work that couldn't help but be worthy of admiration…

A tall man from the north had such a wildly prominent chin that it was obviously nature's way of protecting an extremely gentle person by conferring a belligerent appearance.

A boy of around twenty, fleet-footed and curly-haired, a spear-bearer.

An Indian woman, gazelle-like with her moist, pleading eyes and soft ashy lips, as if asking for a little human kindness.

…When Anna awoke and sat kneading her neck, dawn was visible through the window. The clouds had separated into layers and curdled and were moving like a mighty ice floe below, beneath the plane's dazzling wing.

The black woman sleeping beside her threw back an arm and a big garnet ring splashed a peacock's tail of rainbow light onto the wall, flecks skittering like sunlit foam in a basin...

∗∗∗

Anna followed Arisha up into the bell tower of the local university church, up the wooden stairs between heavy joists and intersecting beams. It smelt of the damp brick of old walls, ingrained dust, mould and fish oil, with a touch of the elusive smell of the circus. Why the circus? Of course, bats most probably visited at night and their scent was reminiscent of the rat's piss that used to eat away at the metal cables in the circus.

"Patience," Arisha muttered, panting, "it's not much further..."

She looked round at Anna, slight and always prepared to soar to the highest heights in a flash, and they both snickered, one at herself, the other at her friend.

Arisha had put on weight in recent years, although her figure retained its stately proportions. What's more, especially for Anna, she had donned a flame-red concert gown that left her back and shoulders bare so that Anna could appreciate the full glamour of her concert.

"I need to lose weight…" she noted sadly, pausing once more.

From there, from high in the bell tower, a wide panorama of sloping hills with the occasional farm unfolded. The whole town was clearly visible with its grey, yellow and pale blue wooden houses, its old university buildings, its cricket pitch and volleyball court. Right below them, a strapping young man rode atop a lawnmower, shiny footballer's knees spread wide, leaving a prickly nap of fragrant lawn behind him—bright, trim, filtered… And lilac-headed couch grass grew wherever it was left in peace, a breath of nostalgia.

"But it suits you, you know," Anna said. "And surely physical strength must help draw out the bells' … voices, do we say? And it's a wonderful dress…"

"No, I still need to lose weight!"

A carillon had been installed in a tiny cell at the very top. From it, ropes ran up to each bell and if you went up another five or six of the steep, narrow wooden steps and looked through the open hatch, you could see fragments of enamel-blue sky between the black bells' cast-iron flanks.

Posters papered the panelled walls of this cubicle—in its own way, another nest. Plenty of them were Arisha's.

"Sit down here on the edge," Arisha said, nodding towards a wooden bench along the wall. It was low like the ones in a sports hall. Evidently, only a select few were invited here for concerts.

Anna took her seat. Arisha sat down as well, in the carillon's smooth seat, polished by the bottoms of its exponents, and half-turned to face her friend.

"I'll explain everything briefly so that you can understand. Here's the upper row of keys, see. They look like choc ices, don't they? Above them, there's a metallic row. They adjust the length of the wires. And underneath are the pedals, one and a half octaves of lower bells."

"And they're like boot lasts," Ann put in and then was embarrassed to have blurted out something stupid.

"Exactly!" said Arisha, delighted. "I just couldn't remember what they reminded me of… Right, so listen. Everything is tuned to the scale. There are forty-nine bells altogether. The lowest is B flat. It weighs nine tonnes. Can you imagine the effort involved in ringing it?"

"Go on then, play," Anna requested.

"What shall I play for you?"

"God, how should I know? Something … imposing."

Arisha chuckled. "Imposing. Okay. Listen. This is the "Minuet and Trio for Carillon" written by my teacher, Gustave Nees… He even dedicated it to me."

She turned back, moved forward, fitting her buttocks efficiently and solidly to the shape of the bench—occupying the bridgehead. For a moment she rolled her head around, clenching and unclenching her fingers, splayed wide in her lap. She lifted her hands…

Anna started and flinched as if someone had suddenly called out to her. A single sorrowful sob shattered the silence above the small university town. As if the sky had shaken from a challenge and Someone had decided to part the clouds, clearing the field for battle.

Rumbling sounds began careering down like slow stone spheres, overtaking one another, gathering strength with each swell, the speed of their descent increasing. And then great boulders came powering down in an explosion of falling rocks. A resounding battle cry cut through the sky, a cry that went unanswered. It was summoning an adversary to battle, an adversary who continued to hang back…

But then, at length, replied!

A thunderous cascade of high-pitched bells rocked the panelled chamber. Someone was striking a gigantic copper disc over and over, summoning witnesses to the battle. A hollow din, stamping feet, screeching wheels and the clatter of the empyrean carriage sounded above the church's roof, swept out of the bell-tower arches, rolled about the hills and lakes, pervading everything in the Vermont area.

Shifting from one thigh to the other on the wooden bench, the artist used the edges of her hands, her fists, her elbows to depress and tug at the keys, leaping up to snatch at those on the upper row of bells, stepping along the row of foot pedals as she did so or rather prancing along like a horse rider, spewing forth a tempestuous throbbing litany, now menacing and potent, now fading away above the hills.

The throbbing suddenly abated, almost reaching the shores of silence, as if ripples of pure spring water were skittering across forest streams…

And the battle cry sounded again! And again that drawn out call … dying away in the mountain heights…

It was a fight between two angels, one white, one black, both cruel and implacable, battling to the last groan, to the last fall. This battle was for her, over her, for her sake...

No, it was her. It was her life being pulverized by a powerful, pitiless force…

The distant hills quivered and divided in a shroud of tears. Anna shut her eyes and *went into the Mirror World.*

Arisha would die in a Belgian hospital in 2015, having gone in for a routine check-up between two tours. She would never know her diagnosis—cancer of the liver—because a wire would catch fire that night in the luxury wing. The fire-alarm system would fail and several patients would meet a tragic end, including a famous and international-prize-winning carillonneuse, by then the wife of the Belgian minister of cultural affairs.

And the fire-engines' wail would be an obscene caricature of the cascading carillon peals the woman had drawn from the bells all her life with her blessed hands...

In the all-encompassing silence of a village noontime, the shouts of cricketers erupted from the pitch, the startled rasp of a jay screeched above the bell tower.

"Great," Anna sighed in unalleviated torment amid the silence. "A triumphant Amazon! You're so warlike amidst these divine lightning bolts and waterfalls. And how well, how very well this fiery flame colour suits you."

∗∗∗

She raced across the bridge, flew up onto the crest of the road. From there, Lake Champlain appeared beneath alabaster stucco clouds in the soaring heights, yachts like white pennants on the ruffled crests of its waves.

It wasn't far now to Rawdon and Senya—he'd managed to get Anna on her mobile about three hours ago—was supposed to be there before her.

She hurtled along at ballistic or as she called it "a decent" speed. Good roads are a blessing—the motorcycle went along as if it was on rails.

She crossed yet another bridge, drove into town and a minute later came to a halt in the paved carpark where two or three buses were usually waiting for tourists. The little town with its picturesque waterfall that could be admired from a viewing point must have been on the tourist route.

Anna took a flattened coke can out of her backpack and placed the motorcycle stand on it. Although the hot day was tending towards evening, these sports bikes' stands were prone to sinking into the heat-melted tarmac and then not even a bulldozer could pull them out. She removed her jacket, gloves and helmet in relief, stuffed them into the compartment on the back seat and set off to the waterfall.

The viewing spot's wooden platform jutted out over the narrow neck of a ravine, into which a small but raging torrent fell in a thunder of frantic beer froth.

A group of Italians, including children and older folk, clustered up there now. They all leant enthusiastically on the parapet, striving to see as far down as they could, to follow the route of the stream as it bounded through the ravine.

If you bypassed the platform and descended a steep path to the side for literally six or seven metres, a tiny glade that gave on to the waterfall appeared in the pine cover but was safely protected from the road by trees and bushes. This secluded spot, which nature seemed to have carved out for itself, had a scenic view of the tumbling falls and the forest, still drenched in sunlight.

Senya had discovered the glade by accident around five years before as he tried to get away from the tourists *to take a leak in the open air*. They had arranged trysts there ever since, when he was on his way from Boston to see Anna and she would go to meet him en route. Or he would go to meet her, unable to wait until she arrived.

Senya was already there, sitting on a spread out blanket.

"You're like a Muslim at prayer time," she said. She plumped down on top of him and for twenty minutes or so they simply lay in a silent embrace, listening to the regular roar of the wall of falling spray-tousled water.

"God," he said finally. "is it really conceivable for a woman to be always wearing these awful boots?" And went on to say, for the umpteenth time, "How I hate that bike of yours!"

"But it got me here quickly," she replied listlessly and sat up, hugging her knees.

The black forest opposite was still entirely bathed in sunshine. The sun darted across the mossy stones and red-trunked pines. On their side, everything was still deep in shadow. The wild waterfall, spewing forth its cold breath of spray, was the fault that split the ravine in two. Solid chunks of yellow-black quartz blazed in the last rays of the sun.

"Oh and about boots," Senya said. "I've dreamt about my grandfather twice in the past week. He stands there, barefoot, offering me the boots of the slaughtered Italian soldier, and says, 'Senchis, you have such hurricanes over there in October, God help you. Take these, warm your feet up…' And I am so surprised in my sleep. 'What do you mean, Granddad? October in New England is the most golden time.'"

"Well, are we off?" she asked. "Do we need to stay any longer?" He said nothing, didn't move. Perhaps he was tired from the journey?

Suddenly he said with unaccustomed gravity, struggling to get the words out, "You know, it's time we got married, Anna…"

It was the first time he had called her by her name. She said nothing, didn't turn around. Her shoulders sagged.

"I've just been pleasantly surprised to discover that I've even built up a small pension," he continued. "We'll rent a flat, wherever you say… I'll play… Good bassoonists are in short supply… Do you hear me?" he said to her back, anxious and demanding. And his voice lacked its usual levity, his eternal irony. "Do you hear me? I can't live without you anymore." She turned, placed a hand on his brow and stroked his face firmly yet gently.

Again and again, like raking snow.

CHAPTER 22

… I never did understand what she saw in those pieces of glass, what properties she credited them with or why she gave them human qualities everywhere she went.

Actually, that's not true. I did once see something and, maybe, understood something as well.

It was the Professor's ninety-fourth birthday. Not a special date nor likely to be his last if his state of health was anything to go by, but nevertheless, no matter how you look at it, at his age any date could become a special one at any time. Julia insisted it was celebrated on a grand scale, with speeches, formal addresses from a multitude of different music academies and the television upstarts and illiterates who could ruin any festivities.

Literally a month before the big day, the Boston police solved the mysterious disappearance of the Stradivarius in a perfectly routine fashion.

Edna's paramour, the dodgy, moustachioed chap from the Mexican back of beyond, who'd been Julia's gardener or odd-job man for a couple of years before quitting out of the blue, was caught on the border with the priceless violin in a cheap and nasty fake leather case. Everything unravelled at astonishing speed. The fact that he was Edna's lover came to light literally the first time he was questioned and it wasn't long before she admitted, with much weeping and wailing, that she was pregnant. Plus, in next to no time, they got out of her that she was the one who tipped the shady character off about her grandfather's violin. How was he to know how much that bit of wood was worth in that strange, hoity-toity world that kept him at such a distance? The love birds were planning to do a runner, I don't remember where to and it doesn't matter now.

The family was plunged into the depths of despair for a few weeks then bobbed up again for the sake of the little mite they'd already raised and the little mite that was on the way...

Everyone was grudgingly reconciled but the big celebrations were cancelled and instead they hired a small room in an Italian restaurant in nearby Newtonville for a dozen of their closest friends.

And if anyone was cheered beyond words by this news, it was my poor sweetheart. I say 'poor' because I remember how inexplicably glum she was the day we went to see Myatlitsky for the first time. I was genuinely perturbed at the way Anna snapped, "Home!" at me. We were ready in a minute and practically fled the field like the Swedes at Poltava.

I remember our silent journey home and her suddenly saying gloomily as we went onto the veranda, "Anyway, pretending to be a corpse is no great shakes. Fairground nonsense. I can do it too."

To which I replied jokingly, "Just not when I'm around, sweetheart. Spare me! Not when I'm around."

At the time, I called myself everything under the sun. Why, oh why had I dragged her off to the Professor's and to face Julia's bigoted judgment into the bargain but, most of all, by what right had I saddled her with a task beyond her strength? Fool that I am, I thought Anna was depressed by her own failure.

It's clear to me now that it was her success that brought her low. But, that's enough. That's not what I'm talking about. It's not for me, pathetic creature, to try and understand the divine gifts she dragged behind her like fetters.

And so it was Myatlitsky's ninety-fourth birthday and Anna, excited and pleased that the Stradivarius had turned up, suddenly announced that she wanted to give the Professor a present. What present? A mirror— what else could it be?

"A mirror?" I said, taken aback. "Are you sure he needs one?"

"Yes," she said firmly and confidently. "That house is utterly unprotected. We'll lock and bolt it against all harm."

I said nothing in reply but when I suggested going to the nearest hardware store that evening or wherever else mirrors might be sold to choose one, she actually recoiled. Was I out of my mind? Surely I didn't think someone could take just any mirror into their home?! And a run-of-the-mill shop-bought one at that, the kind sold on every street corner?

I bit my tongue at that and thanked the heavens for the marbles that remained in my greying skull… No, she would order it herself, of course, and I knew where from—Edouard's mirror workshop in Montreal—she'd been working with him for many years and trusted him implicitly—the exact mirror the Professor's living room required. Above the fireplace. Only Edouard was capable of having everything done to her order at short notice and of sending it by courier...

I was instructed to take the measurements and I did, sniggering cryptically and self-consciously under the Professor's bewildered gaze as I teetered on a wobbly stool dating back to the American Civil War and put a finger to my lips in response to each and every question.

The day before the gala gathering at the restaurant, the mirror was delivered to Myatlitsky at home as scheduled. He was already up and dressed as if for a concert in a dinner jacket, a dazzling dress shirt and a bow tie. The couriers brought in a huge rectangular box, Anna signed for it and set about removing the cherished infant's swaddling wraps. Finally, the last strip came off... Everyone fell silent.

I don't understand how that piece of glass was able to incorporate the Professor's living room with all its tiresome little tables, trays, candelabra, jewellery boxes, sofas and carpets, and still encompass the hallway in a protective side reflection and even, which was quite remarkable, a corner of the main door via a small mirror in the hall.

It was my mirror girl who had pulled off this mesmerizing feat.

In addition, the mirror possessed some kind of extra depths, greenish, moisture-laden depths, imbued with such underwater silence that I wouldn't have been surprised if some great ghostly fish had floated past behind us with a flick of its tail... I swear by all the gods, that mirror could breathe. And, most importantly, not only did it *reveal* the living room, it gave it a theatrical gravitas as well. A solemn import, equal to and worthy of the man of the moment's long life.

It had an ordinary frame, dark cherry, almost invisible.

"God," said the Professor, fascinated. "What a dunce I am! Why did it never occur to me to hang a mirror there?"

And smart cookie Julia replied grandly, "It has always hung here. You simply couldn't see it!"

But I stood and thought that *she* had never, ever had her *own* house to decorate with such mirror amulets. Can it really be that she never will? And—my love! My heart clenched with such longing, as if she wasn't beside me but already far away. Irretrievably far.

***

Her indifference to where she lived always puzzled me and sometimes baffled me altogether. Especially if I had rooted around the Internet before we met up trying to find some treat, some unusual cosy little place.

That's not right, though. It wasn't indifference but kindness, equally approving of any location. The circus's nomadic willingness to be accommodating. If I proudly threw open the door for her into our room in a delightful old villa near Florence with a winery and stables to hand and asked, "Well, what do you think?" she would readily and gladly reply like an obedient child, "It's wonderful here!"

And she would just as readily and gladly say exactly the same at the door to some random third-rate motel on the Belgian-Dutch border, where we had collapsed, exhausted from the journey. "It's wonderful here!"

"What's so wonderful here, damn it?" I would roar, hurt. "You little gypsy. You circus scum!"

Was it Guryev perhaps rearing up to its full height at moments like this?

Although I was lucky enough on one occasion to drag her into a truly magical place which filled her with indescribable childish delight.

It was in Karlovy Vary. The Grandhotel Pupp—eighteenth-century pomp, opulent Baroque, festooned with stucco, the gilded arabesques of cast-iron railings and cherubs with harps on the pediment.

Something had gone wrong with my booking of a relatively cheap but still incredibly expensive double room and, all apologies and smiles, they explained as they shuffled the electronic key cards that they were obliged to put us in the Dvorak Grand Suite appropriately enough—this with a nod at my bassoon case. Sod it, I said to myself, if it's a suite, it's a suite. If it's Dvorak, it's Dvorak...

It turned out to be two high-ceilinged ballroom.

Garlands of leaves and moulded alabaster roses wreathed the ceiling's stucco skies. Bottoms jostled breasts, ribbons and flowers trailed between someone's legs and the whole celestial Bacchanalia swirled around a low-hanging crystal chandelier...

The slender-legged Italian furniture seemed ready to launch into a quadrille. Pretty decent paintings in gilded frames and drawings of Mendelssohn, Chopin and Smetana looked melancholically down from the walls.

The glazed tiles of an old-fashioned stove like an immense block of butter gleamed in the corner of the drawing room, its two bronze bolts shot home for good. In the manner of a pastry chef, a pastry chef, some wag had attached entire bouquets of glazed-tile cream roses and lilies in wicker baskets to its roof, curved in the manner of Chinese pagodas. He had stood back, assessed his work, clicked his tongue and squeezed one last quivering leaf from the tube...

I threw open the tall door and went out on to the balcony. Its flower planter was woven from spreading iron leaves and two caryatids, one male, one female, rose fluidly from the two side columns. Each bore an ornate capital like a basket of fruit on its head. Both, arms stretched behind their heads, were gazing at their own underarms shyly and even guiltily, the man with a rather fastidious grimace on his bearded face, and the Greek girl in a tunic, a delicate spider's web already fluttering between her jutting chin and the peaked nipple of a small breast.

I leaned my elbows on the railing. A group of five Arab women, enclosed in black dresses and black headscarves, paraded along the promenade beside the steaming Tepla River and I remarked over my shoulder that the Prophet Mohammed himself had evidently ordered an immense orgy to take place here at the spa.

We roamed around the two spacious rooms, vanquished by all this palatial splendour, switching standard lamps and lights on and off, contemplating drawings, peering into a wardrobe, discovering a special safe one minute and another mysterious fixture the next. What was it for?

Finally, we peeped into the bathroom.

It was entirely in keeping with the apartment, huge, marble, slightly gloomy, styled to resemble a Roman bath-house. Mirrors stretched the length of the room, bronze light fittings attaching them to the walls.

"Oh," I said, "this is where you're meant to slit your wrists and expire after a letter from Caesar..."

She stopped in front of a marble panel bearing two mosaic sinks, on which stood baskets full of scented bathroom nonsense and candles in bronze candleholders. She glanced in the mirror and exclaimed merrily and excitedly, "Dear God. What on earth is going on in there? Such debauchery! You can't imagine!"

I embraced her from behind, drew her close and asked softly, "What? Rome at its pleasures?"

She laughed. "Yes!" just barely uttered as if responding distractedly but in time to the caresses of my hands that had stealthily and swiftly removed her top...

And as always, that sudden languor, as if she was losing consciousness. "Yes!"

"And this?" I asked, pressing my lips to her hot bare neck while my
hands, moving as familiarly as they did over the keys of my bassoon,
felt for the button and zip of her jeans.

"Yes…" she moaned, shakily, melting.

"And this?"

"Yes, yes!"

"And this?"

…And over and over again in her hot, parched voice, more and
more wildly and rhythmically, "Yes, yes, yes, yes!" Two musical instruments that were instantly in tune at the merest hint of a note, the harmony of the duet honed over the years: a brief exchange, two or three
tentative bars and the sweet melody, piercingly beautiful even when
known off by heart, hastening into *allegro vivace*…

In this, she was always uncommonly musically-attuned and I
handed control of the whole piece to her sensitive hips that were able,
almost imperceptibly, to tell the strings to slow down and switch to
adagio or even *largo* … and then moving freely and expansively, now
staccato, now *legato*, to develop this unexpected woodwind theme and
allow the bassoon its virtuoso *solo* … let it hold the note *fermata* … a
moment of lasting weightlessness … especially in the build-up to the
coda which … which, as you know, is precipitous and inexorable and
there … there … and there now … *tutti*, the whole orchestra together
in the final bars…

At that moment, I transferred my gaze from the impossibly curved
bow of her back to the mirror and suddenly realized that we weren't
playing a duet. Oh, no! It was a quartet and the couple in the mirror
were moving at a slightly different pace, a fraction of a second later,
like a mirror echo, repeating and committing to memory the tiniest
movements of our hands, bellies, thighs, nipples… It meant the score
was more complex that I'd thought… And the musician in the mirror,
a brazen satyr, his shirt unfastened in such a hurry over his grey chest
that not all the buttons were undone, even seemed to wink at me with
a fellow player's eagerness to keep in time…

… but the draining and sustained rondo was already speeding towards the final movement; the musicians' breathing, the tension in
their bodies, were focused on the agonizing bliss of the final ascending
passage…

A fanfare from the brass section.

The power of the last chord, lingering for a few more moments as it died away in the very fibre of their beings…

And then a fleeting moment of repose….

The tumultuous applause came as I turned on the magnificent shower with its Italian fittings.

PART FIVE

You wait where that lantern softly gleamed
Your sweet face seems
To haunt my dreams
My Lili of the lamplight
My own Lili Marlene

CHAPTER 23.

She dozed on the plane and in her sleep she was flying once again beneath the sky over a water-surface mirror, sheened with the scarlet dawn of the last remaining sun.

When she opened her eyes, she could see hilly islands through the window, floating below with their cobwebs of roads, like the relief models she and Arisha used to build for their geography lessons: green plasticine spread onto cardboard for a plain; brown squashed into a lump and moulded into camel-back mountains. Islands were indicated by walnut shell halves. They placed them, outer scarabs upward and thought they were oh, so lovely. Arisha was covered—fingers, nose, chin. She sat, motley as a clown, squinting slyly and plaintively asked a laughing Nyuta, "Am I pretty?"

And through her laughter, Nyuta replied, "Awfully pretty!"

A young missionary had the seat next to hers, a Baptist, by all appearances. He read or leafed through a book throughout the journey. Anna sneaked a peek. It was a manual on how to increase his flock. The chapters had touching titles: Soul-Striving for Heaven; Seeing Clearly Through Prayer... A good, gracious, empty little book.

They exchanged a few sentences at the start of the flight and, fearing a heart-to-heart, Anna quickly closed her eyes. Now though he ambushed her, or perhaps he had noticed her fleeting interest.

"Would you care to take a look?" he asked with obliging alacrity.

"No, thank you," she said, too hastily. It was rude.

But not for nothing had the young man taken courses in fishing for men.

"You cannot imagine what enlightenment, what clear, acute vision the Lord grants in response to sincere prayer," he said with feeling.

"You don't say?" Anna remarked politely.

"No, really, you'd be amazed. Your senses become so much keener, you can read people's minds!"

"That's going a bit far, pal," she replied wanly. "Who's going to believe that?"

And she turned away.

There was a tiny ship below on the blue ocean, its wake a white feather behind it.

It was dark when they came into Indianapolis. The city sparkled below like clusters of beads and blazing woodchips that seemed to have been swept into a corner of the earth by a giant broom.

As usual, Eliezer picked her up in his old Ford. He was old himself now too, and fat and bald...

When she had first tracked him down there, it had taken her several hours to come to terms with the striking changes in his outward appearance. It turned out that his massive head had been merely a small flower pot for his magnificent clump of black hair. And now that the bush had lost its leaves, the pot was exposed in all its cheerless decrepitude. Only his large nose and the ironically protruding cherries of his eyes remained the same...

He was flustered, lumbering heavily along as he walked beside her. As always, he attempted to take Anna's light-as-a-feather backpack off her and once in the car started trying to cover her legs with a blanket.

"I'm telling you, you'll catch a cold, Nyuta. It's such a shit climate over here."

"Never mind, it's brilliant that you've learned to drive, you know," she remarked as usual.

"It's all since Abram died. I've had to learn to live by myself." He gave her a sideways glance and ended with the childlike boast, "And I have."

They rattled up to the Park Regency, a two-storey building of the kind that used to be called "hostels of the hotel kind" in her old circus life: a long corridor with doors opening onto minuscule apartments—two rooms, a bathroom, a little nook with a hot plate and a tiny cupboard.

Up on the first floor, they walked slowly along the corridor. It was evident now how hard walking was for him. Eliezer never let slip an opportunity to show Nyuta off.

"Is this your daughter, Eliezer Markovich?"

"Indeed it is. My daughter."

"And what's a daughter, you silly old fools? Someone completely other, born of your body's cloudy emission… This isn't my daughter. It's my soul reflected in a mirror."

The doors to many rooms had been flung wide open and Russian was being spoken inside.

"She had an iron will! Ninety-five years old!"

"She wanted to die and that's what she did!"

"No, but *come on*, what does that mean, she wanted to die? Everyone wants to die!"

"It's quite simple. In the evening, she said, 'That's it. I'm tired of living. I'm done.' And the next day she was found dead in her apartment. She'd left the door open so that they didn't break the lock."

"No, but *come on*! What did she do?"

"Nothing. She died. She had an iron will. She wanted to die and she died."

"You know," Eliezer said proudly as he turned the key in the lock, "I ordered lunch from a little Chinese restaurant just near here. And it looks appealing."

"Great!"

They went into the room he called hers. It had a couch, a round dining table, a sideboard and chairs. A door to the right led into the bedroom which was just as small, spick and span, the furniture antediluvian. The very picture of a neat and tidy Kiev flat.

There was a photograph of his late brother on the wall, looking even more like a negative of Eliezer in this two-D image and seemingly pleased at such a full and definitive incarnation. Anna always averted her gaze.

"So, you did fall off, white head…"

"I didn't want to drag you into our canteen, you see," Eliezer said, tying an apron over his belly. "It's the usual American grease trough. So, wash your hands and sit at the table. I have everything ready."

While she was washing her hands, he shouted from the tiny kitchen.

"It's half board here and sometimes I eat the free grub they give you. But, I thought, it isn't every day that Nyuta, my angel, comes to visit. Isn't that right?"

"It is," she said emerging from the cubbyhole of a bathroom.

The main thing was to keep up the cheerful tone and make herself eat something at least. Chinese cooking can be perfectly fine.

She tried to visit at the slightest opportunity. She didn't see even Sen-ya more frequently. And every time she listened to a run-down of all Eliezer's news, beginning in 1978 when his brother forced him to go to divinely-favoured America. If anyone had said that Eliezer was rapidly developing Alzheimer's, she would have spat in that person's face.

"I get by," he said, still shouting and taking no notice of her. "Once a week, they bring along a bus with a Negro driver we're not allowed to call a Negro for some reason. What are we supposed to call that idiot then? And he takes us food shopping."

"I can hear you," she said. "Come on, what have you got to eat?"

"You'll laugh," he said, "but the dill's mine. See the little box out on the balcony? Fools plant flowers but what I plant's useful."

She closed her eyes and thought, God, there must be no one, no one at all bar me who knows that this fat half-crazy man with this little box of dill on the balcony could have been a great scientist… Or that his genius, the trusting, touching essence of him was stamped out by a jealous and cruel white shapeshifter.

"That's such a great idea!" she replied.

"I hope you'll be staying for a few days at least."

He hoped she'd be staying for a few days every time.

"No, dear… I have to be in Chicago tomorrow. The bike's already ordered."

Over lunch, she recounted what she had been up to. He demanded the smallest details. *And how did you answer him?" "Well done, you. And what did he say to that?" "Rubbish! It can all be calculated to the milli-metre and everything built on concave and spherical mirrors, basically!" "Good for you! And when is he back from America?"*

She played along enthusiastically, answered, parried, asked questions. She often felt as if she was talking to herself. And he to himself. And this light, insubstantial, seemingly almost soundless conversation had been virtually the only one able to console her in recent years.

He was interested in such drivel that Anna could only marvel that this brilliant brain, capable of the most complex reasoning, could in-quire so intently as to why Cirque de la Lune contract workers had no paid leave. What do these contract workers have to do with anything? she wondered. You're fixated on them. And she discovered, as had been happening recently, that she had only thought these things, not said them out loud.

"So how do you like the duck?" asked Eliezer, chewing with gusto, which made his three chins quiver and quake. "Not bad, is it?"

"Amazing!" No, this was one restaurant that truly couldn't boast the best examples of Chinese cuisine.

"Would you like a rest?" he asked after they had eaten. "Have a lie down on the couch. I'll bring you a blanket."

She said as he went, "There's no need. I'm not tired..." But, no, again, she didn't say it, only thought it.

He came back into the living room once he had found a blanket in the cupboard. Nyuta was already asleep in an armchair, head thrown back, like a child that had done too much running around.

Eliezer gently covered her up, sat in the armchair opposite and began to look her over.

Sometimes it seemed to him as if she hadn't changed at all. She certainly hadn't experienced any of the annoying physical changes that affect most people after forty. It was down to her circus training, of course, the motorbike, a lifetime of stunts... Stupidity, when you came to think about it. God, this precious girl's whole life had been stupid. And even now, even now ... these celebrated, stupid shows—were they really what her unsparingly clear, acute, split-second thinking was created for?

Was it really for this that such outstanding examples of humanity were honed on the divine lathe?

He kept his eyes on her and could have looked forever, experiencing only peace and happiness that she was here. Sometimes, bizarre as it might be, he felt as if he was looking at himself, that he was the one whose hand had just twitched, who had just let out a sigh without surfacing from sleep. It was strange. Despite being a twin, he felt that his true spiritual reflection was not his brother but this girl he had run into by chance at the Milk Factory Club thirty years ago. She reflected his soul so fully, so soothingly. No one knew that he would occasionally say her name when he talked to himself during all the long years of separation. "*See, Nyuta, I've managed to wash the dishes and run the iron over my trousers.*"

She slept for about twenty minutes and was woken by a loud voice in the corridor.

"Now you mind, Fanya, I owe you one and a half dollars."

"Aw, forget it!"

A table lamp had been switched on in the room. Eliezer was sitting in the chair opposite, quiet now and sad, the negative version of himself behind him.

Suddenly she was assailed by the stale smell of the dark confusing hallway of his communal flat in Podol. A vile musty mixture of shoe polish, ski wax and burnt porridge from the kitchen. Furtive footsteps behind her and a sudden terror that chilled her scalp.

"Stop!" the shapeshifter intoned dully, catching up with her at the door and plucking at her shoulder. "Don't move!"

They stood in the dark corridor, both breathing hard, as if they had been running a race: her breathing irregular—a line of dots—as she tried to escape—his a malevolent wheezing.

"I have forbidden you to come here! I have ordered you to leave my brother alone!"

She said nothing, incapable of taking her eyes off this nightmare: white hair glinting in the darkness of the blind hallway and two white eyebrows floating in the void.

"Did you hear me? Don't you get it, you pushy bitch? I won't let you drive him out of his mind altogether! I'll take him away, understand? Far away and for good!"

"For good!" she breathed, horrified that she was about to break a taboo, to say what mustn't be said but could not go unspoken. "It won't be long before you die over there. He'll be left alone. And I will find him."

The darkness cracked from his slap to her face, flared up in the mirror so blindingly bright that, to begin with, she didn't even realize she had been struck.

"Cunt!" he gasped then turned and retreated rapidly down the hall.

"No, Fanya, I don't like debts."

Eliezer bent the plastic stand of the old table lamp from his Kiev days so that the light didn't shine in Anna's eyes. He sat, propping up a fat, flabby cheek and looked at her with concern.

Poor soul, he had been so looking forward to it and once again she had only dropped by for a day and even then she had fallen asleep.

"You look tired," he mumbled. "You never rest, never. It's been many years since you took some leave."

"Leave? What are you talking about?"

"You need to go to a health camp."

She grinned. "'Leave,' 'a health camp.' You've never really left Kiev, have you?"

He smiled like a child and said, "I recently remembered how surprised you were as a child that I couldn't read your mind. You thought that somehow the mirrors were linked to..."

"I really am very tired, you know," she said, cutting him off. "I've got an awful headache. But that's not the main thing."

She hesitated, looking up at him. "That's not the main thing. The mirrors are dimming, Eliezer... Oxide film, maybe..." She snorted, wanted to add something but broke off. "They're old mirrors, they can't be replaced..." she said pensively.

He brought in Gzhel teapots, poured already brewed tea from one and boiling water from the other, cut a thin slice of lemon and flicked it off the knife and into her cup.

"Eliezer..." she said suddenly. "Why was I even born?"

And he didn't smile in response as he usually did. His heart ached.

"It must be to show what people can be like," he managed after a pause.

"What they're like? Really?" She pulled a face. "But I'm a monster, you know. I drove my parents to their graves, innocent people who took me in, saved my life and loved me unguardedly. I drove Mashuta out of her mind and my father, a man of infinite love and kindness, simply went into a decline when she died, unable to live without her. I abandoned him to see out his days alone. The main thing, I told myself, was that Khristina was washing his underpants and making him porridge. Oh, and I sent them money. That's something I never begrudged—but what's money? Just bits of paper... The mirrors, they were the real thrill. They're the essential me... I haven't brought anyone the slightest bit of joy. Only grief. People are scared of me now, you know. They think I'm a witch. They're not saying it to my face yet but a lot of people think my involvement in anything is bad luck. Even Philippe Gauthier's wavering about whether it's worth having anything to do with me."

She raised her head and gave him a gentle smile. "Tell me, Eliezer, have I really been hanging around here just to perfect a few circus routines and come up with some mirror illusions? Is that it? A twenty-one-gun salute in honour of absolutely zilch?"

"What do you mean?" he interrupted indignantly at last. "You're wrong, quite wrong. You have no right to judge. And you're not a free agent in anything!" He stood, a fat and foolish man with shaking hands that he was waving with such abandon in that little room that it was amazing he didn't sweep the lamp off the table or knock the photos of his brother from the wall. "And what if you, you just the way you are, are the hope of a future life? Perhaps you are a kind of greeting from the Creator, his smile, a ray of sunshine, that he's sent to earth, like a child, playing with some divine mirror of his own, attempting to draw people's attention to him?"

She burst into a cheerless laugh that made him terribly angry.

"And you're forever putting yourself down. Why do you do it?" he yelled. "You're lovely! You're an honest person, straight as a die. You've simply never told a lie and that's that. That's your whole problem!"

"I have told lies," she demurred. "Only today I said nice things about that awful duck from the restaurant."

"There, you see..." he said wearily. "You can't keep quiet even about nonsense like that."

They stopped talking. They sat in the semidarkness, listening as the sounds faded away in the corridor.

"You know," he said, "you're the only person I can say this to: It's been much easier for me since Abram died. Is that blasphemous?"

"No."

"You're the only person I've brought myself to say it to."

"Because I'm cynical and cold, like a swamp, and will swallow up any confession?" she said with a wry smile.

"No! Because you're serene and deep as an ocean trench. Everything, any confession of mine, drowns in you," he said. "Yes, a judgmental pair of eyes that had watched me all my life has disappeared... All my life, I lived under the fixed gaze of my own reflection. Anyone who thinks twins have it easy doesn't understand a thing. And now I say to him, 'Rest in peace, Buma,' and I help myself to another sweet."

"No need to overdo it, though," she remarked.

He gave a sudden sob and hurriedly rubbed his eyes with the flat of his hand.

"Apart from Abram, I have only been attached to one person in the world," he said. "And that's you."

"I know."

"I even cried when he took me away."

"Now, now, hush. It's all in the past."

"I could never understand what use you had for that boy, your husband..."

"Drop it. That's in the past too."

"...Not to mention your pointless relationship with that middle-aged musician, no home, no future, no..."

She said nothing.

"No," Eliezer checked himself. "Of course, he has talent. That CD, the Vivaldi concertos, you brought last time, I've worn it out. What a pleasure to hear him on the bassoon! Actually, as an instrument, it's like someone still talking as you leave, saying goodbye over and over again... An endless goodbye..."

She still said nothing, eyes closed.

"But all the same, what I meant to say is that you're still young, full of creative energy and there's no way an age gap like that... You need to think about the future, Nyuta..."

"Not any more, I don't," she cut in in such a tone of voice that Eliezer said no more.

They had breakfast as usual next morning and pored over the calculations she had prepared for Philippe. And as Eliezer would later recall in his conversation with the Interpol investigator, she was pleased with his praise. She jotted down some minor comments. Overall, she was her usual calm self.

As if the previous day's conversation had never happened.

After twelve, some young Afro-American dimwit, with astonishingly sagging, wide-leg jeans, arrived with the sports bike Anna had ordered. Eliezer made her have a cup of tea "for the road" and a piece of Kiev cake bought at a Russian shop.

"Call this Kiev cake?" he said. "Do you remember the real thing? They used to make it at the Karl Marx factory in these ancient stoves that were black with soot. They were two hundred years old. And when the factory was being reorganized and renovated, the CEO, sensible chap, had everything replaced bar those stoves. He'd worked out that they were the secret to the taste of a real Kiev cake..."

Finally, they went outside. They kissed one another goodbye on the steps. She wouldn't let him go down so that he wasn't in the way in the last few minutes as she checked the tyres and made sure the oil wasn't leaking.

Eliezer loathed the moment that she donned her helmet and those huge great padded gloves, turning into an extra-terrestrial right there and then, retreating from him even before the time came for the motorbike to snort, roar and sputter out a bark ... and not a word could be heard any more. Not one word...

Her only thought right then, however, was that he would now ask his usual question...

And he did ask his usual question, looking at her beseechingly, "Nyuta, my angel... Will we meet again?"

She climbed on to the bike and sat down, kicking away the stand.

She looked round.

"No!" she said.

She started the engine and set off but, after slowly circling the courtyard, she went back to him as he stood, a lonely crumbling mountain, on the steps.

"Something about your legs, Eliezer!" she shouted across the back of the motorbike. "Take care of your legs!"

He stood and watched her slim figure, which was eternally dear to him, receding along Colby Boulevard in the direction of Eighty-Sixth Street. At the junction with Meridian, Anna drifted the corner as if she'd hit an invisible obstacle, ripped through it and vanished.

***

René Bourdier was standing by the counter and speaking into a telephone in the foyer of the Cirque de la Lune office building. When he saw Anna, he faltered and raised a hand, welcoming her at the same time as trying to hold her off. She stopped, waiting for him to finish his conversation. She didn't look towards a portrait in a black frame that had been placed on a tall tripod between two potted palms, deep inside the foyer.

She wondered whether René was there on his own or with Sophie.

Both dancers were already over sixty. At some point in their youth, they had appeared in Europe's famous dance halls. They were both toned, svelte, limber... For some reason, whenever she saw the dark-skinned Sophie with her permanent copper tan Anna was reminded of a cello, the one that had stood in a dark corner of the communal flat, its lacquered flank propped against the wall.

Some bright spark in casting had used old posters to track down the two dancers, who had long since gone their separate ways. They had been invited to take part in an erotic show, which the director and choreographer envisaged as depicting all ages of love. And this ageing couple had thrown themselves into the venture with residual ardour so great it appeared to have rekindled their erstwhile passion.

René was an amiable guy who preferred to spend his free evenings drinking with friends whereupon he became a little wearing. He claimed that as a young man he had been friends with Edith Piaf when she was already past her prime and he was constantly insinuating that they had been very, very close. And why not? He still had a fabulous body. His face a mesh of fine lines but such youthful bearing. There was a sense that inwardly both he and Sophie were tightly wound, like a music box on the brink of over winding as it played a loop tape of some "Oh, my darling, Augustin" or the old favourite, "Lili Marlene".

Anna enjoyed watching their act which they performed nude: the strong, fluid interlacing of hands, hips and backs. At those times, she always thought about Senya and herself.

At last René put down the receiver and turned to face Anna.

"Do you already know?" he asked, gesturing towards the portrait on the tripod and peering intently into her face. He had probably decided to find out straightaway on the grounds of being a friend. Everyone would be peering into her face now and seeking some dark portents for themselves although many others would prudently opt to keep their distance just in case.

"What do you mean?" she asked as calmly as she could.

"Haven't you read the papers?"

"I don't read the papers, René."

"How can you not read the papers in this day and age?"

"If you want to tell me what's in them, go ahead, otherwise I'm in a hurry."

He started at her impenetrable expression with increasing anxiety. Now even the girls on reception were keenly listening in to their conversation.

And *so were those others over there...*

"Are you serious?" René exclaimed. "Helene's dead. The new Russian gymnast. She got caught up in the safety rope. Strangled!"

"Oh!" Anna raised her eyebrows, remembering as she did that the dead woman had done the same. "That's terrible. Poor woman... But, René, why are you staring at me like I'm the Prophet Elijah?" For a moment, he was embarrassed, looked away even, but said stubbornly, "Everyone already knows you predicted her death, Ann."

"So that's it. Thus spake Zarathustra?"

"Genevieve swears you knew. To be fair, she's completely lost the plot and is saying terrible things about you, basically... But she swears by all that's holy that you knew Helene was going to die. And if that's so, Ann, don't you think you should have warned the girl?"

"Don't you think, René," she said, "that I'm about to tell you to go to hell?"

Philippe's secretary came down to the foyer.

"Madame Nesterenko? Mr. Gauthier will see you now."

And that's it, she thought, following the secretary up the stairs. It's strange: Why do you need the last scene this fox is about to play out? What's it about? A ridiculous sense of obligation? A misguided desire to finish what's been started? Or the mental laziness that makes you watch some dumb serial through to the end because you can't be bothered to reach out and turn the video off?

The secretary picked up the receiver on her desk. "Mr. Gauthier. Madame Nesterenko's here now … okay … okay…" And to Anna she said warily, blatantly attempting to ingratiate herself, "Please, go through."

She bumped into Philippe in the doorway is all one word. He had stood up to welcome her. She almost fell onto his chest as the door opened abruptly.

"Ann, delighted to see you. Have a seat, my dear. Shall I have something to drink brought in? Sandwiches? Coffee? As you like… What news? How was the trip to Europe?"

And so on and so forth…

They talked about the state of Europe's small itinerant circuses. Philippe sat, his expression interested, the tip of his shoe tapping out some little tune or other. No, he was no homespun smooth operator. He was a high priest of dirty dealing. He wouldn't be where he was otherwise. Weirdest of all, he liked Anna and he liked her idea best of all. But Philippe was never governed by his initial instincts. He didn't even have any. He couldn't afford the luxury. Philippe developed a large-scale battle plan, taking the slightest particularities of the terrain into account, working out which way the winds were blowing and he always won!

If you only knew, she thought, how easily in the space of three minutes I could turn you into someone who thinks exactly like I do, who is so passionately on my side that you couldn't wait to start urging me on: Come on! Hurry up! When do we get down to work?

A year. A whole year she'd wasted on maintaining good relations. On ensuring they retained their respect for one another. And really it was clear that his courtesy was a cowardly prelude to turning her down. Why was he squirming like a lizard in a tin? He should tell it like it is. Nothing out of the ordinary. Ahh! So, he was scared of her too.

"I had a meeting with David and Mark the other day, Ann. We discussed your plans. We would have been happy to ask you along too but you were in Europe. I make no secret of it. Your proposal is extremely interesting. Extremely ambitious and interesting. If expensive. But cost isn't the issue. What we need now is to see how well it fits with the overall concept of the show. The guys aren't sure about turning the whole thing into a huge illusion."

"It's not an illusion," she objected. "Not purely and simply an illusion. We've discussed this already. It's a mixture of genres. Isn't that one of your principles?"

Suddenly, she felt terribly tired. As had been happening in recent months, she broke off the conversation, convinced that she had brought it to a polite conclusion, said goodbye, left even, only to find herself still sitting in the same chair, devoid of all words and strength... The line between words spoken inwardly and words spoken aloud was fading... *The mirrors* were worn membrane-thin.

She sat, examining the big coloured show posters on the walls, saying nothing to Philippe who was disturbed by her silence.

"Remember, this is far from a no," she heard. "We just have to figure out the costs, weigh it all up... Give us time!"

Anna stood and headed to the door.

"Ann," he called. She turned.

His face was pulled into a nervous smile. He was smoothing his beard with two fingers the way a diligent pupil smooths down her skirt. Of course, the conversation had to end on a friendly, upbeat note... No, it was something else... He wasn't sure ... his thoughts tattered, as tattered as old socks... Amazing: such a shrewd strategist of multi-layered intrigues and such inarticulate thoughts.

"There are various rumours doing the rounds ... that our gymnast, the unfortunate Russian girl ... do you know?"

"I've heard," she tossed out, her look planting him firmly back in his chair. All she needed now was for him to shake her hand before she went.

Philippe shifted restlessly, fidgeted ... and stayed seated.

"I'm sorry ... but I'd like to understand..." he offered at a loss. "To be honest, it's been a bombshell for all of us. And I can't even imagine how the performers will treat you now if we do decide to go with your arrangement... Would you care to offer some explanation?"

"I would," she said and she *explained* in a long sentence, accurately translated into French, that could only have been properly appreciated and applauded by her drunken circus brethren and, of course, the drivers from the milk factory on never-to-be-forgotten Zhilyanskaya Street.

And she felt better for it.

Afterwards she left for good, politely pulling the door to behind her.

∗∗∗

When she reached Genevieve's flat, she paused and plumped suddenly down on the last step to wait for the tingling in her heart to come to a stop.

She had begun to experience this fitful quivering behind her ribs only recently. It was painless, ticklish even, as if a baby bird was trying to fly, fluttering its featherless wings. It lasted perhaps five minutes, no more, and left a tiresome incapacity and deadened mirrors in its wake.

The door jerked open. Genevieve appeared. She looked pretty much the worse for wear—tatty denim shorts with a fringe and a red tee-shirt, something spilled down the front.

"I saw you through the window," she snapped, brokenly. "Why are you here?"

Anna stood up from the step. It was clear that Genevieve had been drunk for several days and not just drunk either. A resinous smell drifted through the open door.

"What are you here for?" she roared. A hoarse echo coursed through the entryway, reverberating to every floor.

Anna pushed her gently into the flat and went in after her.

"We have to have this out, Genevieve."

Howard heard her voice. A rasping shriek went up from the cage which was covered by a dark-blue scarf.

"Anna! *L'horreur! L'horreur!*"

Genevieve had apparently covered him up so that he didn't interfere and God knows how long the hapless bird had been sitting there, locked up and in the dark, nourished only by the toxic smell. Such a weird smell. Hashish? No ... you chill out on hashish and marijuana whereas right now Genevieve was like a Fury. Anna pulled the scarf off, opened the cage, poured seeds from a paper bag into his little bowl. The poor dishevelled parrot rushed out immediately and settled on her shoulder, saying something over and over in a great hurry, complaining and pecking his beloved's earlobe.

"Put him down!" cried Genevieve. "Don't you dare! Put that bird down, you witch! Witch!"

"Calm down." Anna put the parrot on top of his cage where he launched into a run, lumbering awkwardly from side to side.

She sank down in an armchair. Ah, so that's what's going on: empty pill packets on the table—speed? Cocaine? So, she's gone completely crazy, mixing weed with any old stuff!

"Why don't you sit down?" Anna asked. "Sit down, Genevieve, for goodness' sake. Stop yelling and flouncing about. I have to tell you something. Are you capable of listening to me?"

"I know who you are!" the girl blurted out. She was breathing heavily, sweat standing on her forehead, an ingrained, greasy film. "And I am not afraid of you!"

"Well, that's great then. Sit down!"

Genevieve continued to stand in the doorway, on guard, as if ready for flight or fight. The veins stood out on her brow, her eyes set in a mesh of thread veins. Poor unlucky Genevieve...

Poor Genevieve who would sadly go on to live a very long, lonely life thinking back all too often to these moments...

"I know who you are!" she said again. "Our Grandma told us about women like you when we were little. First they worm their way into your heart like serpents and then they strike! You wicked black witch, you invoke death! You radiate evil! Nothing but evil! And me, pathetic imbecile, I didn't know... So many years..."

Howard's claws plucked restlessly at the bars of his cage. He flapped his wings and opened his beak wide, muttering his "Spare-the-parrot-*l'horreur*, Anna, *l'horreur*," clucking and fussing, not understanding what was happening between these two women whom he loved so much.

"Shut up!" Genevieve yelled at him, eyes fixed on Anna as if she was afraid to miss her slightest movement.

"Listen," Anna said. "We talked about it once before, many years ago. I told you what happened at the Circus School... I'm just a mirror, you see. Nothing more. Sometimes I'm shown something but I'm not allowed to put anything right. I can only reflect it... We can never change anything, Genevieve. It's just that everyone reading the book breaks it down, word by word, line by line, hesitating over every letter. Whereas I know everything in it. But I can't force the author to rewrite the page."

"No ... no..." Genevieve muttered. "You're putting me under a spell, witch! I only realized when it was too late, when my beloved died! I don't want to live anymore!"

The baby bird in Anna's chest began to flutter its tiny wings again at her cry. She pulled a face in spite of herself and this drove Genevieve especially wild.

"It was you! You sent her to her death! You cold-blooded, evil, envious snake, as hard as stone. You unfeeling bitch! Sorceress!"

Right, Anna thought, it looks as if she's been shut up in here for a few days already and she's strung out on all kinds of crap. She's already really aggressive.

"Give me your hand," Anna said, reaching towards Genevieve. "You'll feel better. I'll bring you down."

Genevieve gave a laugh. She sprang even further away.

"Do you think I'm a total fool? You've wound me around your little finger for so many years! For so many years, you were the apple of my eye. How I used to wait for you to turn up! How I used to lie, gnawing my pillow, as you roared away on your bike. I would go over and over your gestures, your every word. For so many years... I kept on hoping! And now that I'm free from you, now that I've dumped you like so much garbage, you won't forgive me. Oh, no, you won't! Even now you're certain that you can do anything, aren't you? If you're such an all-seeing Morgan le Faye, tell me what I'm planning to do right now? Go on, tell me! Look into your mirrors! You can't? You can't..."

"Why can't I?" Anna said with weary pity. The *mangy ennui* had descended again and was turning her this way and that, trampling her underfoot. "You're planning to kill me."

Genevieve shook her head as if she'd been slapped across the face and leant against the wall. Only Howard's muttering and Genevieve's ragged, drugged-up breathing could be heard in the silence. She made her way in tiny steps along the wall until she was behind Anna ... who sat still, not looking round, the back of her head, her shoulders and neck sensing every movement Genevieve made... She ought to put a stop to the lunacy of the drugs talking, to get up and leave this house for ever as well...

But her pulse was already slowing down, her temperature plummeting, her body sinking into viscous ice-cold clay. As usual, it was her feet that froze and stiffened first.

Genevieve jumped onto her back. She used all her strength, hands clasped around Anna's throat.

Anna didn't flinch, didn't twitch... And that's how she stayed, unmoving, only her neck growing colder and stiffer in the hands of the groaning, wailing Genevieve... Howard began rushing about the bars of his cage in a fearful flurry. A woman's weeping, groans, the trilling ring of a telephone were added to the elderly squawking and rasping shrieks of his repertoire of sounds... And when Anna was frozen, hard as stone, in the armchair, when the hollow silence of the plaster walls reigned, in which Genevieve whimpered like a luckless puppy, Howard flew up and plunged his beak into the back of his owner's neck.

She didn't appear to feel it. Her limp hands clamped around Anna's throat, she kept trying to press harder and harder but, as in a lingering nightmare, the stony neck did not give. Howard flew down and struck Genevieve on the head, in the face... Something hot oozed over her forehead, flooding her eyes, dripping crimson onto the top of Anna's red hair... And Genevieve could no longer unhook her pincers. Only when the distraught Howard began to hammer her hands did they relax their grip.

She slid to the floor behind the back of the chair and curled up, protecting her face with bloodstained hands. And she lay still for a long time, whimpering softly... She felt that she was the shaft of a merry-go-round and that someone was having a ball, spinning her room on, faster and faster around her. Even with her eyes closed she felt she could see the chair in which sat... But who was it, sitting in that chair?

Eventually, the spinning of the merry-go-round and the room and the chair that *someone sat in* slowed ... and came to a stop. Genevieve opened her eyes, trying to clear them of blood.

The chair stood like a solitary cliff at the middle of the universe. It was really important to remember *who was sitting in it.*

Severe nausea ripped through Genevieve's entire body. Even her hands and feet shook with it. And where had this hellish darkness come from? Where was Howard? And was it daytime, night-time, dusk? How long had she been lying in this puddle that had come from somewhere?

She struggled to rise onto all fours ... froze... She grasped the tall chair back and at the third attempt was on her feet. And then her gaze landed on the unmoving back of Anna's neck. Using both arms to balance, Genevieve tiptoed around the chair.

Before her, slightly slumped towards the chair back, sat Anna, stone-cold dead.

Horror surged through Genevieve at the sight of her face, eyes frozen open. She staggered back, started yelling.

"Anna, Anna!" she hiccupped in a weak, heart-rending cry. Urine streamed down her shaking legs. "A-a-a-n-na-a-a!"

The nightmare was swiftly becoming more solid, an undeniable reality. Only now did she realize what had happened. Her many days of horror and pain, her delirium of hate, her ridiculous fantasies were manifest in the dead Anna's lifeless eyes. Eventually, beside himself, Howard joined in Genevieve's sobs, running through the entire range of voices and sounds available to him.

She stepped backwards, stumbled over Anna's backpack, fell, leapt up again...

She was sick on the carpet. And as she backed away, unable to tear her eyes away from that ice-cold face, she reached the hall, bumped into the door and tumbled out of the flat.

And then Howard calmed down.

In the utter silence, he flew down onto the dead woman's shoulder, opened his beak and bent his head, peering closely at her ear lobe as if measuring it for size so as to give it a more delicate nip...

"Anna..." he cooed. "Anna, boy! Let me give you a kiss."

***

Her hair was still wet. Fighting down her lassitude, she had washed it under a tap in the bathroom of the Greek coffee shop she'd ridden to, not entirely sure as to why.

From the street, she had simply spotted a comfortable corner through the window, made up of two benches covered in woven fabric and a cage beneath the ceiling. In it sat a small yellow bird of some kind, persistently repeating the same little ditty. It was tuneful and lively, at least. Most importantly, the place was quiet and empty. Not a soul present.

A waitress brought over a glass of brandy and a cup of coffee on a tray, set everything down in front of Anna and suddenly said, looking at the top of her head in alarm, "Is that a cut on your head? You must be able to feel it. It's bleeding!"

"Oh, thank you!" Anna covered her head with her hand, lifted her hand to her head and looked at it. "Yes, I... I've hurt myself."

"Should I fetch some antiseptic?"

"No, thanks. A towel, if you could..."

After washing her head, she rested up for a long time in that corner, beneath a photograph of a little girl with curly hair and bare feet, who was sitting on the steps of a Greek church. The little girl was very like Arisha as a child. She even seemed to have a squint.

A round mirror stuck out from a column by the entrance to the coffee shop, a tired street mirror that had swallowed such a great number of cars and pedestrians in its time that a different one would have been suffering from severe indigestion.

To be honest, Anna couldn't remember how she came to be in that narrow sloping side street in Outremont. Howard, the clever boy was a true friend: She wouldn't have *come back* so quickly without his sympathetic nips and long phone trills... And a good thing too that it wasn't her brain that was in charge when she was driving but clearly something else. Right now she had only a vague understanding of how she had found the strength to crawl down from the fourth floor and climb onto her motorbike.

A three-storey brick house opposite (two curved stairways forming a semi-circle like arms akimbo) was home to a framing workshop. The owner, a fairly inventive chap, had come up with an entertaining device. He had hung a multitude of large and small squares, trapeziums and rectangles of framed bits of mirrors completely haphazardly in the window and on the walls leading to the back of the shop.

Each piece reflected a fragment of the street: a street light on the corner of a building, a turnstile, the window of a women's lingerie store with two dismembered mannequins and an autonomous upside-down leg, standing securely on its stump and stretching up a blue-socked sole. (Remember, it said, the funeral of the hero's false leg on the waste ground when you were a child? And look at the interesting social life *I* lead over here.)

The biggest acute-angled mirror fragment reflected the sign over the door of a Chinese restaurant and the window of the coffee house Anna was sitting in. Or rather, the mirror captured only the curved back of the empty chair opposite and hands holding a cup of coffee. Topsy-turvy shards of this world, destroyed, unhinged, the pieces piled into an enormous heap.

She was seized by an unendurable desire to scramble, burst, and fly out of this useless heap.

She called the waitress over, paid her bill, stood up and left.

She needed to crash somewhere. The only flight to Frankfurt was in the morning and although the idea of taking a plane had become intolerable of late—as indeed had ideas about anything—Anna still hoped that in Frankfurt she could lie low for a few days in the loft that was, *but wasn't really*, hers. But there—for troubles never come singly—October was already on the horizon, October with an unprecedentedly early snow-storm beyond which nothing was visible in any case.

At this point she remembered that the evening fireworks on Ile Sainte-Helene were due to start in ten minutes' time. A festival of fires of heaven, the vital background for her future show at the Casino Mon-tréal.

Let's see the fun one more time, she said to herself with a grin.

She reached the Old Port in the damp, indigo dark: the blank con-crete cylinders of grain elevators, cranes like giant grasshoppers.

She had barely made her way to the multi-storey car park where she planned to leave the motorbike when the sky overhead thundered, boomed and blazed into sprays of gold and everything in the the shoot-ing range of black sky suddenly started to spin at the same time.

Anna came to a halt.

She had loved aerial fireworks since she was a child. On official holidays, she and her father had always gone to watch the display on Vladimir Hill beside the monument to Saint Vladimir. The whole city could be seen from there. The right and left banks of the Dnieper would flare up, a vast panorama laid out like a medal, reflecting the glitter of the festival fireworks. But she would be enraptured too by a single rocket or solitary shooting star, compelling its enchanted path to be followed until it faded away, leaving invisible ripples on the black water of the sky...

The fireworks of her childhood, however, bore no resemblance to the sublime Bacchanalia of the Old Port festival.

Bouquets of whirling fire tornados rose and fell at a thunderous rate from behind the trees and houses. Crimson, bright green and yel-low spheres exploded, then were overlaid by a purple rain of small beads sliding down the black mirror, waves of bright blue already in pursuit. Individual white and indigo flowers flared up and a giant green palm rose fluidly above them at phenomenal speed in the eerie silence where it swayed then collapsed onto the city and scattered into the bay...

A low forest of white sparks spread across the horizon, sizzling their last in a hollow groan. For a moment, stillness reigned, seething with anticipation, then out of the blue, a hundred sheaves of golden fire surged upwards and the sky gasped over and over again, convuls-ing in explosions of delicate Persian tracery that expanded to split the vaulting sky, embroidering ever more lilac and azure on the cosmic canvas. While somewhere on Ile Sainte-Helene, a whole team of pyrotechnic wizards made all the preparations for the next round of the wild fire dance.

The arc of the Gulf of Saint Lawrence could be seen from where Anna was standing and, suspended above it, the fishing net of Jacques Cartier Bridge twinkled with lights. Woven from a multitude of glow-worms, the ghost ship of the Casino Montréal on Ile Notre-Dame floated above the water. The enormous transparent sphere of the US Pavilion, Expo 67, stood solidly beside the Ferris wheel...

And, meshed with the black mirror of the night sky, the black convex mirror of the gulf throbbed amid the fierce lightning of the flashing fireworks.

Anna stood, head thrown back, drawing in a long breath of the scent of reeds from the direction of the water, blinking at particularly loud bangs from the fireworks and letting out a soft, "Wow! Bravo!"—and then another "Wow! Bravo! Bravo!" as she marvelled at the purpled silver of the soaring birds and succumbed to each heart-rending swell of delight.

Out of nowhere it seemed as though her unremitting vigilance had loosened its iron grip, as though she had been abandoned ... given permission ... set free! Faint with hope, she swayed as if testing the boundaries of freedom for her newly liberated heart, numb from its fetters, not daring to believe, heart pounding, that it might all be over, time served, everything annulled—the harsh sentence and the snowstorm and the oppressive delusion of vagrancy ... that any moment now a certificate of freedom would fall right into her hands amid flashes of fire, into the golden garden echoing with painted nightingales, to the chamois-soft sound of Senya's bassoon in love!

"Can you imagine? They've even fetched up here! Honestly, I was so taken aback. Where is this, I thought, Montreal or the embankment in Sochi? The point is I saw just which thimble that damned ball was under. I really did."

"Idiot, they base everything they do on you being certain. God himself sent fools like you out to forth and multiply... But, hey, what nimble fingers that redhead had? Did you see?"

"If we just whisked him away from the cops, the company could take him on as head of sales!"

Someone roared with laughter and said, "Selling fresh air!"

Just then, Anna heard her name being called. In Russian.

A little way off beside a car, in the dead yellow light of a garage, stood a fat albino in a crumpled Tyrolean hat. He was obviously tipsy, hovering around the car, trying but failing to open the boot and gesturing comically to Anna to ask her to lend him a hand and lean on it, all friends together.

Anna staggered back. She caught her breath: It was all clear now. *No chance, it won't fall off...* There's your certificate of freedom. The only kind possible.

Right then, she said to herself.

She sat on the motorbike, wheeled it out of the car park, took it into overdrive (Khristina started screaming enough to rouse the dead, "Don't do it, Nyuta. Don't!"), did a wheelie in the middle of the bridge and, soaring over the barrier, raced along the mirror corridor between the black Gulf of Saint Lawrence twinkling with lights and the black, firework-gilded gulf of the sky...

CHAPTER 24.

So what's the time? I don't believe it! We've been here a good long time now, Robert... I didn't even notice it go dark. It has to be time to call it a wrap now... See, the kids are already piling in. Their music gives me a splitting headache. I've talked you to death today, right? I can tell by looking at you. You look kind of ... strained.

Just a minute, now, where the heck did I put my bag? It's a small packet, really, with the logo of that patisserie, you know, on Saint Denis Street... There, got it! I hung it on a peg when I came in. I would have forgotten it. I wanted to give you something you haven't seen before. You can't have. Last time I didn't think it would add anything to the investigation. And also, everything in me objected—didn't want anyone to touch it, to read it... But now, I think, so what? You're not going to arrest me for concealing vital evidence, are you? Good. There you go. And there.

What are you looking at? You can rest assured, they're letters. Senya's letters to her. See how heavy they are? He wrote to her for years. He obviously had a gift for it, enjoyed it, writing that is—not like me.

Hang on and I'll explain how they ended up with me. Yes, I know you searched the loft. But I was there before you. Remember, after she disappeared, you tracked me down in Berlin. I was filming there.

Right, well, that same evening, I took a train to Frankfurt. I had the key to the loft. I stayed there sometimes when she was in Montreal or wherever. I felt as if I and I alone would be able to discover ... pick up the scent ... find out where she could have gone... I was like a madman! Anyway, I arrived ... rootled round all night ... didn't find a thing. Then I opened our old wardrobe trunk... It's a huge circus suitcase, like a chest... More history than the Titanic. Do you know how many cities it travelled to with us? Anna adored it. In fact, when she crept out of hospital to Bluvstein, the Trotskyist, she used to sleep in it. Isay Borisych had let our old cubbyhole to an old maid of a librarian by then. He had absolutely nowhere to put Anna unless it was top to tail with him. Then the guys brought the trunk over and—she was tiny, like a little kid—she slept in that.

Anyway, I opened it and there were photos, costumes—the whole of our life! Everything except her. Except Anna... I'm standing there looming over our life together and ... okay... Okay! I remember her opening it when it was standing on end. She stood between the two halves and threw her arms wide, as if an angel with purple wings had come to earth. And it suddenly seemed ... I had this bee in my bonnet—that if I lay down and curled up myself, I would immediately find out everything about her—where she was, where she'd gone. And I lay down and I curled up and, d'you know, I started howling like a stray dog. What's it called? An "affective state," huh? In short, I lay in our trunk and wailed for all my past life and all my life still to come. And well, that's where I came across a thick bundle of letters from Senya, neatly fastened with a rubber band. And y'know what? They were all unopened. I sat for a good hour with that bundle in a complete stupor: What could it mean? Why hadn't she opened them? And what did I come up with? Just don't take me for a fool, okay? So, I thought, she didn't need to open them, did she? See? No? She barely had to pick the envelope up *to know* what the letter said...

Basically, I didn't want anyone sticking their unfeeling nose into them or opening them in her place. So, I just took the bundle with me. And didn't say anything to Senya. He was racing around the whole of Canada like a madman at the time. He flew from Indianapolis to Boston, from Boston to Montreal, and then wherever hope beckoned. He also felt as if only he ... he alone... And then he passed away.

And then there's this green notebook... Hold on, don't open it. Let me finish. This green notebook turned up at his friend's, old Myatlitsky, the famous violinist. It was just when Senya was planning to move into another flat and had left his travel bag at Myatlitsky's and headed off to that blasted concert... And then, after that, I set off on what you could call my own private investigation as well. I went to Myatlitsky's, saw his daughter—you know, the famous American TV journalist. She's at the centre of every political scandal. It was nice, spending a bit of time with the old boy, heart-warming. He even had a little cry. His daughter said, "Daddy, that's the first time I've seen you in tears. You didn't even cry at Mama's funeral."

To cut a long story short, they gave me this notebook of Senya's as a keepsake. I was about to dive in ... then started back like a scalded cat. It was all about her! I closed the notebook and it's lain there ever since. And that's fine. I'll collect everything from you later on but, in the meantime, read away. Maybe it'll produce a lead of some kind. As for me, though, I've stopped hoping...

Monsieur, le compte, s'il vous plait!

No, no, why? I might have needed this meeting more than you did. Let me pay... Ah, I see. Well, then... How nice it is to have expenses, very nice indeed... In that case, Mr. Kerler, may I leave the ring, as we used to say in the circus? It's been a pleasure...

But no. It hasn't actually. Not at all. You've discombobulated me! Or else that's what I've done to you ... I'm outta here. That's it, I'm gone. All the best!

...Sorry. Don't be surprised that I'm back. No, I didn't forget anything. I've made up my mind. There's another letter for you.

It's his *last* letter, written when she'd already disappeared. It was in his inside jacket pocket. Which means he kept it on him, took it every-where... Myatlitsky gave it to me. And this one I did read, the only one... Because what it says wasn't addressed to a real woman but to an angel somehow. I know it off by heart. I can tell you how it starts.

"Little one, some Interpol investigator has tracked me down in re-hearsal and told me you've disappeared. What does it mean?"

CHAPTER 25.

Dear Arkady Viktorovich,

I am terribly embarrassed. It's already nearly two months since you left and I still haven't written. Time really does fly. It seems like only yesterday that you were here, telling me, "Robert! You bat-eared loser! Your job's a gold mine! Interpol! It's one subject after another! Sit down and write a detective story. We'll cook up a bestseller and have it out there in a fortnight!" I remember tossing and turning all night, thinking, Fancy just dossing around when you're related to the head of one of Russia's major publishing houses.

I must admit, I do sometimes flick through your output: all these ladylike forays into crime fiction. It's not Dostoevsky. But you know that yourself. It's all formulaic plotting, dull, clichéd situations. It's boring! I know on page one what the criminal's going to do and where they'll be found bang to rights. Believe me, life's far richer in this area too. And people more complex. The things that crop up sometimes! Even when a case seems to be closed and you're up to your ears in work, you keep on thinking and thinking about those people.

So, I've been carrying the idea around with me and it's true, I really do have everything at my disposal when it comes to real-life stories from my own work. And style's neither here nor there in this kind of writing. At the end of the day, if you have editors, literary experts of some kind, if anything's not right, they'll correct it. Generally speaking, I think my Russian's pretty good. My parents brought me to Canada when I was fifteen and I've always loved reading and never lost the language. Of course, it pales and becomes impoverished in a foreign-language environment but that's not a disaster in today's Internet world. Not like it was in times gone by.

And as soon as I started thinking seriously—about a book, I mean—a case from four years ago popped into my head. An unusual one.

A woman, fairly well-known in her own circles, vanished without trace and the police submitted a request to Interpol. We came on board. And it all got off to a very strange start. An individual covered in blood raced into one of Montreal's police stations. Not a girl so much as a ... a Pinocchio of indeterminate age. She ran in and collapsed on the floor. Here's what was discovered as she was being brought round—a real creep in urine and vomit, you should have seen her—as her wounds were being treated (strange wounds as if someone had used pincers to tear her flesh out), all the tests done and the levels of alcohol and drugs in the blood of this deranged personage ascertained ... while things were still unclear, in short. Her wounds had been inflicted by her beloved parrot, what a delightful little bird. Its owner turned out to be even more delightful. She reported that she'd just strangled her friend in her flat and that the friend was sitting there in an armchair, choked to death and "hard as stone"! Well, she sobbed and she tore her hair and as she started to sober up she became completely unable to cooperate. She was asked when she'd strangled her. Just now! So how come she was stiff? Nothing added up.

The cops took hold of their bandaged-up criminal and went off to her flat. Sure enough, there was no sign of a corpse although the flat was in utter chaos. The parrot was flying around like a hawk and attacked again the moment he set eyes on the crazy woman—the police struggled to fend him off and to stuff him back in his cage. I'd have shot him my-self, to be honest. Beak like an eagle's.

In short, not a corpse in sight and the only blood was the owner's. The lady needed to go into detox. So it was cheers, folks, job done.

That same evening, however, a German tour group (they were there for the annual firework festival—the fireworks launched from Ile Sainte-Helene every day from the middle of June to the start of August would blow your mind!), Russian-speaking tourists too, led by a local guide who went to the police—gave evidence that a woman on a motor-bike had driven off Jacques Cartier Bridge right in front of them ... and flown away. What did that mean, 'flown away'? Exactly that, flown away. Across the sky. On a motorbike? Yessir, on a motorbike. And comparing all the evidence suggests that this motorbike Valkyrie was highly rem-iniscent of our runaway corpse from earlier. Do you like this plotline, Arkady Viktorovich? Uncle Arkasha, if I may—after all, you are my dear wife's dear uncle...

Given all this information, I set out to investigate. I'm not going to bother you with it for long, it's already late and I have to take my youngest girl to Scout Camp tomorrow. The divers didn't find anything. Diddly-squat, no matter how you look at it.

Incidentally, a special committee was set up here a few years ago to prevent suicide attempts on the bridge which has a cycle lane and pedestrian walkway as well as the road. It issued a recommendation to erect an anti-suicide barrier on each side of the bridge. Anyway, repair work was underway on a section of the bridge. And there was a mound near the barrier, which our heroine-to-be used as a launch pad.

And now, be honest with me, Uncle Arkasha, do you believe in parapsychology? All that gobbledegook: reading minds, seeing into the future... I don't, essentially. I'd say that parapsychology has as much to do with ordinary psychology as the electric chair does with an ordinary chair. And where parapsychology begins, the need for ordinary psychology and its insights automatically falls away. So there I was, hanging around asking questions in the midst of these miracles, wondering from time to time whether I really was the normal one or not. It couldn't be that these people, telling me God knows what about the missing woman, were all nuts. Then again, hand on heart, were the four apostles crazy? And yet we read that He walked on water as though on dry land and we've been lapping that up for 2,000 years... So, let's think of this as the birth of a contemporary myth... But where's the hero? Or, heroine, in this case. Or rather, a perfectly average person, in age at least, but, hey ... I'm not going to describe my feelings. This is evidently where you'd need those expert editors of yours. Such a strange, moving, solitary image emerged from all these accounts... Basically, on more than one occasion, I've been sorry not to have known her. I would give a lot to meet her.

Naturally enough, we conducted a thorough search of where she lived in Frankfurt. She rented a small loft in one of the respectable houses on a quiet little street in a nice area. I swear I've never encountered anything more ascetic. She had no things of her own, you know, the kind women take around the world with them. Just a big old circus suitcase, nearly empty, the remnants of their props and some magazines about optics. There were booklets, too, with mindboggling titles: "A Guide to Fractal Physics," or better still "Guidelines on Tensor Analysis and the Visualization of Space-Time Curvature." Not bad for a circus girl, is it?

But back to business. No one ever found anything, try as they might. She had disappeared. Ascended, if you like. It depends what we set our sights on: a whodunit, a thriller or mystical fiction. Let me know what's required.

As soon as I remembered that mysterious woman, I asked one of the witnesses in this long since closed case to meet me—to refresh my memory and well, I had to resort to a bit of a ruse. I said the case had been referred for further investigation. He wouldn't have come otherwise, her ex-husband. You should have seen him, what an ox: head shaved, burn scars on his face, muscles like balls of iron. He looked like a criminal, to be honest. But he turned out to be very gentle, sensitive even. He looked away three times or so during our conversation so that I couldn't see his tears. First time round he claimed to be her circus partner, a colleague, an old friend and then it hit me out of the blue. I asked him outright what he meant. Some partner! It's eating him up even now.

He spent three whole hours with me in the café, talking about their life together and then gave me an entire bundle of letters written to her, not by him but by her lover, a musician. He played the bassoon. Plus, there's the bassoon player's notebook, full of fairly paradoxical reflections.

So now I'm thinking why don't we push a novel out about this, Uncle Arkasha? Using all the letters and notes—especially since the musician has also gone to a better place. There's no one to bring a complaint. We can leave the ex-husband out of the equation.

But the main thing is to come up with a suitable ending, right? A killer ending of some kind. So you bring your editors on board and in the meantime I'll put my thinking cap on as well.

Oh, yes, I forgot to say: There was another witness in the case, a ridiculous fat old man who'd known her since she was a child. In the space of a few years, he drummed a university maths and physics degree into our girl genius and then they spent half his life exchanging letters in the back-to-front handwriting that even criminologists in the previous century thought of as code. (It would be good if the cover of the future novel—and this is just me dreaming now—was illustrated with a couple of sentences in that "Leonardo's handwriting").

Huh? Well, after all, it's a separate strand of the book!

The main thing though is that when I was talking to him in his neat little room in a typical home for single seniors, he assured me in all seriousness that "Nyuta," as he called her, had been transported into another, "mirror" universe. I'd realized I was dealing with a madman and innocently inquired how it had happened, via what gate. Not via a gate, he replied, cool as a cucumber, via a mirror corridor, formed from mirror matter. And then he gave me an entire lecture, of which, unsurprisingly, I didn't understand very much. Here's the outline in the event that we decide to give the story a silly fantasy aspect.

A man named Everett came up with the idea a long time ago that there are a multitude of parallel universes. More importantly, David Deutsch, a serious theoretician, has proved that mathematics based on that idea unexpectedly gives rise to the famous formulae of quantum physics. As a result, the notion of parallel universes arose in cosmology. They are reached by some kind of "space-time tunnels" or "corridors" formed inside black holes by a particular type of energy that blows the black holes apart.

Anyway, the suggestion of moving not just into a "parallel" but into a "mirror universe" is a frequent theme. Because each elementary particle has a "mirror double." This is my rambling and chaotic rendering of what I can remember from talking to the old crank.

When, hiding a smile, I asked for clarification about tracking down the entrance to such a "mirror corridor," he explained just as seriously that for many years he and "Nyuta" had discussed the creation of an "interdimensional machine that would affect the transition between different dimensions." Pretty amazing, isn't it? Anyway, something of the kind. Are you still awake there, Uncle Arkasha?

If we developed the theme for real (something I'm not sure about) we would have to speak to experts to avoid showing ourselves up.

Nevertheless, some ending that makes sense will have to be contrived.

In a novel, the heroine cannot vanish without trace. That only happens in real life. It's only in the real life of that young man who is in bits because of her that she's flying through the sky on a motorbike. Still flying and flying, on and on and on...

P.S. I forgot to say that her backpack was found on the bridge. A pathetic little backpack, almost empty. And it's strange: Did she drop it at that speed or what? Or just throw it away as no longer necessary? But does it make any difference what luggage you take with you when you vanish into the water forever? The fishy customs officers will let anything through.

Can you believe it? It's like being under a spell, the way I think about this. Can it really be the case that she simply dumped the ballast off her shoulders before taking flight?

Damn! Strangest of all is the way I can't let it go...

     LEONARDO'S HANDWRITING

CHAPTER 26.

Little one, some Interpol investigator has tracked me down in rehearsal and told me you've disappeared. What does it mean?

I actually asked him what it meant.

I don't want to give in to such nonsense because I know such a thing could never happen. You promised you'd be with me when... Anyway, it just couldn't!

Little one, listen... Listen, my darling... I'm writing to you in Frankfurt as usual and I beg you to respond straight away. Your mobile's switched off again, which is nothing new.

I'm not so much at a loss as irritated somehow by that investigator's stupid phone call. But none of it concerns us.

The point is that the longer this goes on, the more I think about You. I think about You all the time. This isn't a love letter, little one. It really isn't....

The thought I can't shake off has nothing to do with desire.

I am trying to understand where, as a young woman, You found the strength to reject all the benefits of your astonishing gift, to turn your back on what dozens of people in Your place would have handled with considerable commercial acumen. They would have rushed to join a travelling show and perform fairground miracles for the audience. In the final analysis, why not make money by reading other people's minds or giving advice on how to circumvent or to trick providence or simply on how to find a lost purse?

You're like the dervish in the oriental parable, visited by an angel in a dream and shown where a trunk full of treasure has been buried under a bridge. The dervish dug up the trunk, sat by the pile of dazzling treasure, ran heaps of gold coins through his wide-open fingers, slammed the lid and buried the wretched riches once and for all.

You're the strongest of all the people I have met in my life, with the greatest integrity. You rejected your divinely imposed gift with glorious disdain.

I think about You all the time.

My grandfather used to tell me the stories of Bible characters when I was a child, the way people tell the stories of the marriages, deaths, cheating and adultery of relatives, near and far. All those ancient heroes in the thick and tattered book seemed weird to me at the time, primitive and even stupid. Nowadays, I return more and more often to those parables which, as I go on, imbue me with some sort of cosmic meaning higher than human emotions.

I can remember that I used to be particularly irritated by the story of Jacob fighting until dawn either with an angel, or God, or himself. "And Jacob was left alone and a man wrestled with him until the breaking of the day." Every word was irritating in its imprecise meaning and indeterminate actions. Whereas my grandfather practically sang these sentences, relishing them, rolling them on his tongue like the sweetest drop of divine nectar. "And he saw that he could not overcome him, and touched the joint of his thigh; and the joint of Jacob's thigh was dislocated... And he said, Let me go, for it is daybreak."

I couldn't understand what delighted my grandfather in this hard-fought battle with an unnamed foe. And this vague, imprecise mention of the lifelong limp Jacob acquired in his night-time combat. "Touched," indeed! And the outcome of the ridiculous duel didn't make sense: "The sun began to shine upon him ... and he limped because of his thigh." Most irritating of all was the completely incomprehensible: "For I have seen an angel face to face, and yet my life has been spared."

I never stop thinking about You, about Your life in which you were alone, always alone—for you chose to be alone, to fight alone until the breaking of the day—and no one was able to be with You in this furious battle with the Unseen.

I am certain now that my whole life ran along the edge of Yours. I was the supporting voice, the usually distant answering voice of the bassoon, playing Your theme. And my music—those were Your lessons in producing the truest, most transparent note.

It was You who taught me to spare nothing for the sake of the crystal note of the heavens, for the sake of the truth as You saw it in those mirrors of yours, which were beyond my understanding... Now, I am in agony as I try to discern what divine voice sounded within You, what You heard in those calls. Who was calling You and, at the same time, not letting You cross the mirror borders that were a mystery to me?

On many occasions, Your aversion to falsehood—seemingly innate—held me back from numerous, perfectly human, perfectly mundane actions and words. But—thousands of kilometres away from You—I would be held back from a dubious joke, from gossip, from lies—by what? I don't know: the mere fact of Your existence.

You were one person with two aspects: You struggled in the iron pincers of the Unseen yet held the person closest of all to You in a ruthless grip. It was You who put the thigh out of joint and You whose thigh was touched. And perhaps we are all doomed to fight furiously hand-to-hand with the people dearest, most precious, to us?

I remember not being able to move away from the Rembrandt in the Berlin Museum, in which an immense powerfully-winged angel holds Jacob closely and lovingly and gazes at him with such tenderness. My beloved son, look at me, look! But Jacob has turned away, reluctant for some reason to look upon that radiant face, full of such heartfelt love. Why? Was he afraid he would falter? Fall apart, dissolve in streams of bliss? Cease to be himself? Was his own individual soul really more precious to him than the everlasting love of God Himself?

I couldn't walk away, I couldn't leave that painting. An avalanche of thoughts—about myself, my grandfather, my mother, You, my anonymously murdered father—descended upon me and spun me around and around like the wild current we writhed in so fatefully on the floor of my hotel room when You came to me for the first time and of your own accord. Do you remember? You announced that we belonged to one another from then on and threw Yourself at me as if into the current, possibly in order to have at least some advantage in the battle... Well, now, I'm telling You: You won. And I can no longer take my eyes from Your face, no matter where You are.

I no longer know whether I'll send this letter. It feels like I've written it to myself. It doesn't matter whether You read it or not. In my mind, I'm just begging You to show up—where You like, how You like, just come—in Your sweatshirt and jeans, on that loathsome motorbike.

But even if You don't reply, even if I've lost You for ever, even if I am doomed to limp until the breaking of the day for the rest of my life, I am no longer scared: "For I have seen an angel face to face, and yet my life has been spared."

CHAPTER 27.

He raced around Canada for two months in a futile search for Anna. He visited every hotel he'd heard of, every motel he knew, pulled into roadside settlements, small towns and cities, checked out shops, bars and cafés...

On two occasions out in the sticks, he was given fairly precise descriptions of a woman on a motorbike and in one dive on the border with the USA he was assured that only that morning just such a woman had ordered coffee and waffles, had sat just there by the window, smoking and drawing something in a notepad. Then she had taken such a tiny mouth organ out of her pocket and played it softly... The waitresses laughed: She hadn't played it with any great skill.

After which he raced off in the indicated direction, without sleep day or night, desperately honking the horn behind any motorbike riders and it seemed as though she was moving further away from him into the misty throat of an endless mirror corridor...

He tore off to Indianapolis too.

Eliezer, majestic and lordly as an elderly patrician, sat in his sagging armchair and referred to him as a "young man" although although they were the same age.

He blathered on about Plato or, rather, his myth of "two halves," saying that we are all one half of a whole in heaven but that whole is split in two before we are born and each half of the soul receives a different body and spends all its life yearning for its lost other half and this yearning is love, physical love. In just the same way, there are "mirror" souls that understand each other as well as they do themselves, for they are in fact "reflections" of one another "in the inner mirror of the soul." And we are captivated by mirrors not because we can see ourselves in them but because, all unawares, when we look into them we see our unknown double, our mystic alter ego. With whom, unlike Plato's "halves" we cannot be joined, precisely because they are mirrors... And this gives rise to a yearning that is not carnal love but some other feeling—"a mystical yearning for the double"...

...and all sorts of similar nonsense that was unbearable to listen to. Three times or so, Senya attempted to stand up and leave and in the end he got to his feet.

"The person who does not know who he is or why he was born," Eliezer said slowly and dispassionately, gazing somewhere past Senya, at the wall, "into which world or with whom he shares that world or what good and evil are ... is totally blind and deaf."

Senya stopped.

"What, what?" he asked, narrowing his eyes. "What did you say?"

"I didn't," Eliezer replied. "It was Rabbi Yossi. 'The Discourses' of Epictetus... Don't waste your time rushing around. Nyuta isn't coming back."

"Why?" Senya roared, irritated by this supercilious blob of lard.

Calmly, the blob replied, "Because she said so."

"What does that mean, she said so? What does it mean? And where is she not coming back from?"

"Don't shout," the old fat man replied. "Get over it. Get over it, like me. Nyuta never told lies."

His contract with the Boston Symphony Orchestra was renewed in mid-October and he couldn't spin things out any more.

He went back.

His old Ford crept on and on beside the elongated intestine of Lake Champlain, which just wouldn't come to an end. Moorings, wooden cottages, overturned boats and yet more moorings flashed by... And during all these miles, restless brown water splashed on his left, tawny as soap suds.

He went back to the bassoon that he hadn't touched for a couple of months and grumbling disgruntledly, coughing and coming round, it began by having its say about the negligence of owners and the neglect of love but gradually it got into its stride, cheered up and began to lift its voice and sing its old tune, its own tune of long drawn out farewells.

There were rehearsals, an interesting new programme, concerts...

The members of the orchestra tuned their instruments back stage before performances. They wandered about in dinner jackets and bow ties, sawing away, turning pegs, giving one another an A, and he would remember how she used to say, "It's like they're lighting each other's cigarettes."

Senya was in a dinner jacket himself—spare, elegant, carrying his magnificent bassoon—he scrunched his grey eyes up in a distracted smile...

In addition to the orchestra, he resumed his relationship with the John Clarke Wind Quintet in Albany, where he was invited to play two major concerts every year. The city held a chamber ensemble mini-festival every autumn. It was necessary to set off two days in advance, which was inconvenient. At least two rehearsals were needed before the concert. All his absences had to be negotiated with the orchestra and Senya had been doing it for years. It was a pity to abandon the fervent and passionate provincials.

This time too he asked artistic director Jacob Ring for three days off. The latter possessed a consummate ability to resolve all adversities, snuff out any squabbles, respect grievances and create an overall mood of "Be embraced, you millions!" Incidentally, Senya had already arranged for a bassoon-playing friend to stand in. The friend was delighted at both the salary and the prestige. Everything was sorted, in other words.

Jacob asked, "Are you going by car then?"

"No, on roller skates," Senya replied.

"Because tomorrow they're promising an unprecedentedly early snowstorm. Seriously."

As if to order, they both looked out of the window to where, on the backdrop of a deep blue sky, a crimson Canadian maple pressed fondly against a golden-headed aspen, and Senya said in Russian, "Storms enfold the sky with darkness."[5]

"What?"

"Nothing," he said. "The weather forecasters can stuff their snowstorm."

Early next morning, he filled up the fuel tank and set off.

In the countryside, the trees were a blaze of vermillion, yellow, copper, red and straw-coloured leaves. The hills bubbled, boiled and spiralled into bushes—a colourfully woven carpet, the golden fleece of New England...

---

5   A line from "Winter Evening" by Alexander Pushkin in Eugene Mark Kayden's translation (*The Sewanee Review*, Vol. 50, No. 4 (Oct. - Dec., 1942), p. 526).

Slanting slabs of black shale gleamed on the slopes beside the road: an open-pit mine, gaping like an eviscerated purse. He remembered that on just such a road as this in the Alps she had once driven through tunnel after tunnel, crying "Yay! Bravo!" each time they were stunned by the sun as they emerged from the dark. And, unusually for him, he now drove almost at Anna's speed so as not to think. Not to think. At all!

...Some forty minutes later the weather began to worsen. Here and there, up in the sky, a beetle gnawed through the endless blue heights, towing a blemish of black clouds, and darkness fell rapidly with a sense of panic. Senya reduced his speed, wiped his glasses and peered more attentively into the sky. Odd, he thought, it's becoming overcast too quickly. *Allegro maestoso...*

The wind grew bolder and more furious over the next half hour, gathering the entire weight of the violet impasto thunderclouds with their putrid yellow bellies into the middle of the sky. Just as the tragic waltz is set swirling in the first movement of Tchaikovsky's Fourth, spinning and fading away. Then the clarinet sings out—A flat minor— and the theme is repeated by the bassoon. Forget ... forget ... forget...

There was a sudden clap of thunder ... and another and another... The world darkened in an instant as happens only in the mountains when evening is drawing in. And, after five or six minutes of seemingly pleading for mercy, the deluge began.

That's all I needed on Route 2, Senya thought. It's bad enough as it is. And with only forty-five wretched miles to go as well.

It was completely dark when he turned onto Route 2 and began following its meanders, repeatedly crawling off to the side to sit out the heavens' torrential downpour. It was hard to believe that it was ten in the morning, that only today he had been contemplating what to wear, whether to bother with a light jacket or whether just a sweater was enough. And he hadn't brought the jacket.

The rain was lashing and lashing down as if being squeezed from a continuously open firehose by the numbed hands of a berserk fireman.

Nevertheless, for the next twenty minutes or so, Senya endeavoured to make headway, advancing slowly along the slippery road. Soon, however, the rain turned to wet, stinging sleet and then into ominously end-of-year-holiday type snow. Bastard weather forecasters, they weren't wrong!

Gusts of gale-force wind hurled ghostly spectres against the car windows in such fits of fury that, wisely, Senya pulled over to the side more and more frequently in the hope of sitting them out. How long could this outrage go on? In October? Bollocks...

Before long, a cracking sound came from the sides of the road. Trees, still in full leaf, were falling, unable to withstand the weight of the snow. Only by a miracle was Senya not hit by a magnificent ... birch, was it? Who the hell could tell in this gloom? It fell right in front of the car, the whole of its quivering body continuing to shudder for a long time on the ground, already being ravenously devoured by the savage blizzard. The road was completely closed off. Snow was piling up in the most outlandish places, swirling a mutinous mass of white above the ground. Like a flock of white geese on the attack...

Beautiful drifts, opaque as candles, built up at precipitous speed on all sides.

Good thing I filled the tank, he thought, turning the heat on.

An hour later, the wind had abated slightly but the snow was still coming down, swamping the car.

Senya hopped outside twice in his thin sweater to scoop out an exit for the exhaust. Strands of ice whipped across his cheeks, sealing his eyes and mouth. He spat and screwed up his eyes, struggling to breathe in the wind, and returned to the car once more.

A translucent winter splendour lay all around, posing an immense threat to his cherrywood bassoon, the priceless bassoon made by master craftsman Peter de Koenig, *a blessing on his hands.*

Well, I've been sitting in this wondrous unexpected snowstorm for an hour and a half now, he thought. I wonder if that lad of mine's split... Just a minute, Senya told the bassoon. We'll have you nice and warm in a minute, my friend! A bit of a play will warm you up... He flipped the locks on the case, opened it, unwrapped the instrument and lifted it out.

In its plush, enveloping, ever so slightly nasal voice, the bassoon recounted the opening of the Tale of the Kalander Prince: dream and oblivion...

And for another ninety minutes or so, Senya worked in quick succession through all his parts in Vivaldi's concertos, Shostakovich's symphonies, Mahler's Symphony No. 1... And that part of the first movement of Tchaikovsky's Fifth where the soul races around in circles and there is no salvation...

Obviously, the snowstorm was so improbably early that the snowploughs weren't ready for use. The mobile phone Senya had forgotten to charge that morning, leaving the charger at home into the bargain, died peacefully. There was nothing he could do except wait for the dullards in some highway department, or whoever was in charge of it, to cotton on.

From time to time, he switched the heating off to avoid suffocating. The snow continued its smooth and measured descent, covering the car. Senya played his entire repertoire over and over again, alone in the world amid this untimely roaring winter and its fragile porcelain silence, in which the plaintively languid, silken, honeysweet voice of his bassoon sought someone out, beseeched someone to return...

Senya had already tired of playing. He was breathing fitfully and couldn't remember how long he'd been sitting in in the torpid snowstorm, in the dazzling winter, shrouded in his bassoon's long, intimate exhalations...

He clambered out again to scrape away the snow around the exhaust. He got back into the car, rubbing his frozen hands with the hem of his sweater.

He took up the bassoon and cast a cursory glance at the rear view mirror.

In the left-hand corner, against the snow-whitened window sat Anna, her legs tucked up comfortably beneath her.

His heart stopped then raced faster and faster, plunging into the turmoil of the furious, churning blizzard.

"Have you been here long?" he asked without looking round. And she said simply,

"I'm here all the time. Keep playing, go on... What was it? Tchaikovsky?"

"It's Stravinsky, you monster!" he said fondly, gasping for breath. "The lullaby from 'The Firebird'."

"Well then, play us a lullaby."

"Have you got your harmonica?" he asked.

"Of course."

"Then, my darling, let's knock out a rendition of 'Lili Marlene'."

"There is nothing rounder than my lovely knees?"

"Your lovely knees, *Ich liebe dich...*"

She took her scuffed looted harmonica out of her jeans pocket, put it to her lips, gave it a trial blow, green eyes protruding, face stretched...

"You wait where that lantern softly gleamed,

Your sweet face seems

To haunt my dreams…"

The harmonica wheezed, coughed and choked.

Senya gave a blissful laugh and lifted the bassoon to his lips...

Some three hours later, a bulldozer from highway services finally made it through from the nearest town.

Spotting a car at the side of the road, a workman jumped down and dashed over to scrape the heavy wet slush off the windows with his hands.

A man sat nonchalantly inside, head thrown back against the seat, holding some sort of enormous saxophone, as if he had just taken the instrument away from his lips and was listening to the notes fade away. And by all appearances, they were sweet notes too, for the network of lines around his eyes still wore a strange dreamy smile.

Taking everything in at a glance, the workman radioed the police. And until the ambulance and police arrived, he sat on the steps of his bulldozer, smoking one cigarette after another, unable to look away from the car's wing mirror which reflected the musician's sunken temple, the grey bristles on a cheekbone and a smiling grey eye.

He was gazing steadily skyward, this dead musician, the way people stare after someone they love...

And there, overhead ... two lakes in the heavens opened wide to form deep blue mirrors, their shorelines interchanging, seductively slow...

Jerusalem 2007–2008

ACKNOWLEDGMENTS

My warm thanks to all my friends and those who have become friends during the writing of this book.

Firstly, my thanks go to Lina Nikolskaya, the brilliant performer who led me out on the wire above the abyss of this novel and made sure I kept my footing.

They go also to stunt performer Dmitry Shulkin;

Kievans Sergey Baumstein, Sasha Khodorkovsky, Svetlana Blaus and Elena Mishschenko;

"mirror women" Larisa Gerstein and Lena Kotlyarenko;

Marina Dudulovskaya;

Raphael Nudelman;

bassoonist Aleksandr Fein;

Aleksandr Krutitskiy;

my sister, violinist Vera Rubina;

carilloneuse Elina Sadina;

Evgeny Terletsky;

Zhanna Pritzker;

Masha and Yulya Shukhman;

Yakov Shekhter;

Sonya Chernyakova;

Shurochka and Manya, African grey and Amazon parrots respectively, members of the family of Lina and Nikolay Nikolsky;

And to my own family—for their infinite patience.

Dina Rubina

Nikolai Gumilev's Africa

Gumilev holds a unique position in the history of Russian poetry as a result of his profound involvement with Africa. He extensively wrote both poetry and prose on the culture of the continent in general and on Ethiopia (Abyssinia, as it was called in Gumilev's time) in particular. During his abbreviated lifetime Gumilev made four trips to Northern and Eastern Africa, the most extensive of which was a 1913 expedition to Abyssinia undertaken on assignment from the St. Petersburg Imperial Museum of Anthropology and Ethnography. During that trip Gumilev collected Ethiopian folklore and ethnographic objects, which, upon his return to St. Petersburg, he deposited at the Museum. He and his assistant Nikolai Sverchkov also made more than 200 photographs that offer a unique picture of the African country in the early part of the century.

This volume collects all of Gumilev's poetry and prose written about Africa for the first time as well as a number of the photographs that he and Nikolai Sverchkov took during their trip that give a fascinating view of that part of the world in the early twentieth century.

Buy it > www.glagoslav.com

I Want a Baby and Other Plays

by Sergei Tretyakov

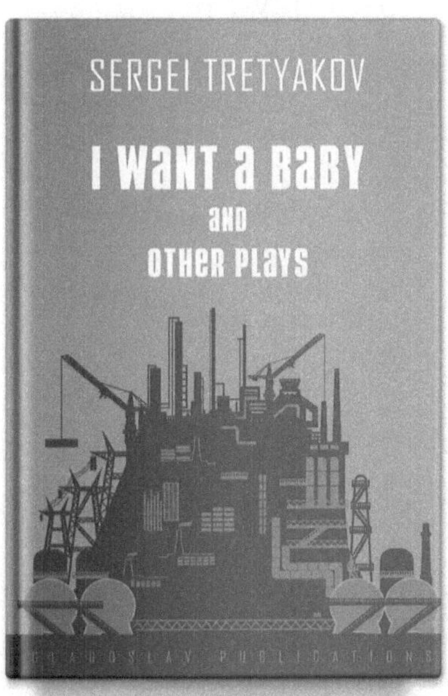

When Sergei Tretyakov's ground-breaking play, *I Want a Baby*, was banned by Stalin's censor in 1927, it was a signal that the radical and innovative theatre of the early Soviet years was to be brought to an end. A glittering, unblinking exploration of the realities of post-revolutionary Soviet life, *I Want a Baby* marks a high point in modernist experimental drama.

Tretyakov's plays are notable for their formal originality and their revolutionary content. *The World Upside Down*, which was staged by Vsevolod Meyerhold in 1923, concerns a failed agrarian revolution. *A Wise Man*, originally directed by the great film director and Tretyakov's friend, Sergei Eisenstein, is a clown show set in the Paris of the émigré White Russians. *Are You Listening, Moscow?!* and *Gas Masks* are 'agit-melodramas', fierce, fast-moving and edgy...

Buy it > www.glagoslav.com

A Brown Man in Russia
Lessons Learned on the Trans-Siberian
by Vijay Menon

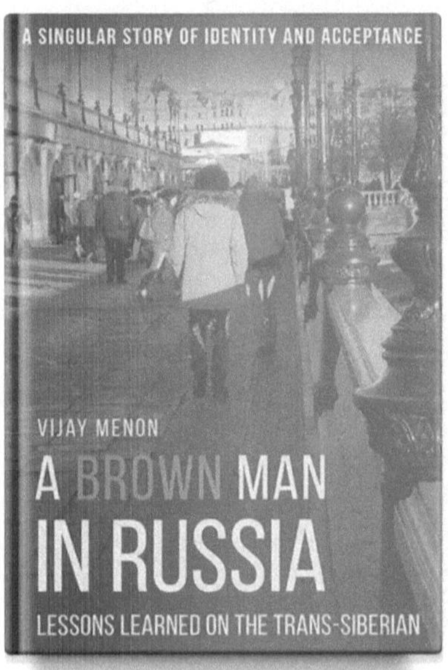

A Brown Man in Russia describes the fantastical travels of a young, colored American traveler as he backpacks across Russia in the middle of winter via the Trans-Siberian. The book is a hybrid between the curmudgeonly travelogues of Paul Theroux and the philosophical works of Robert Pirsig. Styled in the vein of Hofstadter, the author lays out a series of absurd, but true stories followed by a deeper rumination on what they mean and why they matter. Each chapter presents a vivid anecdote from the perspective of the fumbling traveler and concludes with a deeper lesson to be gleaned. For those who recognize the discordant nature of our world in a time ripe for demagoguery and for those who want to make it better, the book is an all too welcome antidote. It explores the current global climate of despair over differences and outputs a very different message – one of hope and shared understanding. At times surreal, at times inappropriate, at times hilarious, and at times deeply human, A Brown Man in Russia is a reminder to those who feel marginalized, hopeless, or endlessly divided that harmony is achievable even in the most unlikely of places.

Glagoslav Publications Catalogue

- *The Time of Women* by Elena Chizhova
- *Andrei Tarkovsky: The Collector of Dreams* by Layla Alexander-Garrett
- *Andrei Tarkovsky - A Life on the Cross* by Lyudmila Boyadzhieva
- *Sin* by Zakhar Prilepin
- *Hardly Ever Otherwise* by Maria Matios
- *Khatyn* by Ales Adamovich
- *The Lost Button* by Irene Rozdobudko
- *Christened with Crosses* by Eduard Kochergin
- *The Vital Needs of the Dead* by Igor Sakhnovsky
- *The Sarabande of Sara's Band* by Larysa Denysenko
- *A Poet and Bin Laden* by Hamid Ismailov
- *Watching The Russians (Dutch Edition)* by Maria Konyukova
- *Kobzar* by Taras Shevchenko
- *The Stone Bridge* by Alexander Terekhov
- *Moryak* by Lee Mandel
- *King Stakh's Wild Hunt* by Uladzimir Karatkevich
- *The Hawks of Peace* by Dmitry Rogozin
- *Harlequin's Costume* by Leonid Yuzefovich
- *Depeche Mode* by Serhii Zhadan
- *The Grand Slam and other stories (Dutch Edition)*
  by Leonid Andreev
- *METRO 2033 (Dutch Edition)* by Dmitry Glukhovsky
- *METRO 2034 (Dutch Edition)* by Dmitry Glukhovsky
- *A Russian Story* by Eugenia Kononenko
- *Herstories, An Anthology of New Ukrainian Women Prose Writers*
- *The Battle of the Sexes Russian Style* by Nadezhda Ptushkina
- *A Book Without Photographs* by Sergey Shargunov
- *Down Among The Fishes* by Natalka Babina
- *disUNITY* by Anatoly Kudryavitsky
- *Sankya* by Zakhar Prilepin
- *Wolf Messing* by Tatiana Lungin
- *Good Stalin* by Victor Erofeyev
- *Solar Plexus* by Rustam Ibragimbekov

- *Don't Call me a Victim!* by Dina Yafasova
- *Poetin (Dutch Edition)* by Chris Hutchins and Alexander Korobko
- *A History of Belarus* by Lubov Bazan
- *Children's Fashion of the Russian Empire* by Alexander Vasiliev
- *Empire of Corruption - The Russian National Pastime* by Vladimir Soloviev
- *Heroes of the 90s: People and Money. The Modern History of Russian Capitalism*
- *Fifty Highlights from the Russian Literature (Dutch Edition)* by Maarten Tengbergen
- *Bajesvolk (Dutch Edition)* by Mikhail Khodorkovsky
- *Tsarina Alexandra's Diary (Dutch Edition)*
- *Myths about Russia* by Vladimir Medinskiy
- *Boris Yeltsin: The Decade that Shook the World* by Boris Minaev
- *A Man Of Change: A study of the political life of Boris Yeltsin*
- *Sberbank: The Rebirth of Russia's Financial Giant* by Evgeny Karasyuk
- *To Get Ukraine* by Oleksandr Shyshko
- *Asystole* by Oleg Pavlov
- *Gnedich* by Maria Rybakova
- *Marina Tsvetaeva: The Essential Poetry*
- *Multiple Personalities* by Tatyana Shcherbina
- *The Investigator* by Margarita Khemlin
- *The Exile* by Zinaida Tulub
- *Leo Tolstoy: Flight from paradise* by Pavel Basinsky
- *Moscow in the 1930* by Natalia Gromova
- *Laurus (Dutch edition)* by Evgenij Vodolazkin
- *Prisoner* by Anna Nemzer
- *The Crime of Chernobyl: The Nuclear Goulag* by Wladimir Tchertkoff
- *Alpine Ballad* by Vasil Bykau
- *The Complete Correspondence of Hryhory Skovoroda*
- *The Tale of Aypi* by Ak Welsapar
- *Selected Poems* by Lydia Grigorieva
- *The Fantastic Worlds of Yuri Vynnychuk*

- *The Garden of Divine Songs and Collected Poetry of Hryhory Skovoroda*
- *Adventures in the Slavic Kitchen: A Book of Essays with Recipes*
- *Seven Signs of the Lion* by Michael M. Naydan
- *Forefathers' Eve* by Adam Mickiewicz
- *One-Two* by Igor Eliseev
- *Girls, be Good* by Bojan Babić
- *Time of the Octopus* by Anatoly Kucherena
- *The Grand Harmony* by Bohdan Ihor Antonych
- *The Selected Lyric Poetry Of Maksym Rylsky*
- *The Shining Light* by Galymkair Mutanov
- *The Frontier: 28 Contemporary Ukrainian Poets - An Anthology*
- *Acropolis: The Wawel Plays* by Stanisław Wyspiański
- *Contours of the City* by Attyla Mohylny
- *Conversations Before Silence: The Selected Poetry of Oles Ilchenko*
- *The Secret History of my Sojourn in Russia* by Jaroslav Hašek
- *Mirror Sand: An Anthology of Russian Short Poems in English Translation* (A Bilingual Edition)
- *Maybe We're Leaving* by Jan Balaban
- *Death of the Snake Catcher* by Ak Welsapar
- *A Brown Man in Russia: Perambulations Through A Siberian Winter* by Vijay Menon
- *Hard Times* by Ostap Vyshnia
- *The Flying Dutchman* by Anatoly Kudryavitsky
- *Nikolai Gumilev's Africa* by Nikolai Gumilev
- *Combustions* by Srđan Srdić
- *The Sonnets* by Adam Mickiewicz
- *Dramatic Works* by Zygmunt Krasiński
- *Four Plays* by Juliusz Słowacki
- *Little Zinnobers* by Elena Chizhova
- *We Are Building Capitalism! Moscow in Transition 1992-1997*
- *The Nuremberg Trials* by Alexander Zvyagintsev
- *The Hemingway Game* by Evgeni Grishkovets
- *A Flame Out at Sea* by Dmitry Novikov
- *Jesus' Cat* by Grig
- *Want a Baby and Other Plays* by Sergei Tretyakov
- *I Mikhail Bulgakov: The Life and Times* by Marietta Chudakova
- *Duel* by Borys Antonenko-Davydovych

More coming soon...